Twice a Duchess

BOOK TWO OF THE
AMERICAN DUKE SERIES

AUGUST JADE STERLING

Published by Krystal Kat Press, New York City
https://www.augustjadesterling.com

Image credits: cover © Envato/Fisher-Photostudio, Rawpixel, Shutterstock/Darya Komarova

ISBN (paperback): 979-8-9863933-2-2
ISBN (ebook): 979-8-9863933-3-9

Library of Congress Control Number: 2023924565

First edition

To the women in my life who hold my hand through life's tougher moments and who teach me to love more, grow larger, laugh often and louder, and become stronger—my sister Quinnette, my cousins Dianne and Jolene, my sisters in spirit Andy, Barabara, Christina, and Tricia, and of course my mother, Marylou.

To all the women in the world who are developing the best parts of themselves, always keep striving.

THE ROXBURYS

Anne Roxbury—American, wife of Avery Roxbury, mother of Sar, Mer, and Beth

Avery Roxbury—British, lived in America, the deceased brother of the sixth Duke of Westmoure, Sterling Avery Roxbury; Anne's husband; father of Sterling Avery Roxbury, Meredith Anne Roxbury, and Elizabeth Beverly Roxbury; co-owner of the Avery Jacob Shipping Company

Charles Roxbury—British, deceased brother of Avery Roxbury and Sterling Adam Roxbury, the sixth Duke of Westmoure

Elizabeth Beverly Roxbury (Beth)—American, the youngest child of Anne and Avery Roxbury

Meredith Anne Roxbury (Mer)—American, the oldest daughter of Anne and Avery Roxbury

Sterling Adam Roxbury—British, deceased, the sixth Duke of Westmoure, lived in England

Sterling Avery Roxbury (Sar)—American, son of Anne and Avery Roxbury

Abigail Donaldson—British, wife of Nathan, mother of Marry Anne

Adele and Laura—British, very young maids of the exchequer's household

Alexius Standerson—British, daughter of Caroline and Sebastian

Anthony Daggs, Marquess of Dearne, Inspector Daggs of Scotland Yard—British, one of the elite operatives who works for Berkley on an as needed basis

Ashby (Ash) Wyndham, Earl of Danford—British, an aristocrat who served in the elite group of noblemen under the command of Berkley during the war

Aston, Duke of Aston—British, Royce's father, special envoy to the king

Aurelia Rothingham, Duchess of Edgerton—British, wife of David, good friend of Caroline Standerson

Babette—British, Madame Burgoff's assistant

Basil Willingham—British, the future Duke of Brockton, nephew of the current Duke of Brockton

Brian O'Keefe—British, deceased, accomplished actor

Captain Coomes—British, sea captain, works for Westmoure Shipping Company

Captain Johnson—British, works for Scotland Yard in Inspector Daggs's section

Caroline Standerson, Marchioness of Broadhurst—British, wife of Sebastian, daughter is Alexius

Charlotte Peach, Countess of Fatson—British, a member of the aristocracy

Chief Red Cloud—American, second in charge of the Avery Jacob Shipping Company

Cintha Eliot, Countess of Wyckham—British, a busybody aristocrat who strongly dislikes people of color, especially Negroes

Countess of Garth and Viscountess of Ream—British, widows of the elite of society

Daniel Gardener—British, groundskeeper for the Westmoures

David Rothingham, Duke of Edgerton—British, an aristocrat who served in the elite group of noblemen under the command of Berkley during the war, married to Aurelia

David—British, second-in-command under Captain Coomes

Diana Ryerton, Duchess of Northampton—British, wife of Marcus, good friend of Caroline Standerson

Dr. Langley—British, physician, a specialist

Duke of Horton—British, son of Hortense Horton

Earl of Morton—British, member of the elite of society

Earl of Severson—British, a wealthy aristocrat

Easton Willingham, Brockton, Duke of Brockton—British, an ally of the Crown

Edward and little Elizabeth—British, street orphans

Ethan Quinn, Marquess of Perth—British, head of the Foreign Office

Evan Marston, Duke of Carrington—British, an aristocrat who served in the elite group of noblemen under the command of Berkley during the war, married to Georgina

Evelyn Quinton, Marchioness of Briarcliff—British, wife of Richard Quinton, Julien's mother

Frances—British, mother of Joycellyn

George Mason—British, worked for Berkley in the Home Office

Georgina Marston, Duchess of Carrington—British, wife of Evan, good friend of Caroline Standerson

Grayson, Duke of Grayson—British, Caroline's father

Henley—British, majordomo of Hampton Manor and Berkley's right-hand man in the country

Hortense Horton, Dowager Duchess of Horton—British, the most revered woman of the ton

Jackson (Jack) Abbott—British, was one of the elite operatives under Berkley's command, murderer, traitor

Jacob Goldsmith—American, co-owner of the Avery Jacob
     Shipping Company
Jacques—French, Rue's son, also in the spy business
James—British, majordomo of the Duke of Hampton's
     household
Jay, Digvijay, His Royal Highness of the House of Ranjea—
     Indian/British, half-brother of Daggs
Jenkins—British, the majordomo of the Daggs household
Joycellyn—British, daughter of Charles and Frances
John Smythe—British, solicitor for the late duke Sterling
     Adam Roxbury
Jonathan Simmons, Earl of Carlyle—British, field surgeon
     and physician, an aristocrat who served in the elite group
     of noblemen under the command of Berkley during
     the war
Julien Quinton, Honorable Earl of Sutton—British, son
     of Richard and Evelyn, one of the elite operatives under
     Berkley's command
Lady Sarah Jersey—British, head patron at Almack's
     along with the other patronesses at the time, Lady
     Emily Cowper, Lady Anne Stewart, Marchioness of
     Londonderry, the Viscountess of Castlereagh, Lady
     Sefton, Countess de Lieven, Baroness Willoughby de
     Eresby, and Countess Esterhazy, arbiters of le bon ton
Madame Burgoff—British, modiste extraordinaire to the ton
Marcus Ryerton, Duke of Northampton—British, an aristo-
     crat who served in the elite group of noblemen under the
     command of Berkley during the war, married to Diana
Marry Anne Donaldson—British, daughter of Nathan and
     Abigail
Mildred Cook—British, cook and integral part of the
     Westmoure household

Miriam Wyndham, Countess of Danford—British, wife of Ashby, good friend of Caroline Standerson

Monsieur Rue—French, Berkley's counterpart on the Continent

Morgan—British, was the man of affairs of the sixth Duke of Westmoure (Sterling Adam Roxbury)

Mrs. Kiggins—British, housekeeper, companion, friend of Lady Hortense

Mrs. Spencer—British, chatelain of the Westmoures' homes

Nancy Smith—British, customer

Nathan Donaldson—British, mason worker, husband of Abigail, father of Marry Anne

Oliver—British, majordomo of the Westmoure household

Otis and associates—British, Basil's henchmen

Padre—British, Berkley's country connection

Perkins—American, Sar's right-hand man

Raymond—British, majordomo of the Duke of Brockton's household

Richard Quinton, Marquess of Briarcliff—British, husband of Evelyn Quinton, Julien's father

Royce Thortonshire, Honorable Marquess of Shone—British, one of the elite operatives under Berkley's command

Sam—British, one of the top bosses in the underworld operations

Samuels—British, soldier, attached to the Home Office, works for Berkley

Sebastian Standerson, Marquess of Broadhurst—British, the senior diplomat in the elite group of operatives under Berkley's command, married to Caroline, daughter is Alexius

Seymour—British, majordomo of the Broadhursts

Sylvia Meacham, Viscountess of Truvo—British, a member
of the aristocracy

***Thomas Berkley, Duke of Hampton, a royal duke, moniker:
the general***—British, head of the Home Office, leader of
the elite group of operatives, cousin of the king

Viscount of Truvo—British, husband of Sylvia

***The Wolfhounds: Duchess, America, Baby, Bella, Oscar,
Felix***—British, trained at Whitehall

Twice a Duchess

——

March 27, 1822

"What?" The Earl of Severson's furor showed in his red face, erratic breathing, and bulging eyes. "You guaranteed me the purchase of Westmoure Shipping Company for my assistance, and I expect to get it."

"Is that a threat, Severson?"

"No. That is a promise." His deadly hiss sent shivers up the other man's spine. They were in the tavern in the East End. One of their favorite meeting places. To the untrained eye, they were two ordinary workers swilling house ale, trying to drink their troubles away.

• • •

A day later in the other house in Mayfair, a messenger arrived and clearly stated what could never be put in writing. "You are to meet him at warehouse number two at nine o'clock sharp next Thursday evening. What we are expecting will have arrived."

The Earl of Severson nodded a dismissal to the messenger, rubbed his hands in glee, and reached for his glass of brandy. He reviewed the memorized agreement. *Due to the illegality of Westmoure's involvement in smuggling and espionage, trafficking of women, and other treasonous activities, the current duke will be hanged.* Upon the demise of Westmoure, he was to be offered the shipping company at two hundred million pounds. Severson couldn't wait—his, all his. He'd own the largest shipping company in the world. He was feeling almost giddy as he wrote the note. The rumors had started about Westmoure. The men in power were beginning to talk about bringing charges. Summoning his butler, he asked that the note be delivered immediately and that he wait for an answer.

• • •

At five minutes to nine the following Thursday, the Earl of Severson was at warehouse number two. His contact, a government official, was already there. Pallets stacked five feet high held everyday statues filled with opium. "Is it all here?" Severson turned to him with a greedy glint in his eye.

"Checked the manifest twice. Ordering a change as we speak. My instincts are telling me Berkley and his group are aware of the smuggling. Doubt if they know about the espionage. Just to be safe with this shipment, we are using a different company. All of this will be out of here within the hour."

He had planned on killing Severson here, but he thought it wouldn't be clean enough. Too many loose ends. Furthermore, with the change, he may have further use for Severson. The blade in his pocket felt as though it were burning a hole through his pants, and he was itching to plunge it into the man. "Delays, delays, delays, but this shipment is worth it.

Millions of kilos of opium. Can you notify your contact of the changes tonight?"

"Consider it done." After memorizing the changes, Severson went to seek out his shipping contact. In his mind, Severson saw the mounting profits. But tonight was for celebrating, and he thought of the women he would have at the Pleasure Palace. *Ah, the Pleasure Palace, where sexual delights of every kind with multiple partners can be found.* He smiled to himself. The Pleasure Palace was the place where everyone was safe and free from the prying eyes of Berkley and Daggs. All visitors would always be safe. It was owned by another high-ranking official of the government.

• • •

On the estate in England in the exquisite, secluded hunting lodge, Boss sat. She was seething. The foundation of her anger was the aristocracy. Every time she saw one of them, Boss glimpsed murder and the body oozing blood. She couldn't forget; she couldn't forgive.

Being locked in her brain for six years, with just memories of the night of her rape by that arrogant pig, gave her time to begin to plot and plan. The child she delivered was nothing to her but a constant eyesore of an outcast, which only escalated her rage. She distanced herself from the child as much as possible.

Now, the half-breeds from America were in charge. They had more status than she did. But they wouldn't be here long. That was guaranteed.

Besides smuggling and espionage, there was the lucrative side business of sex trafficking. So far, the bastard children were being pawned off as aristocratic children of deceased parents with sundry side benefits.

No later than September of next year, Jack would have returned. Along with Sam, the three of them would own Westmoure Shipping Company and command the world. To hell with the rest of them, including Sylvia and Severson.

Boss studied the red leather murder book—the list of assassinations of aristocrats, *le bon ton*. Besides Avery, there wasn't a Roxbury among them. She thought about the plans that had gone awry. Always something or someone interfering. She would meet with the exchequer tomorrow. They would come up with solutions. Boss slammed her book shut and waited for the dark, sinister silence to totally consume her thoughts.

• • •

In a study in another house in Mayfair, two men nursed their brandy. "I don't like what is going on. Fortunately, the last two shipments of women reached our buyers safely. Dressing them like men and darkening their skin worked perfectly. We have to establish ourselves as the premier trader of women. We have already done that with opium."

"It was Sylvia's idea to darken the skin. Remember the Viscountess of Truvo is a vicious murderer. She kills first and never asks questions. But she can make your release and hers come three times in an hour." Both men reflected on the time they both had Sylvia in front of panting footmen. They couldn't move when she finished with them. Then she rode all the footmen, and they had her every way possible.

"We will continue with our new shipper. I am thinking we need to ship more. Our current profits are extraordinary. Find another carrier."

"Not to worry—I will. Jack returns next year. He can handle business from England. After that, we will be in better shape than ever."

They raised their glasses and toasted their success.

"Must go. There is a certain widow I must ride. Just thinking of the viscountess has caused me to swell."

As the other gentleman was being let out the door, the man in the study looked down at his pant placket. He too had to have a woman tonight. When the door opened and the saucy fourteen-year-old maid walked in, he beckoned to her. "How many men are you servicing, Adele?"

She looked down at his pants, which outlined his engorged rod. Adele moved closer as he reached out and felt her hardened nipples.

"You love pleasing me and getting pleasure yourself, don't you?"

The young maid nodded her head yes and started rubbing her nipples and love spot. "I'll call the other maid."

"Please let me." As he pulled the correct bell, she gently started removing his clothes.

Laura quietly locked the door behind her and took her uniform off as she walked toward them. Her bare skin glistened in the candlelight.

"My lord, how may I help you?"

"I need both of you all night. Look in my pant pocket. Take all my money."

She did as he instructed and helped Adele remove the remainder of his clothes. With glazed eyes, Adele started to suck on Laura. They found each other's centers, and wet sounds pierced the silence. They made sure he saw everything. All the exchequer could do was watch before he joined in the fun. They turned their attention to him. One covered his mouth, and the other inserted his stiff member into her center.

"We must make sure you last all night, my lord, so we can make you come over and over again." Laura slid partly down his chest, leaving her essence on him and putting both of her nipples in his mouth.

He bit the nipples and tried to speak. "Tonight, I want it

all. In the morning, I want you both gone. You will live in my country house and be available to me at all times. I want you two to practice your art on each other, my staff, and anyone visiting when I am not there."

"That will cost you a lot more, my lord."

He stood up, opened his safe, and pulled out five hundred pounds, then gave it to Laura. "Split this and whatever you pulled out of my pant pocket. My carriage will be ready at six. Take two other girls with you. I wouldn't want the two of you to get bored with each other."

He came and came and came. Their nectar was in his mouth, their mouths, and all over his body. As dawn approached, Adele rode him as he supped on her friend. He felt the strong contractions of both; he knew he had reached heaven.

By six o'clock, the carriage pulled out of the drive. Four half-exposed women opened their legs and bodices for each other. They played all the way to the country home.

When helped out of the carriage, they were turned over to the housekeeper. "They are here to please themselves, the staff, anyone who stops by, and of course the master. Insert the tubing every day to make sure they are clean. Let them ride the water. They are to have their release at least twice a day." Amos and the other outriders then returned to London with the carriage.

The housekeeper looked at their wilted bodies. "Let's go to the tub." The large round tub had holes in the side. "Put your legs in those holes and move your love centers to this opening." Their arms were tied under tables. Their hair flowed behind them. She put tubing in each of them and allowed the warm water to flow. The bath maids scrubbed the four and left the room. The women were bundled in warm robes and carried to their suites by the footmen, who gently placed them in the middle of their beds.

Adele's footman was broad, with arms and thighs like tree limbs and stumps. Like the other footmen, he was assigned to one particular whore to cater to her every whim and make sure she obeyed all house rules. He whispered in her ear, "There is a price for my service." He spread her secret passage and inserted a finger. "You are still wet. Your honey is still flowing. Do you want more?" Adele nodded yes. "You know you will have to have another bath." Adele answered by putting her nipple in his mouth.

Oh, she was ready, so he pulled back. "The rest of the rules: You will not get the pox here. If you get the disease, it means you have cheated on Master. Then you are tossed out. No one uses protection here. We spill our seed. I am assigned to you. You will please me when Master is not here. I will spill my seed whenever I want. If you become with child, you will get money and a house, and what you decide to do with your life is up to you.

"Naturally, we want to see you ripe and make love to you up to the last moment and then send you away. How long have you been pleasing the master?" He bit her love button.

"I might get you with child today. That may not please you. If you want to become heavy and ripe with child, let the master do it."

He opened her wider and pushed his way in. He glided in and out. Her muscles pushed against him again and again. Raising her hips, she pleaded with him to go deeper. He did, and she shattered.

"How many times do you want to come today? I get to bathe you in the bath chamber, and I will have you again." He ran his finger across her mons. It was still large and sensitive. "You still want more. And you will be with babe if you keep this up."

The next week, the lord of the house arrived. He found Adele. He suckled her breasts and ordered her footman, Bemis, to take her to the bath chamber and close it to everyone except his two outriders. In the chamber, Adele took the exchequer until he screamed from the release that caused him to ask the outriders to service her completely.

"My lord, we wouldn't know whose child she would be carrying."

"So true. Tell Adele and Laura I want them in the morning. I want them increasing at the same time."

Well satisfied, the exchequer climbed the stairs. *I will fill the country with aristocratic bastards and sell some to my friends. Already I have dozens of my bastards satisfying some of the highest members of society and governments around the world, thanks to Westmoure Shipping.* He couldn't wait until Westmoure was his. The women he would have, the bastards he would make, and the women he would sell to the highest bidder. And then of course there were the other side businesses, but selling sex slaves was more lucrative. He laughed to himself.

CHAPTER 1

Breakfast with the King

Her Grace, Anne Roxbury, the Dowager Duchess of Westmoure, skipped softly down the stairs of the Duke of Westmoure's townhouse in London. She stopped midway and turned her head to listen to the snores of the men.

Her mind wandered to everything that had happened since the end of last year. First, it was the murder of her husband, Avery, in America, along with the shocking surprise that he was a duke. Two things precipitated his murder—their marriage and the heir apparent, their son, Sar. Being a Negro in America was never less than hard, but in addition, being married to a white man set her up for instant lynching and death.

Their marriage on the high seas on a British ship was upheld as legal by the British high court, which enabled Sar to legally inherit the dukedom. Then there was the secret flight from America one night and the voyage to England. Upon arrival in England, Sar was shot, and they found three operatives dead as they sped to London.

Was that all? *Oh no.* There were deceit and betrayal, more murder, attempted murder, and smuggling and espionage. But most of all there was love. It made her heart sing. She sighed and continued down the stairs.

His Majesty had decided to spend the night. Besides her son, Sar, the current Duke of Westmoure, also present were Sebastian Standerson, the Marquess of Broadhurst; Grayson, the Duke of Grayson; Richard Quinton, the Marquess of Briarcliff; Royce Thortonshire, the Honorable Marquess of Shone; Ashby (Ash) Wyndham, the Earl of Danford; Marcus Ryerton, the Duke of Northampton; David Rothingham, the Duke of Edgerton; Evan Marston, the Duke of Carrington; and all the wives.

In house also was Thomas Berkley, a royal duke and cousin of the king, who was already up, pacing the floor. His moniker was "the general." This name had been given to him by the group of elite operatives he'd commanded during the war. Many of his operatives were wealthy members of the aristocracy who wanted to do more than carouse, chase women, and gamble. Some of these operatives were upstairs, asleep.

As head of the Home Office, his job was to keep the Roxburys safe from the growing number of threats. One of his constant thoughts was how to protect the Roxburys and the woman he believed to be the love of his life—Anne. *Humph, she's doing a damn good job protecting herself.* He chuckled. *Those daughters of hers aren't too bad either.* Berkley wondered if he could sneak downstairs and kiss Anne senseless, but he knew better than that.

The physician, Simmons, the Earl of Carlyle, was also on the second floor, as was Lady Hortense Horton, queen of the ton and the most revered of the elite. Yesterday, they had all witnessed the marriage of Anne's older daughter, Meredith, or Mer as they usually called her, to Julien Quinton, the son of the Marquess of Briarcliff.

The last guest had left at three thirty that morning, but Anne was wide awake, as though she had slept for eight hours. She had dismissed the house staff and ordered them not to appear until two that afternoon. Her Grace was even able to give the footmen a rest. With the king in residence, literally all the king's men were guarding the house.

Anne had promised everyone her American-style celebration breakfast. Anne hummed her way to the kitchen, checked the clock, and donned an apron. For a moment, it felt like being back in America, preparing Christmas breakfast. Everyone would still be upstairs as she scurried to make the best meal ever. Then she thought of Avery, and tears formed in her eyes.

With all the hustle and bustle of the wedding, the quiet seemed odd. Breakfast for forty. Laughing to herself, she got to work as she replayed the events of yesterday. Mer's walk down the aisle with her father's ghostly apparition on one side and Sar on the other was one of the highlights of Anne's day. Even though Anne was the only one who could see him, she was always grateful when he appeared. *Thank you, Avery, for giving your blessing. We wish you were here instead of hovering about with angel wings.*

I wish I were there too. She heard him and felt a soft touch on her cheek. Then he was gone—receding from the niches of her mind. Her Grace perceived people would think she was crazy if they knew she communicated with her dead husband. *But that's our secret, isn't it, Avery?*

Every day brought new challenges, heightened awareness, sorrow, and incomparable joys. She didn't want to think about murder always lurking around the next corner—or the smuggling and espionage.

"Your Grace. Please let me help. I couldn't sleep. Too used to being up at this hour." Cook was tying her apron.

"Cook, are you sure?" Anne knew Cook had worked long hours to create the perfect wedding party and an incredible cake. Anne also realized Cook would feel shamed if she didn't help. "All right then, can you wash and split the blueberries in half?"

"Of course, Your Grace."

"You and the rest of the staff did an outstanding job yesterday. You made Mer's day perfect."

"We appreciate that, Your Grace. I'll make sure the rest of the kitchen staff knows how pleased you are. Now, how many for breakfast?"

"Just forty." They both laughed.

Ignoring the stirrings from upstairs, Her Grace went about her business. The batter for the cinnamon blueberry pancakes was done. Bacon had been started. The perfectly seasoned small steaks and eggs would be last. Glancing at the clock gave her assurance that the first meal of the day would be on time. Cook was slowly adding batter to a hot pan. Anne looked up and then suddenly ran from the kitchen. She got as far as the hallway and deposited everything in her stomach into the umbrella stand and hung on for dear life, shaking worse than a crème à la vanille.

Sar saw his mother pitched over the umbrella stand, trembling and crying. "Perkins, get Berkley and the rest of the men." Gently, he picked her up and headed toward the beckoning couch.

Anne had become their human barometer. Whenever this happened, someone was about to die. Guessing who would die next had become an art form. When the rest of the men arrived, one look at Anne confirmed they were being stalked by murder once again.

A cool damp cloth was draped over her forehead. "And before you ask, there was no warning. I found myself hurrying out of the kitchen. My only thought was to make it to a dustbin. As you can see, I didn't." Anne shifted to a more comfortable position.

"Berkley, let's get her upstairs. I want all the men to meet me in the kitchen." Sar ordered everyone about and watched as Berkley gingerly lifted Anne from the couch and carried her to her bedchamber. The Duke of Westmoure headed to the kitchen and donned an apron.

"Cook, I'll need an apron for all the men here, even His Majesty. Her Grace taught me how to make celebratory meals. May not be as good as hers, but we will survive." Sar smiled at the thought of the scrumptious meal he and the other men were about to make.

By the time the women descended the stairs, the scent of burning pancakes and the stench of overcooked bacon wafted through the air. Knowing something was wrong, they headed directly to the kitchen. There, standing at the stove, was the king, trying to flip pancakes, and Sebastian turning the charred bacon. Cook; Mrs. Spencer, chatelain of the Westmoures' homes; and Kiggins, the longtime companion and confidante of Hortense Horton, were leaning against the wall laughing.

"Ladies, I think we will wait in the blue room and let the men have at it." Caroline wondered if Cook would ever get her kitchen clean again. With the rest of the ladies in tow, Caroline turned and found the safety of the blue room before laughter took over.

"Did you see them?" Aurelia's bouncy red curls were doing a happy dance of their own. Aurelia, the Duchess of Edgerton, was part of Anne's protective inner circle. "It appears most of them have never been in a kitchen before. His Majesty looked a little out of his league. That pancake almost hit the ceiling before it hit the floor. Can you imagine pancake batter on the ceiling dripping?"

"Thank goodness Cook won't let this get too out of hand or the kitchen staff will be cleaning for days. We'll have our morning meal shortly." Miriam had no idea how they were going to fake enjoying the meal, but what a story this would make for future generations. "Should we ask Sar to bring Her Grace down? This might just be the thing to cheer her up."

Just as the women predicted, the meal was a disaster. The only thing that could be said was that the men had cooked it. The women listened as the men told of their part in making the disaster.

"Never done anything like that before, cousin. Remind me to give the royal cooks a raise. I can only imagine what it takes to prepare a feast." The king sat back and marveled at what their morning endeavors had produced. The ladies looked politely at the mess the men had created and served. It took a lot of stamina to pretend to eat and enjoy the meal.

As the men finished their breakfast, Sar brought his mother down. Her Grace looked as though she hadn't slept for a week. Shaking hands demonstrated how deeply these bouts before someone died affected her. When she was settled in the most comfortable seat, Cook brought weak tea and toast.

In the study, the men were more than puzzled. For the first time, Her Grace had seen still people in smoky, shady shadows during this spell. "Were they dead? Were they only men, or men and women? Anne is becoming more and more ill each time she has one of these spells. Let's keep her more closely guarded. She'll have a fit and accuse us of all sorts of things, but that is the best thing to do for now. Simmons is with her at the moment." Berkley's voice was edged with concern.

Julien strolled in and stopped. He could feel the tension like an oppressive ton of bricks on his chest. By the looks on the faces around him, something had clearly happened.

"Gentlemen, I take my leave. Keep me posted, my cousin. Let me know what you need from me."

As His Majesty rose to leave, Berkley said one word, "Gossip."

"What say, cousin?" The king leaned in closer to hear what Berkley was saying.

"We need to know as much gossip as possible. Who has a lover or lovers in the highest realms of the government? Anything that seems to be a little off, we need to hear it. Regardless of how insignificant it seems to you; it may be a link to us. My men and I might be able to connect it."

"Done." The king took his leave.

"Now, is there anything else?" Berkley looked at the men around him. "Okay then, let's go and talk to the women. We will find out all about the wedding and what people were really thinking. Also, we can check on Anne; she may have remembered something more."

They knew where to find the women by following the trail of their noise and laughter.

"Perkins, make sure there is plenty of brandy in the blue room. It appears the women have decided to roost there." Sar and the other men headed straight to the front of the house.

The women were doing exactly as they thought, dissecting the wedding from top to bottom, left to right, laughing, and throwing out bits of information here and there. When the talk turned to local gossip, the men listened more intently.

Even though there was laughter all around them, Berkley took one look at Anne and knew they needed to talk, alone. The haunted look in her eyes scared him. The slight trembling of her hands indicated how distressed she was by this latest episode. He would meet her tonight in the kitchen, if the staff could get it clean.

• • •

On the ride to Whitehall, Berkley couldn't help but chuckle remembering one of the first times he had met Anne in the kitchen. He had ordered everyone to dinner at His Grace's house and didn't show up himself. He thought back and smiled. His men had been in Sar's study discussing the latest murder. When Berkley left the meeting, he had come around to the front of the house to be let in.

Perkins had answered the door with a raised eyebrow and said, *"Did you come for dinner?"*

Berkley was in no mood to banter with Perkins. He had simply stated, *"I would like to speak to Her Grace. Can we cut to the chase? Perkins, I need to speak to Anne."*

Without so much as a twitch, Perkins asked, *"Why didn't you just come through the back of the house? You were already here."* Perkins raised his eyebrows. *"I will see if Her Grace is receiving."* Perkins had closed the door in his face.

The general had chuckled. He had just received his set down. Perkins was all you saw and more. He was there to protect the family in every way, at all costs.

Minutes later, Her Grace had opened the door and taken one look at him. She hadn't offered the normal salutations but immediately started to put him in his place. She had said things he would never forget. *"You haven't eaten, have you? We can have our little chat while you eat. And you know what little chat I am talking about. The kitchen, now."* Berkley had responded like a child in leading strings.

Berkley laughed at this memory, wondering how many more memories they would create.

That night she had given him an earful. Laughing again, which was completely out of character for him, he didn't notice he was close to Whitehall. Berkley replayed everything in his mind's eye. He had literally been stuffing his mouth when Anne's deadly whisper reached his ears. *"Don't ever use your high-handed methods with me again. I am not one of your elite operatives."* He had wanted to grin, but he knew she would shoot him with her little pistol.

Ah, the beginning or close to the beginning of his love for Anne. She made him whole. There was never a day he could go without her. Until she came into his life, he was nothing. He was without a heart. This was something he could fix. Now, it was the business of the Crown. The rest he would take care of later.

• • •

The night of the breakfast fiasco with the king, shadows danced along the corners of the tavern in the East End. Two laborers were in their usual spot—heads hunched, solving their worldly problems. Jerkily, they stood. Staggering, they gave the impression of drunken men drowning their sorrows. They dropped the act as soon as they were safely enclosed in the warehouse.

Pallets of statues filled with opium stood in the middle of the otherwise empty room. The Earl of Severson was leaning forward, examining the pallets, thinking about profits, and about sampling the delights of Sylvia Meacham, the Viscountess of Truvo, later tonight. For a second or two, he only felt the pain of the sting of the cut and a neat zip across his throat.

"You will never threaten me or anyone else again. Can you still hear me, Severson? I want you to go to the devil remembering that." Blood dripped on the floor; a thud was the only answer as Severson's frantic eyes and long talon-like fingers clawed at his throat as he struggled to grapple with the reality of the moment.

How many minutes had passed? The earl realized he was on his stomach. How? He didn't have the strength to figure it out. He thought he heard a rustle of fabric and something being stuffed around his throat. Severson felt he was being lifted, or was he floating? *So, this is what death and hell are like.* Then nothing.

• • •

In the opulent study on Grosvenor Square, the exchequer sat at his desk in his private office. Checking his transportation schedule for the women, he thought of all his future plans. It was time to leave England. There was nothing much left for him here. He would be gone within the week.

The two women already in France would be sent to the sultan when he arrived. Adele and Laura would leave for France in the morning. They would be waiting for him at his French home. As discussed with Boss, the exchequer would run the business from the French and Italian side. Double-checking everything, he summoned his valet to pack his things and his man of affairs to make sure all was in order.

• • •

The next morning, Caroline and Alexius came for breakfast. Anne didn't know how she and her family would have been able to maneuver through the ton without Caroline Standerson, the Marchioness of Broadhurst, and her daughter, Alexius. *What a disaster that would have been.*

"Your Grace, are you receiving?" Oliver presented a card on the silver salver—the Countess of Wyckham.

"Yes, Oliver."

The effervescent, elegant Countess of Wyckham, Cintha Eliot, strolled into the room, engulfing all with a vitality that made everyone want to follow like the Pied Piper. Smiling, she thought to herself, *I hate Negroes. You see one, you've seen them all. They're all the same. Thank goodness I don't know any, but rules of society require I stop by. And I won't get to know these either. Why should I? They aren't white. It is disgraceful and shameful for one of the richest families in the world to have Negroes as a part of their lineage and claim them.* She assured herself that someone in the ton would take care of the matter. Never questioning her thoughts, she continued playing nice with her best smile in place while thinking of ways to make sure they were eliminated.

"Your Grace, Caroline, excuse me for intruding like this, but I've just returned, and I wanted to welcome the new aristocrats to England and our rarefied world." Cintha glanced around the elegantly appointed room, approving of the taste.

"Cintha, allow me to introduce you to Her Grace and her daughters." Caroline hid her surprised look that someone else was out and about so early, and she wondered why. Not knowing Cintha well, she had no idea what the countess really thought of the new duke and family.

Was she an ally or a foe?

Anne almost stopped mid-smile. Cintha's smile was there, but Anne felt waves of hatred. She inwardly cringed. *This is what most white people do. They smile in your face, but inwardly they're saying how much they dislike Negroes. They think Negroes don't feel it, but Negroes do and become more distrustful of them than ever.* The visit only lasted a few minutes, but Anne had that feeling she was staring at her enemy in the face.

Shaking Cintha's image away after her departure, Anne realized she needed to do something productive. "Oliver, will you summon the girls?"

"Caroline, who would have ever thought that our girls, with the help of your father, would develop his original concept? Working girls can walk in, try on clothes, and walk out with a dress. Our seamstresses keep replenishing the racks. We can also do a simple nip and tuck in the store." Anne pushed all thoughts of Cintha to the far corners of her mind and focused on all the good that was happening.

◆ ◆ ◆

The Viscount of Truvo, Sylvia Meacham's husband, thought his wife was at her girlfriend's in the country preparing the hen night party for her daughter. In reality, Sylvia had been spending the last few days with the Earl of Severson, believing she was ensuring her ownership of Westmoure Shipping Company. After the incident, Sylvia Meacham stitched the Earl of Severson's neck back together. The cut hadn't been deep enough to cause much harm. When healed, there wouldn't be a scar. *Too bad he won't live long enough to see that happen.*

Sylvia obliged him because she had what she wanted. The trade-off had been simple—her body for complete ownership of Westmoure Shipping Company in the event something should happen to him. *Men are so easy, especially older, single ones.* Her solicitors and his made sure all was in order.

Sylvia smiled to herself. Finally, she would complete what that fool hadn't finished the other night. *Thank goodness my man was tailing Severson. Now, let me eliminate this worthless piece of mankind.* He had already slipped into a natural slumber. She turned him on his side, which woke him to a degree. "This is for you," Sylvia whispered and plunged the blade between his ribs. Laughing, she got up and continued to clean out his safe.

Boss looked around, making sure no one was about as she hurried to the trade entrance of the Earl of Severson's house in Mayfair. What she was wearing covered her from head to ankle. Adjusting the veil, she daintily climbed the stone stairs. Her little chat with Sylvia Meacham was long overdue. *Should I kill her now or let her live?*

The door was opened by Sylvia herself. They both sensed this was no afternoon social call.

"Come into the bedchamber. I need to tidy up. We can talk there." Boss was led to the bedchamber, where the body of Severson artfully decorated the center of the bed.

Boss took one look at the bed, and Sylvia shrugged. "We

had an agreement and both of us lived up to our end of the bargain."

Turning to Boss, Sylvia pronounced in a brittle voice, "No one tells me what to do or what share of Westmoure's I am entitled to." Sylvia stared at Boss with hard, glassy eyes. "Severson signed Westmoure's business over to me in case something should happen to him." She pointed to the bed. "As you can see, something has. What you are entitled to will be given to you when I take over the company."

"I came to you with this plan over six years ago. We agreed that this would be split between us, and we would equally share any additional expenses as they came up. Now, now, Sylvia, no need to get greedy. We will be rich beyond our wildest dreams." Boss cocked her pistol. "However, since I was trained by the old duke himself, it is best that I take over now. Your ambitious tactics worry me. Hand over the note Severson gave you."

Sylvia extended her arm and handed over a copy of the note.

"Let's not have this discussion again. Next time, I won't be this lenient. Clean up this mess and destroy everything. Sylvia, if I were you, I would leave town for a while."

Boss shivered as she got into her coach. *I should have killed the little upstart. Next time I will.*

Sylvia lit the pile in the attic, ran down the stairs, grabbed the bag with all the valuables, threw the lit candles around the bed, ran to the basement, and ignited the oily rags. Then she raced out the trade entrance. Once in the carriage, Sylvia smiled and blew a kiss to the house that would soon be rubble. She and her husband would make it just in time to board the ship to the Continent.

• • •

The Duke of Aston slowed his horse in the courtyard. One of the king's men caught the tossed reins. He had been away since last December on the king's business, and he was glad to be back on British soil. He lifted the diplomatic pouch and headed for the king's private chambers.

"Your Majesty."

"Aston, commendable job as usual. Your reports arrived by the various couriers. Is there anything to add besides what is in the final report?"

"No, Your Majesty." The Duke of Aston, Royce's father, traveled as special envoy for the king. Both father and son were in service to the Crown. Ever since Royce's mother died, neither wanted to stay in the empty house she had once filled with love and laughter.

"We have another kettle of fish that needs your immediate attention." All Aston wanted to do was to go home, see his son, and rest. But that appeared not to be possible at the moment.

The king continued. "We have a problem that implicates someone or several people in the higher echelons of government. They will need to be weeded out and eliminated quietly. Your job is to gather all the gossip going around the palace grounds and other places the elite gather. You are to report only to Berkley. This very secretive matter must be taken care of as quickly as possible. It involves our newest aristocrats, smuggling, espionage, hate, and murder. We have proof. Now we must find those involved.

"That's it, Aston. Go see your son and Berkley. They are at Westmoure's house. My cousin will fill you in."

As Aston arrived at the Westmoures', he noticed smoke coming from a house somewhere in Mayfair. Thinking nothing out of the ordinary, he climbed the stairs and knocked. Perkins took one look at the duke and knew he was one of Berkley's elite operatives. "My lord, they are in the study." Perkins followed him to the study and became one with the door.

. . .

Samuels thought his next job might be with a circus. Jumping on and off horses was a specialty anyone who worked for the general must possess. He rapidly knocked on the door. Oliver saluted. With one look at Samuels, Perkins could see there was urgency stamped on his face. Without being told, Samuels headed straight to the study. Perkins silently opened the door.

"Sir."

"Speak, Samuels." Without asking, Berkley knew something was wrong.

"There is a fire at the Earl of Severson's house. Daggs and your men said to come quickly."

By the time they reached Severson's house, the fire had been extinguished. Daggs was getting a report from one of his men. "It appears the fire was started in three different places. The deepest char marks are in the attic, basement, and around the bed. The body was found on the bed. You might want to take a look at it before it is moved."

Daggs picked up a piece of the charred debris and turned it over. "Did someone speak with the neighbors?"

"Johnson, he's over there."

As the captain finished his report, Daggs issued his order. "Thanks, Captain. No one is to touch the body until I say so."

"Right, Inspector."

"Johnson."

"Inspector."

"You spoke to the neighbors? Can you tell me exactly what they said?"

Johnson glanced at his notes and gave his report to Daggs. "The housekeeper in the house on the right claimed she saw a woman climb the stairs earlier this afternoon. It was very early this afternoon, probably late morning, she said. She had seen the woman come many times before. Today, she never saw her leave.

"The upstairs maid was looking out the window of the other house, and she saw a very well-dressed woman climb into her coach. The maid did not recall seeing any smoke or fire or flames. Shortly thereafter, another woman emerged from the trade entrance at the back of the house; she got into the other carriage. She was carrying a large bundle, and that was it. The maid might have smelled smoke, but she didn't see any flames or fire. I asked them each several times, Inspector, but they could tell me nothing more. Their names are here in case you want to question them further."

"Thanks, Johnson."

Berkley had been beside Daggs all this time and knew it was the moment to examine the body. "Let's go, Daggs; there's a body to examine. Where's Simmons?"

"Right here, General." Simmons was making his way through the rubble.

Back at the Westmoures', Cook and the kitchen staff waited dinner for the men. After they washed the soot and smell of smoke off them, the men headed to the dining room. Beside each man's chair was an empty one. Before they could speculate, the door opened and the women walked in, all looking as beautiful and colorful as birds of the most prized aviary. Perkins took up his usual position, with his ear becoming one with the door.

"We need to know what is going on and how it affects us." Anne's voice carried that *I'm your mother, so you had better tell me everything* tone. Before Berkley, Sebastian, or Aston opened their mouths, they took a hard look at the women. They were serious.

"If we keep this up, pretty soon you'll be asking for positions as ambassadors for the government." Berkley's only thought was that they'd be damn good at it.

"Oh, don't be daft, Berkley. Since the king now spends so

much time here, we've already asked him for positions as ambassadors at-large. He has agreed. His Majesty thinks women have an interesting perspective on most things." Anne smiled her prettiest of smiles.

"But it's dangerous out there. You could get killed." Berkley's food was flying all over his plate. Why would his cousin do that? *He doesn't know what these women are capable of.*

"May I remind you who saved Sar twice?" Anne looked Berkley directly in his eyes. "And I could get killed right here."

Berkley looked at Anne again. He wondered why he was always losing battles to this pint-size woman. "The men and I will think about it." Before the words were out of his mouth, he understood it was the wrong thing to say. He knew he had just stepped into the hornets' nest with bare feet.

Sar looked across the table and raised his eyebrows, knowing Berkley was going to get a dressing down like a four-year-old. His mother was wise and smart. No one told her what she could or couldn't do. She would dissect the problem and find a solution. If she wanted to become an ambassador at-large, she would. And there was nothing Berkley could do about it. Sar wanted to be there when it happened. He chortled to himself. *The general as a five-year-old before the headmaster. That will be something for the books.*

Berkley knew there was nothing they could do but tell the women everything. "We found the body of Severson in his bedchamber. The fire would have burned him to a crisp if it hadn't been put out when it was. We were able to examine the remains. He died before the fire was started. We found the stiletto point of insertion between the ribs. There was enough thrust to pierce the heart.

"Beth, some time ago you told us there was a woman or women at the center of this. They were devious. Then your mother and the other women told us what to look for—vicious, angry, and a marriage for everything but love. Unfortunately, based on everything we learned today, you may be right.

"The housekeeper on one side of Severson's house witnessed a woman enter late this morning or very early this afternoon. The upstairs maid in the house on the other side of Severson's saw two women leave. One left earlier than the other. The second woman left carrying a large bundle. No one saw any flames or smelled smoke."

Daggs picked up where Berkley left off. "The fire appeared to have been started in three separate places in the house. It would take some time for anyone to notice smoke, flames, or fire. We are dealing with an expert who knows about creating fires that cause the most damage before they are detected." Daggs was pacing a kilometer a second.

"Is there anything else you might be able to tell us that would help us to identify this woman or women?" Caroline looked at Sebastian.

"Now you want us to help you, but only when it is convenient for you. Darling, it doesn't work like that. We're either in this all the way or not at all." Caroline and all the other women smiled sweetly.

"No, I won't have you involved. This is too dangerous. No, no, no." Sebastian almost pounded his fist on the table.

"Well, Sebastian, I'll be spending a lot of time at Her Grace's house in the country. Anne, do you have a room I could use for a few weeks?"

"Caroline, I just want to keep you safe; I love you so much. If something should happen to you, I would die." Sebastian sighed. "You want to help clear this up, don't you?"

"Yes, dear. I know there's Harson's, Paige's, Cummings, and whatever else we come up with, but this must be done. Too many people are being murdered, and this is directed at us."

Sebastian knew when he was defeated. He looked at his wife and just said, "Be careful. I would be nothing without you."

Caroline understood how much it took for her husband to say that in front of this group of people. She would remind him tonight how much she loved him.

CHAPTER 2

A Different Perspective

Later that night, Berkley stealthily made his way through the trade entrance of the Duke of Westmoure's London residence. The back of his neck was tingling. It always forewarned him of danger. The love of his life was angrier than a charging bull. He guessed he deserved it.

Of course, I shouldn't have said what I did at dinner, but she doesn't understand; she is my life. Now, how should I approach this? Just go into her bedchamber and make love to her before she says anything? Of course, that won't work. I promised her a relationship in which she would be equal to me. Maybe I had just better go in and face the music.

The room was still except for the flickering candle on the table next to the chair in which she sat. Berkley approached her, not knowing what to say or do. The general, a man of many words with diplomats, armies, government officials, and operatives, didn't know what to say to the love of his life. The only thing that came to mind was what was on his heart, and he could never say that to a diplomat. *Be honest, Berkley; if you are going to spend a lifetime with this woman, only honesty will work.* "I'm sorry. I should have never said what I did earlier tonight at dinner."

Anne stared at him for a moment. Her face was without expression. It was as though he were looking at a stone wall, no emotion, no affection. When she spoke, her voice was flat as the top of a barrel and as welcoming as a forty-day rainstorm. "An apology like what you have just said is unacceptable. You do not understand the depth of what you did. Don't ever tell me what I can do and what I can't do."

He took a step closer and was stopped by the frost of her voice.

"I didn't come to this country to be told how to act or how to live. This business of murder, espionage, and smuggling affects me directly. It's up to us, not you and not me alone, to try to stop this if we can. This can't be done if you think you are in charge of me, or if you think you can tell me what to do. You agreed to discuss things with me, but I'm not going to try to confer with you just to have you say, 'Oh no you can't,' before we talk it out."

She continued before he could say anything. "You have no idea what it's like to have people tell you what to do, where to do it, and when. That is America.

"There, when Negroes leave home for the day or for a minute, they never know if they will get home again. During the moments out in public, some people may determine that they don't like that person because they are different, and they are going to create a situation in which that person won't exist any longer.

"They're accused of stealing, doing things they've never done, and then tried and convicted on the spot. Punishment could be anything from chopping off a hand to lynching, just to enforce that the white man is superior to the Negro. This is what we live with, this is what we must do to survive. We must bow our heads, keep silent, and hope we continue to live, due simply to the idiocy of many white people.

"Here in England, white people spit on you, throw refuse on you, and ignore you. You aren't seen; you can't participate. This isn't freedom either. People call me *Your Grace* when they don't want to, they bow when they don't want to, and they think I am nothing. Berkley, in order for me to live, to live a life of freedom and to be as free as I can, it is essential I do everything in my power to ensure I can walk on the streets and to guarantee I can live and love. If I don't do this, then what will my children have after I am gone?" Anne hung her head and softly sobbed in her hands.

"What else is it you are not telling me?"

Anne looked at Berkley, and the sob turned into a deluge.

"You won't have me because I am white?"

The tears kept coming. Her Grace shook her head no.

It was just as Berkley thought—haunting memories. He held her closer. "Anne, my love, what is it?" He kissed her softly.

"Nothing, just nothing." She looked up at him, and a tear traveled slowly down her cheek. Knowing she could neither lie to him nor herself, the tears came in a rush like a waterfall. The general had been an operative for too long to accept her willing excuse. There was something else disturbing his love intensely. His mind flashed on everything he knew about her—the flight from America, the death of her husband, being a Negro, the Underground Railroad, trips to the South to lead slaves to freedom. He knew horrific memories were assaulting her.

"It's the Underground Railroad, isn't it, Anne? Talk to me please. Tell me more about what you saw and felt." The tears started flowing even faster. He held her tenderly and sensed he was not going to like what he was about to hear. The pain in her eyes spoke volumes. She had to let it out at some point, and this was as good as any.

"It was even worse than I had ever imagined or anticipated." She stopped, doubled over, and held her stomach as if to ward off excruciating pain. Her Grace's body fell into him as if looking for security.

"There was no turning back for the slaves. It didn't matter whether they were caught, lynched, or beaten to death. The life they had been living was that of pure torture and unspeakable horrors. Life was always spent on guard, on edge. If the overseer or master had a bad day, it was taken out on the slaves. It didn't matter whether the slaves were from Africa or Ireland. They were slaves—the master's property to do with as he chose. It is hard to comprehend for those who are free. Slaves had nothing and were nothing—no rights, no property, no life. They were at the whim of whoever owned them. Nothing, Berkley—nothing. Can *you* begin to understand? You lived your entire life like that.

"These were not indentured servants whose fathers or family needed money. In exchange for the daughter working for several years in America to pay off the debt, the family was given the required funds. After the debt was paid off, the indentured servant went her or his own way.

"These were slaves—the property of another, not human, but property like a piece of clothing. From Africa and Ireland, the slaves were sold to slave traders.

"The property was bound, put in manacles, and many times branded. Branded like an animal and put on boats in a most inhumane manner. If they made it, they survived in filth. Starvation and disease resulted from the neglect, and no one cared. Women were raped. As you know, if the ship was about to be seized by the navy for violating the law, or if the ship and its crew were running out of food, they thought nothing of tossing the slaves overboard. Some women from Ireland couldn't take the misuse. As I have told you before, they drove nails through their brains—*nails*. Killing themselves. Overboard they went. Vanished. Gone forever.

"In America, the slaves were put on auction blocks, inspected, and sold like horseflesh. How could someone do that? Don't tell me it's business or economics; it's beyond inhumane. Humans are humans—flesh and blood." She was enraged. Thoughts of what she might have gone through zoomed through his mind.

He pulled her closer to him as if trying to protect her from the onslaught of memories and what might have been. Just like his missions, what one witnessed was etched in the deep recesses of one's mind, too horrible to ever be brought to the surface—*the chilling haunting memories of war, the only spoils one ever earned—unspeakable spoils—no honor, no glory.*

"The runaway slaves were human beings; many had lost arms, hands, and other parts of their bodies due to someone else's cruelty—many times without cause. It was just because the owner could. But it was the vacant look in their eyes, and the fact they were the living and walking dead, that scared me the most. The slave men and women had been abused in so many ways, including repeated rapes, and there was nothing left of their souls. They had to get out, one way or the other. It was horrible." The sob that erupted from her was pure agony.

"A few in the group had been the object of . . ."

Berkley stopped her with a kiss before she continued. He had a feeling he knew what was coming next, and he didn't want her reliving that horror. Working in Whitehall, along with his position, made him privy to many things, including the dark whispers of acts too horrible to comprehend.

One was the diabolical slave practice in the Americas called buck breaking—the use of demeaning sex and violence to emasculate male Negro slaves. Although mostly practiced in the Caribbean, he had heard of instances in the former colonies. *If she witnessed one, I will personally travel to America and rip the slave owner to shreds.*

"What these men endured was the most degrading act that could be inflicted by another human." Anne's tremble was the indicator she was well aware of this form of indignity.

"No, you don't need to explain. The utilization of buck breaking is one of the most debasing, belittling, depreciating, and cruel things one man can do to another." Berkley's mind focused on what he knew of the practice. *Sex used to control men and others.* Calling the other slaves to watch, the slave owner or master usually picked one of the strongest slaves, had him tied to a stump, stripped him, and had another slave flog him. When that was done, the slave owner would sodomize the beaten slave. To make the humiliation, shame, and mortification worse, the slave owner invited neighboring slave owners to watch. They could also sodomize the captive slave if they chose. Reports had reached his desk stating that many of the slaves subjected to this form of inhumanity were so disgraced and mortified, they committed suicide. This intimidating punishment kept the other slaves in line and instilled the practice of Negroes beating each other as an acceptable form of control. This idea was lodged deep in the caverns of their minds and passed down to their children.

"Hush now, I have read reports about this practice. It is beyond comprehension." He ran his hand over her hair such as a mother would soothe a child.

"How could someone treat another human like that? It was horrible. The men were broken. They felt less than whole. Even worse, the slave masters instilled the same hate in their children and passed these notions down to them. Slaves were nothing but their property. You can do your worst. No one cared. They were thought of as inferior and stupid. African or Irish, you were theirs." She rocked back and forth in the world of the past, having witnessed the reality of man's inhumane treatment of another of God's creations.

Looking at her, the general comprehended on some level that he should not touch her again right now. He had seen this of his men at war. Not realizing what she was doing, Anne would lash out at him with all her might. It was the spell of the trauma. Slowly and carefully, he walked over to the side table. Knowing her, Her Grace had to have something stronger than sherry in her chamber. She did. He poured two glasses.

Berkley was always ashamed and astonished at what one man would do to another for power and greed. It always boiled down to the same core factors. Unfortunately, it would probably never change. As he approached the bed, he cleared his throat to get her attention. She had lived through hell, and damn it, she was going through a living hell now in England.

Anne glanced up, gazing at him as though in a trance. He had to make sure she saw him and recognized him as a friend. A muted "Anne" escaped his lips. Extending the glass, all he said was "Drink."

She didn't reach out to him. Her Grace was frozen in time—a horrible time. From experience, he understood what she was going through—reliving the horrendous moments. The scars of her war. He would wait, and they would drink brandy together—probably for most of the night. How fortunate he was to have such a woman in his life.

She has been through the worst situations to help right an injustice and live a free life. Man's fatal flaws repeated over and over again, and inhumane treatment of others was one of those major failings. Stranger yet was how man thought he was always in control of everything and right . . .

Just watching her made him reexamine his life choices. And he knew. *It isn't about how you look; it is about the heart that beats under the exterior. It isn't about how much money you have; it is about how much more you have to give.*

Isn't America ashamed of itself? Will a Negro ever feel he can trust a white man? Is white America so unconscious of its behavior that they think they are right?

In England it is the aristocrats who think they are above all other people and hate Negroes because they are different. They pass this hatred down to others by their actions. This is just like America. We don't own Negroes, but we treat them abominably. And the king is part Negro. We owe much of the root of this hatred to that ridiculous writer Edward Long, who wrote The History of Jamaica, *and people actually believed it as though it was the gospel. Foolish, foolish mankind.*

These are the wounds of life, and the aftermath—how you choose to deal with them determines your course. Is it with a heart full of hate or love? He acknowledged love was the only answer. Sighing deeply, he sat on the edge of his chair to watch his beloved; he would do so for the rest of his life if need be.

Berkley kneeled beside her and held her tenderly. "You know I can't make the world right for you. All I can do is love you forever and create a life for us and the children that is as good as possible. You realize I don't understand, because I've never had to look at a problem like this from your perspective. Call me as foolish as the others to never look at the different perceptions.

"You are my all. I didn't know you were going to walk into my life and be the love I've never had. At forty-nine, that's quite a shock for an old man." Berkley tried to make the moment a little lighter but not less important. He wouldn't diminish her love or his love for her in that manner.

"Beloved, my love for you goes beyond all time, dimensions, and beings. Right now, I want to make love to you, but that won't solve the problem. Just promise me we can talk about everything regardless of how painful it is, or how much joy it has brought into our lives. Note I am neither changing nor do I ever want anyone else's love but yours. Speak to me, my love; let us figure out how I can become less of a horse's arse."

For the rest of the night, Berkley held her and they talked.

Just before dawn, he tucked her into bed and gently kissed the top of her head. Before the day staff arrived, Berkley let himself out the same way he had entered. He had a lot of thinking to do. But most of all, he felt he had to find out for himself the truth of the matter. *Could it be that bad?*

Her Grace awoke to an empty bed, an empty brandy decanter, and a pounding head. She had heard his whispers and promises as they floated in and out of her brain. Only one who truly cared would have uttered such assurances.

CHAPTER 3

I Am Who I Am—Maybe

Frances arrived at Paige's before everyone else. She needed the quiet time to make a general list of what was to be done and a purchase list of any additional items they might consider for the grand opening. Her daughter, Joycellyn, was dancing around like a two-year-old although she was approaching thirty. Somehow, they had made it with the help of the old duke. They had a place to live and a place to work, and Frances had a business of her own, Winters.

Joycellyn was the bastard child of Charles Roxbury, the middle son of the family. At the age of eleven, Frances, who worked as a servant in the duke's residence, was molested. Charles framed his younger brother, Avery, for the deed. Not knowing the truth, the old duke had been mortified and had banned Avery to America.

For six years after the molestation, Frances was locked in the chamber of her brain. When she saw Charles again, it sparked something. Whatever *that* was made her scratch, claw, and grunt at him like an animal. Finally, when she was able to speak again, she told her tale. Charles was exiled from the family from that moment. A few years later, he died. But his death could not erase the horror of that night and its plaguing lingering thoughts.

The shop door opened and in walked Georgina, Aurelia, and Miriam. They were followed by the queen of the ton herself, no other than Lady Hortense Horton, who used her cane as though it were a scythe. She had been known to say, *"I clear all the rubbish that's in my way with my secret weapon. People pay me respect because they think I am old and can't hear. Infirm, many say."* She cackled. Caroline arrived next, along with her daughter, Alexius. Then Anne walked in with Beth, Mer, and Evelyn. Duchess and America, the four-legged protectors, trailed behind.

"The men will be here shortly; let's see how much we can get done before they arrive. We'll have them do all the heavy lifting." Anne was looking around at the partially decorated shop.

The dogs were comfortably settling into a morning snooze. Upon hearing her mistress's voice, Duchess perked up her ears. Sensing she wasn't needed, Duchess sighed and tucked her head under America's chin. America was Mer's little wolf. Well, it shouldn't be said *little*, but they were the smallest wolfhounds Whitehall had trained.

As the morning progressed, the men appeared; the ladies with their lists showed them what to do and what to purchase. Perkins stood at the ready to help but mostly directed the other men. Cook brought lunch and set up the tables so they could see what it would be like when the patrons in the store took time for tea and pastries.

This was a trial run. Seamstresses were working; their area looked comfortable. Next, the women attempted the artful arrangement of the ready-made sample dresses. "Who ever thought this would become a reality from a loosely formed idea—or be so helpful for women who work?" Aurelia showed her delight as she examined the dress closely.

"These are extraordinary." Miriam was looking at the stitching and pulling on the seams to see how well everything withstood the abuse. She understood that these dresses would have to endure washing after washing after washing and repeated wearings. A new dress for many workers was a treat, and she wanted these garments to live up to their expectations.

"I, for one, think it is time for something stronger than tea. We can continue this tomorrow." Evelyn's announcement had the other ladies nodding in agreement.

Dinner was a lively affair. No one knew how Paige's would turn out. It could be a failure or a success. They were being judged by not only the working girls who came into the shop but also the ton. Judged they were and judged they would be. There was no way around it.

"The best thing to do is to listen and to make any adjustments quickly. This way we will keep everyone satisfied and learn how to make better patterns. I never knew this was possible." Caroline marveled at all the things that were happening: ready-made dresses, an awe-inspiring new concept; Harson's, the school teaching women how to run a business, become accountants, handle accounts receivable, and run an office; and the growth of Cummings. Cummings, which was the brainchild of Caroline's family, thrived. It had been passed down from one generation to another through the women of the family. No one in general society knew it was run by women. Alexius was in charge. The company supplied high-end soaps and lotions for the mistresses of the wealthy, along with fabric and distinguished buttons. It was growing faster than Alexius could handle. Beth and Mer had joined the company. Along with this came Paige's. Of course, there was the joy the Roxburys brought. She wondered what other fabulous things were in store for them. Caroline smiled and whispered, "Can't wait."

• • •

On the other side of town, Berkley was quickly changing his clothes and being transformed. One of the actors Scotland Yard depended upon for certain information was an expert at makeup. Berkley's white skin was now a dark chocolate brown. He would find out for himself what it was like to be a Negro.

By nine o'clock, all was in order. Berkley was ready to take to the streets where vendors sold fruit and flowers and women sold themselves. He strode along the streets with a jaunty step, never thinking something could go wrong. *Will I prove Anne wrong, or will I find out things are worse than I imagined?*

Berkley walked the streets near the theater district. He was pushed, spat upon, and had refuse dumped on him. *Well, Anne was right about that.* He wanted to throw the jacket in the garbage right then and there. But as the actor had warned him, the general had to stay in character. Daggs was working close by, keeping an eye on everything; Julien and Royce were milling about as well.

Then, like lightning, it happened. "Stop t'at man! Stop 'im, t'e Negro! Stop 'im. 'E stole oranges from me cart. Stop 'im." For a split second, Berkley wondered who the vendor was talking about. He didn't see any Negroes. Then he realized the cart seller was pointing at him.

The crowd came upon him from nowhere. Someone wielded a stick to his ribs, and punches were being thrown. Then there was another cry.

"T'ere, she's with 'im, t'at little un. Git 'er." The anonymous voice from the crowd had everyone turning on the little child who couldn't have been more than six. Wide eyes locked on those running toward her; she searched for an escape.

Somehow Royce and Julien separated the crowd and grabbed the child.

The general headed into the free-for-all; it was mayhem. A heavy work boot connected with his ribs. Another person beat him with a stick. The crowd was kicking and punching. Daggs broke everything up with a sound of authority, his whistle.

In a well-sprung duke's carriage, the child was rushed to Berkley's house, where Simmons was waiting in anticipation of something happening. The bleeding child was gently taken into the house and put into the capable hands of Simmons. The doctor had been Berkley's right-hand man on the field during war, and when there was trouble anticipated while working for the government, he was still.

Meanwhile, somehow Daggs extricated Berkley from the crowds and got him into a coach. "It looks like you need to see Simmons. You have a gash on your head that is bleeding, your clothes are ripped, and I can tell by the way you're holding your side that your ribs are at least bruised. If this is the way Negroes are treated, then the citizens of England are more foolish than I thought—turning on another because of the color of one's skin."

"You're right, Daggs. If everyone wants power over someone else, then the world is indeed a conflicting place. The injuries are nothing, nothing at all. Where is the child?"

"Royce and Julien got her out of there and took her to Simmons. He's probably working on her now as we speak." Daggs looked at the general and realized he had passed out.

Samuels, Berkley's military attaché, was at his usual post when the general was gone—standing guard outside the front door. Before Daggs could get the general out of the carriage, Samuels was banging on the front door. It instantly opened. The general came to as they were helping him up the stairs, but then his legs collapsed, and he lost consciousness again. Samuels and Daggs carried him into the house.

"Mobs can be brutal. You never know where the hits are coming from, and people are fueled by the perceived injustice of the incident, which makes it worse." Samuels talked as he helped to gently place Berkley on the bed.

"What was he doing out like this? What was he trying to prove? What was he trying to discover? Hate without fact, especially with a crowd, is one of the strongest motivators for trouble." Simmons examined Berkley; he knew without a doubt the general had been working, but why and for what?

"You'll have to ask him. All he asked me to do was to be his cover, and believe me, I got to him as soon as I could. But what I can't understand is why people would inflict this amount of damage over an orange. When he was talking in the coach before he passed out, Berkley couldn't believe it either and expressed the same sentiments." Daggs was striding the width of the floor, as usual.

"It was worse than he described. I watched it all. People were going crazy over the theft of an orange. When the vendor said 'Negro,' it was as though someone had unleashed a tidal wave of hate. Someone stole a damn orange, a piece of fruit worth two or three pence, and they were going to kill Berkley and the child. Would you believe the mob thought they were together? They thought they were together because they both had dark skin. They were going to kill them. The sad part is no one would have cared.

"Where does this hate come from? Where do we get this foolishness over an orange? Does this extend to other things in life? Simmons, don't answer that. I know the answer—of course it does. A killing for an orange. We have gone crazy." Daggs continued to talk and pace.

He was like a hoop picking up speed as it descended a hill. "My men have the man who stole the orange in custody. Of course, I'm going to let him go once I find out if there's anything we can do to help him get a job, so he doesn't have to do this again."

"Was the man a Negro?" Simmons waited for the answer to that all-important question.

Daggs shook his head. "If he had been a Negro and the crowd discovered that fact, they would have categorically accused all Negroes of being thieves. Then they would get on their high horses and become avenging angels—saving our city and the world from the worst of the worst. Life is tough for one whose skin isn't white. We seem to forget that we, the white race, caused the problem." Simmons wobbled his head. He never thought much about the different people he treated for free. He didn't care. That was what one could do if one had money—the defining differences were the color of his skin, an aristocratic title, and a sense of fairness and justice.

The rapid knocks on the door probably meant the other men had arrived. When James opened the door, his jaw dropped. Not only were the men there, but the women were beside them.

"Where is he, James?" Sebastian didn't recall having ever seen the general hurt, and he was worried.

"He's in the makeshift hospital, my lord."

They all hurried to the back of the house. When Anne saw Berkley, her breath caught in her throat. She looked at the dark-toned skin applied by makeup and knew he had done it for her. He had wanted to know for himself what it felt like to be different from others. Love poured from her heart. She hoped he could feel it. Anne loved this man far more than she could ever explain to someone else.

"What do you think, Simmons?" Sebastian looked at the general and understood the damage injuries like this could cause.

"Let's wait and see. Hopefully, all of this is more external than internal. However, I am worried about the little one. She took many punches thrown by the crowd, and she's so small and thin." Simmons's trained hands poked and probed the general.

"Cook has already decided the little one is her responsibility and is in the kitchen now making a hearty broth. They will both need it." Simmons looked at the group surrounding him and smiled to himself. Whether they were on the battlefield or at home, adventure always pursued them. But here on the streets of London, you never knew who the enemy was.

"I don't understand. They could have been killed for an orange. Yes, I know this happens more than we'd like to think, but an orange. They appeared to be Negroes, so they were fair game for everyone. Isn't that a little preposterous? I don't understand what's happening to us. I need someone to explain this to me." Daggs was still pacing, fuming, and wondering what he had gotten himself into trying to protect the streets of London as an inspector at Scotland Yard.

Berkley woke shortly after their arrival. He took one look at Anne and felt his head. "Never run into an angry crowd. You would probably come out on the losing end. Where is the little one?" Before he could utter another word, he fainted again.

"Where is the little one, Simmons?" Her Grace was methodically looking at the bruises on Berkley's skin, which were already changing colors. She was one hundred percent sure he was going to have bright green skin in the morning.

"In the bed in the other room." Simmons could see the worry reflected in Anne's eyes. "Don't worry, Your Grace. Daggs will find her parents.

"As for Berkley, time will tell if there is any lasting damage. No, we don't know anything about the child. From what Daggs said, she was suddenly there in the middle of the crowd. We'll discreetly ask around. If she belongs to someone, they will also be looking for her. I hope this is not another abandoned child on the streets of London. From the looks of her, she was dressed too neatly to be a street urchin." Simmons chatted as he worked.

Then the general started babbling, but he wasn't making any sense or connecting what he was saying to reality. "If the rest of you will excuse me, I think I need to find my bed and take a nap." The general tried to stand but abruptly stopped. He paused in that position for a second or two and then plopped down.

"Why don't you spend the night in here? I will better be able to keep an eye on both of you then." Simmons looked at Berkley and knew he was going to be a difficult patient.

"No, Simmons. I am fine." Berkley curled up on the bed and went back to sleep.

"Now, as for the rest of you, leave me alone with my patients. I promise I will get word to you if anything happens during the night. Both need rest. Inspector, please find out if she has parents who are looking for her.

"We'll see everyone tomorrow. I know you will all be here at some time. Don't make it too early." With the help of Perkins, Simmons was able to get everyone out of the general's house in under two minutes.

• • •

By the time Anne returned home, she was drooping. She went straight to her room and sat in a chair by the fireplace. It was a cool evening, and the fire was brightly lit, but she felt nothing. It was as though part of her life had been ripped away from her. All she could do was cry. People were cruel—and many times, without reason. Her body shook from thoughts of what might have been.

Climbing into bed with a glass of brandy, she put the glass on the nightstand and fell asleep immediately. Shortly thereafter, Anne sensed someone else in the room. When she opened her eyes with *Bessie* in her hands, she was staring into Berkley's face, or she was dreaming.

"No, love, you're not dreaming," he said and kissed her. The tears she thought she no longer had rushed forth.

"I know you did that for me, but don't ever do anything like that again. I almost died when I saw you on the bed. Your eyes were closed, Berkley. Closed. I can't take the death of another person I love. Why would you do something so stupid? I told you what it was like, and when you must live this every day, it's ten times worse." Anne was hugging him and kissing him at the same time.

"It was worse than you described." The events of the evening had stretched his nerves taut. He thought of the little girl. In his mind's eye, he saw the teardrops splashing down her face and her frightened expression. She was unprotected.

Berkley couldn't believe it. What was left of his little innocence about humanity had been forever stripped away. He hung his head to hide his tears.

"Shush, my love." Anne wasn't able to comfort this weeping man. She sat silently with his head in her lap.

"I had to find out for myself. I now know more, but I understand less. How could people be so cruel to other human beings? It must be hell in America." Berkley held on to her.

"It is hell. America is a living hell for Negroes, Indians, and anyone else of color. Just think if you were considered chattel, property of another, not human." Anne thought of the fear and danger they always lived with. Now, she wondered how they did it and survived.

"And it seems to be hell for Negroes here. We have committed terrible acts against mankind throughout the world. Anne, I apologize for all the misguided souls. Must the white world always have to try to be dominant over someone? My love, this is so disgraceful.

"We'll talk. I'll try to understand more. The importance of preventing British ships from transporting slaves was significant. I don't know how the sixth Duke of Westmoure did it, but he understood the meaning of freedom and fought for it, beginning with the act to prohibit transportation of slaves. He should be applauded for that.

"Simmons thinks I'm in my office taking care of a matter. I told him I'd be back quickly. I don't want him to send anyone to come looking for me. He thinks I passed out this evening. Ha, ha, I bet you would tell me I did.

"I love you; remember I have plans for us. Anne, I don't care what color you are, you are mine." Like the superspy he was, he disappeared into the inky night.

Anne chuckled out loud. She would leave it to the other men to tell him he had actually passed out several times. Her Grace felt loved to the tip of her toes; she sighed and fell into a peaceful slumber.

The next day was a busy one for the ladies. They went to see Berkley and the little girl. Simmons threw them out again. Then they worked on Paige's until someone announced it was time for afternoon tea—champagne for the ladies and brandy for the men. There were still things to do, but they could wait.

Perkins and Cook had anticipated their needs. The *London Daily* was open to the Society News. Removing her shoes, Caroline announced, "We might as well see how much of the Society News is about us."

Today's column didn't disappoint.

The London Daily

Society News

Dear reader,
The ton has been desecrated again with the marriage of the Duke of Westmoure's sister to Lord Julien Quinton, one of the ton's most

eligible bachelors. Will we have more mixed-breed aristocrats or will the two be smart enough to not have children?

"The Society News editor goes on to describe Mer's dress again and the decorations at the church. Everyone wanted to know why the queen of the ton was sitting with the family. Are they always this nosy?" Beth continued to read more of the pertinent paragraphs of the article.

> *My sources tell me the king spent the night after the reception at Westmoure's house. In the morning, he and the other men made breakfast for the women. On the menu were burned blueberry pancakes and charred bacon. Batter dotted the ceiling and the king's head.*
>
> *Paige's is still scheduled to open on Friday. We wonder what the concept of ready-made dresses is really about. We will find out. At least the Westmoures are not involved.*
>
> *The Earl of Severson's house was nearly totally destroyed by fire. The earl was allegedly found dead in his bedroom. Rumor has it the fire didn't kill the earl; he was dead before it started. At the scene were Inspector Daggs of Scotland Yard and Lord Berkley, head of the Home Office. The Duke of Westmoure was there also. How much more secrecy will surround these recent deaths? It seems the Westmoures are involved in some manner. Does it happen to do with smuggling and espionage? Probably.*
>
> *One other bit of startling news, the exchequer has left his position. He contracted the consumption disease. According to his*

physician, if the exchequer wants to heal, he must move to a warmer, drier climate imme-diately. Wherever he goes, we thank him for his years of service to the Crown.

Beth glanced over the remainder of the article. "Well, that is all I need to read. We know everything else. How does she know so much? It's as though she is watching the house."

Joycellyn almost danced into the room, followed by servants carrying boxes. "I have something to cheer all of you." Joycellyn started passing out the boxes. Fluffy green bows decorated each one. "With the wedding and the opening of Paige's, not one of you mentioned the ball on Monday. The dukes would be extremely upset if you weren't there. Caroline, you can't disappoint your father."

"How did you remember, Joycellyn? It is the time the reigning dukes of the ton give their annual ball. It's just the two of them, Aston and Grayson. To the disappointment of most women, Berkley is not considered one of the reigning dukes. Although he should be. He outranks them all.

"The main object is to find a suitable bride. Unfortunately, Berkley is too formidable. He would interrogate the women and have them running for the hills. Too bad. That is one very handsome, honorable, wealthy man who would probably be a little difficult to live with. The right woman would straighten him out." Caroline chuckled at the image of the women running for the hills. "This is Aston and Grayson's moment. Everyone wants to be invited."

"You forgot your father's ball, Caroline, and you and the rest of the ladies must outshine them all." Joycellyn and the servants were still passing out boxes.

"No, no. I just pushed the ball to the back of my mind—okay, I forgot." Caroline laughed again, and the sound of crinkling paper filled the air.

Each of the ladies had a dress in a different hue of green. The most amazing part was the lining. They each ranged from a rich purple to a waterfall of cascading blues.

"Joycellyn, with the dresses for the wedding and preparing for the opening of Paige's, how did you find time? Are we overworking you? Thank you. These are incredible, as usual. We should all stand together at the ball. What a sight that will make. I am paying for my dress. No more free talent and work. All of us appreciate what you do." Caroline's words of praise put Joycellyn over the moon. "Now, show us your dress."

The rest of the afternoon was spent talking about the upcoming ball and the women who would make passes at Grayson and Aston. They also spoke about the lack of suitable candidates.

"My father has been alone long enough. He misses my mother, but he needs to be loved again. I see the lonely look in his eyes. Royce's mother died many years ago. Do you think that's the reason Aston travels all the time, so he doesn't have to face the loneliness?" Caroline almost cried thinking about her father.

"If we ever find any suitable candidates, we'll push them their way. Now for our one-pound bets of the women who will make passes at Aston and Grayson." As usual, the one-pound bets were in place by the time Perkins announced dinner.

• • •

Berkley sat at his desk doing something he hadn't done in a long time—nothing. The new duke and the nasty business following in his wake took up most of his time. *Is it really, though?* He was restless and unnerved, and for the first time in many years, he questioned his life. At forty-nine he had felt extremely old and dried up, until Anne came into his life. How could he have walked around so empty?

Anne had triggered these feelings. The general always assumed he would live and die for the Crown and that would be his everything. Now, he realized how wrong that was; something was off.

He wasn't worried about his title, nor the included properties; his closest relative was primed to take over. As a matter of fact, he rather liked Henry, although he didn't know him well. Their chance meetings over the years had left him with the impression of a boring man settled into an equally tedious routine. Maybe that wasn't as bad as he thought.

A year or two younger, his first cousin was the only child of his late uncle John. As far as Berkley knew, his cousin rarely came to town. Henry was a personal friend of the exchequer and was always kept informed of what was going on in the capital. He had a keen head for business. Berkley's cousin was a classic study in stately nature and well settled with his wife. Their son and daughter were doing what most people in their class did, a grand tour for him and husband searching for her. *Good luck on that one.*

The general was closely examining other things. Was it always living on the edge of death, or doing the killing for the Crown, that was making him feel his own mortality? Was it dying without leaving a piece of himself behind? Or was it loose ends, strands of clues, and a family to protect?

With an introspective telescopic inward look, the twinges of incompleteness coursed through him. There was no cook with a hearty meal waiting for him. His staff never anticipated his arrival. They ran an empty house. *Maybe I should get a dog.* Owning a dog would only get him bitten one night if he came home late and the mutt thought he was an intruder. Was this mess he was living called life—his life? Shaking his head, he looked to the future.

Did those he worked with think of him as a stodgy old man with nothing but an office and an empty title? He answered his own question—*yes*. Sighing, he picked up the missive on his desk and just as quickly dropped it as though it had singed his hand. Reaching for pen and ink, he mentally started composing words for one who would never read them.

> *Dear Anne,*
> *I don't know how to express my love to you. All I have done is dedicate my life to the Crown. What an imbalance this has been. It will take a moment, but please let me show my love to you with all I have and please you.*
>
> *You remind me of a little imp about to wreak havoc on a totally unsuspecting ton. You are one of the most interestingly preceptive individuals I have met in quite a while. I laugh at night when I recall some of the things you said. Always remain the way you are. Don't let our crazy world change you.*
> *With affection,*
> *Berkley*

Berkley read the note again, thrust it into an envelope, sealed it with wax, impressed his seal, and went back to work. The nagging voice in his head refused to stop. *Couldn't even address it. Worst note in the world to ever write to a woman. Old man, you have no idea how to just tell someone you love her. She knows you care, but you have to let her know that yours is a love that will endure forever. You'll never send it. It's not the right expression for the love of your life.* Berkley wondered how he had created his world like this.

That starless night, Her Grace sat at the kitchen table with enough food for three before her. She sensed the shift in the air before she saw him. As quiet as the dark, he slipped into the chair beside her. He turned to Anne and tenderly held her face in his large hands. He kissed her until she nearly fell out of her chair. She was panting when he softly whispered, "I owe you my life. You're more than I ever wanted. If I get to do this again as a reincarnated Berkley, I will find you when I turn sixteen." She knew he meant it.

Later, when he slipped into her bedchamber, he looked like a man possessed by love. Before he could do anything, she softly said, "Stop." The glowing fire and branch of candles backlit her like a serene goddess. She summoned him like a mythical creature.

He understood he could not wait, but did she? The boundaries of his love had no limits. When he reached her, he started a total assault of her senses. Covering her body in the softest of kisses, he worked his way across and down her torso. Her nipples had pebbled. She leaned back to offer him more. "Come." He sat in the chair and placed her astride him.

She was hot as the fire itself. Her body was flexible enough for her to bend back and touch the floor. He started to sup on her sweet nectar and run his tongue over and over her mons. Anne spread her legs wider, and his tongue plunged deeper. Over and over again he pleasured her with this motion.

Her Grace was wild—pulling on her nipples and begging for more. She twisted and turned, totally out of control. Her dripping center almost put him over the top. The contractions were beginning. He wanted her like this and nipped her mons lightly. The pressure was enough to have her pleading with him to enter her. She was holding back, but he wanted her at a point where she could hold back no more. He nipped again, and she started moaning and reaching for her nipples. Berkley wanted more—for her to understand she was his.

Anne reached for her center to spread her nether lips wider. He welcomed the access. But she was getting to that point. The next contraction was a little stronger. The storm was about to break. He pulled her up and sat her on his swollen staff; he touched her center once, and she started to twist and turn on him. She pulled him in deeper and deeper. Grabbing both breasts, he placed one nipple in his mouth and rubbed the other over his hairy chest. Both sensations had her riding him harder and harder. He rubbed her center, lifted her off him, and covered her with his mouth. He plunged in with his tongue and then brushed her mons; now he wanted her to shatter. He placed her on his stiff member again; she leaned back. He rubbed her love center and then rolled her nipples in his hand. Her hard, sensitive peaks couldn't stand the sensation. They both shattered together.

Anne fell onto his chest, crying out his name. For a moment, Berkley couldn't move. When he could, he lifted her, turned down the counterpane, and placed her in the bed. He climbed in on the other side.

Before dawn, he whispered, "Again." He started with the lightest of kisses and then suckled while his fingers found her center. He was slowly inching his way down her body. She was trying to move her hands but discovered her hands and feet had been tied to the bed—legs spread apart. She was totally exposed to him.

Berkley looked at every inch of her while rubbing her nipples in his hands. They peaked like grapes. Her center was getting wetter from his gaze. He lowered his head, and his tongue found the entry it craved. As she started the ascent to their world, he untied her hands.

Anne wanted it all again. She couldn't stay still. Her hips rose to meet his tongue. He entered her. Her Grace placed a nipple in his mouth, and she toyed with the other sensitive tip, wet with her own essence. As she pulled him into her, the contractions held him in hot velvet. And then she lost all control. She begged for more as her release claimed her. Berkley spilled the hot seed of love in her center and drained her of every sensible thought.

When Her Grace awakened, all she wanted was him.

• • •

Fourteen sat down to dinner that next night, and that number did not include Berkley. Anne set the tone for dinner with her bright smile, and most of the talk centered around the grand opening of Paige's. Everyone laughed and relaxed. There were tales of the new aristocrats in London, and their snafus. There had been many glitches, but they hoped they had handled them in a reasonable manner. Anne thought, *If we didn't, I really don't care. It is a strange world, but we'll figure it out eventually.*

Of course, the conversation moved to the topic of men. "There are men who are reprobates and gossips; they are unfaithful everywhere. However, it appears the men of the aristocracy have an open-door policy to act any way they wish. They arrogantly flaunt their station—above everyone else. It seems many of the wives and other women willingly ignore it. I guess they must in order to keep their titles and status in society. What happened to the cast-iron principle?" Anne looked thoughtfully at Caroline.

"What? What did you say?" Caroline questioned, as if the wine had affected her hearing.

"The cast-iron principle—a greeting from a wife with a seasoned skillet after a husband's night out usually ends all of his shenanigans."

Caroline almost fell sideways out of her chair laughing—very inappropriate behavior for a lady. But she was with the Roxburys—the refreshing down-to-earth aristocrats who were bringing joy to her life. Oh, how she loved the American Roxburys. "Sorry, Anne, won't work. First, most women in the aristocracy don't know what a cast-iron skillet is, and second, most can't even find their own kitchens. Any other ideas?"

"I wonder if Lady Horton will ever tell the story. Her

husband used to parade his mistresses in front of her. It is rumored she creatively took care of the problem. We will probably have to wait until her next-to-last breath to find out." Caroline didn't know whether the story was true or not, but if it were, what a tale it would make.

"It is absolutely crazy how the aristocracy behaves and believes they are correct or arrogant enough to know everything they do is spot-on. Just teach me how to ignore them and continue doing what is right to survive." It was hard for Anne to believe what power a title had.

"Anne, just follow your instincts and heart. You know what is wrong and what is right. That will be your guiding beacon. Do not worry, Anne. All of us will be right by your side. Trust me, there is nothing you want from reprobates and cheating husbands."

"We have this dangerous game of murder, and I don't want anyone to get in harm's way. It's almost impossible to believe this is happening to our family." Anne reached for her wine as the tear rolled down her cheek. *Avery, I need you.* She felt a soft touch to her cheek, and the tear stopped its journey.

• • •

A couple of nights before the opening of Paige's, everyone joined Caroline and her family for dinner. At least tonight, Her Grace wouldn't have Berkley in her kitchen consuming leftover puddings. Anne was somewhat perplexed by what was going on in her personal life. Should she even have a personal life? She caught herself halfway sighing. *But oh, I live for those moments in the kitchen.* There was the ease of completion. No, no, that couldn't be possible. *Avery completed me.*

At the Duke of Hampton's house, the general was restless. It had been a bad idea to decline the invitation to Sebastian's house for dinner. He had work to catch up on. But he couldn't do anything but think of those moments with Anne. *Living without her is impossible.* In the morning, he'd procure a special license. *I must marry in order to have a heart, a life.* Work was the furthest thing from his mind. He pulled out a piece of paper and started to write.

> *Anne,*
> *Moments with you are almost impossible to describe. Without a doubt, you are one of the kindest people I have ever met. I know you are still grieving Lord Avery, but you are facing life with a determined will to make the most out of all things new to you. Being around you lights up my world. Your gentle love and understanding of all you care about eases into my life and offers a comfort I have never felt before. Please always stay the way you are.*
> *At your service,*
> *Berkley*

The general tossed and turned. This time it wasn't the memories of war but of Anne. He'd be damned if he was going to look at one more report. Taking out ink and paper, he started writing again.

> *My dearest Anne,*
> *To me, you have become "my dearest" in such a short period of time. You make my day richer. When I hold you, my soul realizes the emptiness of my life—the void which may be an unfamiliar feeling to you. But for me, it is the only feeling I have ever known. Now, I appreciate and*

grasp the gift you bestow upon me—love. Not the fleeting infatuation of those of our class, but the feeling of knowing someone on all levels of their being. What a precious gift. Thank you.

    At your service,
Berkley

CHAPTER 4

Berkley and His Edicts

It was a pleasant day to be on Bond Street. The sun was shining, and the air was warm. Walking leisurely, Anne and Caroline chatted about everything as they approached Madame Burgoff's shop. They had almost reached the door when the hiss of a ball whizzed past Anne's ear and shattered the window of the shop.

"Behind me, Caroline. Back into the shop." In a flash, *Bessie* was in Anne's hand.

Caroline fumbled for the doorknob as she continued backing into the shop. With a sigh of relief, Caroline grabbed Anne and pulled her through the open door with her. A stunned Madame Burgoff stood staring out the window.

"Away from the window. Please hang up your CLOSED sign. We will wait for my son." Anne sounded more like the general than she wanted. She would think about that later.

Madame Burgoff took one look at the pistol in Anne's hand and fainted dead away. She hit the floor with a hard thump.

"I guess we will have to put the sign up for her." Anne hung the sign and thought of the scandal this was going to cause. *Thank goodness there were no clients in the shop.*

In a matter of minutes, Anne and Caroline heard pounding hooves and the tinkling bells of a carriage. Sebastian, Sar, and Berkley were together.

Before Berkley was off his horse, he was barking orders. "Get the area cleaned up, board the window, do not let anyone come close to the shop. Samuels, get a detail and secure and guard the perimeter." Just as they entered the shop, Simmons's carriage rounded the corner.

Sebastian and Sar searched the atelier and made sure the back door was secure before joining Berkley.

"Okay, Anne and Caroline, tell us what happened."

"Caroline and I were approaching Madame Burgoff's shop. We had just passed the front window and were close to the door. I heard a hiss, and the window shattered. I told Caroline to get behind me and back into the shop. *Bessie* was out. We moved backward into the shop. I didn't see anything except the carriages on the street." As Anne finished, Simmons walked into the atelier, looked around, and headed straight to the form on the floor.

"Caroline, what do you recall?" Berkley was in his general mode.

"It is just as Anne said. We were coming upon the door of the shop when a ball shattered the front window. Anne told me to get behind her and back into the shop. I fumbled and found the doorknob, opened the door, and pulled Anne in with me. Anne turned to Madame Burgoff and told her to move away from the window and put her CLOSED sign up. Madame took one look at *Bessie* and fainted dead away. She hit her head quite hard. Simmons, you should probably take her to Berkley's hospital. Madame isn't coming around." Caroline was talking like Daggs paced. Sebastian knew she was in a state of shock.

"Simmons, I want you to examine all three women. Glass might be embedded in their hands or faces. Have them rest for a while." Berkley had reached the same conclusion as Sebastian; Caroline was responding to the attack with enough nervous energy to probably install a new shop window by herself, and she didn't even know how.

Berkley's questioning continued on the ride to his house. Caroline was heard snorting more than once. Anne told the general she wouldn't answer any more questions that she had already answered. Madame Burgoff was with Simmons. She wasn't talking. Being unconscious usually rendered one speechless.

By the time they reached Berkley's, the other women and their husbands were there. Perkins had somehow notified everyone immediately. "Just doing my job, General." The other women were there to make a fuss over Anne, Caroline, and Madame Burgoff.

"Does news travel any faster, Perkins?"

"I do admit I was a little off my stride today, Berkley."

The general caught himself rolling his eyes.

That night at the Duke of Westmoure's house, a weary Anne climbed the stairs. She knew what to expect—he would be waiting. He was. She opened the door, and she was staring directly into his eyes. This was a man on a mission.

There was no preamble, no small talk, no sweet promises. Just Berkley trying to be a general in his love life.

"We shall marry tomorrow. I want you under my protection in a place where no one can get to you or even begin to think they can. Do you hear me?" The whisper of his voice was most deadly.

Anne sized him up. *"Humph!"*

"It's time, Anne. You could have been killed this afternoon, and how dare you '*humph*' me."

She turned on him like a lioness protecting her lair. "Don't you dare think I am one of your operatives or under your control. I could have been killed at any time during the past few decades. You think the danger here is any different than the danger in America or the danger of being a part of the Underground Railroad? There is no protection for me besides common sense and being alert. Yes, you help, but I can't be cosseted."

"I can't lose you." The look on his face was one of sheer despair.

"In case you hadn't noticed, we all lose things in life, Berkley, especially you. Every time someone does work for you, death goes hand in hand with the assignment. I lose, because I am a human being. It's the chance we take for waking up. Some are in more precarious positions than others. So do not—I repeat, do not—try to order me about."

"Anne, we will marry in the morning. I have a special license. Right here, in this pocket." He patted his jacket. "Look at you. You're losing weight from worry. You sense when someone is to be killed. Your premonitions have been occurring since you arrived in England. Unfortunately, you have been right every time. You become nauseous and must go to bed for hours to regain your stamina. No, today."

"Well, Berkley, you didn't hear me. No! Out! Get out, and don't come back." She opened the door, checked the hallway three times, and pointed. There was nothing the master strategist could do but retreat. One recognizes when one has lost the battle but not the war.

Too wound up to sleep, Anne stared at the sliver of moon. She wondered what life was like for those who were white. Did they understand the strength it took to be a person of color? To be able to survive? How it felt to be considered less than a human being? The dark thoughts kept pursuing her. Ultimately, she hoped there was a better way. People had so much to give to each other to enrich their experience in the world. *Avery, is this what it has boiled down to for man—greed, fear, and hate? If so, most of us won't make it to where you are.* The brush of the wind on her cheek was her only answer. Satisfied *Bessie* was in place, Anne crawled into bed.

The general was at home deep in thought. Could he really have a life with this woman? The notions of what he would put her through opened the closed, locked vaults in his mind. He was a master spy and lived for the Crown. What he had done for his country sent a chill through his body. That door of the closed vault opened a little wider. What would she do when he screamed out in the night, his body drenched in sweat, vomit covering his nightclothes?

One of the many pictures tucked away in that forbidden compartment came to the fore. He was lopping the head off an enemy opponent. He did not have a choice. As the head rolled on the ground, the vacant eyes stared up at him, detached from the rest of the person. Blood was everywhere, and he walked away.

According to Simmons, battle doctor beyond compare, the name given to this condition was Da Costa's syndrome or soldier's heart. It was believed to have been caused by an overstimulation of the heart's nervous system. Berkley had to clamp his mouth shut from the scream that was about to erupt.

Maybe I work all the time to keep these recollections at bay. How do you tell someone or explain what you have to do to survive? After war, there is nothing but bottles, pints, work, and occasional empty encounters with women. Men returning from war are all damaged, fractured. Am I fit to be a lover and a husband? What would she say? How would she react? Would I be able to continue to live as I do now? The nightmares will be a constant companion until I leave this life. I have killed sons of mothers and fathers, and all the training didn't prepare me for the fallout of the aftermath.

Berkley was on his third glass of whisky. If he kept this up, he would drink the entire contents of the decanter. What had he been thinking? It struck him like a thunderbolt. For the first time in his life, the general was scared. He would have laughed at the irony of the situation, but he couldn't. He sent men to war; he went to war, and he never felt like this. God help him. That woman owned his heart and soul.

And, like any other fool in love, Berkley started making plans to make amends. Should he strike fast or slow? Or use a combination of both along with any opportunity that came his way? He would have to speak to Sar and the girls. They needed to know his intentions, but first he had to speak to Anne. Anne must come first. He started to sweat as though he were in India on a record-breaking day of heat. What would his love say?

After another glass of whisky, the reckless general threw on some dark work clothes and headed to the house of the Duke of Westmoure. *She could really be angry, old man. Maybe now is not the time to talk. Oh hell, I'll never be able to sleep.*

Anne didn't even bother to reach for her pistol. She knew who it was the minute the door started to silently open. "Didn't I tell you to get out? I didn't ask you to come back."

"No, you didn't, Your Grace, but I need you down to the bottom of my toes and my soul. I am groveling here, Anne; I will grovel for the rest of my life if I must. But I am here and willing to lay everything out for you to take and plunder." Berkley inched toward her. "I also think I have had one whisky too many." He fell into her bed and started snoring.

"Men!" Anne rolled over and fell asleep smiling, knowing she was safe and wanted, but she wasn't going to make it easy for him. *"Humph."* When she awoke, he was gone.

The march of Her Grace's quick cadence bounced off the walls and echoed through the lower floor as she made her way to the small dining room. Speaking to the empty room, she knew he would hear her. "Perkins, please let Sar and the girls know I would like to speak to them in my study in thirty minutes."

"Sar, your mother would like to speak with you in a half hour in her study."

"Do you know what this is about, Perkins?"

"No, I don't, but she appears to be in one of her *do as I say* moods."

"If you knew what this was about, you wouldn't tell me anyway. Would you?"

"That's right, Your Grace, especially when she is in one of her moods. I love my head exactly where it is."

"Which indicates to me you realize exactly what is going on, and I may not like it." Sar was talking to empty air, but he heard a faint whistle rapidly fading.

"Oh good, I found both of you together. Your mother would like to see you in her study in twenty-five minutes."

"What is it about, Perkins?"

"I'm not at liberty to say, Mer. But please be on time. Her Grace is in quite a mood." He was gone before they could question him any further.

"What do you think, Beth?"

Beth was beginning to gnaw on her bottom lip. "When it is something like this, it always turns our world upside down once again." Mer's foot started tapping on its own volition.

Her Grace was sitting majestically behind her desk when her children arrived. As they entered, she looked at each of them carefully. The weight of everything happening rested on Sar's broad shoulders. Mer was the glowing newlywed. How could they have missed her happiness? And Beth was a strong, sensitive young woman waiting for the next adventure on the divergent path of life. She was so proud of them. Each one was different yet caring and kind. A parent couldn't ask for more.

"There is something I need to discuss with you. It is

important, and it may come as a surprise." Without any other words, Anne simply stated, "Berkley wants to marry me."

Mer's suspended foot dropped to the floor with a thud. Beth gasped. Sar went to the sideboard and poured a brandy. Before he said anything, he turned toward the door. "Perkins, I can hear you smiling from here. Please come in; I want you to witness everything in case I need to call out the general."

"Your Grace, I think I shall stay where I am. Calling out the general would not be a good idea. We would probably lose both of you. I wouldn't be able to bear the grief."

Sar coughed to prevent his laughing. The opportunity to question the general at length was near at hand. "You are right, Perkins. In thirty minutes, send for the general." Sar needn't say more; Perkins heard every word. Then, he turned to his mother.

"Mother, did I hear you correctly?"

"Yes, and before you attempt to act like lord and master overall, remember I am your mother, and you will listen to what I have to say." Anne held up her hand to stop any further comments.

"No, your father has not been gone long. Do I miss him? Yes, but our lives are moving forward. As you know, I was eighteen when I married your father—young and very trusting. He was an honorable, loving man. Sar, he taught you to be the same.

"Did I expect Berkley to come along? No. I didn't expect nor want to have feelings for anyone. I just wanted to get through the days and make sure my family was safe. But he did come along. He did not offer a starry world of perfection but a relationship—one we would work along in together—and a love that would grow and be enriched by the joys and sorrows of living. Your father gave me that, and I didn't expect it to happen twice, but it has. I am willing and able to take the chances that come with this marriage.

"I love all three of you so much. If you object, I won't marry him."

Her last words lingered over the room. Sar reached for another brandy and looked out the window, watching the sun bless each bit of nature it touched, and then he heard it swirling in his head. *Sar.*

Dad. His mind responded just as quickly.

I know you weren't expecting this, but life goes on. No man wants to see the woman he loves marry another, but I am not there. Berkley will make your mother happy. Give them your blessings. Just don't make it too easy for Berkley. I will settle this with him when he reaches my new home. Avery laughed that rich, robust sound of joy.

I talk to your mother too. Wanted you to know just so you don't think you are going crazy. The first time I spoke to you, I felt you wanted to believe it was me, but you were hesitant and unsure. I will always love you, Sar. You carry me in your heart. But, right now, I think you need to duck.

The push to the floor was like a strong wind. There was a crackle and a shatter of glass. As Sar was being shoved to the floor, a rock flew over the top of his head. When he looked up, two shocked faces were grinning at him.

"Edward, little Elizabeth, in here now!" Sar smiled inwardly as he thought of the two abandoned street children who were now under his protection. They had been hired by an older boy to deliver a message that Sar would be dead soon. A search for their parents had been futile. The little ones had become part of the family. Their favorite sport was breaking glass.

"Elizabeth was showing me she didn't throw like a girl. But she does." Knowing they were in trouble, all Edward could do was explain. "Girls, they always try to show you they are right."

"And why aren't you in the schoolroom?" That was the only thing Sar could think to ask.

"Rock throwing is something Elizabeth must learn to do

properly." Edward wiped the dirt from his hands all over the front of his shirt. "Are girls always this difficult?"

Sar snuffed a chuckle. "They become more complicated as you get older. Little Elizabeth, do you have anything to add?" Sar was trying to keep the laughter from his voice.

"Of course, I have something to say. I throw a rock better than he does." Sar wasn't going to refute that. Little Elizabeth was going to be a handful, just like his sisters.

"Perkins, will you make sure these two get cleaned up and into the schoolroom? We'll discuss their punishment later." Sar knew, as did everyone else, he would talk to them to explain what they did wrong, and he would explain the consequences of their actions. Then they would probably go for a ride on their ponies, or go to the pond to fish, or stay in and make cookies. That's what his father had done with him, and that was what he did now with these two who now belonged to him. He choked up at that thought and issued a silent thank-you to his dad.

"Now, about this matter at hand—Berkley. Mother, do you think he will make you happy?"

"Are you asking if he is your father? No, he is not. Avery will always hold a special place in my heart. But he is Berkley, an honorable and loving man in his own right. Perfect, no, but perfectly imperfect.

"He will ask you and your sisters for my hand. He respects each of you. What you say is up to you. I shall not influence you in this matter."

"Berkley will be the most honorable and loving of men. Look at who he has trained. When Caroline looks at Sebastian, she smiles; her eyes light up. The general expects his men to live honorably in all areas of their lives. I am expecting the same from Julien. Twenty years from now, I want to look at him the same way."

Sar glanced from Mer to his mother. His chest constricted.

They had both found love. How was he going to handle this? If some man asked for Beth's hand, he was going to hit him first. Damn the questions.

"All we ask is that you be happy." Sar gulped to chase away the tears.

"Happy, yes, definitely so. Adjustments, many. As we all know, the general can be rather high-handed in his manners. He believes everyone should obey him, just because he is the general. Everyone must learn a thing or two, including him, and we are just the group to teach him. After all, he may be a part of us." Anne laughed out loud at the thought of them teaching Berkley a lesson.

"Mother, if you are sure, we will welcome him to the family. I can't think of a better man to have in our lives." Mer grinned as she thought of her honorable husband. Words echoed in her brain—*All cut from the same pattern and stamped by the ethical man who trained them.*

"Thank you all."

Berkley arrived at the Duke of Westmoure's house at exactly nine thirty. Perkins opened the door with a verbal quip at the ready. "Who do you wish to see this morning, Her Grace or His Grace?"

"His Grace."

"Good choice, Berkley. You may make it through the day."

Ignoring Perkins's banter, Berkley followed him to Sar's study. Oh hell. They were waiting for him—the three children—and they did not look happy. *Can't back down now, old man. It is obvious they know your intentions.*

"We've been expecting you. Do you have something to say?"

The general wanted to clear his throat, but his neck was paralyzed—it was stuck and wouldn't move. *I will bet my bottom pound that Anne left the decision to them. If they say no, there is always the parish of Gretna Green.* "I came to get your approval to marry your mother, the consent of all three of you."

"Our mother has left the decision as to whether she will marry you up to the three of us. Do you understand what you are asking of a woman who loves—I said *loves*, Berkley—with all her heart and soul? She is not like the ton women who marry for title and money. Regardless, she already has both."

Before Sar could continue, Beth chimed in, "She loved our father dearly. He was an honorable, trustworthy man who loved all of us deeply and entirely. When he died, we each lost a piece of ourselves. Do you understand a love and death that is so intense, profound, and sincere?" She chewed on her lower lip.

Did he? Berkley thought about that for a quarter of a second. "I can't live without her. All of you make my days better."

"You work too much. Our mother needs to be cherished. Despite what is happening, she still must have priority in your day and your heart. Do you understand what that means to a woman?" Mer's foot was tapping in rhythm to her words.

The general wondered if in their spare time they held inquisitions—torturing each other just for sport. He understood that siblings could be quite terrifying. Never having had one, he wasn't quite sure.

"I only want to make your mother happy for as long as she is on the face of this earth." *Weak, Berkley, weak. Can't you think of anything better?* The look on his face was one of desperation and anxiety, and he realized he was losing his request.

Sar's eyebrows arched of their own accord. "Is that all?"

"Let me make this very clear to the three of you, I shall neither live nor go through life without Anne by my side. She shall, do you hear me, be mine."

That was what Sar was looking for—conviction and *damn what you say, she is mine.* "Perkins, will you show Berkley out?"

Oh hell, is that all I get? What is it about this family? They execute orders in a fashion more deadly than even me. Berkley was mute. He dutifully followed Perkins to the door.

"Good day, my lord."

"Now is not the time to 'my lord' me, Perkins."

"Yes, my lord." Perkins's smile almost went from ear to ear as he watched Berkley mount his horse and ride toward Whitehall.

Anne exited from the room adjacent to the study. "Well done, my children, well done. But don't let him stew too long. He may take the heads off his staff until he hears from you. If he goes home, the entire household will quit en masse.

"Now, after you finish punishing Edward and little Elizabeth, head to the kitchen. It was mentioned that Cook was baking up some new treats; she needs people to sample her creations. I also understand she requires a helping hand."

Her Grace left the study feeling happier than she had in weeks. *Thank you, Avery. I can tell you spoke to Sar.* The soft brush on her cheek was the only answer she received.

Sar sat behind his mother's desk and quickly penned his notes as they had discussed. The first note was to Berkley; the next messages went to Sebastian, Julien and Julien's parents, Royce and his father, Daggs, Quinn, the ladies, and last but not least, the Dowager Duchess Horton. His sisters looked on, adding a thought here or there.

"Perkins, make sure these notes are delivered at once, and have the messengers wait for a reply from everyone, especially the general. Here is a list of what we will require. Tell Her Grace we must leave by ten thirty."

"Yes, Your Grace." What passed as a smile for Perkins adorned his face.

• • •

The messenger in Westmoure livery stood in front of the Duke of Hampton's desk. Berkley almost ripped the missive in two trying to open it. He looked, read, and looked again . . . *name your seconds, midnight tonight, the West Green.*

"What?!" exploded from the general's lips.

Berkley knew in that moment his life was over. Dueling was basically illegal, and those children of Anne's would make sure he never got off his shot. Sar would send one of the sisters onto the field to shoot him. And the code the operatives lived by would be in full force and effect . . . never harm a woman, especially the child of the woman you loved.

The messenger waited silently, observing the Duke of Hampton carefully. As his stomach churned, his reply was only one word—*midnight.* By himself again, Berkley quickly penned a note to Sebastian. There was no way he could whisk Anne away from all this now. Those children of hers probably had her under lock and key. Now, he was more certain than ever they held inquisitions.

The day dragged on. No word from Anne. *Midnight it is, and I'm breaking the law I swore to uphold.* He could hear death approaching.

At the Duke of Westmoure's house, preparations were being made for the midnight rendezvous. When the messenger returned, he was questioned relentlessly by the family. Satisfied, the children went to dress for the evening adventure.

The group gathered on the field and were milling around when Berkley arrived. The general's entire life flashed before him. As his steps drew him closer to Sar, he realized the entire group was there. *Well, if you are going to be disgraced, you might as well do it in front of your closest friends.* Looking toward the night sky, he silently summoned Avery. *Avery, you and I are going to have a little chat when I join you shortly.* The general was so fixated on the situation, he didn't notice the wives.

Sar approached. "Berkley, welcome to the family."

As the group parted, he noticed a table, candles, and an evening repast fit for a king. Beaming at him was the love of his life. "You didn't think I would let you get away with your bossy attitude, did you? Berkley, I warned you about your high-handed ways."

He laughed, swooped in, and kissed Anne soundly on the lips. Whispering so no one else could hear, he chuckled, "Wait until you experience my high-handed way in the bedroom. You haven't seen anything yet. I bet you ten to one you will change your mind."

Anne laughed and blushed. Night prevented anyone from seeing that. Turning, he looked for Sar. The general wanted to thrash the lad within an inch of his life.

They met at the tree known as the lover's knot for its beautiful intricate patterns. "Sar, I probably would have done something similar if it were my mother. I'll treasure her."

"If you don't, I won't have to do anything. My sisters will take care of you, and then Perkins will have his turn. By the way, it was my impression that you wanted to keep this new little development a secret until after you were married. Everyone has been sworn to secrecy. Tonight, we celebrate; later today, we make sure we have plans in place to catch a murderer, a spy or two, and smugglers.

"Damn it to hell, Berkley. Is your life always like this?"

"No, Sar, there are moments of pure, unadulterated joy. Those happen because of you, your sisters, and Anne. Thank you." The two men walked back to the gathering, talking quietly.

Berkley's mind was swirling with thoughts of his new family. *Yeah, you'd better get used to it, old man. You have a family. And no ordinary family it is. Sar is a good person. Just like the son you would have wanted—kind, honorable, and protective of what is right. As he grew into the dukedom, his father could not have asked for a better steward. And the sisters—they are beyond bluestockings—brilliant, inquisitive, caring, and thoughtful.* He thanked whoever was responsible for handing out abundance and joy and sat down to eat next to his beloved.

CHAPTER 5

Paige's Grand Opening

The ladies were as nervous as though it were opening night of the theater season and they had the starring roles. Everything was in place. The girls were pacing back and forth as though they were Daggs. Precise steps echoed throughout the room.

"What if no one shows up?" Anne glanced around the newly renovated space. Everything was welcoming, open, clean, and fresh. Someone working here on a daily basis would find it a pleasure to come to work. Someone passing by would not be intimidated to walk in and purchase. "Just remember the shop is new. There will be a lot of curious people. On top of everything else, ready-made dresses are an unfamiliar concept. Women will want to see the dresses to understand. Girls, you did a great job."

The store had been open for an hour. There were no customers in the shop. Tea, sandwiches, and pastries were placed artfully around the garden. Stems of flowers added to the festive ambiance. Everything was clean, pristine, and hospitable.

Now it was two in the afternoon, and they hadn't had one shopper.

"We'll just have to grow on the public and keep doing this until we get customers." Beth was chewing on her lower lip.

"Look, customers approaching the shop. I am going to welcome them." Beth grabbed Alexius by the train of her dress.

"No, the world can't know we are involved. Notice how our mothers and the other ladies have disappeared? Out the back. At closing time, we will return."

Frances threw open the door and invited everyone in. That was all it took. One group followed another; tea and finger sandwiches were consumed. One order was placed, and then another.

By the end of the day, Frances couldn't believe it. "We have six orders; these are for the styles we sold out of. Off the racks they went. The ones on order were purchased from displays in the store. Maybe ready-made dresses will catch on. It's almost closing time. Let's get cleaned up and prepared for Monday."

A customer slowly meandered in and looked about; she was ready to turn and leave. The young woman had the most gorgeous auburn hair. "Don't go. Maybe I can tell you a little about what we are selling and why." Joycellyn smiled her biggest and most friendly smile and offered a soap sample.

"Do you mind if I just look? I have never been in a shop like this before." Her smile was as large as the one given by Joycellyn.

"Please feel free to look. We're here if you have any questions."

The customer looked at everything and marveled at the gas lighting on the wall. As she was about to leave, she turned and said, "Unbelievable."

"I'm exhausted, Anne. It turned out better than we thought. This is hard work." Caroline gave the shop a cursory look, noting everything was clean and in order. The two of them had returned just as the front door was being locked. "My place. Cook will have dinner ready, and we can talk about next Saturday. Even though the shop will be open to the public, members of the ton will be stopping by to see how miserably the shop is failing."

"Yes, that is what the ton does. It's a game. They make judgments and spread their declarations. It is always a negative at best." Miriam smiled at the thought of great success.

"Enough. I need food before I can even begin to think of next week's onslaught." Anne hadn't been this hungry in ages.

Dinner was a mix of conversation about the success of the opening and Anne's upcoming wedding. There was a lot to do. And there was no one better to put everything in order than the Dowager Duchess Horton herself—the little general.

Anne didn't make it to the blue room before she ran to the nearest dustbin in the hall.

"Sar, Anne is sick. In the hallway." Perkins needed to say no more and went to get all the items Sar or Berkley would be demanding momentarily. As Berkley picked Anne up, he shouted for cool towels, warm blankets, brandy, and the other ladies. By the time he reached her bedchamber, Perkins had caught up with them.

Anne's body trembled in his arms. "I have sent for the other ladies. Did you see still bodies and smoke again?"

Her Grace nodded as she was placed on the bed.

• • •

The following night at Le Havre, France, the second-in-command, David, checked the Ships at Sea Report handed to him by one of his men. It was there, the extra pallet of goods not listed on the original manifest. Doing his usual walk around the ship, he had spotted the pallet. Identifying the pallet and noting the men standing around, he continued on. On the trip back to the deck, he would make a closer inspection.

As he checked the other areas of the vessel, he mentally went through the protocol for getting information to Berkley immediately. On his way back, he found three men with their throats slit from ear to ear—two were his comrades from Daggs's office.

Sounding the alarm, he followed the procedures for murder at sea with a few exceptions. Back at the ship's helm, he summoned the cook's aide. "Tonight, something to take the crew's mind off murders. Sailors are a suspicious lot, and rebellion could be sparked at any turn."

Sending the cook's aide to the store, he took over at the helm and let Captain Coomes proceed with the investigation. The words of Inspector Daggs rang in his ears. *If there is a problem, let Captain Coomes handle the investigation. His ship found the actor Brian O'Keefe floundering in the water; that linked us to Jack. Jack was part of Berkley's elite operative team. With the help of O'Keefe, Jack faked amnesia, boarded a ship to America, and pushed O'Keefe over the side of the ship to eliminate any connection to him. O'Keefe died. It appears Jack is working for the group involved in smuggling and espionage. He's wanted for murder and treason among other things. The captain is thorough. He was trained at the Yard.*

As the aide entered Le Serveur, the clerk looked up and was clearly disturbed that his reading of the local newssheet had been interrupted. *"Commande spéciale pour Monsieur Rue, si'l vous plait."* Not knowing this was something more important than just filling an order, the clerk reluctantly rose and went in search of Monsieur Rue.

"Viens par là. Il est occupé, mais il vous recevra à l'arrière." The cook's aide followed the clerk to the back.

"Oui?" Monsieur Rue kept working without looking up. He put his finger to his lips to stop the aide from speaking.

After being sure he heard the rattle of the newssheet, he stood up and greeted his old friend. Moving deeper into the office, the old man began to speak. "Some things never change. It's been a few years, my friend. The message and goods must get to Berkley immediately."

It was a routine they had enacted many times during the war. The aide just nodded his head. "Tonight then, my friend. Same place."

The cook's aide picked up the supplies for the special dinner and headed back to the ship.

Captain Coomes had the cargo unloaded and stacked for the buyers except for the extra mystery pallet. He had off-loaded that pallet to a Westmoure warehouse.

Monsieur Rue was waiting deep in the shadows by the time the second-in-command arrived. Quickly and efficiently, the sequestered goods were loaded. Monsieur Rue quietly guided the wagon down the alley and headed to the next rendezvous point for the swift journey to England. On top was a case of the best French brandy for the general.

The fastest sloop available was waiting at the dock. No words were spoken. In a flash, everything disappeared into the mist. It was as though nothing had ever been there. Signals had been sent, received, and understood. All was ready in Portsmouth. Everyone realized the general was waiting.

• • •

The second set of signals reached Berkley as he dined at the Westmoures'. There was no need to summon everyone; they were there with him. Excusing themselves from the table, the men headed to Sar's study. The women followed.

Berkley knew there was no need to object. It would get him nowhere. Decoding the signals, he simply stated, "Nine o'clock, Daggs's secret office, including those women who want to join us." *That will fix them*, he thought. *They don't get up that early. Smart move, old man, smart move.*

• • •

Six hours later, the sloop slipped into Portsmouth. Dawn was fast approaching. With the cargo secured, two dockworkers were on their way to London within ten minutes. Fresh teams of horses awaited along the way. Not a word was uttered as horses and men were tested and pushed to the maximum.

By nine o'clock, Daggs had worn a new groove into the wooden floor with his pacing. The office was packed. The women sat together, smugly looking at him. The air was heavy with unspoken tension.

The wolfhound Bella saw her mates from Whitehall, and they spent time cavorting around. Now they were all hunkered down. The wolfhounds were snoring quite loudly.

First, ears perked up. Then the humans heard it at a distance. The sounds became louder and louder. The wagon pulled into the back. Drivers heavily laden with road dirt jumped down and quickly unloaded.

"Quick trip."

"Almost, General. We had to circle a couple of times. Felt as though we were being followed. Perkins helped us lose the tail." Julien reached for a towel to wipe off the dirt and some of his disguise. Royce was doing the same. Perkins had his ear pressed to the door.

"Perkins, do you wish to come in?"

"No, General, I'll be able to tell you everything you want to know from here."

"Before we dismantle the pallet, let's see what Bella thinks. She found the other drugs. Was that a fluke, or does she really have a talent? Jacob?" All eyes shifted from the general to the beautiful Bella.

Jacob, partner in the Avery Jacob Shipping Company, stooped down next to Bella. "Okay, girl, tell me if you like that pallet." Jacob walked toward the stacked goods with Bella by his side. Before they took another three steps, Bella started to whine. Sensing it was time to go to work, the other dogs followed Bella. All of them were whining except for one—Duchess. She sat on her haunches and looked at the rest of them as though they had gone mad.

Then Duchess circled around to the back side of the pallet. She started scratching, pawing, and gnawing on the back side. Her bark was like an ominous warning followed by a cacophony of sounds from the other animals.

"Duchess, let's see what we have here." Anne had followed Duchess and hugged and petted her for alerting them. Berkley, Sar, and Julien took the back apart. The others started sawing off the heads of the statues.

"Ah, my missing document. Thank you, Duchess, for ensuring it was returned safely." The general rubbed her coat as she grinned from ear to ear. "Good job, girl; good job."

"No surprises, Berkley. Kilos and kilos of opium. Let's get everything cleaned up. We'll meet at Sar's if that is okay with everyone." Quinn interrupted what he was saying by sneezing.

"Amazing, we have drug-sniffing, document-retrieving dogs—spy dogs that sense everything around them. Keep them close. The opium will be removed to the vault.

"Good job, Perkins. Let's make sure we are not detected when we leave this place. There are three layers of protection besides Perkins—my men, the men from Quinn's office, and Scotland Yard. You won't even know they are there." Berkley's nose was also twitching from the dust lingering in the air from the opium.

He looked at the women. *Ha, no one would guess they are anything other than what they look like.* They were dressed in work pants and shirts with hats and gloves. Each carried a shovel or broom—street workers. When Perkins gave the signal, they headed out in their work wagon, driven by the duchess herself. The dogs traveled in a closed coach with the duke's seal. The human bodies kept stacking up.

• • •

In Sar's study, the women sat pertly waiting to hear what Captain Coomes had written in his report. With a swift movement, the twine was cut. Berkley spread the sheets out. Quickly, he glanced at everything. Until he came to the last paragraph. Berkley stopped and started reading aloud:

"'Two women were taken into custody. They only spoke English. They were dressed as sailors. We had to turn the two women over to the French authorities. They were destined to some sultan in the Near East.'

"It appears you have another business, Sar—trafficking of women."

Berkley continued reading Coomes's report. "'We need your help to get the women released as soon as possible. Since the contact did not find the woman as planned, my feeling is that they will be killed to prevent them from talking if it is discovered what happened.'

"Royce, send a message to Rue: 'Get the women released immediately. Very dangerous situation. Need the women back on English soil safely as soon as possible. Please advise.'"

For a moment, there was stunned silence. Royce went to start the signaling process. The general cleared his throat and reached for a brandy.

"Sar, at this time, it is obvious we don't know how long your ships have been used to transport women. This form of trafficking has been going on for centuries. Excuse me, ladies, but you should understand that many of the women are used and abused in the most primitive ways. Now we must dig through the layers surrounding this person or persons and put an end to their participation in this endeavor. Danger will haunt us. If you don't know how to shoot, please learn immediately. Always carry your weapon." They all knew Berkley had just issued an order.

"I must find Quinn to see how we can expedite this matter."

Daggs came rushing into the study and felt he was walking in on someone's funeral. He was informed of the latest development.

"This is not good. The people behind this will kill all of us. The profits in this type of business are huge. I will have two of my men tailing you at all times. As for the women, there will be three men. Please learn how to shoot." Another order issued.

"Now, for a bit of good news, I have found Marry's parents. They have been looking everywhere for their daughter, and they were worried sick. That night, they were on the streets trying to buy what food they could; the little one wandered off. The father does masonry work. Because he is a Negro, most people won't hire him. The parents seemed to be honest and hardworking. Sar, could you use some extra help at Ivy Hall? I thought he could help at Rushton also."

Without thinking or hesitating, Sar nodded his head yes. "We can give them a better life while the father practices his skill and earns a living for his family. Bring them in. Let's meet them. I am sure refreshments are on the way."

Mr. and Mrs. Donaldson followed Daggs into the study. After them came trays and trays of food. As everyone introduced themselves, the Donaldsons told the group about themselves and the hardship of living. It appeared Daggs was right—they were hardworking, honest individuals.

"We have a house in the country that always needs masonry work. Would you consider working for my family there? Next door to us is Rushton, the ancestral home of my sister's husband. I am sure they have work also. Your daughter is at the Duke of Hampton's house being spoiled. After you finish eating, we can all stop in and pick her up."

"Is it true what you say about this job and living in the country?"

"Yes, it is. We will send you to the country immediately. As a matter of fact, Perkins, get me a messenger. We'll send word to let them know to expect you tomorrow. Tonight, we would like you to be our guests here if we can pry Marry away from Cook. I should ask you what her name is."

"Marry Anne Donaldson. We would love to accept the chance to live in the country. Are you honest? What is your name again?" Mr. Donaldson was looking Sar directly in the eye.

Sar thought not many people would have the nerve to ask those questions. Then he heard his father's voice. *You make me proud, son. Continue to help others in any way you can.* Then he was gone. Anne looked at Sar and knew he had heard from his father.

"I am Sar, and this is an honest offer. This is settled if it is okay with you and Mrs. Donaldson. Come meet my mother and the others."

"Settled it is." He extended his hand to shake Sar's. "My name is Nathan, and this is my wife, Abigail."

When James opened the door at the Duke of Hampton's house, beside him was his new helper—Marry. When she saw the men, she did what James had taught her. A little voice was heard. "The general is in the study."

"James, we are here to speak to little Miss Marry if that is acceptable with the general?" Sar's smile went from ear to ear.

"My lord, I believe the duke would allow that."

As they crowded into the house, Marry saw her parents and ran to them. "I'm sorry, sorry, sorry. I didn't mean to wander so far off." Then Marry was smothered in kisses.

•   •   •

Quinn dipped into the inkpot again, then signed the letter. The knock on his office door startled him. His clerk announced Berkley. "The Duke of Hampton, my lord."

Berkley took the seat Quinn offered. Making sure they couldn't be heard, Berkley started explaining the situation in Le Havre. They discussed tactics and the best way to handle this delicate situation.

"Okay, Berkley, I'll go through official channels; ask for immediate release and have them get word back to me by the end of the day. Everything must be done by the signaling system. I know you already have your operatives and connections on the ground going into action."

"That should cover it, Quinn. Get word to me if you hear something before I do."

Quinn sighed after Berkley left. "Problems, problems, problems." This fell within his jurisdiction as head of the Foreign Office. He and Berkley had worked together since the war. *Now look at us.* As he thought about the best way to deal with this state of affairs, he wrote another note, leaned back, and put his stubby legs on his desk. The English women in Le Havre were the last thing on his mind, and he laughed to himself knowing the matter had already been taken care of. *One up on you, Berkley.*

•   •   •

In the other opulent house in Mayfair, preparations were underway. Everything was checked and double-checked. The plan was gone over again and again. "We're ready. No link, no trace. Our man is already at the ball." As she rubbed her unclothed body over his stiff member, he promised things he would never live up to. He let his body use hers.

• • •

A sea of green descended on the Duke of Aston's London residence. Standing next to him was Grayson, Caroline's father. "Father, you look particularly spectacular tonight." Caroline had that mischievous look in her eyes.

"How many bets did you place tonight, my darling daughter?"

"Now, Dad, you know me. Maybe this year I did not place enough." They both laughed.

As the other ladies passed through the receiving line, they noticed that the dukes looked husband worthy. The many widows of the ton were going to be chasing the two like the proverbial fox and the hound.

Grayson claimed Caroline for the first dance. For some reason, whenever someone looked at the two of them, she was laughing like a debutant. Then Sebastian stepped in, and one could not miss the look of love. Anne sighed wistfully.

Anne felt as though tonight she was one of the special few in the world. But Her Grace knew the difference. Here, she and her family were totally accepted.

"Your Grace, may I please have this dance?" Berkley's strong hand placed hers on his sleeve.

"It's a waltz. That's like declaring your intentions right here." Anne looked into his eyes and knew she had found her everything.

Then Berkley pulled Anne a couple inches closer. His mouth was next to her ear, uttering the most delicious, decadent things for future times together. "And when I am making love to you, you will scream my name as I take you any way I want. You will beg for more and live for me to come in from work and be inside of you. Steps during your day will only whisk you closer to the moments you have been craving—that is all your mind's eye will see, think of, and desire. Do you understand?"

Anne looked up at him. "You're too old."

For the first time ever, a booming laugh exploded from the general. This caused one lady to drop her glass. The Dowager Duchess Horton slipped her quizzing glass to her eye and mouthed a silent thank-you to Sterling. Caroline thought, *My, my, my, my, this is more than interesting.*

A woman leaned over to her companion. "It laughs."

Her Grace smiled and ran her hand across Berkley's chest. "But I look forward to your imagined efforts."

The second laugh erupting from the general had half of the dance floor stopping. But his mind was reeling. *What if she won't have me for forever? What if she is repelled by my body? One night here and there is totally different than the day in and day out business of marriage. I am older, not sleek like Julien, Royce, and Daggs. Scars, rigid raised lines from knives, hot solutions, and gunshot wounds mottle my body. How does one survive? Will she be willing to take a life's ride with me? That* old thought circled in his head again. *Will she leave me? This isn't a siege. It's not a campaign. It is my path to heaven on earth. She knows; I don't have to guess. This is our now. Can we both handle it?*

Her body is not one of a green girl but a woman. She has a pouch for a stomach and breasts that have probably been suckled by children. He thought of their bodies melding into each other. *We are perfect, simply perfect.*

But the internal demons and terrors of the matter were worse. A soldier never knew when the sneaky, terrifying tentacles of war would overtake him and capture his senses, leading him down that crooked, slippery road to a living hell. He relived everything down to the most minute of details—feelings, sights, smells, and an opponent's last breath. Always a captive—never to escape.

The music stopped, but he held on to her a second longer. Reluctantly, he placed her hand on his sleeve and escorted her to Caroline.

"Was that you I heard laughing, Berkley? Impossible, you never laugh." The Dowager Duchess Horton cackled as she passed by. She stopped and adjusted her quizzing glass. "Love gets us all in time, doesn't it?" The old harridan kept walking and didn't seem to give one hoot.

. . .

In the ladies' withdrawing room, a widow balled her fist. "I will have him whenever I want with no interference from you. I will wed Aston by next summer."

"You're out of your mind; he would never have the likes of you. You spread your legs for anyone who is wealthy with a title." The second widow turned to leave but was stopped and turned around by the other, who raised her arm and swung to slap her face.

At the same time, the door opened. Beth and Alexius walked in. The widow who was about to leave ducked. The momentum of the arm of the other widow could not be stopped. Beth was hit with the total hand on the side of the face and fell back into Alexius. The other women helped them both to a divan.

. . .

"Caroline, let's get some punch. For some odd reason, that

last dance left me parched." Anne's eyes held the look of love. There was no denying the sparkle.

Caroline looked at Anne. She was glowing. *I would be glowing too. Whatever Berkley said to her on the dance floor must have been for the bedchamber only.* Caroline smiled. *Ah, love in bloom.*

The two of them glided across the floor, acknowledging those they knew, and they talked like two schoolgirls without a care in the world. Anne reached for a glass, picked it up, and started to take a sip when Aurelia, excited and out of breath, whispered, "Come quick, ladies' withdrawing room—Beth has been slapped."

Putting their drinks down, they casually strolled across the room. As soon as they were out of sight, they lifted their skirts and ran as fast as they could.

• • •

In the ladies' withdrawing room, Beth and Alexius sat on a couch. Someone had brought a cold towel for Beth's face. "Beth, let me see. We will fix it. You'll be all right." Anne hugged her daughter as she gently removed the towel. An exact handprint in bright red was on the side of Beth's face. On the other side of Beth, Caroline was trying to comfort Alexius.

The door opened, and in walked Lady Hortense Horton. Her presence silenced the room. "The two of you who hurt these innocent young ones shall forthwith be banned from all social gatherings of the ton. Who did this?" The husband-hunting widows, the Countess of Garth and the Viscountess of Ream, stepped forward as everyone else stepped back. That was it; the queen of the ton had determined their fate. "Disgusting conduct for members of the ton. Out, now!" Hortense turned her attention to Anne and Caroline.

"Come, I know the back way down to the kitchen, and I know the cook. She will help us. Aurelia, as soon as we are in the kitchen, let the men know." Like a general, Lady Horton led her troops.

• • •

In the ballroom, the Earl of Morton picked up Anne's glass of punch and drank. About fifteen minutes later, he started gagging, foaming at the mouth and turning blue. Julien, Royce, Sar, Berkley, and Daggs helped him to a secluded area of the house. Simmons followed.

A quick look at the earl was all it took. "Poison. Tell Morton's doctor to meet him at his house immediately. Also, I would suggest inserting a tube to cause him to vomit. Otherwise, I can guarantee death." Simmons doubted that Morton could be saved, but inserting the tube would be the best form of treatment. Perkins was gone the second Simmons uttered the last word.

• • •

As soon as Aurelia glided into the ballroom, she was assailed by the gossip. *Morton was poisoned; Beth and Alexius were detained for attacking two ladies of the ton.* Aurelia found Georgina, Diana, Miriam, and Evelyn. "We'll talk later. Right now, act as though nothing has happened. The Duke of Westmoure's house." The ladies smiled and danced with those they knew. No one questioned the absence of their husbands.

• • •

In the other fashionable house in Mayfair, she paced as she waited. They had to have succeeded. Following the directions, she had personally sealed and wrapped the vial and placed it in his pocket for delivery.

He burst through the door. "Done, but not done. Our footman put the poison in Her Grace's glass and watched. She was about to sip when all hell broke loose. Someone had slapped her daughter. The Negro duchess set the glass down and never returned to the spot."

He gulped down a brandy as his mind furiously worked on alternate plans and scenarios. Tonight, there was nothing enticing about the naked body undulating in front of him.

• • •

The next day, Anne and Caroline were doing a postmortem on the events of the party. "Anne, you think this is something?" Caroline's eyes wandered from the newssheet. "I hate to be the bearer of bad news, but it is going to get worse. Much worse. Sebastian feels as though the poison was meant for you or Sar. Think, Anne. Do you remember anything about reaching for a glass or putting a glass down?"

"Once I heard about Beth being slapped, that was all I focused on. I don't think I thought much of my movements." Anne was running the events of the evening through her mind.

"Yes, that's it. I was ready to take a sip from a glass when Aurelia came into the ballroom. I put the glass down and opened my reticule to be able to pull out *Bessie*. I never picked the glass up again. Oh, my goodness. That poison was meant for me."

"Come, we must let Sebastian and Sar know now!"

That night, Her Grace found an uncaged lion in her bedchamber. This was not a happy man. "You shall not put yourself in danger like that again. Do you hear me?" The low growl with a hiss was worse than out-and-out yelling. "Do you hear me? From now on, until this is settled, I do not want you eating anything outside of this house nor anything inside of the house unless it is given to you by a trusted servant. And going about in the park, even if it is a sunny day, is out of the question."

"Are you crazy? I shall not live a half-life." Anne responded in a deadly cold demeanor.

"I shall not lose you. There are committed criminals out there ready to strike; they know where you are. They can get to you." She could see the sheen in the general's eyes. "I can't lose you now that I have just found you." His lips covered hers and silenced her next retort.

"Berkley, what are we going to do? One moment I am as happy and as giddy as a seventeen-year-old virgin, and the next minute I am scared witless."

He wanted to affirm life with her. This vibrant woman in his arms carried the message of forever love. As his kisses warmed Anne's body, Berkley knew this was the heaven he would come home to for the remainder of his life. He asked the one up above for a long life and then blanked everything out of his mind except the pleasure he could give Her Grace.

As he covered her in kisses, Anne felt the rough hands on her body. He was sending tingles of sexual energy through her body. Her secret garden screamed for attention. Reading her mind, he touched her mons and pulled out fingers covered in her nectar.

"You know, if we were younger, you would have been in-creasing by now at least four times over." Then his tongue dove into her center and massaged every inch he could reach.

Anne wanted more. He could feel her release coming. She was shaking. He pressed down on her mons again, and she exploded. Her release was so strong that the pillows flew off the bed, and she was pulling on nipples that were hard peaks. Tossing and turning, she continued to flow.

"My turn, Your Grace." Berkley entered her as a slight contraction subsided. He was ready to explode watching her pulling on her nipples and trying to get closer to him. As he rubbed her center, he could feel her excitement building. She wanted him.

Her first deep contraction hit him like a tidal wave. With the second one, she tried to completely engulf him. Sweat dripped off his forehead; his entire body glistened as he moved in and out. She hugged him with her velvet sheath, and he emptied his hot seed into her welcoming vessel.

• • •

On Wednesday, the Society News was all about the Westmoures. Their lives were laid out for inspection and dissection once again.

The London Daily

Society News

Once again, dear reader, the news is about those half-breed Americans who lay claim to a place in the aristocracy. As we know, it must be the blood. Less than pure blood is the reason for their outlandish behavior and lack of acceptance. It shows how little those people cherish the sanctity of pure bloodlines and heritage. They are trying to force their way into the ton.

As reported earlier, the oldest sister married Lord Julien in front of His Majesty and half of the ton at St. George's on Hanover Square.

There have since been three more murders. Somehow, the Duke of Westmoure is involved. From our sources, we understand a Westmoure ship was docked in Le Havre, France. We have been told that three men were found with their throats slit from ear to ear. Two of them were in service to the Crown. We have it on the best authority that the ship is involved in espionage and smuggling contraband. How deeply involved is the Duke of Westmoure? It is clear to us; the Home Office and the Foreign Office need to do something immediately.

However, there is one other sideline the Westmoures are involved with—trafficking of women. Two English women were found on the ship dressed as sailors. They were destined for a sultan in the Near East. The women were detained by French authorities. Is there any degrading and demoralizing activity the Westmoures are not involved in?

At the ball given by the two dukes, our beloved Earl of Morton drank a glass of punch and had to be escorted from the ballroom. A physician was present and examined him. Lord Morton had been poisoned. He is at home in the care of his physician and not doing well, according to all accounts.

If that is not enough, Lady Beth, the younger sister of the Duke of Westmoure, and Lady Alexius, the daughter of Lady Caroline and the Marquess of Broadhurst, attacked two ladies in the ladies' withdrawing room at the ball. They tried to blame it on the ladies. Of course, that is not true. Our ladies of the ton do not go around attacking others. It's the mixed blood, readers. Why is Lady Alexius associating with the Westmoures? Do her parents understand the social consequences of this action?

The store Paige's has opened. It is the shop selling ready-made dresses. Of course, the Duke of Westmoure's family is involved. The manager of the store is Frances Thomas. This is the woman who gave birth to Joycellyn, the child born on the wrong side of the blanket. They were both present at the store on Saturday and are connected to the Westmoures. From what we understand, Frances claims that Charles, the brother of the former duke, was the father of Joycellyn. Sometimes hired help will do anything to entice their employer or a family member.

Saturday, there is another opening celebration for Paige's. It is our understanding that some ladies of the ton have been invited. If you have secured an invitation and you choose to go, please send your report of the event to the London Daily. As you know, firsthand information is always the best.

My dear readers, the aristocracy cannot allow lower classes and mixed breeds to smudge the integrity of the elite of society. Something must be done as soon as possible. Teach your children well that the races cannot mix and the lower classes do not belong with the upper class. They work for us and should not become a part of us. This is the only way we can preserve the pure.

"Enough, Caroline. The Society News goes too far. Their insults demonstrate the general lack of understanding about people. Obviously, there are some in the elite of society who want us gone as soon as possible. It is also apparent they have not been around people who are different than they are." Her Grace was beyond vexed. She was pale, her complexion sallow. As she opened her mouth to say something else, Anne abruptly pushed back her chair and promptly emptied everything she had just eaten into the nearest dustbin. Anne was simultaneously shaking and crying.

Scooping her up, Berkley carried her to her bedchamber, barking orders as he went. "Cold towels, smelling salts, warm towels, extra bed coverings"—and the list just kept going on and on and on. "Shush, my love. I know; everyone knows someone else is about to die."

"It came on suddenly. Right after I read the Society News. I am so helpless. Someone is going to die, but I don't know who, and I can't stop it." Anne's tears were flowing like water, her body wracked by sobs.

Sar and Perkins were right behind him. Berkley turned to Perkins. "Perkins, send Caroline up in another ten minutes. Sar, we are about to have another murder. We need Quinn here as soon as possible. When Caroline is with Anne, have everyone meet in your study. Make sure the ladies join us. They may have a clue or something we can go on. Ring for her maid and some strong spirits."

Berkley was pacing almost as fast as Daggs when a worried Quinn entered the study. "What do we know?" Quinn tossed his gloves on the side table.

"Our human barometer for predicting murder is upstairs in her bed very nauseous and sick. Her Grace is extremely distraught and upset because she is utterly powerless. Anne has no idea who will die or when this will happen. And, before you ask, she had just read the Society News, then ran to the nearest dustbin." Berkley crushed the cigar in his hand.

"Ladies, can you think of anything? I don't care how insignificant you may think it is, just anything." Quinn looked from one to the other.

"There is so much we must do that we were just going from one project to the other. Quinn, Berkley, nothing stands out. First it was Mer's wedding, then the opening of Paige's, and then the dukes' ball." It was as though Aurelia's bright red hair was dancing, just as fiery as the flames in the fireplace.

"Nothing. I have nothing. It came on Anne suddenly. She finally fell asleep." Caroline reached for Sebastian.

"Go through the day. See if anything comes to mind that wasn't quite right. Just tell us. We will see if it is a tiny missing piece of this puzzle." Berkley didn't know how he was going to protect the ladies. But this was what he did know—he would catch the culprits. They would pay.

• • •

The next morning, a very shaky Anne made it down the stairs to the doorway of the breakfast room. Grabbing the knob for support, she surveyed the scene before her and swayed. Perkins braced himself as Her Grace fell back into him. Sar was on his feet before Perkins could open his mouth.

"Are you making it a habit to swoon so people can pick you up and carry you around?"

Anne tried to smile at her son, but it was just too much effort. As he turned to take her back upstairs, she feebly shook her head. Carrying her gingerly, Sar headed to the table.

To Sar, she felt as light as a feather; it reminded him of when he was sick as a child. Dad would carry him to the table just like this. *Dad*, his mind shouted; there was no reply.

Tea and toast were placed in front of Anne, and she nibbled silently. No one spoke; everyone was guardedly watching the duchess. A few minutes later, Berkley strolled into the room. He opened his mouth and just as quickly shut it when he eyed Sar's imperceptible shake of his head.

"I must get strong enough to get through this week and next." The voice coming from Anne was barely recognizable. "To make things easier, I will stop in at Paige's at closing time on Saturday. Today, I will work on getting ready for the second and third grand openings of the store. We will also work on my wedding. Caroline will stay with me all day.

"Don't, Berkley." Anne held up her hand in protest. "This will pass." She glanced at Sar and then the general. "Believe what you might, I am fine and will be much stronger shortly." She stood; before she fell, she was scooped up once again.

"You are very stubborn, Your Grace."

"Ha, this from the man with the high-handed ways."

All Berkley could do was chuckle and hold the love of his life near.

For the next few days, everyone tiptoed around Her Grace until Anne ordered the general back to Whitehall and sent Sar with him. As she had stated she would, the duchess made the final changes on the meal and menu for the third Saturday for Paige's; the workers were prepared as well as could be expected for the assault from the ton on Paige's this Saturday. She also tried to picture a life with Berkley sneaking into her bedchamber, and she started the preparations for her wedding. *It will be one adventure after another, Your Grace.* Avery's robust laughter echoed in her brain. There was no need to silently ask what he meant because Avery was already gone.

"If you come into this room one more time, Perkins, I am going to shoot you. I know Sar told you to keep an eye on me, but Caroline is here. Go. Catch up with Sar and the general at Whitehall. That's an order. Now! You have ten seconds to get out of this house before I start shooting, and I don't miss. Also, I am giving the staff a week from Saturday off. With Mer's wedding and the opening of Paige's, they deserve it. Let everyone know."

"Yes, Your Grace."

"One . . . two . . . three . . ." Before Anne reached seven, she heard the front door quietly close, followed by the crisp, precise steps of Perkins leaving the house.

Caroline was doubled over from laughing so hard. "Don't know how you do it, but they all obey you."

"I have a hair-trigger finger. It works every time. I believe some very strong tea is in order." The two friends settled in for an afternoon of relaxing.

Upon their return, the men found two very regal ladies who could barely stand. "I knew you shouldn't have left them alone, Perkins." Looking at his mother, Sar shook his head. Sar and Berkley were both laughing.

"Didn't have a choice. I like my head exactly where it is. The duchess was in one of her *shoot now, ask questions later* moods." Perkins hadn't bothered to shut the door. They were all staring at the empty decanters.

"Perkins, ask Sebastian to join us for dinner." Sar shook his head. "Do you think you can find a decanter with spirits in it for Berkley, Sebastian, and myself? Maybe you had better join us also." The slight stirring on the couch confirmed the ladies had no idea the men were even there.

• • •

The Westmoure ship guided by Captain Coomes slipped into Southampton. He had double-checked everything and was ready to disembark as soon as most of the sailors had taken leave. The locked and chained waterproof chests never left his sight. Daggs, the general, and the Duke of Westmoure awaited his arrival. Before he left the ship, he sensed the two men waiting for him.

He never thought his years in service would lead to a position as an operative for the Crown. The captain touched the wheel for the last time and headed down the gangplank. Coomes had the description of his escorts committed to memory. Not a word was uttered as the chests were placed in the back of the coach with the second man guarding them. Within minutes, they were on their way to London. It was also clear there were additional bodyguards hidden within the traffic to the capital. The horses strained as the rush to London was inevitable.

• • •

As was their habit, the men were gathered in Sar's study. Jacob was there. The general was barking out orders as though they were in battle. "Jacob, Coomes has delivered the trunks from the ship in Le Havre. Along with two men from the inspector's office, who had been on the ship in Le Havre guarding the pallets of opium, there was the man we knew nothing about, and the two women who had been bought for the sultan. Unfortunately, we were unable to rescue the women in a timely fashion. They were poisoned.

"Jacob, I need you to sift through everything. The trunks contain the personal effects of the murdered men and women. Find my link, Jacob. Find the missing pieces so we can find the culprits. Too many people have been killed; too much opium is being smuggled out of the country; there's espionage and trafficking of women. This points to high government officials. No one else could have these connections.

"Walk carefully and quietly. We don't know who is involved yet. Daggs will have men tailing you twenty-four hours a day," Berkley continued as he quietly snapped the cigar in half.

"Daggs is at Southampton now waiting for David, the

second-in-command on the ship, and the remains. If possible, Simmons, I will need you to examine the bodies. Wyndham, go with him. We might find something." Berkley was always pleased when Wyndham joined them. This elite operative was an expert on ways the human body could be injured. His munitions factories supplied the government.

• • •

Daggs and several of his men were waiting at the docks. For once, Daggs was not pacing. Solemnly, they watched and bowed their heads as five coffins were unloaded and put on the waiting wagon. The pall for two of the coffins was Britain's flag. Daggs felt his stomach clench; he attempted to adopt a stern demeanor. But grief took its own path. His stomach churned once more, and he upcasted his meal. Two more of his men dead. Slowly following the procession was the second-in-command of the Westmoure ship that was still tied up with French officials in Le Havre.

"David." Daggs saluted the man who had been at the center of the operation. "We're meeting at His Grace's. Everyone is waiting for us." The inspector could see the toll of the operation etched in the hollow look on David's face. And Daggs knew only too well how hard it was to bring home your own in a box.

"Good. I have a written report from Captain Coomes for your eyes only." David turned over the oilskin-wrapped, tied, and sealed missive. After thanking the captain of the ship, Daggs and David headed to His Grace's.

CHAPTER 6

Everything Happens at Once

At the London residence of the Duke of Brockton, the butler and staff were still having a go of it. Basil was the worst type of aristocrat ever—ill-mannered, drunk most of the time, loud, and boorish. The weeks he had been in residence seemed like years. Thank goodness his comrades had not arrived.

The pounding on the door stopped Raymond, the duke's butler, in his tracks. With an abrupt turn, he reached the front door as the next bout of thumping started.

He opened the door and took one look at the unkempt man on the stairs, smelling of strong spirits. The sneer on his face and the quality of his clothing announced he was a member of the upper class and a difficult one at that. "Can I be of service to you, my lord?"

"Here to see Basil. Let him know Lord . . ." Before the

visitor could get out another word, Basil stumbled unsteadily down the stairs.

"So, you are here. Glad you came so quickly. Come upstairs, we'll have a drink. You can give me the latest news about what's going on in town." Once again, Raymond and a footman helped a very unstable Basil back up the stairs.

Closing the door tightly, Basil reached for the stiletto on the desk and turned on the man. "Dead, do you hear me? She is supposed to be dead. You can't get the job done? One woman, one death, with no links to me in any manner. If I find someone else to get it done, you are just as dead as she." It was done in a flash, without notice; all he saw was his right lapel falling to the floor. Seething, Basil grabbed the man's neck cloth. "We need a new plan; shooting didn't work. The wrong person drank the poison and died yesterday. Something that sets her up, so she can't escape."

The more he dealt with Basil, the more he was convinced that the future duke should be committed to one of the mental asylums. If he didn't do something soon, he would be the one with a blade sticking out of his chest. "I will have my contacts keep their ears to the ground. There will be a way if we just stay watchful. It will happen, Basil; it will happen."

"I want everything tied up—shall we say before fall? A Christmas here in the capital satisfying my every wish and desire is what I plan on having. Stay for dinner. Then we will take on the prostitutes at Les Dames de Bois d'Ebène de la Soirée. It's better I inflict harm on a dark prostitute than you." His laugh was just short of demonic. "No one takes from me what is lawfully and rightfully mine."

• • •

At Sebastian's house, there was a polite knock on the front

door. Seymour, Sebastian's butler, took one look at the man before him and knew the matter was urgent.

In the front room of the house, Sebastian and Brockton had just settled in for a long chat, when two sharp raps on the door interrupted them. That meant Seymour needed to speak to Sebastian immediately. "Enter."

"Your Grace, your butler needs to speak with you." Raymond was three steps behind Seymour.

Raymond twisted his linen square in agitation. "I am so glad you are here in the capital."

"Raymond, what is it?" The Duke of Brockton eyed Raymond carefully. Stress and anxiety were written on the face of this sad man.

Sebastian was easing his way out of the room.

"Stay, Broadhurst. Something tells me you need to hear this." His Grace sadly shook his head. "Raymond?"

"Basil, your nephew, is still at your house. As you know, he was drunk when he arrived and has been drinking ever since. Today, we just managed to get him upstairs when an associate appeared. Neither are the most pleasant of chaps."

• • •

In the study of the Duke of Brockton's house, the heir apparent to the title seethed. Basil needed it all—the entailed and unentailed wealth. By coincidence, he had found the actual accounting from the moneyman. Damn his father for leaving what was his, as the heir, to a stranger—a woman, a Negro. There was no clue why his father had done this; Basil had searched relentlessly for the answer. The current Duke of Brockton, his uncle, was childless. Besides some other cousins, there was no one else but him.

Another friend in crime had joined them. Looking at the

two men, Basil turned the stiletto over and over in his hand. He wanted to skewer them.

"What do you mean you missed? You are expert marksmen. What's the problem?" Basil sat back, glared, and reached for his whisky.

"Couldn't get any closer." His henchman caught the dribble of his drink with his sleeve. The other man simply nodded. It was best to placate Basil when he was infuriated. During his rages, they had witnessed him destroy rooms and derive extreme amusement out of beating women—especially dark prostitutes.

"There have been too many near misses. Too much suspicion is being raised. We don't want Berkley and his merry band hunting us down. No one survives Berkley."

Basil loved the sound of his title, the Duke of Brockton. In his head, he was plotting how to bring this craziness to an end. After his uncle died, which wouldn't be long if he wasn't dead already, and the Negro woman was eliminated, everything would be his. He cackled as thoughts of great wealth and visions of unlimited dark prostitutes to use and abuse danced in his head. As the duke, he could do whatever he wanted. He would live in that rarefied air. Negro women were put on this earth to please his every whim and fantasy. What he did with them was up to him.

• • •

At his house, Sebastian the operative mentally switched into gear. The Duke of Brockton stared intently at his butler. "Raymond, please start at the beginning and leave nothing out. We need to hear everything."

As Raymond relayed the story, the Duke of Brockton hung his head in disgust.

"Raymond, I am counting on you not to say a word about this to anyone. Of course, this includes seeing me. You must promise me this again."

"Of course, Your Grace." After Raymond left, Brockton shook his head as though he had been defeated in battle.

"Broadhurst, I must tell you a little story."

The tale of a privileged young aristocrat who was only interested in wine, women, and the most depraved behavior poured forth from the lips of an incredibly sad uncle.

"After Basil's father died, it was as though Basil thought a future duke was above the law, that he didn't have to listen to anyone and could do as he wished. He had an inheritance left by his mother and a future dukedom." As Brockton continued telling the story about Basil poisoning him and the duke's escape from his ancestral home, Sebastian was brought to tears. *It's the same old thing*, he thought, *greed, arrogance, and domination over another—the Roxburys and now the Duke of Brockton.*

The old duke continued. "I fear the worst is yet to come. My brother made the request that his unentailed property go to another. As this was his last request, I am honor bound to see if I can legally fulfill it."

"I sense there is more, but speak to your solicitors and get an idea about what can happen. Berkley needs to be involved. He will have ideas, and if you need them, some of his men can be added to your staff." Sebastian started to rise to get Seymour, but he decided to see if the Perkins School of Eavesdropping was teaching Seymour the fine art. And it was. The messenger appeared before the note was completed.

• • •

On the other side of town, two men exited Les Dames de Bois d'Ebène de la Soirée and took note of the Duke of Brockton's coach. "So, this is where the old duke seeks his pleasure. Probably needs the excitement of dark beauties. What man wouldn't want that pleasure?"

The man popped into his carriage and made a mental note to make sure this tidbit got to the right ears. One little mention in the Society News would be all that was needed. Who would have ever thought the kindly old duke was a reprobate?

Just as Basil and company stumbled from their coach, the other vehicle turned the corner. Before Basil could finish climbing the stairs, thoughts about the pleasures awaiting within made the remaining final few steps uncomfortable—big breasts, dark nipples, and a passage dripping with anticipation. The tassels on his special riding crop and a few slaps would bring added carnality and thrills. His stinging thigh made him smile as images of unbridled lust and hedonism danced in his head.

• • •

At the home of Lady Horton, Kiggins, her lifelong companion, asked if she could bring her a glass of brandy. Nodding yes, Hortense pulled the blanket under her chin and reached for the silver box.

How many letters had she read again and again? The dowager duchess didn't know. Dare she read the last one again? Would she be able to hang on to him through the night if she did? Hortense took a deep breath and focused on the worn words before her.

> *Oh, my dearest,*
> *We have let time slip away from us. I can't live*
> *forever, but I am making this promise to you.*

The letter floated noiselessly from her trembling fingers.

She repeated the rest of the memorized letter. *Oh, Sterling, why did we wait? I will love you forever.* In a whisper, she reverently spoke out loud his declaration of love. "I give you my heart and soul. I pledge myself to you." The remainder of the note brought more tears to her eyes of what could and should have been. Shortly before he died, the old duke had snuck into her bedchamber. In their stolen moment together, Hortense had finally understood why a woman would do anything and everything for the right man.

Clutching her ring and crying, she fell asleep, and she dreamed of him. The smile he gave her could have melted the sun. When she woke in the morning, she could smell the scent of his cigar. He had been with her.

The old duke's words uttered to the niches of her mind were swimming in her head. Parts danced about clearly. *Well done, old girl. They'll grow to love you . . . not your time yet . . . be there for the other . . .* She was drawing blanks, but what he said before he kissed her good-bye made her smile. *I'll be watching and waiting for you. I'll love you always and beyond eternity.*

She glanced down at the band with five two-carat sapphires winking back at her and thanked whoever was in charge for their time together.

• • •

At the Westmoure household, Anne barely made it up the stairs before nausea overtook her again. Locked in her room, she felt everything about her was shouting *death.* What were they going to do?

Tuesday dawned with Anne ready to tackle any task. As she started to dress, something struck her as odd. The house was too silent. Queasiness and a cold numbness hit her from head to toe. With a certainty as sure as her name, she knew death had struck again. Heading downstairs, this fact was affirmed when she saw Berkley, Quinn, Sebastian, Sar, Daggs, Julien, and Royce quietly talking in the front hall.

Anne didn't even bother with a good morning. "Who was it this time and where? Don't try to soften the blow. Out with it, Sar."

"The gardener, the shy one who always coughed or cleared his throat before he spoke."

Anne found the nearest open container and promptly threw up everything in her stomach. Before she could move, she realized she was being carried into the front parlor. Looking past Berkley's shoulder, with distress, she simply said, "Sar, tell me everything."

"I was up looking around just after dawn. He was on the ground, in the garden, face down, shot between the eyes. The note said, *Does this remind you of America?*"

Anne flinched as the tears pooled in her eyes. "Perkins, have my maid lay out proper mourning clothes; have Cook prepare a large hamper of food." Knowing the task was being done as she spoke, she quietly asked, "Does his family know?"

The men shook their heads.

"Is he in the icehouse?"

"Yes, Mother."

"Sar, Julien, please escort me to the gardener's house. We will discuss possible plans for the family along the way. Daggs, have your men do what is necessary with the help of Berkley and Quinn. Royce, please watch over the girls until we return."

"Mother, you don't have to do this."

"Oh yes, I do. I have been in this woman's shoes. I'll be ready in thirty minutes. Daggs, we'll find out from his wife how she wants us to proceed."

Her Grace hurried upstairs and didn't hear the comments.

"Sar, is she always like that? Her Grace took over as though we were children. She ignored us and ordered us about." Berkley loved the take-charge attitude of his love.

"Always, Berkley, always. When she is in her *do as I say, no nonsense* mood, we just follow her lead. For some odd reason, and the heavens only know why, she is usually one hundred percent correct."

"Gentlemen, let's do as the lady said. Daggs, please conduct your investigation as swiftly as possible. I assume you sent for the coroner." The general pushed back the lock of black hair threaded with gray from his forehead.

"My men are still investigating the scene. We will be out of here within the hour."

"Good, I don't want anyone else to know of this. Quinn and I will be in my office."

• • •

In the other house in Mayfair, the disguise of a common laborer was being removed. In the book, another check mark was placed indicating one more death. Killing was such a powerful aphrodisiac. "Oh, what a glorious day" echoed off the walls of the empty room.

• • •

The plain carriage pulled up to the entrance to Daniel Gardener's house. Even in its plainness, the carriage shouted upper class in this working-class neighborhood. Three very sad figures stood at the entrance. The door opened. A woman took one look at them and screamed. Three children rushed to their mother.

This time it was Sar who picked up the distraught woman and carried her to the couch. She was sobbing and trembling.

"Tea immediately please. If there are spirits in the house, please bring the bottle." Her Grace motioned for Sar to take a seat in a chair. Anne's arm went around Daniel's wife, and they cried together.

The duchess and the commoner clutched each other, sharing their grief and losses. Pain brought them together as one, because death had no boundaries.

Sar and Julien took care of the children and, as tactfully as possible, explained that their father had died. Leaving out as many specifics as possible, they tried to assure them everyone could go on without worrying about a roof over their heads and food on the table.

On the ride to the house, Sar's mother had proposed several plans for the family. Taking a look around the cottage, Sar sensed they used every penny he paid to the family. *Damn it, they shouldn't be living like this.* He made a mental note to give everyone a raise. Looking up, he saw his mother had never stopped embracing the widow. He realized there was so much comfort in a loving touch, the human bond—what counted most.

"Now, do not worry about a thing. When you are ready, send for me. We'll discuss everything then. There are a few ideas floating around in my brain."

"I have never been without Daniel since the day we married ten years ago. He was everything to our family. It hurts so much my heart is on fire with pain."

As the woman touched her heart, Her Grace knew only too well the feeling that your heart had been ripped out of your chest while it was still beating. Avery had taken a piece of her heart with him—*a piece removed from her heart left to mend.* Anne dabbed her eyes.

"Sar will return tomorrow with the things you requested. Daggs is from Scotland Yard. He and his men will see to the arrangements as you wish."

Daniel's wife balled Her Grace's tear-soaked lace handkerchief in her hands and stared through stormy eyes. "One of our staff will be here within the hour to help in any way possible. If there is anything else we can do right now, please let us know."

The ride back to the duke's residence was undertaken in complete silence except for the occasional sobs of the three passengers. With the honor and dignity afforded royalty, the entire staff lined up in silent greeting out of respect for what the family had done for one of theirs.

Nothing could stop the day from marching on. Time progressed at its own speed. Lady Hortense sensed the grief and took control as any good general would, with the other ladies falling in line, executing their duties to perfection.

As strange days went, this one was one of the strangest. First murder and now this—all seven patrons of Almack's stopping by for a little chat again. Anne thought everything had been settled about Beth's come-out.

"Wanting to be received, Oliver?"

"Yes, Your Grace." Oliver was also curious.

The Dowager Duchess Horton heard the news, and the sly grin that she conjured up on her face spoke volumes for the entire group. Then she broke out in one of her notorious cackles. "Okay, girl, let's find out what the infamous group wants this time."

Her Grace turned to the other ladies. By the looks on their faces, they were just as curious as she. "Well, we should get to it. Our popularity knows no bounds." Anne stood and walked from the room.

As the patrons were leaving, Anne just shook her head. "The patrons of Almack's keep shocking us. First it was the official sanctioning of Beth's come-out and now this. They want to have lunch with the king to show him they support the Westmoures. That was something I wasn't expecting." Anne turned to Lady Horton. "Tell me what you think."

"Oh, they are gloating. The come-out and lunch with the king is just their way of saying we are the elite of the elite. I wonder what they will think up next just to stop in and chat. This way they can claim they are in on everything—*ha*! Now, let's get on with receiving these insufferable afternoon bores. Too bad they don't have anything else to do."

After Lady Horton's statement, which dumbfounded the other ladies, the doors for receiving were flung open.

Her Grace sat there and listened to the endless chatter. She had no idea what the gossip was about or who. What she did know was that all these visitors were really there to get gossip about the Westmoures. Anne smiled and prayed for an immediate, abrupt end to the receiving hour. Her prayer sadly wasn't answered.

By the time dinner was over that evening, Anne was weary down to the soles of her feet. She didn't know how she knew, but she sensed Berkley was waiting for her. It had been a long day, and she needed him.

Anne reached her bedchamber and crossed the threshold, and he pulled her to him. Not a word was said. The general stopped any talking with his lips. He was well aware of the emotional drain the day had taken on Anne—murder, a visit to the widow's house, planning, the visit by the patrons of Almack's led by Lady Sarah Jersey herself, and receiving the nincompoops of the ton. He was emotionally spent just thinking about it.

"Now it is my turn. You have let everything and everyone have at you all day long. I'll now show you what you are missing as my duchess. We'll talk later." He removed every stitch of her clothing and reverently placed her in the middle of the counterpane on her stomach. He had taken out the scented hot body oil, and with long strokes, he began a full-body massage. Each of his movements created an abrasive touch against her nipples and the very heart of her center. Working his way down her body only ignited a maelstrom of desire. When he turned her over, passion was raging in her eyes. But he wouldn't stop until every inch of her body had felt his magic touch.

By the time he reached her center, she was panting and beginning to lift off the bed in search of more, the elusive *it*. "Not quite yet, Your Grace. This is the way you will be each night after we are married. Do you understand the pleasure I must give my one and only true love?"

All Anne could do was nod her head in agreement. As the oil glazed her body, her nipples pebbled. Berkley suckled each one until they were as large as grapes. The sensitive nibs had her seeking her release. "Not yet, Your Grace. I need to watch you shatter without me touching any other part of your body."

As Her Grace started losing more and more control, oil and touch became her aphrodisiacs. Anne's body twisted, begging to be fulfilled. "No, Your Grace, like this." He continued to whisper the most wonderful things in her ear as she lifted off the bed. Her essence was everywhere.

Berkley gently nipped her left nipple, and she exploded. Contractions long and deep claimed her. He rubbed her mons and entered. He massaged her again, and both of them went to the stars as her contractions kept coming and coming.

As she went over the moon, her overactive mind was blank. Anne's breathing was almost normal. He held her like she was richer than the most expensive cargo—wanted, loved, protected, and cherished.

"Now we talk." Berkley ran his hands through her hair, massaging her scalp as though it was a forgotten part of his seduction. Her Grace could only sigh. "It's been one of your rougher days to say the least. I could patronize you by saying it will get better, but I won't diminish your worth. It was hell. Tell me about Daniel and his widow."

Anne wondered if all she would do in this country was cry with intermittent moments of loving to make it all tolerable.

"Daniel was always shy. Never looking me in the face. To get my attention, he would cough first. We went to his house, and when his wife saw us dressed as we were, she screamed. Berkley, I was in the same position several months ago as she is now. The pain . . . is indescribable. When Avery died, a friend of mine wrote this for me, and I carry these words close to my heart . . . *Take my love with you to the heavens, take the wonder of us, my friend, my lover, my husband, a piece removed from the heart left to mend.*

"That's the sum total of what it is, Berkley. A hole in the heart. I don't know if it is ever completely repaired. Sar has asked Daggs and his men to take care of the arrangements. We will talk with the widow when she is ready to give us some options. There are a few ideas swimming about in my head to make the family's life easier."

"You know, you don't have to do anything, but I realize you must."

"You're right, General, I must. And, speaking of generals, did you teach Hortense, or did she teach you how to take control?"

"Your Grace, I thought I learned everything from you." Berkley's deep chuckle was music to her ears.

"You order us around like we are still riding our first ponies, and I love it."

He rolled her on her back and proceeded to demonstrate just how much he loved her. "There is something about you. I get uncomfortably hard when you are stripped bare. I can't do anything but love you." Her release came almost immediately. "Three weeks, Your Grace, and then you become mine."

"Insufferable man." He just turned, gave her a grin, and became one with the shadows.

The next morning, Anne rang for her maid and focused on the day—Daniel's funeral.

The full recap of their actions at the service was the next

article of the Society News. It broke Anne's heart that some-one could find enjoyment in mocking a funeral service of any-one all because the Duke of Westmoure was present.

The London Daily

Society News

*Yes, there is more news about the Duke of
Westmoure and his half-breed family. They
have found their place—among the common
folk where they belong. It's apparent they are
more comfortable among the lower classes. The
Westmoures were seen conversing with every
commoner at the funeral of their gardener
Daniel and sharing a meal with them. This is
not the behavior that is expected of one of the
richest families in England, let alone an aristocrat. This is what happens when we pollute the
lines of the upper class. Don't the Westmoures
understand we cannot have this happen?
We are pure, above the rest, the arbiters of
society and all that is right. Those beneath
us will always be below us. Those of you who
understand the elite, please let us figure out a
solution soon. This is getting out of hand.*

As Beth finished reading the article, she burst into tears. "What's wrong with these people?"

Daggs watched the woman he had been admiring since she arrived in England. *Such a strong, sensitive woman. What a cruel article.* He stopped his perpetual pacing, turned, started to reach for her, and stopped. What did he think he was doing? Sar would make sure he wouldn't live past this day.

"Oh, my darling child," Anne said. "Beth, I know people can be mean. Why people hate and try to divide people by color, class, origin, or religion is beyond comprehension by those of us in this room. We may have some theories, but our ideas and thoughts do not rule the world." Anne had a few thoughts, and stupidity was at the top of her list, but she didn't voice that.

In his mind, Daggs finished Her Grace's thoughts—*Most or many in the white world believe they should be loved unconditionally, but they do not love others that way. The aristocracy leads the pack—they dislike for no reason, and many can't think beyond the spitefulness taught to them. The world can be full of ugly and evil notions.*

Daggs was pacing while watching Beth and Anne. *How could someone hurt others like that?* He stopped, and once again his thoughts took over. As he strode around the room, the ugly truth marched in time with his steps. *There is very little kindness connected with what you do, Inspector. And that is a reflection of the world. You know that as well as the others at the Yard.* Once again, his eyes swept over mother and daughter. It was his job to protect all of them.

The inspector thought of his half-brother, Jay, and the cruelty inflicted on him. He was Indian and white British. Daggs never really considered the differences except when blackening someone's eye when they were kids. To him, they were brothers.

The last few weeks had taken a toll on everyone. After hearing the article in the newssheet, Anne felt deflated and somewhat defeated. Understanding mankind was beyond her comprehension at times.

• • •

Later that evening, Her Grace was upstairs preparing for bed. As an afterthought, she asked her maid for a glass and a bottle of wine. She probably wouldn't see Berkley tonight. The men usually worked as long as necessary, and tonight was one of those nights. Her eyes were closing when she heard his familiar voice: *You are doing the right things. Our lives are very different now, but I am so proud of you and the children. My brother sends his regards. Oh, Anne, if you only knew the half of it.* He laughed, and at the same exact moment, Her Grace fell into a deep slumber.

Anne felt she was being lifted from her bed. As she floated upward, a cool breeze hit her face. She reached for her pistol, but there was no pillow.

"I have never made love to you outside." The deep rumble of a voice she would know anywhere assured her she was safe. He gently placed her on a couch he had moved to her balcony. When she looked down, she noted he had created a nest.

As he heated her body, what nightclothes she was wearing seemed to disappear. Sensations were playing counterpoint as they skipped across her body—the heat of his tongue on her nipples and the rushing air of the early morning. She was willingly being assaulted. His tongue touched her center, and she exploded. He quickly entered her, felt the powerful contraction, and followed suit.

"You know, Your Grace, I see you in all your glory, and I spill my seed. When I think of you during the day and someone is in my office, I have to control myself. The thoughts are for me only, and I don't share." He continued his whisperings as the two of them moved the couch back into her room. When she turned, he sealed his lips with hers, then disappeared.

Dawn was quickly appearing. Secrets of the night made everything more mysterious, but the reflections created days of wonder. Her Grace knew she would not be able to fall asleep. She was tingling down to her toes. Anne rang for her maid.

"Well, that was a great start to the day." The smile wreathed her face. "Better than the last couple of weeks." Her voice bounced off the walls of an empty room.

• • •

In her study two weeks later, Anne was busy consulting with her four-legged confidante. "Well, Duchess, what do you think? You believe we can get this done?"

Duchess looked at her mistress as though she understood every word uttered, nudged her head into Anne's hand, and gently licked. It was their own form of communication between the two of them. And on cue, Her Grace offered the magnificent beast a treat.

"Always spoil her, Anne, like I plan on spoiling you. How are you?" The general leaned down and kissed her. "Can we talk for a few minutes? I need to say some things out loud and hear responses from someone I trust."

"Of course, Berkley, but I have a request first. Can we postpone our wedding for five weeks? There is just so much happening that our wedding would not come together properly."

"Are you telling me you are leaving me at the altar?"

"Yes, for five weeks."

"For five weeks and five weeks only. I must make you my duchess. Even though I have been distracted the past few days, you are the love of my life. We need to talk about the distractions.

"Are you feeling all right? No more bouts of nausea? The last incident was at the time Daniel was murdered about two weeks ago. You are the gauge for predicting murder."

"I'm fine, General. I will only keep you waiting five weeks longer. It looks like we are in for one adventure after another."

"Anne, somewhere deep within Whitehall there is a spy who is well connected and knows our every move. The murder of Daggs's two men emphasizes that point. I have turned everything upside down and inside out. I came up with nothing. This can't go on. Too many bodies are in the wake."

"This makes what? Seven, eight, or nine murders? Do you have any other information about the two men? Anything that would alert you that something was not quite right?"

"Nothing. They were two dedicated men in service, trying to make the world a better place."

"Berkley, if nothing in the present is sending up red flags, then look to your past. Look for someone seeking revenge, someone who didn't make it as an operative, or someone right beneath your nose. The answer is probably there."

"Are you sure you don't want to work for Whitehall? I know someone who could get you a position there."

"You're funny, Berkley. I have all the positions I could ever . . ." Before she finished her sentence, the general captured her mouth.

"It's been too long since I have held you and touched you. Come, let's get out of here so I can have my way with you."

"You had your way with me this morning." Anne laughed at her husband-to-be.

"That was far too long ago." He sealed her lips with a steamy kiss.

"Berkley, five weeks from now. Since you're here, take this list and see if I have left anything out." Grumbling, Berkley set about his task.

Her Grace indelicately snorted. "You're so typically male, Berkley; that is why I love you so."

"Do you really love me, Anne?"

"Without a doubt." She reached up and kissed him on the cheek. "Now, work!"

CHAPTER 7

Another Celebration

Digvijay, called Jay by his family and the king, stepped out of the coach and stared at his family home. He had left England when he graduated from university at the age of nineteen. That was eight years ago. One of their father's final wishes was that he learn about his Indian roots. *"Son, your English blood runs as deep as your Indian blood."* He remembered the excitement he had felt when his father had uttered those words. That was it; when he graduated, he went to India.

His brother was two years older than him. Their father died when Jay was ten. His mother, a royal princess of the House of Ranjea, had left this mortal realm when he was two. His brother's mother had died in childbirth. It was the two of them after their father died until his brother graduated university. He had gone to work for Berkley. Digvijay guessed that's where he'd find his brother today—with the general.

When his mother died, Jay became one of the two royal princes or royal highnesses of the House of Ranjea. Working beside his grandfather, uncle, and cousin, Jay learned every aspect of the family business. Knowing England better than other family members, Jay's job was to establish trade relations with Westmoure Shipping Company. Jay's family business was precious gems and exquisite fabrics. The types of goods the rich and elite craved.

As Jay climbed the stairs, he wondered if Jenkins, the majordomo, would recognize him. Now twenty-seven, he had changed a lot from the knobby-kneed child of nine and the young man of nineteen he had been when he left for India. All manner of thoughts swirled through his head—would he still be welcomed, had society taught his family not to accept him, could he adjust to England again? Making his way up the stairs, he almost turned and went the other way. When he attempted to knock on the door, one of his entourage wouldn't allow him to do such a lowly task.

The door opened. Jenkins stood there as erect and imposing as ever. He was about to say *my lord* when he looked again, smiled, and wrapped his arms around Digvijay. "Welcome home, son of this house."

Tears pooled in Digvijay's eyes. "Jenkins, I have missed you too. Is all well with you?"

"Your Royal Highness, all is well with me and this house. It is much better now that you are home." Looking around him, Jenkins noticed servants carrying all sorts of things. "What can I help you with?"

"My Indian grandfather designated certain things from his estate for Anthony. Most of it is for Anthony's future bride. Grandfather wanted her to feel and understand our culture also. May they be brought in? We can go to the trade entrance."

"No, no. Bring everything in here." Magically, the underbutler appeared with help, and everything was whisked away as though it were never there. "Are you moving into your late mother's house? Should I have your room prepared here?"

"I'll move into my mother's house. It's being cleaned as we speak. Do you know where my brother is?"

"Probably at the Duke of Westmoure's house. You can catch up with him there. If he is not there, Perkins will know where to find him. Your brother will be glad to see you. If I may say so, he has missed you."

"Thanks, Jenkins."

• • •

Perkins took one look at the man standing in front of him and knew as sure as his name was Perkins that this was the half-brother Daggs talked about when he wasn't busy trying to make his country and London a better place to live. "Your Highness, this way please."

The men and ladies were in the conservatory. Evelyn said, "Enough. We have been going round and round with this all day. We need to step away from the problem for a while. We will figure it out. Now, we need afternoon tea and something much stronger than tea and sherry to revive ourselves." Evelyn said what everyone was thinking.

Perkins miraculously appeared bearing gifts in hand—champagne, brandy, and whisky. As usual, he had reminded the cooks that their mistresses might be less than steady by dinner. Behind Perkins came trays of tasty food.

When the door to the conservatory opened again, no one looked up. Perkins cleared his throat and simply said, "Daggs, your brother is here."

Daggs was standing next to Beth, deep in conversation. It took a few seconds to comprehend what he had just heard. He looked up, and a smile erupted on his face. "Jay."

The two met in the center of the room. It was a meeting of brothers who genuinely loved each other. "Let me introduce you to those you do not know. Over there next to Berkley is

Sar, the eighth Duke of Westmoure. Next to Caroline is Anne, Her Grace, Sar's mother; sitting next to Evelyn is Mer, Sar's sister and Julien's wife. I was speaking with Beth, Sar's other sister. And of course, there is Perkins, who is outside being one with the door. His gift. He knows everything."

As Digvijay made his way around the room speaking to everyone, it only took one look to realize he and Daggs were brothers. There was only one difference. His Highness had a rich light coffee complexion.

"Please join us, Your Highness." Anne smiled, and Jay knew he was welcomed. "Eventually, they will fill you in. We are up to our necks in murder, espionage, smuggling, and trafficking of women. But tonight, we are so happy to have you home."

"It's Jay. Thank you for welcoming me to your home. Berkley, I am at your service."

"Thank you, Jay. Welcome home." The general knew he needed as much help as possible.

As everyone was getting to know each other, Mer wanted to finish her conversation with her mother-in-law. "Do you think Julien and I will make a good team?" Mer stared at her as the silence lengthened.

Evelyn's mind battled itself as she watched Mer in what felt like a deep probe of the truth.

When they started their conversation, Mer was searching for the unspoken—did her mother-in-law resent the fact that she was Negro and white? Would she completely accept her new daughter? With Jay's sudden appearance, the afternoon turned into a welcome-home gathering. Mer's thoughts had been pushed to the side. Now that things had settled down, Mer had her mother-in-law's total attention.

"Well, I don't quite know how to answer your last question. If you are asking about differences in people, in my opinion, that is what makes a marriage work. I am different. I walk with a limp and pain. Others no longer consider me as whole or a beauty because of that. Damaged. That is what many call me.

"Don't frown, Mer. I was once a silly twit who also believed everything the ton holds true without question. Life has taught me a few invaluable lessons, which I hope I have instilled in Julien.

"As a wife, I am counting on you complementing my beloved son. His love for you is like none other I have ever seen. Oh, you will have discussions at times, sometimes major discussions, but the two of you will see it through and be stronger than ever. There is just one thing I ask—don't let Berkley send him away on a long mission. Keep my son at home with you."

"I will do everything in my power to keep that from happening. Thank you, Lady Evelyn."

"Do you think you can consider calling me Mother Number Two?"

"Why don't I just call you Mother and have the two of you figure out who I am talking to if we are all together in the same room."

Evelyn just nodded. She couldn't say a word. Her husband handed her his linen square.

Lady Evelyn limped over to Anne. "Anne, I had a conversation with Mer a few moments ago." Evelyn was still dabbing the tears from her eyes.

"I can't imagine what she said to upset you so, but you know our Mer. She is always direct and to . . ."

Before Anne could finish, Evelyn interjected. "It's better if I continue. Mer is a perceptive, intelligent young woman. The ton will never get used to the likes of her. Never." Pausing, Evelyn took a deep breath. "Mer wanted to know why many of the aristocracy, and white people in general, are cruel, unjust, and unfair.

"I wasn't expecting a question so on point, insightful, and piercing. Searching for an honest answer, I repeated her question my way. *You mean, why are so many people idiots.* Anne, the words hung between us like an oppressive shroud. You see, I didn't know how to answer her at first. I was brought up with these rules I was supposed to obey. After my carriage accident, I started to see how foolish these rules were, and I finally started to look around. My eyes began to open and see, Anne, really see.

"This country and world are so mixed up. There are things we should never assume, ways we should never conduct ourselves. There are manners that should be extended to all, rather than a select few. How stupid are our actions?

"I wanted to deny everything and avoid the truth of the matter. But you, Mer, and your family deserve nothing less than total honesty. I do not know why we act the way we do. We were raised to think of *us*, and then there is the rest of the world or country. We perceived things unconsciously, and these things shaped the way we lived and who we accepted. No rhyme or reason—just because someone else acted in that manner, we should also. We were able to exert and enforce superiority. It wasn't questioned, because we presumed; we were superior and everyone else knew that.

"I have changed, Anne. The carriage accident set everything in motion. With the birth of Julien, I knew I did not want my child raised in this closed-minded world with an equally closed-minded attitude. Sometimes it was a struggle, but it was well worth it. You should hear my description of the ton and most of England." Evelyn's light laughter was like that of the softest wind, gently swaying the crystal on a chandelier.

"Evelyn, I have always wanted to know what other people thought, but you can't ask. Everyone is so different. There are few words of kindness when people talk about others who are different than them. I will never understand why we pit one class or color against another. *Cruelty* is just one word for it.

"If Mer's question offended you in any way, I know that was not her intent. She has always asked very pointed questions. She expects truth in return." Anne also wanted to know the answer to Mer's question. It was one of those things that haunted your thoughts and fashioned the way you approached the world—less than whole, less than free.

"I am glad she asked. Mer made me think, really think. Why can't we make the world a better place for our children?"

The question was out there for inspection and change. Both women looked at each other knowing they had crossed a divide, and now they were closer to being one.

"We'll get there, Evelyn, someway, somehow. In the meantime, there is much to do. Let's expect wonderful things for our children and from them." Anne turned and realized they had an audience. The men had stopped what they were doing to listen.

"Unfortunately, we can't take on the world. Let's do our part to make it a better place. I am proud of the two of you. Groundwork for better understanding is essential. You just can't dismiss another because his or her experience is different than yours. Now, I say a toast is in order to new beginnings." Richard said nothing else. Instead, he held out glasses of champagne for everyone, and the talk turned to lighter things, but they all realized the foundation for something greater and deeper had been forged.

The remainder of the day and evening turned into inquiries about Jay's Indian family and tales about the mysteries of India—foods, spices, customs, exquisite woven fabrics, arranged marriages, magnificent structures, and weather. Business was mentioned. As the wine flowed, so did the laughter. Everyone politely and intentionally skipped around the current problems.

"Tomorrow, ten, here. I'll see if the king will join us. Jay, please notify the proper officials that you are on English soil if they don't know already. Until tomorrow."

Then Berkley disappeared into the night.

———

CHAPTER 8

Links

Everyone was in Sar's study before ten, waiting for Berkley when Jacob burst through the door. "Glad you are all here. Where's Berkley?"

"Behind you, Jacob." Beside Berkley was the king.

The king spoke to everyone, especially the ladies. He then turned to Jay and gave him the official welcome befitting his status. "Always Jay, Your Majesty."

"Glad you are back. This is nasty business. We must make sure you are protected on English soil. I know your men are all over this place, but a few of my men are also watching your back. My cousin is in the middle of this muddle.

"Do you want me to give a ball in your honor? You will have your choice of women who will be vying for your attention."

"Thank you, Your Majesty. Due to the gravity of this situation, we will celebrate when the culprits are brought to justice. I understand this is to be done in the quietest manner possible."

"Jay, I always did like your thinking. Will you and the rest of this group pay a formal visit tomorrow at six? This will give the busybodies enough to chew on for a week and let them know you have paid the proper visit to the king and have been received. We will have tea and dinner."

"It will be our pleasure."

"Now, down to the business at hand. Jacob, what did you find? Not much, but it will be the beginning of closing some gaps in this puzzle." Jacob and the two inspectors opened the trunks of the women.

"Gowns. Only an expert modiste could have executed these."

"Jacob, let me see." Miriam spoke as she and Joycellyn started inspecting the gowns. Seams were pulled, designs were studied, and the quality of the fabric examined. The two whispered between them before turning to the group.

"You had better get Madame Burgoff here immediately. We suggest that she close her shop and move in here. She made some of these gowns. An apprentice of hers made the others. You need to find the apprentice and bring her here also." Joycellyn's tone was serious.

Before the order could be issued by Berkley, Perkins had sent for a messenger, along with outriders for protection. A soft knock on the door signaled the messenger was ready.

"What else do you have, Jacob?" Berkley's cigar was dancing across the desk.

"This is a very distinctive piece of stationery, and the trunks are also unique." Handing the piece of paper to Berkley, Jacob continued, "Only a lord of the realm would have paper of this quality. It had to have been made specially for him. Find out who made it. The same for the trunks."

Anne couldn't hold back one second longer. She stood and ran to the nearest dustbin. Sar grabbed her before her shaking body hit the floor. Then he sat with her on the divan.

"Do you want to go to your bedchamber?"

She shook her head no.

"Did you see something this time?"

Her "yes" was barely audible.

"Mother." Sar was wiping her tears.

"Still people, smoke, and fire."

"Was this the same as before?"

A visibly shaken Anne clung to Sar. "The same."

Someone handed Sar a cool towel. "Is there anything else?"

"No, Sar."

"There we have it. Someone is going to die or has already died. We don't know who, where, or when. It could be anyone in this room or someone connected to these crimes. Anne, is there anything else?"

Before Anne could answer Berkley, there was a soft knock on the door. Perkins opened and announced Madame Burgoff.

"Thank you, Madame Burgoff, for joining us so quickly. We need you to tell us about these garments and for whom you made them if you please. This is critical." The room echoed silence as everyone waited for answers.

"Your Majesty, Your Royal Highness, my lords, it is hard for me to reveal who my clients are. The men especially trust me to remain silent as to their identity and entrust me with complete confidentiality as to their requests. Most of the time, the items are for their mistresses. Today, I must break that silence. Something tells me this may have something to do with the shot that destroyed my shop window."

"You are right, Madame. Everyone in this room is in danger, and that might include you." Berkley puffed on his unlit cigar.

"I started making dresses for the exchequer about ten years ago. The dresses were always for his mistresses. There were always two sets of garments. He would come in with precise measurements and specific designs. As you can see, they were very scanty.

"Over the years, the measurements changed, but the requests were always similar. In all these years, not one of his mistresses ever set foot in the shop. I would have known immediately because of their measurements.

"Besides being scanty, they had two other things in common. The tops were very large in proportion to the lower half of the body. The lower half of the body was exceedingly tiny for such a ratio. To me this indicated these women or young girls developed early, and they were between the ages of eleven and fifteen. I never really questioned that until now, but I believe the exchequer was using *très jeunes filles* for reasons I would not like to think about.

"Then, about three months ago, he asked if he could have one of my assistants exclusively. I was taken aback by this request, thinking the exchequer wasn't pleased with my work.

"He assured me my work was exquisite, but he needed a lot of garments made. The making of so many garments would interfere with my normal business. I asked Babette if she wanted to consider this position for two or three months. The pay was extraordinarily good. It would be difficult for anyone to turn down what he offered."

"Do you have Babette's address?" Berkley had an uncomfortable feeling about what they would find.

"Yes." Rummaging around in her reticule, she pulled out a little green book. "Here it is. She usually comes by the shop at least once a week, but I haven't seen her in about ten days."

"Simmons, Jay, take four of our strongest men and go to Babette's. Daggs, you had better take a couple of your men and go also." Berkley barked out his order. One glance at Anne completed the story.

"Daggs, find out discreetly where the exchequer's staff is now. We must interview all of them immediately." Then he turned to Madame Burgoff. "Madame, please tell us more." Berkley was in his predator stance.

"There is not much more to tell. He was polite and always spoke in French, which made it easier for me, and he paid his bill in cash when he picked up the last garment."

"Madame, I am going to have to ask you again to start from the beginning. Feel free to add anything you think you may have omitted the first time." Berkley had started pacing.

"Please call me Yvette."

"Thank you, Yvette." As Yvette went through her story again and endured endless questioning by the general and other men, a feeling of extreme sadness washed over her. Babette might have taken a job that led to her death.

There was a knock on the door, and the messenger handed the note to Berkley. It was in Daggs's scrawl. Berkley would recognize it anywhere. He didn't want to open it, but that wasn't an option. Slitting open the envelope, he took a moment to read the note and then read it again.

"Yvette, ladies, gentlemen, Daggs found the body of Babette draped over a dress she was working on. Cause of death, a knife slipped through her ribs. I am so sorry, Yvette."

The women did what all women have been doing since the beginning of time—console the bereaved.

"Where are her relatives?" Berkley looked at the women surrounding Yvette and knew any further questioning would have to wait.

"There are none. I only hired bastards, for I am one also." Yvette hung her head and sobbed in shame, grieving for her friend.

"Perkins, I need a messenger. If you do not mind, we will take care of all the arrangements."

Joycellyn was softly crying.

"General, we will adjourn to the blue room. I know you

have a thousand things you want to ask Yvette, but that will have to wait." Anne had begun to recover from her earlier spell.

"*Humph.* This is the real reason the exchequer left for a drier, warmer climate."

"What did you say, Beth?" The general looked at his daughter-to-be and caught himself almost smiling. *She is brilliant.*

"Just repeating what I read in the Society News."

"What was said?" Berkley puffed again on the cigar with no smoke.

"Let me see. The exchequer has contracted the consumption disease. According to his physician, if the exchequer wanted to heal, he must move to a drier, warmer climate immediately. That's it."

"Thank you, Beth."

"Just one last thing. Yvette, I cannot allow you to go back to your shop. We are trying to keep everyone alive. So, my men will move your shop to a room in my house. As for any altering of your garments, I believe we can work something out.

"At first, I thought the ball that shattered your window was meant for Anne. After hearing your story, I am more inclined to believe that it was meant for you. Keeping everyone safe is our priority. We are sorry for your loss. Thank you for hiring the women you do." Berkley stood, as did all the other men, as the ladies left the room.

Yvette felt numb. *Did he just thank me for hiring bastards?* Her tears started to flow anew. *What did I do to my friend?*

In the front room, refreshments appeared along with wine, whisky, and brandy. This was not a day for champagne. No one seemed to miss it.

Back in Sar's lair, the master strategist was at work, barking out orders in a tone that was sharper than usual with an undertone of warning—a death warrant had been issued.

His Majesty rose. "Bring everyone tonight. Cousin, I know

the punishment of death will stalk someone. Do it discreetly, on English soil if possible." Everyone stood as His Majesty left.

"My gut is telling me that the former exchequer is in France. He speaks French well. He may also speak other languages. With his side endeavors, he is close to a discreet port in the north or south of France. There are so many coves and inlets that drugs and women can be shipped out of easily. This is a job for Rue and his men."

"Royce, get the signals started. Tell them 'urgent message to follow shortly.'" A messenger was waiting by the time Royce sealed the envelope.

"'Former government official wanted for treason, trafficking of women, murder, et cetera. Reason to believe in France near coast. Speaks French. Proceed with extreme caution. Very dangerous. Want him back alive on English soil if possible. Advise. Will forward additional information as we receive. Do you need Royce, Sar, Julien, and Jay?'" Sadly, Berkley dictated the message.

"That should do it, Royce. Signaling to start immediately. Urgent. The four of you be ready to leave within five days." Berkley impressed his seal on the envelope, and the chain of command was put in motion. "Also, I want the exchequer's former staff here by tomorrow morning. Arrest them if you must."

Making sure his commands were understood, Berkley joined the women. "Well, if we are having dinner with the king, we had best get ready. Yvette, you are to come also." Berkley chuckled to himself. He couldn't wait to see who his cousin would go after first.

• • •

All the trappings of court were in place. Jay presented himself to the king. "Now the gossip mongers will be happy." The king laughed at that thought.

After that, the evening was a casual affair of old friends, if one can have a casual dinner with the king. The king set his sights on Anne, which put Berkley in a royal snit. When he pulled Her Grace away from everyone else, all the general could see was red.

"Your Grace."

"Your Majesty." By the look on Berkley's face, one would have thought the king had summoned Anne to his inner chamber.

"Wanted to talk to you and Sar about the ridiculous notion that the aristocracy is pure white. As you know, there were two Negro queens to our knowledge—Philippa and my mother, Charlotte. They were both Moors. It is as though their families don't exist. The royal family will always have Negro blood in its veins. I have sent my men to fetch my mother's relatives and bring them to court. That should at least set the ton on its ear.

"I need to see them and know them. I do not understand why people believed that reprobate author Long, but they did. Now we have this big mess. We need to sort this out as much as we can. If you and Sar would be so kind as to attend me next Thursday at two, I would appreciate it."

"We would be pleased to, Your Majesty."

"Anne, can we keep this among the three of us?"

"Yes, Your Majesty. It's late. We've had a wonderful evening, but we must leave. Thank you so much for having us."

"As you wish." They returned to the group. "Until Thursday." His Majesty bowed and joined the rest of the men.

• • •

The message arrived from Monsieur Rue while they were enjoying brandy in Sar's study. They waited for Berkley to read the missive. *Message received. Proceeding with extreme caution. When we get pigeon's location will notify, then send your men.*

"Royce, short message needs to go out tonight." The general wrote, *Received. Understood.*

"I told His Majesty at dinner we would be using our usual training ground. Let's make it seven tomorrow morning. After tomorrow, it is six in the morning. We will have many late nights.

"My instincts are telling me we need to have the ladies join us. They must be prepared." The general was barking out orders, but when he mentioned the women, he softened his tone.

"Mer, if you follow us when we leave English soil, I will shoot Perkins for insubordination. I know you are out there. You tell the women everything we say." Berkley thought he heard a soft laugh. Before Berkley could get out of his chair to open the door, Mer tiptoed soundlessly away.

As Mer briefed the ladies on the men's next move, the wheels were turning as to what the ladies could do. "We will have to go. Who else is going to protect the men and bring this culprit home? We'll meet tomorrow and come up with a plan that is flexible enough to work."

All agreed with Mer.

The ladies were enjoying champagne in the blue room. The men walked in as one. *Oh, oh, there is an edict coming.* Anne felt she could lay a bet on that.

"You are to train with us starting tomorrow morning at seven. We will be using our usual training ground. Sar, you and your group meet at Sebastian's about six fifteen tomorrow morning. He will show you the way. Ladies, wear britches, heavy boots, and scarves, and bring pistols. Yvette, we will bring several extra pistols. I suggest that we all adjourn for the evening. Until the morning." The general was gone just as quickly.

• • •

At six fifteen the next morning, Sar, his mother and sisters, Joycellyn, Yvette, and Lady Horton were in front of Sebastian's house. By the time they reached the usual training ground, they were in awe. Within the grounds of the palace was a secluded park of acres and acres of virgin land with a lake.

"Everyone is here. Ladies, you will train alongside the men and do everything they do." As usual, the general was barking.

They attempted to scale walls and climb ropes. Swimming in the lake and shooting moving targets were much easier. The ladies were given lessons on how to deflect the advances of men. Lunch was eaten as if they were with troops at war.

"Never knew I had it in me." Lady Horton was laughing with glee.

"Just wait until tomorrow morning. We won't be able to move." Caroline snorted.

The afternoon was the same. At about four, the ladies demanded tea. Of course, Perkins was at the ready. Champagne, brandy, and finger foods appeared.

Everyone adjourned to Sar's for a very early dinner. It was a subdued meal. All talk was about the day. One by one, the exhausted ladies let their heads meet their food. The men were betting on who would succumb next.

The next day was more of the same, only more intense. On the third day, night training started. Doing as the men did, the women were beginning to improve.

The second grand opening of Paige's came and went as well. On the fifth day after the grand opening, the message arrived.

> *Pigeon found in Caen. Morning routine the*
> *same. Men watching. Meet 22 Jardin, two days*
> *hence. Will be waiting.*

"Well, the former exchequer isn't in the south of France.

Men, we leave for Caen at eight tomorrow tonight. Would like the pigeon on English soil within four days.

"Royce, send message. 'Message received. Leaving tomorrow night at eight. Note very dangerous situation.'"

Mer was at her usual place—outside the door listening. As she noiselessly made her way back to the women, she wondered if it was possible. She had always wanted to go to France.

• • •

Rue and the General arrived at 22 Jardin at the same time. The house was as quiet as a tomb. They found Rue's three operatives slain—a stiletto slipped between the ribs.

They glanced around, looking for clues. Finding nothing, they knew it was imperative to secure a safe house. *Hors d'ici maintenant! Mes hommes vont nettoyer. Suivre!* Immediately pushing Berkley out of the house, Rue whispered, "My men will clean up. Follow me." Sticking to the shadows, they wound their way through the backstreets of Caen.

"Someone knows our every move. We won't be able to get close to the pigeon. Okay, let us come up with a plan. Rue, let us know if we can do anything for your men." Berkley didn't bark out orders this time. He was deadly quiet with his pronouncement. He knew there was a spy among them, but who? Was the spy with them now?

"The women can do it." Sar saw it clearly in his head. "The women are the only ones who can get close to the former exchequer. He'd be dead before he could open his mouth."

"No, won't have it. Too dangerous," Berkley barked.

"Sar does have a point." Rue could imagine French women doing this. They would be vicious.

Outside the door of the safe house, Mer listened intently. She quietly left and returned to the hotel they were staying at. Perkins followed.

"Once again, it looks like we need to rescue our men. This is the situation." Mer leaned in to whisper low what she had just learned.

With clarity and authority, Anne quickly came up with a plan. "Okay, easy in and out. We are having our boat moved to the closest café on the waterfront as we talk. Let's entice the former exchequer with breakfast and young flesh for his inspection. We will easily get him on the boat. Once he is on the boat and we are headed toward England, we'll signal the men. I want to be out of here tomorrow morning.

"Hortense, you and Caroline write the note. Read it to all of us before Perkins delivers it in disguise. Miriam, Aurelia, and Evelyn will be the backup for tomorrow. Beth, knives ready. Miriam, Aurelia, and Evelyn, pistols cocked and ready to be fired at all times. Georgina, you are going to be the prey.

"Alexius, Joycellyn, Yvette, make sure you are hiding in the least expected places just in case. Do not be afraid to fire if you must. These men will kill first and keep walking. Don't even question what you need to do. Is everyone clear?

"Once the pigeon is on the boat, his hands and feet will be tied. We'll place a scarf over his mouth until we are away from the coastline. The same men who tied the boat will throw Perkins the ropes. We should be able to set sail immediately."

"What about his two henchmen that follow him all the time? They are big and will stop anyone who gets in the way." Beth was beginning to gnaw on her lip.

"This is where the mission relies on Hortense. Once the former exchequer is on the boat, his henchmen will move forward. Hortense, we need you to fall to the ground without hurting yourself. They will run to rescue you, as any man would. In place, before they reach you, will be a rope high enough to trip them. The rope will be a good ten feet away from you, Lady Hortense. They will trip. Mer and Beth will take care of them. Hopefully, the general or Rue will find them and discover if they are French or English. They will decide what to do with them.

"Let's talk this through again and see where we might fail, find hiding places, and make sure weapons are prepared. Everyone carry three pistols at the ready."

Anne and the women went through everything again and again.

The answer to their message arrived within the hour: monsieur would be pleased to meet with madame at six in the morning.

At six, madame, a.k.a. Anne, was looking as enticing as any madame of a house of prostitution, as were the women surrounding her. Breakfast looked like a leisurely affair, as the exchequer was a man on the prowl for his next mistress.

"*Monsieur, chair fraîche. Trop jeune pour moi. Anglais, très bien proportionné. Vierge. Droit pour un sultan. Treize ou quatorze. Comprenez-vous, non?*" Anne could almost see Monsieur Solange rubbing his hands in anticipation. Her Grace told the former exchequer, now going under the name of Monsieur Solange, about the thirteen- or fourteen-year-old English virgin who was proportionally very large on the top. Anne could see him salivating. She wanted to skewer him.

The former exchequer signaled his henchmen. "May I have the pleasure of inspecting this English beauty?"

"*Oui, mais bien sûr. Notre transaction doit être de la plus grande discrétion. Comme vous le diriez privé.*" Yes, yes, Anne thought. *This must be done in private with great discretion.* Arm in arm, they strolled to the boat. Anne almost recoiled at his touch. Perkins watched their backs.

Everything went as planned. The henchmen saw Hortense fall. They ran to help her. Tripped over the rope. Before they could say a word, each one had a pistol in his side and was being trussed up like a roasted turkey. Caroline, Alexius, and Lady Hortense helped. They rolled them to the nearest trees and tied them.

"More parting presents." Instead of speaking, Beth wanted to pull out one of her knives and teach them a lesson they would never forget. But following the plan, Mer and Beth gave them right hooks with brass knuckles and knocked them unconscious.

On the boat, as soon as the signal was given, Anne said to the former exchequer, *"Venez, me laisser vous montrer un cadeau précieux, oui."* He stood. In a flash, the chair was kicked out from behind him; he heard the cocking of pistols. His hands and feet were being tied. Someone with a knife shredded his clothes. The exchequer stood there in his smalls. There was a scarf around his mouth. He felt the boat slowly pull away from the dock.

Caroline looked at her *Bessie*, and with a sense of pride, she joined the other women in saying, "We arrest you in the name of the Crown on the charges of murder, espionage, smuggling, trafficking of women, and treason."

Perkins started the signaling to Sebastian. *Pigeon in cage. Headed to English soil. Meet at designated spot. Please inform Rue and men. Thank Rue for his assistance.*

Three hours later, when Rue received the message, all he could do was laugh and hand the note to Berkley. *"Les femmes sont belles. Celle-ci, je ne la mettrais jamais trop en colère."*

The general knew women were beautiful. Rue was right. *I can't make Anne too angry. She'd probably make me walk a plank for fun and push me into the channel.*

"Oui, Oui. Je vais me chercher les femmes qui sont anglaises dans la maison de Solange? Merci pour votre aide. Jusqu'à ce que nous nous retrouvions." Berkley wanted to have a little chat with Anne right there, right now. How could she put herself

and the other women in such extreme danger? Steam was coming out of his ears.

"I will get the English *femme* in Solange's house to you *demain*. Remember, Berkley, don't make her too angry." Rue stuck to the alleys as he went to rejoin his men. Berkley and the rest of his operatives were on the boat and on their way to England within the hour.

When their boat was deep in the channel, the women approached the former exchequer and repeated the arrest. He was attached to the yardarm, literally sailing across the water. When they landed, Sebastian and Daggs were waiting at the designated point where they officially arrested him.

Sebastian hugged Caroline, then Alexius. "Well done, wife and daughter of mine, even though you two scared me to death. Try not to do that again. Two of my favorite women were on this mission."

Samuels and some other soldiers were securing the former exchequer.

"Shall we wait for Berkley? He will be here in about three hours. I can hear him now. This is going to be interesting to say the least." Sebastian was grinning from ear to ear.

CHAPTER 9

Back on English Soil

The women washed their feet in the water of the English Channel, let their hair down, and ate the delicious food Sebastian's cook had made. They lounged in the coaches Sebastian had brought. Simmons examined the women. "Not a scratch, Sebastian, not a scratch."

Sebastian nodded his head in appreciation that they were all well. He couldn't speak. There was a lump in his throat as he thanked the Almighty that they had returned safely.

Anne stretched out in one of the coaches and was asleep as soon as her eyes closed. Berkley threw a couple of blankets on her and let her slumber on. He had to see for himself that she was fine. Most of the women were asleep, being watched over by the men. Nothing would harm them now.

Daggs, Royce, Julien, Sar, Jay, and Sebastian went with the general to have a little chat with the former exchequer; they didn't get far. He kept saying, "You can't stop the plan. You mixed-breed pieces of scum. There will always be murder, smuggling, espionage, and trafficking of women. You can't stop that either." He repeated that over and over again.

"Men, he is not going to give us anything more. Clearly, he is losing his power to think rationally. The king wants this matter taken care of discreetly. Make sure the beach is cleared and everyone is enjoying the meal and wine."

Two hours later, the general awakened the exchequer. "Time to go for a walk." Berkley gave him a choice. "You can either blow your brains out or take a walk in the channel. The choice is yours." The general laid the gun on the beach and walked away. Twenty minutes later, the former exchequer stepped into the channel.

"Samuels, there is enough light from the torches. When his body washes ashore, get Simmons." The general turned, checked on Anne, and found a coach and blankets. He fell asleep instantly.

When Berkley woke, Samuels, Jay, Simmons, and Sar were pulling the former exchequer out of the water. The general walked to the shore. They turned the former exchequer over, and a loaded pistol was aimed at Berkley's heart. "Science is an incredible thing if you know how to use it properly." The former exchequer let go a demonic sound.

No one seemed to notice Anne and Caroline standing there. All eyes were focused on the drama being played out with Berkley.

"Shall we, Caroline?"

"Target practice, Anne."

As the former exchequer cocked his pistol, two reports were heard. He fell backward with blood spurting from his chest.

"Simmons, do what you need to do. Keep their names out of this. Samuels, bring the coffin. As soon as Simmons finishes, let's get out of here." The general was barking orders again.

Sar and Sebastian were with Anne and Caroline. Berkley joined them.

"Mother, are you all right? Do you remember what happened?" Sar was holding her tightly.

"I am fine, and of course I remember what just occurred. You didn't think I was going to let any harm come to you, did you? We will just let the general get on with his questioning when he is ready." Anne crossed her arms and stared at them all.

"*Humph*, you don't know us well if you think we would let that happen. Are you sure he is dead? If not, we will shoot him again—target practice." Caroline actually glared.

"I think it is best if we get back to London immediately. I will question the ladies along the way." Berkley should have thanked them for saving him. Instead, he was angry. They had put themselves in harm's way again, and there was nothing he could've done about it. If anything had happened to them, he would have become a raging lunatic without a heart. He would have taken aim at everyone.

For the next two hours, he questioned them relentlessly. The general was all general—ruthless. From their landing in Caen to the shooting of the former exchequer, every angle was examined over and over again. When Berkley had finished, he understood two things—their plan was brilliant, and he had gone too far with his actions. *Anne might never speak to me again.*

As Berkley replayed everything in his mind, he realized he would have had to send for them eventually to ensnare the pigeon. *Why can't you just admit you are jealous of them? They came up with a plan that was executed flawlessly. You couldn't have done better. But they could have been killed. But they weren't.*

The coaches came to a halt in front of Caroline's house. As she was about to step out of the carriage, she turned and hugged Anne. "Great job. We couldn't have done it without you."

Berkley uttered a *"Humph."* Both women turned and glowered at him.

"Caroline, I believe we need to be seen out and about tonight. I fear the Society News may find out what has happened. Being about town will help to allay any thoughts about us being in France. The other women must come with us also. I'll check my invitations."

"You're right, Anne. I'll send you a list of my invitations, and please send me a list of yours. We'll compare. We probably need to go to a function where all the gossips are in attendance."

"Good thinking, Caroline. I'll get you the list as soon as I am home. Then, I am going to bed until about two this afternoon."

The footman was assisting Caroline. "Anne, don't move. Wait here. I have something I must give you. It's important." When Caroline returned, she had a small packet in hand.

"Here." She gave the packet to Anne. "Make sure you give this to Joycellyn. She wouldn't accept payment for the dresses she made me. She must be paid. Now to bed."

"I'll get it to her graciously. See you tonight, Caroline."

Anne was never so thankful to be home. While her bath was being drawn, she wrote down the invitations for the evening and sent the list to Caroline. Bathed and wrapped in warm nightclothes, she tumbled into bed and slept for the next six hours.

They decided upon an evening with the Earl and Countess of Fatson. Most of the gossips within the ton would be there. The appearance of the Duke and Duchess of Westmoure, the Broadhursts, and the rest of the group would be the talk of the town before sunrise. Everyone counted on the Fatsons to bring the latest on-dits to the ton.

The group in all its finery descended upon the Fatsons en masse. Caroline watched as the countess's eyes almost popped out of her head when she saw them. In the glow of the candlelight, no one commented on the sun-kissed skin of Anne and the group, if anyone even noticed. All eyes were on the group and their exchange with the earl and countess.

"Please excuse the lateness of our acceptance of your kind invitation. It was something we had most ungraciously overlooked." Sar turned his most sincere and winning smile on Charlotte, the near-swooning countess.

"We are so pleased you could join our little gathering." With three hundred plus people in attendance, *little* was the operative word. Sar simply smiled at their hostess.

When Charlotte looked up again, she was staring in the face of the royal duke, the Duke of Hampton. "It was so kind of you to invite me." Berkley's smile was also one of heartbreaking quality. He did not even address the lack of his acknowledgment.

Charlotte was gulping like a fish out of water. For the first time in decades, she could find nothing to say. Berkley had moved on before she could think of anything. *What will happen next? Will the king appear?*

It was like a play in Covent Garden. The Fatsons greeted the Broadhursts and other esteemed guests. Then trumpets blared, and His Majesty stepped through the door.

"Peach, I hope you don't mind. Just wanted to be with you, my cousin, and the rest of this revered group tonight." The king was his most affable self as he spoke to the earl.

"Not at all. Not at all." The Earl of Fatson bowed and watched his wife sink to the floor. The king's men surrounded her. Anne and Caroline saw what happened and casually walked over to offer any aid possible, along with smelling salts.

As her name implied, the Countess of Fatson was a little on the heavy side. At approximately twenty stone, Charlotte was a challenge to lift. With some huffing and puffing by the king's men, the countess was finally upright.

Like the fairy tale it was, the evening progressed. The king circulated and danced with the hostess, Anne, Caroline, and the rest of the ladies. In their circle of friends, the ladies remarked on the number of messengers who were seen leaving the ballroom with notes in hand. "London will be abuzz tonight." Aurelia's curls were bouncing to the music.

When the first strains of a waltz were heard, Berkley walked over to Her Grace. He placed Anne's hand on his sleeve and covered it with his own. "Your Grace, may I have this dance?" As he spoke, he pulled her slowly to the dance floor.

Anne's glower was not welcoming. "I thought you did all your talking in the carriage on the way to London this morning. You treated Caroline and I as though we were criminals."

"Anne, we need to talk." Berkley negotiated the turn expertly and pulled her more closely into him. "Tonight."

He returned Anne to Caroline and the other women.

"Men." Anne wanted to stomp her foot, but this was not the place.

By the time they reached home, all she wanted to do was climb into her bed and sleep for the next twelve hours. But he was waiting. Anne could feel his heat radiating through the door. *Might as well go and face the lion at his worst.*

Her Grace quietly closed and locked the door. Berkley turned away from the window. "I think I might have overstepped my boundaries in the carriage."

"You think you might have overstepped your boundaries? You acted as though you didn't have any. *Sorry* won't be enough. You must quit acting like a petulant two-year-old. You and Sar take action as though this is some type of competition. This is about staying alive, staying one step ahead of whoever this is."

Berkley took one look at the love of his life. *How do you tell someone you love them so deeply and completely you can't live without them—never ever. Can I make her understand that my heart dropped through my stomach when I received the note that the pigeon was on his way back to England, and she and the other women had him?*

"Anne, at first all I thought about was losing you. The jeopardy involved in this mission was at the highest level of danger. I couldn't lose you, and I felt responsible for you and all the other women. If something had happened to any of you, I would have died.

"Then I took a closer look at my motives. I was jealous. You executed a plan perfectly that I could not have. You're right, this isn't a competition; it's about defeating the enemy."

"Berkley, of course you wouldn't have been able to execute that plan. One, you aren't a woman, and two, you had to find the vulnerable spot of the enemy. He was only interested in the flesh of young girls. You would have figured it out eventually, but you would have pondered too long about using women for the mission. This is a battlefield. Indecisiveness loses the war. We will never be able to use that element of surprise again—they will always be on the lookout for women. It was a one-time plan. We surprised them.

"Sometimes we move forward based on what they do or the information we get. Mostly we use our abilities to outwit them. They create situations that have us thinking in ways we never thought of or understood. You're right, we are dealing with people who think nothing of killing first and moving on. No questions asked. It's all about greed, ignorance, hate, arrogance, and money.

"Now, please leave. I'm exhausted. It's been a long day. Berkley, the questioning of Caroline and myself is over. We have a lot to do for next Saturday at Paige's, our wedding—if I still want to marry you—and of course there is Cummings. We also have interviews for new applicants at Harson's. The ladies must get back to their routine on land. Good day, Berkley."

Berkley quietly let himself out only to return an hour later to hold his ladylove for the remainder of the fleeting night. "I must keep you safe if it is the last thing I do on this earth." The candles caught the glistening of the tears forming in his eyes. Berkley had lost his heart, and emotions surged to the surface.

She didn't want Berkley crying or pretending not to cry, so Her Grace softly kissed him. Unable to say another word, there was only one thing left to do—show her she was his everything. He gently held her shoulder and pulled her into him. His lips explored her neck while his hands rambled over her breasts, sending quivers running through him. The general knew he would never lay out his heart again. The one and only one entitled to it was Anne. Life was too short. He would gladly give her all he had.

"That, Your Grace, is what we will share." He rolled over and fell asleep.

Before dawn, he whispered in her ear, "Do you think this will keep you during the remainder of the day?" He had been using his fingers like his tongue before he woke her fully. Her Grace's release came just as he entered her.

Anne had a few things on her mind that day. *When can I have Berkley deep inside of me, making me scream his name and giving me shivering releases like I have never had before, and who is trying to kill me and why?*

The next day was as busy as the days before Mer's wedding. It started with Beth being summoned by Sar into the men's lair—his study.

"I have something to ask you." Her brother explained the ransacking of Berkley's office and the lace handkerchief found stuck between a file. Giving her all the background he could, he explained their thoughts. "Beth, what do you think?"

She looked at Sar and chewed on her lower lip. The men waited to hear. Daggs slowed his steps to look closely at the woman he was more than enchanted with.

"Well, I may be stating the obvious again. General, you have a spy in Whitehall. At the center of this is definitely a woman with her own plan for revenge. She will kill everyone in her way. Now with the exchequer dead, you will have to find the other government official or officials she is working with. A very high official in government. You have a spy within this small group of men. I doubt if he is with the group present now. Is that all, Sar? I have things to do for Paige's." She left the study with her head in the ledger.

Sar held up his hand to stop the questioning. "My sisters have an uncanny way of looking at things. Beth may not be one hundred percent right, but she'll be at least ninety-eight percent correct. What she said we could wager on and win."

"Has she always been like that?" Daggs wondered if she would be interested in a job at the Yard.

"Both of my sisters can get to the heart of the matter quicker than anyone I know except Her Grace."

Berkley marveled at the family he was marrying into. "Well, I know I have a spy in Whitehall. This makes me ponder what we were told by the prisoners at Newgate: 'a soft female voice and very light footsteps.' When the assailant attempted to shoot Sar at the Broadhursts' ball and Mer shot him, I speculate when their plans went awry, a female stepped in to take care of the potential murderer. If it was a woman, she has a lot of power within the group. Given what the maids saw at Severson's house, two women, my feeling is that we are dealing with some very malicious and violent women. Your sister may be on to something."

"The females of this family are always on to something, especially Mother. She can ferret out a secret faster than anyone else. If she was in a *you had better tell me what you know about the matter in ten seconds or less* mood, we would be telling her everything. When we were in that foot-stomping stage, that was when she really knew she had us. Dad would just chuckle and leave her to it.

"We have very few connecting pieces to this puzzle, but take what Beth told us and keep it in the back of your mind. We will pick up a trail eventually. Hopefully, before someone else is murdered."

"It would be hard to believe there is a spy in this group. Besides Jack, there couldn't be anyone else. No one knows who will be killed next and where our criminals are going with their plans. We are still sifting the clues, trying to find leads and answers." Berkley thought about what he had just said. He thought he knew Jack also. Another traitor? He looked at the men in the room. Impossible.

The men eventually invaded Paige's. Instead of helping, they got in the way. Jay wanted to know if Beth and her mother wanted to attend the theater. Daggs glared. They all ended up going. Berkley invited his cousin the king, which created pandemonium at the theater—a lot of royalty in the house. At intermission, the king's men had to bar entry to the royal box.

• • •

The next day was filled with work and new adventures for Cummings. The business had expanded to the Americas, and they needed Sar's and Jacob's help. The wheels were put in motion to use the ground carriers that Westmoure's and Avery Jacob had in place. A property closer to a major railroad line was purchased, and a new line of lotions was introduced. It was then decided that Cummings and the two shipping lines would consider a joint venture and buy several of the ground carrier companies.

There were sixty applicants for Harson's. "Word has gotten

out. Women want to be more than just governesses. How do we accommodate as many of them as possible?" Caroline reviewed the applications.

"Take them all, girl. The ones who want to do it will stay and work hard. The others will drop out along the way." Lady Horton was keen on making sure more women could run a business. She was waiting for the right women to go to work in her family's businesses. *Oh, this is going to be so much fun to watch.* Suddenly Harson's had expanded by twenty additional applicants.

"Do we have any Negroes, East Indians, and others from Asia?" Anne wondered if the meetings to reach out to various groups had had any impact.

"Yes, some from most groups. All in all, about twenty women. People are aware of us, but we must do it again. It's amazing what women can do, including making a quick trip to France to arrest a criminal." Caroline patted her reticule, and they all laughed.

Unexpectedly all the patrons of Almack's stopped by for a visit. "We haven't heard from you, and we wanted to know what help you needed from us." Lady Sarah Jersey was in her element when she saw all the elite ladies of the ton together. The patrons' underground sources reported an elite group of ladies of the ton had crossed the channel to catch a criminal. The patrons wanted to find out for themselves if there was any truth to this matter. As usual, they were all sure the Society News would give a detailed accounting of the scandalous event.

"How nice of you to stop by. We were just discussing Beth's come-out and were running into problems with the arrangement of tables, colors for decorations, and placement of the orchestra. You understand how important it is to get the details right. We were just sending a message to you."

As if on cue, Perkins opened the door. "Your Grace, the messenger is waiting."

"Thank you, Perkins. I won't be needing him now." Anne smiled at the patrons.

With Lady Horton leading the charge, they placated the women from Almack's for the next two hours. Then Evelyn announced it was time for tea. *Now we find out what these meddlesome buzzards really want.*

It only took a couple glasses of champagne and tongues started wagging. Lady Sarah was smiling from ear to ear as though she had the best secret in the world that she couldn't hold any longer. "We heard that a group of women sailed the channel and arrested a criminal. Can you believe that?"

"What brave women. A criminal, you say? Was it anyone we know?" Caroline, acting like the proper aristocratic wife, sat a little taller. "How could they do that?"

"We don't know. What women would pull a stunt like that?" Lady Sarah looked closely at Anne.

"Lady Sarah, was it you and the patrons? Is that what you are trying to tell us? Which criminal was it?" Lady Horton urged them on after making sure they had more of the bubbly stuff.

"Lady Horton, we know it wasn't you. You are far too old and sensible for such an adventure. We don't want to spread tales, but some things some ladies do are almost sacred. One must do what one must for one's country." Lady Sarah and the other patrons were suddenly taking credit for this caper with the encouragement of Anne and group.

"I am sure the Society News will report everything in detail. How exciting was it, Lady Sarah?" Georgina couldn't wait to hear what they would make up.

"When people are evil, you must bring justice to the fore. No one wants to live in a society with individuals whose goal in life is to hurt others. Let's just say he was a very bad man. Oh, look at the time; we must be going." After two more glasses of champagne, the patrons waddled to their carriages.

"So that's what the old bats really wanted. Unbelievable. To think they want the world to believe they pulled off that caper." Lady Horton hooted with glee. By dinnertime, the ladies were unable to stand. The men ate and watched over their women.

When morning rolled around, a group of ladies with aching heads could barely move. They tried and went back to bed. Joycellyn and Yvette finished the orders for Paige's. Beth's come-out dress was fitted, and fitted, and refitted again.

"Are we done yet? All this bother for one evening. Enough!" Beth started pulling the dress off.

"Almost. It's not that bad, Beth. One little tuck here and we have finished for the day. We will have your final fitting next week. That's a promise."

Joycellyn, with the help of Yvette, carefully removed the dress from the young woman she now thought of as her little sister.

• • •

In America, Jack waited for the message. It should have come the week before. He thought of what he had accomplished during his time in the former colonies. The connections for widespread use of opium were being established step by step. Many of the companies and other businesses were greedy for the money. Certain groups of people hungered for opium. And Jack and his group were willing to get it to them. Thank goodness they would shortly control Westmoure Shipping.

When the mail pouch was opened, the message was there. Separating himself from the crowd, he opened the missive.

Shipment safely arrived in China. Present delivered to sultan. Papers delivered to correct person. Boss.

• • •

At the Westmoures' house, Anne and Caroline were trying to figure out the menu for Saturday's luncheon at Paige's. They understood some of the young workers came for the food. Others came for food and to shop. The pastries and tea were a big hit so far.

"I suggest meat and vegetable pies. Cook can make several varieties, and they can be quite fancy. They are also easy to eat. If someone sneaks one or two into her reticule, it won't be messy."

"Great thinking, Caroline. Cook can add to the menu as she sees fit."

Perkins entered and laid the newssheet before them. It was a special edition of the Society News.

"That bad, Perkins?"

"That bad, Your Grace—not that you had anything to do with this."

The London Daily

Society News

Special Edition

Dearest reader,
This news demanded a special edition. We thank our sources for giving us this information and the London Daily *for indulging us.*

Several days ago, a group of the Crown's elite operatives, under the command of Berkley himself, sailed the channel to capture one of the Crown's most wanted criminals. Unbeknownst to them, a group of elite ladies followed.

Once on French soil, Berkley connected with his French counterpart. Upon arriving at the safe house, they found all the operatives dead. Cause of death has yet to be revealed to us. However, according to rumors, it was a stiletto slipped between the ribs and into the heart.

It appears the women who sailed the channel had a spy system of their own. Undetected, the women followed the men until they knew what the men had planned and where the pigeon to be caged was. Pigeon was the code name for the criminal to be caught.

After getting the needed information, the women devised their own plan. This included enticing the criminal with a young woman to be used for baser purposes. For some reason, this was all the criminal needed to know. The plan involved a fake injury, trussing up the pigeon's two henchmen, giving them black eyes with brass knuckles, and rendering them unconscious.

Once the pigeon was on board the boat of the women, he was tied and stripped of all his clothing except his smalls. The pigeon was then attached to the yardarm. It was at this point the women arrested the pigeon in the name of the Crown.

The women signaled their contact that the

pigeon was caged and to notify Berkley and his French counterparts. This was done immediately. Upon receiving the message, Berkley and the men set sail for English soil.

Arriving safely on English soil, the women were greeted by Inspector Daggs of Scotland Yard and the Marquess of Broadhurst. Inspector Daggs officially arrested the pigeon in the name of the Crown. The women washed their feet, let down their hair, and fell asleep in the waiting coaches.

When Berkley and his operatives arrived, they checked on the women and went to have a chat with the pigeon. After getting all the information they could from the pigeon, Berkley gave him no choice—death by suicide. A pistol was left on the shoals, or the pigeon could take a walk in the channel. The pigeon chose the channel.

My dearest reader, this is where this epic caper becomes more interesting. When the body of the pigeon was pulled out of the channel and turned over, the pistol was pointed directly at Berkley. The pigeon was heard to say, "Science is an incredible thing if you know how to use it properly."

No one noticed the two women standing there observing them. When the pigeon cocked the pistol, two shots rent the air. From the force of the shots, the pigeon fell backward and gasped his last breath. The two women were questioned extensively by Berkley on the ride back to London.

Was it the half-breed aristocrats who were

at the center of this? It sounds like something they would do. However, it is rumored that the patrons of Almack's are responsible for this caper. Or is this the way the patrons are showing support for the half-breeds?

Simmons examined all the women and pronounced them "fit and without a scratch."

On a sad note, we are sorry to announce that the former exchequer died in a boating accident. He dedicated his life to the Crown until declining health forced him to resign. We will always be grateful for the honesty and integrity he brought to his position.

"Caroline, this would almost be funny if it weren't for the seriousness of the matter. Can you imagine thanking the former exchequer for his integrity? *Humph*, unbelievable."

The next morning, a very shaky Anne made it down the stairs to the doorway of the breakfast room. Grabbing the knob for support, she surveyed the scene before her and swayed. She had to keep the pretense up. No one knew how all of this was affecting her.

CHAPTER 10

Another Berkley Order

Berkley sat at his desk thinking. All he could see was Anne and her diminishing spirit. She smiled and pretended all was well. It was too much even for the strongest of men—attempted murder on her life and those of her family, worry about her children, the quick trip to France, her waning strength every time someone was about to die. In his mind, the list went on. He had to do something.

That night, when he appeared, she walked willingly into his arms. Her brow line was etched with worry and concern, her bright expressive brown eyes held no joy, and the tracks of her tears were obvious.

The mere thought of losing her brought out emotions the general didn't realize he had. Holding her, he now clearly understood the power a woman could have over a man. With his bare hands, he would kill one and all who tried to harm her. Berkley was overreacting, but he couldn't put the reins on his feelings and emotions. She was safe; he could feel every inch of her. *I would die without her. My life would not be the same. All the sun and joy would be gone. I would go back to being half a man.* With that thought, he shuddered.

What she needed more than anything else was to feel loved and to be taken care of. Being shot at shifted one's perspective on life. He should know. The general had been a hairsbreadth away from death on one too many occasions.

"Anne, listen to me." She had been shaken by all the events to the tips of her toes. He could tell. There was no smile—just a distant look. "I need to make some things crystal clear to you. I am lost without you. You make my days brighter." Whispering in her ear, he stated his intentions.

Her Grace couldn't hold out against the assault of the last few weeks and the words being uttered by the man holding her. Both taxed the deepest recesses of her being. Emotionally, she had been wrung dry. Now, listening to the declarations being softly uttered to her, she felt scandalous yet thrilled and exhilarated. The mixed emotions—death and delight. Who would have ever thought the general could make her forget everything but him for a moment?

"When I tell you something, you can bet your life on it. I want to make love to you right this minute, right here, right now. However, this is not the time. I am going to own and possess every inch of you from your head down to your toes and every inch in between." He ran his hands over her hardened nipples and caressed her breasts. Fingering them, he announced, "These belong to me." Lowering his head, he laved the fabric covering her luscious orbs.

For a quick moment, Anne had a flashing insight about what the man Berkley was all about. He stamped and imprinted *him* on all he loved and trained. That was how he knew one of his men had betrayed him.

His hands moved lower to the juncture of her thighs and started slowly sliding her chemise over her nether lips. All thoughts flew out of her head but for the moment and the man. Anne's breath now came in short pants. He didn't stop. She swayed to move closer.

"This too is mine—luscious, wet, and hot. You will be hotter when all your clothes are off and I am kneeled before you, tasting your center. When you fall apart, you will scream my name." He wondered if he would have to fight Avery for her in heaven. *What would Saint Peter think of that?*

The feel of the wet chemise spurred him on to demand more as she swayed. Anne was ready, ready for him to take her to new heights. His stiff arousal begged to slide into her hot passage.

This time, pleasure first. Berkley slowly slid himself down her body, making sure she felt and understood, on the most fundamental level, his desire. On his knees, he raised her chemise, tugged the ribbons of her undergarment loose, and slipped his tongue into her center. Feasting, his tongue swirled, and Her Grace braced her hands on his shoulders, offering all she could.

She was dripping wet. His flicking tongue started her contractions as she moved herself forward, silently begging for more. He had to stop. Her release would come soon. His tongue found her inner folds and felt her first pull. One more taste, and he would ease back up her body so they could talk. *Not likely.* He could no more halt than keep the sun from rising in the east. His need was as strong as hers, and he wanted her now.

Anne's mind was reeling. Her only thoughts were what he was doing to her. She was tingling to her soul. *Oh my, my, my, please don't stop.* She wantonly showed him that she wanted more by spreading herself wider.

With more control than he thought he ever possessed, his finger replaced his tongue, and he stood. "That is just a sample of what we shall share together." She was fatigued, and he understood. Kissing her thoroughly, he turned and silently let himself out.

On the way home, he shifted their clues repeatedly. He didn't want to admit it, but the truth was becoming patently obvious. These acts were linked somehow with some very well-connected people. He didn't question the motive. It was always there—power, greed, arrogance, and money. However, he didn't understand the vicious attacks on Anne. That seemed like a separate crime. His mind shifted again to the uncomfortable ride he was experiencing. If he ever again did what he had done tonight with Anne, he would have to take up residence in a cold lake.

Berkley strolled into Sar's house the next morning to check on Anne. They would talk over the morning meal. Seeing her would reassure him that all was well. When Anne descended the stairs, he took one look into his ladylove's sad, listless brown eyes and equally lethargic movements and realized she was reaching a breaking point. He could tell. Many a man in battle had the same look.

Without looking up, he shouted, "Perkins, tell Her Grace's maid to pack her bag for two days. I am sending her to my housekeeper at my country home. Make sure Duchess has everything she needs. Her Grace needs time to relax. Tell Sar I will send six of my outriders along. Is there anything else I should do, Perkins?"

"No, that should be it, General. Give us two hours." Perkins went to make sure the order was executed exactly as given.

Turning to Anne, he tenderly said, "No, I am not asking you. You need to be indulged by my staff. Go and get ready. I'll wait here."

While waiting, Berkley debated whether he should join her in the country and marry her there. He didn't know how she would react. No, that wouldn't work. She needed to have Sar, the girls, and the ladies present. What kind of wedding would that be without any gossip among them? The general laughed and shook his head. *I can negotiate with the toughest of men, command a group of elite operatives for the government, but I can't talk to this half-slip of a woman without quaking in my boots.* As she came down the stairs, his breath caught. On the most fundamental level, he knew Her Grace was a part of his life now and forever.

"Before you leave, you should know I am honored to have you in my life, but it is more than that. I need you." He was tongue-tied. Berkley couldn't think of anything else to say. Thank goodness he heard the coach behind him at that moment.

As ordered, precisely two hours later, the four-in-hand bearing the royal crest of the Duke of Hampton appeared in the courtyard of the Duke of Westmoure's London residence. Berkley helped to hand her and Duchess into the luxuriously appointed, leather- and velvet-adorned, well-sprung coach and watched until it was out of sight. The general turned on his well-shod Hoby boot and ran smack-dab into Sar's fist.

"I take care of and protect my own family. You had no right to send my mother away." Sar was heaving after the punch he had thrown.

The right hook came so fast, Sar didn't even see it coming.

"Sorry, Sar; it's an automatic reaction. Protection is always a concern, but I didn't send her away because of that. I packed her up for a couple of days because she has reached a breaking point. Have you noticed the puffiness around her eyes?"

Sar stared at Berkley as though he should be committed to Bedlam.

"No, I didn't think so. It usually means a woman has been crying. She has a bluish tinge underneath her eyes, and Her Grace is losing weight. A couple of days at my country home and my staff will have her on the road to recovery. God knows they need someone to fuss over."

"*Humph*, but don't ever do that again without talking it over with me first. She's not yours yet. Understood?"

The general nodded and gingerly touched his aching jaw, which he knew was already turning black and blue.

• • •

Following the duke's coach at a distance were two men on horseback. "Too many outriders. We'll see how close we can get at the duke's home." The two fell back even farther to wait for a timely moment. Behind the two riders rode Perkins in disguise. He turned back to locate the general.

• • •

Perkins found the general with a cold, wet towel on a black-and-blue jaw. "Ran into Sar's fist, eh?"

Berkley glared. "You could have warned me."

"Now, General, what fun would that have been? Two men are following behind your outriders. I think they are waiting for the right moment to harm Her Grace."

Berkley nodded. "Of course."

"Of course, indeed, Berkley. You're welcome."

Barking orders to have his bag packed in twenty minutes, the general scribbled a note—*Do not let Her Grace out of your sight. Two men minimum. Should arrive within five hours.*

Turning the missive over to his fastest messenger, Berkley emphatically stated, "There may be danger. This note must reach Henley. Take two others with you. Hurry." When Berkley looked up again, the room was empty.

By the time the general arrived at his home in the country, Her Grace was abed. A quick chat with Henley, his butler, told him all was in order. Reaching for the brandy on the sideboard in his library, he wondered what it would be like to find someone waiting for him at the end of the day. *No, not going down that road. But you can. The love of your life will be waiting for you. Things have changed, Berkley. Thank goodness.* He gulped down the amber liquid and headed for the ducal chambers.

Early rays of sun were streaming through the windows on what had been a peaceful, quiet country morning; unfortunately, the pounding on the door was loud enough to wake the dead. Henley opened the door to see a disheveled young man road weary and covered in dust.

"Sar, I presume. Your Grace." Henley bowed respectfully.

"Where is my mother?"

"Well, she was sleeping before that pounding loud enough to raise the dearly departed probably woke her. Would you like breakfast or a bed?"

Berkley descended the stars. "Sar."

"General."

"Oh, here she is now."

Having hurriedly dressed, Her Grace was rapidly running down the stairs. The worried look on her face spoke volumes. Looking frantically from one to the other, she hesitated before she spoke. "What has happened?"

"Just checking on you to make sure you're all right." Sar almost blushed at the idea of checking up on his mother.

"And you? When did you arrive, and why?" Anne's impaling look made the general feel as though he was standing before one of the school masters.

Berkley shrugged.

"Perkins."

Perkins stepped out of the shadows.

"Yes, Your Grace."

"Where's Mer? If anything happens . . ." Anne didn't get any further.

"Behind me. I have two men following her. Julien is behind

my men. I understand she left her husband a note telling him where she was going."

"This game is too dangerous to be played here. Berkley, this is what they do. Where one goes, the other follows. They call it *The Game*. Mer is seeing if she is as good as Perkins and can follow without being detected. It started when Mer learned how to ride, and of course Perkins encouraged this by teaching Mer the fine art of eavesdropping—a long story. Can your cook accommodate all of us for breakfast?"

"Mrs. Jamison will be thrilled. I'll let her know there will be six for the dining room and two additional for the kitchen. Should we say in an hour?"

"Thank you." Her Grace turned and ascended the stairs. As she properly dressed, Anne tried to figure out what she was going to do with Sar and Berkley.

Anne caught up with Sar near the stables. "Sar, I know you miss your father, and you are trying to do what he would have done. This is all so new to you. I miss Avery more than you will ever know or imagine. You don't spend thirty years with someone, and then one day he is suddenly gone forever, and life just goes on as normal. It's like having your heart ripped out of your chest while it is still beating. My dearest son, we will get on, and we'll find our way. You'll be fine. Every day you are more and more like your father."

Sar felt the moisture in his eyes.

"But you and Berkley must quit acting like schoolboys in the play yard. I don't care who threw the first punch, this simply won't do. Do you understand who the two of you are? Also, I believe you are grown." Anne stood on her tippy-toes and tenderly kissed her son's cheek.

"I love you, Mother." Sar's whispered endearment brought tears to her eyes.

"I love you, Your Grace."

Sar turned upon hearing his mother's words before the tears ran down his face.

They heard Mer admonishing Perkins for having two men follow her. *Ah, the trials of a mother.* Anne followed the voices to have a little talk with Mer and Perkins.

• • •

The two men on horseback who were following the coach transporting the Duchess of Westmoure were now throwing back whisky in another stylish home in London—the in-town residence of the Duke of Brockton.

"It was the right thing to turn back."

"I trust he will return soon, but in the meantime, we will do as he requested and take any opportunity that comes our way to kill Her Grace. A mixed blood in the aristocracy. Who would have ever imagined that? We both know he won't be happy about what happened today. She should be dead."

"Agreed."

• • •

The general found Anne near the waterfall of the man-made pond that meandered aimlessly through several acres of the estate. The sun glistening off the tumbling water set her hair aflame. He wanted to touch and possess, but first things first. Berkley didn't know what it was, but the back of his neck was tingling.

Anne didn't even glance his way. She felt his presence and power. Berkley turned her around and reverently kissed her. Her Grace's toes curled, and she wanted more. But not now.

Looking at him with that *mothers know best* stare, she quietly asked, "Do you always act like a child when things are not going the way you think they should?" She didn't expect an answer. "You and Sar can't go around throwing punches at each other when you need to let off steam. Both of you are doing your best to protect Mer, Beth, and me. But this competition as to who can do it better and faster must stop. Do you hear me? *Humph.* Men!" Her Grace wanted to stomp her foot and throw a first-class temper tantrum herself, but then she would be acting like them.

Berkley was trying to figure out what it was about this woman. He was smiling; she was piqued.

"It's hard for everyone. Listen, Berkley, people have been killed, we're hated for the color of our skin, and someone is using our ships to transport heaven knows what. There may be even more to this when the many layers are peeled away. You are now the predator—the protective predator. I understand. However, the juvenile reactions must stop. Believe it or not, this is not some type of contest. There will probably be more bloodshed and angst. The two of you shall end this now. Have I made myself clear?"

Berkley looked at her and didn't even bother to question the power this tiny woman had over him. No one ever stood up to him that way. Of course, he had been acting like a horse's arse, but that had never made him stop and take note of what he was doing before now.

Using her most aristocratic demeanor and voice, Anne announced, "I would like to leave in the morning. With the upcoming ball, and the children working on Cummings, there is much to do." Her Grace kept walking toward the field of fragrant violet lavender.

He watched her walk down the gentle slope. The general knew one thing as sure as his next breath—she would be his until he cocked up his toes. Like a green lad watching her hips sway, he wanted to discover all there was about her in a field of English lavender. Scanning the area, he noted his men discreetly watching over her.

He turned and walked back to the house, and along the way, he stopped to pick the early blooms for the woman who had stolen his heart. Upon entering the house, Berkley thrust the blossoms into the hands of the housekeeper and muttered, "Thought you would like these."

Even though Anne was angrier than a disturbed beehive with him, he had to be with her. When the general quietly opened her bedchamber door, he stared into the eyes of his beloved. Turning, he locked the door. Turning again, without saying a word, he walked into her silent embrace.

Slowly he removed her nightclothes, using the fabric to create arousing friction across her body. At the same time, Berkley's clothes disappeared. He suckled her sensitive nibs while his fingers played with her love center. She pulled her nether lips apart so he could get to her pleasure spot. With an open invitation, he plundered. Her head was moving back and forth, her hands locked over his, and together they tweaked her nipples. "Hold back until the last moment. I want you to remember this all day tomorrow. I want you wet until I reenter you tomorrow night in all ways."

Anne held back. The pressure built and built until she broke like a dam. Contraction after contraction flooded her as she lifted and pressed her center against him. She didn't calm down. Berkley rubbed the counterpane over her sex to stimulate her again. The abrasions from the fabric had her unknowingly raising her hips. He leaned over and kissed her center and gave her what she wanted.

"I am still angry with you."

Berkley kissed Anne one more time, laughed, and disappeared into the waning night.

• • •

The early morning ride back to the city was done in almost complete silence. Berkley sat opposite Anne with a half-silly grin on his face. Mer slept with her head on her mother's shoulder. Her Grace, through tiny slits of her eyelids, observed the general. Really, she couldn't take her eyes off him.

The next day, Mer, Beth, and Alexius were extremely busy at the office of Cummings. The business was expanding so quickly. They were trying to decide how to make products faster and more efficiently while still maintaining the quality the company was known for. Expense, time, production techniques, and supplies were the major topics being hashed out. The Duke of Grayson had joined them. Rolling up his sleeves, they worked side by side. He felt his wife, Violet, would be so proud and offered up a silent prayer for their success and protection.

Berkley appeared in his usual manner that night. The table had been laid with the leftovers from dinner, which was fine with him. He was with Anne; that was all that mattered. But first, he had to taste her. She was waiting, looking directly at him, when he walked in. The general hungrily kissed Anne as though she was the only woman in the world. Well, she was for him. He held her, savoring the feeling of being loved.

Knowing everything had become more serious, Berkley felt it was necessary to get the rest out. *She has to know. But how will she react? Out with it, old man.*

"All of us are trained to kill. We protect with our lives everything with which we are entrusted. It is horrifying to take another's life. The stain of blood and the memory is always on your soul. You need to know that this is something my job includes. I walk away from the enemy and continue with my life. But I am never the same.

"Sometimes I thought I never could love. You have changed my perspective on that matter. It may get jumbled in my mind at times. I need you to know you are making me complete and more able to do my job. Now, I will have something to come home to."

He pulled her toward him and started kissing her to show her some of the good in life. Their tongues dueled for superiority, and the kisses became deeper and more poignant. The agonizing pain of want versus lack clashed as they headed toward the flames of passion. His hands slowly traced the sides of her neck and breasts. He could not stop. Anne wanted this as much as he did and leaned into him. Breathlessly, she pulled away, took one look at him, and held out her hand.

In her bedchamber, the general looked at Anne as though he had never seen her before. Each touch was as smooth as velvet. "I love you, Anne, more than anything else in this world. I can't live without you, and I'd die without your love."

With his tongue, he brought her to the breaking point. "Let me satisfy you more." He nipped her mons and massaged her center. Her sweet nectar flowed like honey amidst her release. Kissing her nether lips again, he helped her climb to the stars.

"Anne, this is what we will share for the rest of our lives." Her muffled screams of satisfaction made him feel as though he was on top of the world, commanding and controlling.

Anne wanted him one more time. She pleaded with her body and said, "Again." Opening her legs wider, she started to rub her center.

"Oh, my love, let me do that for you. Your release will come quickly, and then I must leave." He kissed her, lowered the covering more, lightly nipped her, then plunged into her center. Rubbing, pulling, and suckling had Anne finding her release immediately, as she craved. He disappeared into the fading night.

The following evening, the dinner party was another one of those meals to go down in the annals of gatherings, the story to be told again and again. It was as though the Westmoures had been members of this group all their lives. It was good to feel wanted and accepted. Adventures were retold with twists and turns that only perspective can create. By the middle of the meal, the hostess was discombobulated, and the guests were listing to the left. Everyone just got up and went upstairs to bed, with husbands carrying wives. No one thought about going home.

CHAPTER 11

Back to Ivy Hall

Berkley was at Whitehall doing what he did best—work. The abrupt knock caught him unaware. "Enter."

"Henry. Good to see you." The heir to the Hampton dukedom walked through the door with his usual affable smile.

"Hampton. Just taking care of a few things in the city, and the wife wanted to go shopping. Women! Perfectly good shops where we live. Like to patronize the local merchants."

They chatted on for the next few minutes about inconsequential matters, and Henry took his leave.

The empty office reminded Berkley he had nothing to do that night—no dinner in the kitchen, no lips to kiss, and no pint-size woman telling him what to do. For the second time within weeks, he realized how lonely he was.

Saturday came and Paige's was busier than ever. The shoppers relished the meat and vegetable pies and roasted chicken. Joycellyn watched as pies and chicken disappeared into reticules. *If I were they, I would have done the same thing. Thank goodness for the Roxburys. They have no idea how this helps.*

There were twelve new orders of styles they had sold out of. The shopper with the perfect auburn hair returned. She wandered through the shop, but she was still hesitant and shy. Joycellyn engaged her in conversation. She was a little more open than on the previous visit.

"Why don't you enjoy a meat pie and some tea?" Joycellyn waited for her to speak. She could see the joy in the other woman's eyes.

"I couldn't. I haven't bought anything." Nancy looked at Joycellyn.

"Oh, that doesn't matter. We are pleased you stopped in again." Joycellyn guided her to a seat at a tea table.

At the close of the day, Anne and Caroline came in by the back door. Looking around, they were pleased. The fitting rooms were in disarray, there wasn't a crumb of food remaining, and Joycellyn was bending over a stack of orders.

"We are ordering you out. Caroline's cook has dinner ready for us. We will lock up after we tidy the place a bit and will be no more than twenty minutes behind you. Take my carriage; I'll ride with Caroline." An excited Joycellyn jumped on the chance for teatime and dinner with the ladies.

"Okay, Caroline, twenty minutes, and twenty minutes only." They worked together efficiently, and twenty-one minutes later, Caroline's carriage was pulling out of the alley behind Paige's.

When Anne and Caroline walked into the house, the sounds of merriment tinkled through the air. The success of the day was evident. It was obvious everyone had had at least one glass of champagne. Laughter, smiles, and stories about the shop were the topics of the evening.

• • •

By the time Anne got home, all she wanted to do was sit. She rang for some brandy. In the blue room, Sar took one look at his mother and realized Berkley had been right. Anne was fatigued. Even though she was as proper as ever, her posture erect, she seemed to slump in her chair, and her movements were without direction.

Her recent trip to the country wasn't much of a rest. It was interrupted by me and my foolish antics, acting like a two-year-old, or should I say a petulant two-year-old. Really, it wasn't a rest at all. He glanced at his mother again. Decision made. They would leave for Ivy Hall in the morning.

"We shall go to Ivy Hall in the morning if that is agreeable with you, Mother. We'll return on Friday. I know you and Caroline like to check on the store at closing on Saturday." Sar poured her more brandy. "Messages will be sent immediately to Ivy Hall, the other ladies, and Berkley. Does that meet your approval?"

Anne was too tired to do anything but nod her head in agreement.

• • •

The sun wasn't even visible when they left for Ivy Hall. Berkley's message had been delivered after Anne had retired for the night. *Meet at church in the morning—Berkley.*

Their standard bearer, the sentinel of tall trees lining the drive, welcomed them home. As the carriage slowed and turned into the drive, Her Grace awoke. Anne inhaled the peaceful serenity of the country air. Her shoulders relaxed for the first time in many weeks.

The nearer they got to the house, the more sounds of

normalcy echoed in her ears—the quiet and easy breezes of the season. At this time of the morning, there were no laughing children, construction noises, or scrapes of repairs to the masonry of the house. The ponies were still in their stalls, and no one was trying to fish from the fountain in front of the house. Even the gardeners were quiet. They had their work cut out for them—furiously laboring to keep up with the denuding caused by energetic little people. To her, all was well.

And then she heard him. *As I have told you before, do not worry. Many things are going to happen, and things are changing. Look at what you did. That quick trip to France was no easy feat. You did well. I am proud of you. Berkley is a good man.* Then just as quickly, he was gone from the recesses of her mind.

Avery? Her silent voice bounced off the walls of the caverns of her brain. There was no answer. Would she ever know all? *Stop coming and going like that with only half answers.* There was nothing, just her tension and her rapid breathing. Maybe she was the one going crazy.

Meanwhile, Ivy Hall's kitchen was preparing the morning meal. The noise was a welcoming balm to Mrs. Spencer's soul. Aromas drifted through the house, along with the smell of clean lavender essence. Her new undercook, Abigail Donaldson, was more than a competent gift.

When Mrs. Spencer had arrived late last night, she had headed straight to the kitchen to get everything in order that wasn't up to her standards. Her mouth had dropped in awe as she inspected the area. It was in precise order. The makings for breakfast and lunch were there, ready to be executed in the morning, the dining room table was set for the duke and guests, and everything was spotless.

She did a quick turn and inspected everything again. With deep confidence in the staff, Mrs. Spencer then went to do something she hadn't done in years—soak her feet and take a long, hot bath.

• • •

The sun was shining brightly. A perfect day for the alfresco lunch after church. As Her Grace entered the sanctuary, she tried to put all thought of what Berkley wanted aside to examine later. But that was impossible. Her thoughts of Berkley were mixed with the padre's words and songs.

Was it her imagination, or had her intuition run amuck? Anne sat in the pew reserved for the Westmoures and observed the reverend. Did the padre know something was afoot? The minute Berkley and Quinn set foot in the sanctuary, the air of this most holy place changed. It was as though the parishioners were on alert, waiting for the first shot to be fired, and everyone was in on the game.

On this Sunday, the service was exceptionally short. As Her Grace stood outside watching Berkley interact with the padre, she understood they were speaking in code.

"Good to see you, Berkley, Quinn. So, family traditions continue, eh? An alfresco lunch, I assume." The minister was shaking Berkley's hand.

"Glad to be able to spend a few days in the fresh air of the country. Yes, lunch. Things remain the same?" These were two old friends speaking a language all their own. Anne assumed everyone had helped in the war effort in some manner; this was one aspect of it.

The reverend smiled. "All is the same except one little thing."

Their code—something was amiss. "Tell me all about it at lunch. We can't wait to hear the news." As if getting much needed information, Berkley moved away from the line of worshippers greeting the minister.

Lunch was a wonderful affair, if you could call the last meal before facing the guillotine a party. The reverend's wife was busy filling the women in on who needed help in the district and what was being done to assist. She looked at Her Grace as if asking for directions and assistance.

"Why don't we do this, for starters? Write down the name of everyone who needs a helping hand. We'll go through the list and see what we can do for them. While I have my closest friends here, they might have some suggestions. Is there work for any of these people?

"While I am on the topic of work, do you know anyone who would like training for a nontraditional position? There is a school that prepares women to work in unorthodox professions, such as bookkeeping and accounting." As Anne spoke, she was watching the men out of the corner of her eye. *So, this is how it is done. The reverend's wife engages the women in conversation while the men talk.* Anne smiled her best smile.

"General, that particular evening was pitch dark with storm clouds obscuring the natural sparkle of the night light. Even though undetected, there was no way he could get closer to the house. The wind obscured the sounds of the assassin's movement from tree branch to tree branch. With feet never touching the ground, the assailant made it back to the end of the long drive leading to Ivy Hall and walked the empty, gloomy road to where his horse was completely hidden."

"What?" Berkley asked in a manner that implied the situation was unbelievable.

"That's right. He jumped from tree to tree, feet never touching the ground. Rufus and I were returning from visiting the sick. The intruder never saw me. You trained me well."

The general looked at the minister and started an unrelenting line of questioning.

"Like I said, we waited until he returned and followed him down the road. He'd secured and hidden his horse."

"Thanks, Padre. The usual precautions." The minister simply bobbed his head as though this were a regular occurrence when dealing with Berkley.

"Sar, we'll need to add a few additional traps as well as additional men. I do not want anyone harmed whether you are here or not." The general was assimilating all that had been said while talking. Sar followed suit and simply bobbed his head also.

Anne only vaguely heard the women talking, making lists, and comparing notes, because she was preoccupied observing the men. The general in action. No wasted words. The protective predator springing to life. He was making sure his orders were understood, which meant something had happened at Ivy Hall. Anne gently brushed the wrinkles from her dress to reassure herself that her second pistol was in place as a shiver ran down her spine.

◆ ◆ ◆

Dinner that night at Ivy Hall was a party with a group of old friends unwinding. Twenty-six sat around the table, and the conversation was lively. The men were acting as though there was nothing more important than the weather.

Anne looked from one man to the other. Tension was written on every face. Would she find out from Perkins, who had had his ear glued to the study door from the time everyone arrived, or from Sar or Berkley, that the situation was grave at best? All Perkins had said was "critical state of affairs." That wasn't the answer she needed. One way or another, she would find out. The voice in her head said, *By the time the women leave, make sure their skills have improved and they can do serious harm to anyone who tries to assault them.*

The men left to savor their port and brandy. With five wolfhounds gamboling about and leading the way, the women strolled the gardens. The men never rejoined the women; the women hadn't expected them to.

A dark sky and shifting winds combined with the thoughts tumbling through Anne's head as she climbed into bed. *Sleep will be difficult,* she thought. Slipping into slumber instantly, Her Grace thought she heard a slight scrape. Impossible. No one could get into this house undetected. Anne closed her eyes again only to sense that someone else was in the room. She slowly reached under her pillow for *Bessie.* When she opened her eyes, she was staring directly into Berkley's face. With a finger over his lips, Berkley motioned and slipped her into her robe. He ungracefully hoisted her over his shoulder and left the way he had come.

The shadowy secret hallway was lit only by the branch Berkley was carrying. He made a couple of turns and kept walking. When he stopped, he slipped open a panel and stepped into another bedchamber. Gently, he lowered Anne onto a thick carpet that muffled all sound. Before she could begin to open her mouth, he swooped down and kissed those lips, ready to ring a peal over his head.

"We cannot be heard. And, yes, we are still in Ivy Hall. This has been my designated bedchamber since the war, so I could come and go undetected, and the old duke and I could meet in absolute privacy. Mrs. Spencer prepares this room herself. It is always ready for my occasional visit. Yes, there is much going on surrounding you, your family, and the shipping business. It all bespeaks of danger and death. Sar will fill you in."

"Take me back to my bedchamber at once. How dare you bring me here? Who do you think you are?" Anne was doing her best *I am going to reprimand you* look of a mother.

Berkley had speculated he would get a response like this to his high-handed manner. But he wasn't most men, and her indignity rolled off him like water off a duck's back.

"I will gladly take you back as you wish." The general

detected the almost undiscernible shift of her shoulders. He read the subtle signal. *She really wants to be here.* He hoisted her over his shoulder and reverently placed her on the bed. Pushing up on his arms, he longingly looked at her.

"I need you, Your Grace. You give me purpose in life—a reason to keep breathing, to work, to protect the country I love, to live. Whether I make love to you tonight, tomorrow night, or next month, you are mine. Do you understand?"

Anne just nodded.

"Now, let me get you back to your bedchamber."

Before he could move, Anne reached up and gave him the gentlest, tenderest, most poignant kiss he had ever received. The kiss was his undoing.

"No, love, can't let you go." Returning the kiss with an urgency he didn't want to examine, he started stoking the inferno. Berkley knew that when he found the love of his life at age forty-nine, everything had to be more than perfect. Every touch and every caress, the multitude of kisses and all the promises, had to carry the silent message of eternal love now and forever, along with the heart he had to lay out there for her to do with as she wished. He had to take them both to places they had never been before.

Love can destroy a man, but the right love will turn an upside-down world upright. If men don't recognize that, they are fools. They will go around drinking too much, gambling too much, being out of sorts, or working instead of living. It is waiting for and finding the right woman, your one and only eternal love. How did I almost miss the most important thing of all?

The worship of Anne's body started with the softest of assaults on her senses. He tenderly kissed her eyebrow, the tip of her nose, and her neck. She stretched up as if asking for more. As his hands held her face, he looked into her eyes for acquiescence.

She was willing. *Any woman would be with a virile man*

tenderly making love to every part of her body. The woman never stands a chance. Isn't that the way the game has been played since the beginning of just about forever? Take the advantage so the woman doesn't have a say in the matter. But is that what I want from this woman?

No, he wanted every part of her she would give willingly, and he would do the same. Agreeing to make love is one thing, but acquiescing to giving one's heart and soul was another. That was everything.

The next night, Her Grace was sitting by the fireplace when she heard the telltale scrape of the opening of the secret panel to her room. She looked up, knowing silence was imperative. He beckoned and started showing her how to come and go undetected if needed in a moment of great danger.

With no light, he quietly whispered the count to the side of the room from the chair and the bed. Using only her fingers, he guided her hands over the panel until he was sure she could find the latch. Comfortable that she had memorized every step and every movement, he led them into the secret passage and raised her arm so she could get a feel for the height and width of the hallway. Quietly, he counted the steps to the first right turn, and did the same for the next turn. Then he counted the steps to his bedchamber.

Once inside the room, he carefully observed. Anne was unperturbed. *Yes*, he surmised, *she has been trained well.*

"That is how to get out of your bedchamber if you find yourself in a predicament. Come, let me now show you how to get out of Ivy Hall. The exit is far away from the main part of the house." For the next hour or so, the general was the masterspy trainer. His pupil was as excellent as any he had ever had.

When Anne was allowed to speak, it was one question, but the right one. "What has happened?"

Mer must have inherited this trait from her mother—direct, to the point. "It appears you had a visitor the other night. One who danced through the trees. We can only speculate that he couldn't get close enough to do what he had come to do—kill you or anyone else. He did not know you were not in residence."

Anne raised her right eyebrow. Berkley had seen Sar do that. *What haven't her children picked up from her?* He would explore that later.

"And how did you discover this? No, don't answer that. The padre, of course."

"Of course." The general's terse reply underscored the gravity of the situation.

"Is there anyone here who doesn't work for you?"

Berkley chuckled and covered her lips with his. The ballet of passion started to build with the kiss. "I'll be gone when you awake. Listen carefully to what Sar must tell you. If you need me, just let the minister know. Please. This game gets more dangerous by the day." Then he kissed her like he hadn't kissed her for ages instead of only a few minutes ago. Knowing that had to be it for now, he hugged her as if squeezing his life into her.

Then she heard Avery. *Like me, he will always protect you. Give him the chance.*

"Now, lead us back." Her Grace graciously led the master spy back to her bedchamber, and just like a master spy, he disappeared into the inky blackness of space.

The sweat started dripping down his back before he was halfway back to his room, and like the other times, the chills would come next. Berkley hurried before he started screaming. The safety of his room was most important—and the decanter of whisky. Throwing himself into the chair, he thrust his feet onto the footstool. A snaking, shaky hand reached for the glass and the whisky. He could reach neither without holding one hand over the other.

Berkley's drooping head, closed eyes, and tears leaking

from the corners was the usual pattern, and tonight was no different. Attacking reminiscences marched to the beat of a death knell through his head as one by one the soldiers passed by missing arms, legs, and heads. He could feel them, touch them, sense the fear, and smell the battlefield—smoke, fire, burning flesh, screams, blood, silence. He had done this—put it in motion. Sons, fathers, his to protect. And he hadn't. And there was the opponent. The worst memories were those of the ones he had personally killed. That was all there was to war— recollections of horror after horror playing through the mind at night, during sleep, at odd moments, at random.

The general knew why he worked as much as he did and usually fell asleep in a chair with an empty glass of whisky in his hand. It was the only way he could get any solace. *What can I offer Anne? A fractured, cracked, broken man?* Bruises from being hit when he lashed out unexpectedly in the middle of the night, or when she naturally rolled over and touched him? Separate beds to sleep in instead of the comfort of being held? Damn, that was no way to build intimacy.

How do other men survive? He knew only too well. *Many don't. Some blow their brains out and instantly end the torment. The majority choose slower ways to die. Some turn inward and glower outward at the world through shrunken eyes, which dart back and forth, comprehending nothing. Many are in institutions, running aimlessly around, screaming, and losing all bodily functions. For others, numbing the body with bottle after bottle of anything drinkable and laughing too loudly is the remedy. Keep memories at bay. Their world is nothing but a hazy, vague existence spent begging for pennies and remnants of dignity. They all silently recognize each other and know— escaping memories of war. The chilling, haunting memories; the real spoils of war.*

No, there is never any "normal" for one who has been to war. Those who adjusted best were married and in love with their wives. Maybe love is an important key, and you find good after the terror, dreadfulness, and awfulness. He would have to ask Sebastian someday. The glass slipped out of his hand; he didn't hear it fall.

By the time Anne reached the breakfast room, the sun had been up at least two hours. There was no one around. Her Grace assumed the general had left before dawn. However, according to Mrs. Spencer, the general was still upstairs. A message had arrived about four this morning. Her Grace knew something else had happened.

"Mrs. Spencer, is there anything we can do to make the staff feel safer?"

"Thank you, Your Grace. As you know, the general himself taught the entire staff how to shoot. He wanted us to be able to defend ourselves if needed."

If Her Grace could wager at White's, she'd bet half of the Westmoure fortune that the general in his usual high-handed manner had trained half of the village if not the whole of it.

"What about the remainder of the village?"

"Everyone was taught by the general and Henley personally."

"Humph!"

"Did you say something, Your Grace?"

"Carry on, Mrs. Spencer." Turning, Anne did not see the smile adorning Mrs. Spencer's face.

It was easy to find Sar. Anne, Mer, and Beth saw Perkins leaning into the door of the study. "Are you waiting for a ducal pronouncement? Open the door, Perkins."

"Sar is in quite a mood, Your Grace." He silently opened the door, and they all watched. Sar was going up and down and round and round the room as though the flames of hell were nipping his heels.

"Sar, please sit down, you are beginning to remind me of Inspector Daggs with all your pacing." Mer and Beth sat impatiently, waiting for an explanation. "Now, tell us everything that has recently happened." Her Grace sat back in her chair and waited for answers.

"We all know what has been occurring. I worry, because it seems as though they are coming at us from all sides, and we do not know who they are. And pieces keep being added to the puzzle." Sar looked as though the weight of the world was bearing down on him.

Anne was about to say something when Sar shook his head and sighed. "There is more. The other night a man was seen skipping from tree to tree along the drive. We can only assume his intent. If we were not here, the assassin would probably kill anyone in the house to send us a message."

Sar told them the rest. "The padre saw him, watched, and followed the man back to his horse. Berkley has his own spy system here in the country. It seems to work well.

"That about sums it up. It looks as though there won't be a dull moment for any of us." Sar stretched out his long legs underneath the desk. He knew it was coming, and there was nothing he could do about it.

"Well, we'll just have to protect ourselves."

"Mother, this is far too dangerous a game. Someone wants all of us dead."

As he continued, Sar fought the urge to take everyone to Scotland until the danger had passed. "We have to carry on as though we know nothing of the shipping crimes and proceed with extra caution."

"Now tell us why Berkley is still here and tell us everything."

Sar let out a deep sigh before he began telling them another complex piece of the matter at hand. "About four o'clock this morning, Berkley received a message. All we know is that Monsieur Rue arrives within two days. He will be brought here. All the arrangements are being made. A message was sent to Rue immediately, inviting him to stay here for two or more days. Mother, that is all I know. Berkley will fill us in sometime today."

• • •

Anne knew what she had to do. The ladies spent the morning perfecting their skills. This time the wolfhounds decided to leave before the first shot. Duchess led the pack.

• • •

Work on Cummings and Paige's continued with ongoing suggestions for Harson's. Absentmindedly, Joycellyn sketched and sketched. She knew why; she was thinking about the past and the future. If she could, she would spin and spin and spin until she fell down. A bastard accepted as one of the family and by their friends—the crème of society. The old duke had told her about the honor and kindness of the Negro American Roxburys. He had been right as usual.

But the darkness always haunted her every move when the reflections of the first six years of her life invaded her peace. The woman she called mother had stared with a wide-eyed glare and only grunted. Things were changing faster than Joycellyn could imagine, but her mother was still "off." She couldn't pinpoint it, but her mother's movements were always guarded and reserved, as though waiting for the next tragedy.

CHAPTER 12

Visitors, Visitors, and More Visitors

Berkley had gathered everyone in the study. Perkins had his ear glued to the door. "This is all I know. Rue and his son arrive within two days. However, I can tell you this, Rue would not cross the channel unless it was of utmost importance. The message could not be sent through the signaling system. Too many people would know. As we are aware, we have spies among us.

"I have invited him here because I felt it was safer. There won't be prying eyes or ears. Sar, Anne, I did not want to wake you at that time of the morning to ask permission. I trust this is acceptable to you." Both just nodded their heads.

"All I ask is that everyone stay on the grounds of Ivy Hall or Rushton. After we find out what is afoot, we will proceed accordingly. I want everyone present. This is going to take all of us to figure out the right strategy. I suggest the women carry on with their training with the help of the men. Ladies, always carry your *Bessies*. Aston and Jay will be here by this afternoon, as will Grayson. Perkins, I will need you to make sure our visitors arrive safely. Dawson will cover you." Dawson, another one of Berkley's superspies, nodded. "The outriders will be men from my group of operatives. They will not be in livery.

"Does anyone have any suggestions?"

"Based on what Perkins has told us, our enemy follows behind. Would it be possible to have some protection that would pick up anyone riding behind everyone else?" Anne realized that, but for Perkins, when she was on her way to Berkley's country house, she could have been harmed.

"I know Perkins spotted those two following you. They could not get close enough to you, but you are right. This is a different operation, and we need all the protection possible.

"Any other suggestions? Rue usually arrives in the night. My message to him was—'Received. Understood. In country. Coach will be waiting. Please stay two or more days.' Royce has already sent the message. Any questions?

"I doubt if anyone can get through the lines of protection here and at Rushton. Be on guard anyway. Don't forget those adorable dogs are trained to protect, and you have the commands. Use them if necessary. Samuels, has the area been secured?"

"Yes, General."

"Unless someone has something else to add, that is all." The general ambled out of the study with his head down.

"Ladies, don your britches, bring your pistols, and wear your heavy boots. Meet at our training ground in an hour." Anne was delivering orders like the general, and she loved it.

Finding Mrs. Spencer was easy. She was next to Perkins with her ear glued to the door. When Anne walked out of the study, she was standing there sheepishly. "Another student of Perkins?"

Mrs. Spencer just nodded.

"She is doing quite well, Your Grace." Perkins stood there as if this were an everyday occurrence. Anne could almost hear him whistling.

"Since you heard what the general said, we have a lot to do. Please send breakfast to Berkley's room if you have not done so already. I assume you know which room Rue prefers. Is the staff prepared for any danger? The ladies and I will be training. Please allow anyone who wants to join us to do so." Anne turned and started to walk away.

Her Grace pivoted. "No, I have a better idea if it is acceptable to you, Mrs. Spencer. Make a schedule that will allow the entire staff some time with us and the men. This will enable them to become somewhat more proficient and more confident."

"That is a wonderful idea. I know the staff will appreciate it."

"Mrs. Spencer, we start training in about an hour. Have the staff wear what they normally do for work."

Samuels stood guard outside Berkley's door. It was as though the atmosphere in the house had instantly changed to war mode. Even the maid delivering breakfast was interrogated by Samuels. When Berkley emerged, he was ready to train with the women.

The general's presence changed everything. Giving orders, he had additional equipment brought out. There were walls to scale, ropes to climb, and different moving targets.

Once everything was in place, all he said was "Let's get to it." He realized he was working off his frustration and making everyone else do the same. By the end of the two-hour session, the staff was literally falling on their faces. "I will see everyone at two this afternoon. We will do the same. Samuels, let Mrs. Spencer know the afternoon schedule and ask her to indulge me and bring the noon meal to my room."

"Yes, sir." Samuels left to do the general's bidding.

The women gathered around Anne. "What do you think?" Aurelia's curls bounced as she spoke.

"I believed he is worried about the news Rue is going to deliver. However, his greater concern is keeping us safe. We must be prepared for everything. Danger may not come this week or next, but it will come. As for our time here, let us make the most of it and train harder than the men." Her Grace realized danger stalked them, and the other women did as well.

They left the training area supporting the staff. Someone piped up, "Is he always like that?"

The women answered in unison, "Yes."

Only the women were at lunch. The men ate in the study, waiting for the next command from Berkley. It was a somber work group.

"Everyone, we will have to be more vigilant than ever now. Samuels is going to make it difficult to get information. He will guard Berkley, a door, or any other place he is commanded. Trust me, someone will be guarding the doors from the outside also. Berkley does not want us to have any information, especially if that means a trip to a foreign land. I don't think he could handle it if we showed up in another country and captured another criminal." Anne tapped her fingers on the table as she thought.

"I believe our key is Perkins. He must understand we can come up with ideas and solutions that are different and will work. If there is trouble, we are the backup. They would feel responsible if anything happened to us, but that is the chance we are willing to take." Caroline knew Sebastian would die if she were injured in any way.

"Caroline is right. If Perkins gives us information, he must do it without feeling he is betraying the men. We will have to promise him something in return and keep the promise if the danger to our men is not too great or we have an easier solution." Miriam looked around at the group and saw every-one nodding in agreement.

"I know he is going to make us swear not to follow them. The adventure to France scared them witless. It is not that we are not competent, but in their minds, they think they should protect us and we should find more ladylike endeavors. Thank goodness we are not the afternoon tea ladies. Could you imagine trying to discuss this with a group like that? They would all say, 'Leave it to the men.'" Hortense let go one of her famous cackles.

"The day of 'leaving it to the men' is over. If we hadn't gone to Caen, they might still be there. I suggest we work with them. That way we will find out all we need to know. We will act accordingly." Hortense talked while caressing her *Bessie* as though it was her best friend.

"I agree with Hortense. That is the only way we can find out as much as possible. The men must still think they are in charge. If we let them believe that, we get what we want." Georgina smiled. "I have been using that approach for years. It works every time."

"If everyone agrees, that is the approach we will take. Now, for an afternoon session with the men." Anne went upstairs to change into clean britches.

The afternoon's session was more grueling than the morning's. Jay stepped in to begin the fundamentals of fighting with a sword. The swords were heavy, and they couldn't swish like the men. Then it was a swim in the cold lake and a one-mile run.

Anne looked at the general and sensed he was scared. *Berkley is acting in his high-handed manner, taking his frustration out on us. The women are doing this, and we will be ready if the time ever comes. Is this his way of trying to make us back off?* Every muscle in her body strained, but she did what she was told. This time, they carried the staff back.

At dinner, the bets were on as to who would succumb first with her head in her food. Surprisingly, the women were as hungry as hibernating bears out for the first time after their long snooze. Food disappeared as fast as it appeared.

Then Berkley entered the room. "Rue will be here tonight or tomorrow morning. If it is not too late, we will meet in the study. Samuels will notify everyone." He turned and left.

As they were about to finish dinner, a plain carriage pulled up to the front entrance. Two people climbed out. The whistle given by Perkins signified that all had gone well. Magically, two more place settings appeared at the table.

"*Bonsoir, bonsoir, bonsoir.*" Monsieur Rue's smile lit up the room.

The noise brought Berkley down the stairs. "*Bonsoir, bonsoir, bonsoir. Sommes très heureux de vous voir. J'espère que le voyage s'est bien passé. Mangeons, puis nous parlons.*"

"*Oui, oui.* All is well, as you would say. *Comment vas-tu, vieil ami?*"

"*Bien, bien.*" The men shook hands with true affection, which was a testament to their many near-death encounters in their efforts for good.

"Rue said the trip over was good. I suggest we eat first and then talk." Berkley sat down at the table.

Anne carefully looked at the two men. They sat and ate as though they didn't have a care in the world. She was beginning to get it. There was only now. No one knew what the next second would bring. In the world of master spies, they had figured it out. Good times were to be enjoyed. Work was one intense moment after another with no known outcome.

"So, you are the one." Rue was grinning at Her Grace. "*Quand Berkley a reçu le message, vous aviez le pigeon qu'il voulait vous donner un morceau de son esprit en utilisant des mots très descriptifs.*"

Rue's son spoke up. "It appeared the general was quite

concerned when he received the note that you had the pigeon captured and were on your way back to England. You might say the air turned blue when my father gave him the message. Really, according to Dad, he wanted to give you a piece of his mind using some very descriptive words." Jacques smiled from ear to ear. Anne raised both eyebrows at the general.

With dinner over, everyone adjourned to the study. The mood shifted instantly.

"Somehow one of our operatives intercepted their signals and was able to decipher their code. We don't have any names yet, but maybe the initials will help if they are using their true names. Though we doubt they are." Jacques spoke for Rue since his English was perfect. He handed the notes to Berkley, and they all sensed a new chapter of death and destruction was about to open.

Not a sound was made as the general read the messages to all—"'Women delivered to Tangier. Very pleased client. Westmoure captain didn't realize women were on board. Smooth sailing from Gibraltar. A. B.'

"The second message—'Come home. Next assignment will be waiting for you. Meet at usual place in London. M. N.'"

"My God, how long has this been going on?" Sar sat with his palm on his forehead. "I am sending for Jacob. We are going to make some immediate changes for anyone boarding or working on a Westmoure vessel. Changes will go into effect immediately. We will improve and modify as the need arises. We'll meet as soon as Jacob arrives."

Berkley's silence was almost everyone's undoing. When he spoke, it was with a hollow tone of disappointment and silent anger. "Beth, you were right. Some very high government officials are at the center of this. No one else could have those connections.

"Royce, Julien, we begin with making a list of everyone at

my level of government or higher. Everyone's name goes on the list, including mine. Investigate every one of them, without alerting anyone outside of this room, nor the other operatives working with us, of what we are doing. I want to know everything about their personal lives from their wives to their mistresses, their homes and their associates who come and go at their residences. They are to be tailed twenty-four hours a day. I feel that searching their offices will be futile. The information won't be there. It will be in a private office or at home. I also want to know everything possible about the former exchequer. Some of our clues may be there. Any questions?" Berkley glanced around the room. He was met with silence. "We start tomorrow morning."

"Rue, join me for a brandy." The general abruptly turned and left the room.

"That, my friends, is Berkley on the hunt. No stone will be left unturned. Woe to the person who is at the center of this operation. Whoever he is, he's already dead. It will be an early morning. I, for one, am for bed." Royce grabbed his glass and climbed the stairs.

"Ladies, we have a lot of work to do. We must remain safe and keep our men protected. Our goal is to be prepared. If tonight was any indication as to the seriousness of the matter, heads are going to roll as Berkley eliminates one culprit after another. This is war." Caroline realized there had been a fundamental shift in the approach to the crimes tonight.

"You're right, Caroline. We now have predatory beasts among us ready to strike at any moment. My study first thing tomorrow morning. Now we must have a little chat with Perkins." Anne stood, and the rest of the ladies followed.

Perkins was easy to find. His ear was glued to Berkley's door. Samuels stood as straight as a rod.

"Your Grace, I assume this is not a social call." Perkins looked at the ladies and understood he was their target.

"Very funny, Perkins. We need to speak with you now." Anne led the group away from Berkley's door.

"Don't you think it is a little unfair that you can eavesdrop on Berkley and Mer can't?" Her Grace was in one of her moods.

"Your Grace, I didn't make the rules. Your future husband did."

"Now that that's established, don't you think it is time to change the rules for all of our sakes?"

"Your Grace, what can I do to help you?"

"Perkins, this is what we need, since you are the only one who can get to a door where Berkley is holding his strategy sessions—tell us everything that is said: the who, where, what, and why."

"But I would be betraying Sar."

"Oh, Perkins, no you won't. You'll be saving him. Who has to rescue the men? We can't have anything happen to them, can we? And you are the only one who can get the information we need."

"Your Grace, Berkley has already threatened to shoot me once for insubordination."

"Don't mind him. He adores you. Now, Perkins, we must work together on this."

"It does appear that you tend to get the men out of their dilemmas. However, if I do this, Your Grace, you and the other women must agree not to follow them if they leave the country."

"Let me speak to the other women to see if they agree." Anne turned to the group with a smile on her face.

"We agree with your terms, Perkins, but we get all the information, not some or part, starting with tonight and what is going on in that room. Are we clear?"

"Yes, Your Grace." Perkins went back to become one with Berkley's door.

• • •

At the London residence of the Duke of Westmoure, the knock on the door could only mean something urgent. The under-butler rang for Oliver and opened the door with a pistol at the ready. He let go a sigh of relief when he saw the messenger in Westmoure livery.

Oliver joined them. "I am to hand this to Jacob Goldsmith directly."

"He'll be joining us momentarily."

"Oliver, what is the problem?"

"It's for you, Jacob, from the duke."

Jacob opened the message—*Need you at Ivy Hall immedi-ately. Carriage is waiting whenever you are ready. Ask Rose, the head office girl, to pick up Bella and take her to the office and bring her back to the house. Encourage Rose to stay at my house while you are away. Coach will be waiting for her in the morn-ing. Use messenger who brought you this note.*

The Duke of Westmoure smiled as he thought of Bella's change in routine. *The drug-sniffing four-legged beast is going to be spoiled by the women in the office without Jacob around.* They all loved Bella.

Jacob found Oliver and the underbutler feeding the mes-senger. "Oliver, I will be joining Sar at Ivy Hall as soon as I can pack. Detain the messenger. I need him to deliver one more note. Rose will pick Bella up here and take her to the office. When Bella returns in the evening, Rose is to be our guest while I am away. We should be back by Saturday."

"Your valet will be informed." Oliver bowed.

Jacob *harrumphed.*

• • •

It was late morning when Jacob arrived at Ivy Hall. The men were gathered in the study. Anne and the ladies were not invited to join. Perkins had his ear glued to the door. It was just about lunchtime when Aston appeared. He was immediately admitted to the inner sanctum.

"Aston, I assume there is something else we need to know. Welcome, always glad to have you involved, along with your son." Berkley was all general. He was in war mode.

"Everyone. No, not a social visit. The king is on his way. He is about four hours behind me. The rumors floating around London have him very concerned. Some people are pushing for charges to be brought against Sar for treason, espionage, smuggling, and trafficking of women. The assumption is that this started when he became the duke. And get this stupid idea—you are a Negro and that is what Negroes do: break laws." Aston sat back in his chair.

"One other thing, the king plans on staying through Sunday."

"Thanks, Aston, this is beyond ridiculous. Someone is out for blood, and so are we. Any ideas as to the motive?" Berkley crushed his third cigar that morning.

"Rumor has it that interested parties want to take over Westmoure Shipping. To me, the most logical reason is that they want to continue their illegal activities. I don't have any names yet."

"This falls right in line with what we had already concluded. We didn't know about the rumors. The information is invaluable." Berkley continued briefing Jacob and Aston.

"These are some of the changes we agree to make immediately. We only use men from established legitimate agencies we have worked with in the past. Everyone must show their papers when boarding. John Smiths will not be hired unless they have worked for us for three years. The watch is doubled.

Anyone boarding or leaving the ship is to show papers and be cursorily inspected. In addition, head covers must be removed. The list of things to look for during the inspection includes hands, facial hair or lack of it, fake beards, wigs, width of chest, et cetera. A thorough list will be given to the captains. Caution everyone to be on guard. These individuals will kill freely.

"Before hiring anyone who claims they are from a legitimate agency, we must check with that agency first. Pay will be increased. Hire one of the ladies from Harson's to be in charge of checking out people who want to work for us. We will help her set up a system to make it easy to confirm with the agency.

"Perkins, I need to see Joycellyn and Yvette."

As the men continued their discussion in the study, lunch was brought in. The ladies sat around the table putting together their pieces of the puzzle based on the latest information. Mrs. Spencer inspected the king's chambers.

"Joycellyn, would you mind returning to London with Jacob? I think we should hold the third grand-opening celebration as planned. We will do something equally exceptional next Saturday when we return. I will send Cook a message so she can start creating a special menu. If you can come back here on Sunday, that would be best. Bring Frances with you. It is important to the men that we are all protected and in one place. Daggs will have his men watching over you." Anne smiled at Joycellyn.

"Since we have let the schools know about the luncheon, it is important to have it. Students might question our intentions. I'm with you, Anne. Let's give the students and shoppers what we intended." Caroline was making a list of their plans as she spoke.

"Going back to the city won't be a problem. I am anxious to see how well we have done." Visions of sold-out goods danced in Joycellyn's head. "Also, Sar has asked Yvette and I to create some type of shield that would deflect a knife being thrust between the ribs. We have some ideas and would like to present them before I leave."

"We need things to do with the king in residence. I know he will want to go to church and do a walk about the town. He likes to meet people and have a pint or two in local establishments. Even on short notice, the local gentry will come to a country dance. We will start on the invitations immediately. I think I have been around the king too long." Lady Hortense cackled.

Evelyn chimed in. "That's about all we need to do. With their meetings, there won't be a spare moment."

"With everything we have learned from Perkins, what should we do?" Anne looked around the table.

"We should send for the Earl and Countess of Fatson and the patrons of . . ." Before Miriam could get out another word, there was a knock on the door.

"The patrons of Almack's, Your Grace."

"Thank you, Perkins." *How do they know just when to appear? One less thing to do.* Anne smiled.

"We were just about to invite you to our country dance. The king is on his way and will be in residence until at least next Monday. We hope you can stay until then." Anne couldn't smile anymore. Her jaw ached.

"Oh, how gracious of you. We will be delighted." If Lady Sarah preened one more time, she was going to receive a collected slap from all of them.

"Out with it, Sarah. Why are you here? We want all the gossip now. Leave nothing out." Only Lady Hortense had the status to speak to the patrons like that. Lunch was served, and for the next two hours, every bit of gossip the patrons had was dissected. "Now, what do you want from us?"

The stunned patrons looked like fish gasping as they took their last breath. "Well, well, I don't know quite how to say this, so I had better just say it. We want to be a part of your next adventure. There must be something we can do to help the Westmoures.

"When you first arrived, we voiced concerns, like many, about Negroes in the aristocracy. Up to that point, we grouped all Negroes together. If one was bad, they were all bad. We had never heard of any good ones. They were never individuals, rather just a group of people that we weren't supposed to associate with or get to know.

"If we talked to any Negroes, we would say to our friends, 'I talked to this Negro.' But when we spoke to people who were white, we would never say, 'I spoke to a white man.' Saying we talked to a Negro was our code for telling someone, 'Don't believe what I heard' or 'I was just patronizing the person.' It was always pronouncing Negroes as less than.

"Then the Westmoures arrived, and all they have done is good, exhibiting kindness to others, even to us when we didn't deserve it. It was unwise to follow the edicts of society. No one should ever be judged as we judged the American duke and his family. All we want is for the ton to see that we must look at every person as an individual, get to know them, and see them for who they are. Things are changing. We have been silly twits."

"Finally, you are beginning to get something into those numbskull brains besides society rules, lineage, and gossip. What took you so long?" Lady Hortense's cackle could be heard throughout the house after she finished commenting to the patrons. "I am going to get dressed."

"His Majesty will be here soon. We are also expecting the Fatsons later today. It's time for all of us to get ready." Caroline rose. "Come, ladies."

The king arrived, and the evening turned into one of jovial festivities. After the Fatsons appeared, the group laughed as though they had all been gathering like this for years. The men adjourned to the study, and the ladies to the receiving room. Champagne became their after-dinner drink. When the men joined them, the ladies were beginning to lean to the left.

For the next few days, it was the same routine. The men worked in the study. Miriam led the ladies on vigorous walks in the mornings. In the afternoons, the king went to the local pub, taking all the men with him. Charlotte Fatson and the patrons of Almack's spent that time refreshing themselves with long naps while Anne held meetings with the other ladies in her study with daily updates from Perkins. Mer spent her time listening at the door of Lady Sarah whenever she had a meeting with the other patrons.

Saturday night was the country dance. On Sunday, His Majesty went to church. Everyone who attended that day was individually introduced to the king. As expected, the king left on Monday. The Fatsons and the patrons stayed until Tuesday. On the Wednesday after the country dance, the ladies were back to training and working. Joycellyn and Yvette presented the men with four designs based on their previous discussion.

The men were holed up in the study still debating over one question. "It's better if we use both approaches. If people continue to believe that Sar is responsible for all the wrongdoing, we can continue conducting our investigations in a secretive manner. At this point in time, it is not necessary we explain the situation to Parliament, the prime minister, and the high court. Eventually they need to understand that Sar and Jacob discovered the crimes, which had been occurring before His Grace became a duke. The two have been working with the Home Office, the Foreign Office, and Scotland Yard to get to the bottom of these matters. With the king backing us, I think this will work." The general was more than sure this was the right approach.

"That may be the better way to deal with those who want Sar brought up on charges. I'll have extra men following him at all times. Someone is going to get anxious and want to put an early end to his life." Daggs was pacing as usual.

"We are returning to the city on Friday. It's time to check in with our underground contacts." Berkley was thinking someone must have heard something by now. "I, for one, think it is time to join the ladies. They can tell us all the latest gossip and give us a line-by-line detailed description of the upcoming edition of the Society News. We can finish in the morning."

Sebastian stood and headed for the door. "Good thinking, General. The ladies might think we abandoned them."

CHAPTER 13

Welcome Back to the Capital

The ride back to the city that Friday morning had been leisurely. Now, Sar sat in the study in the London house writing the note to his man of affairs. Without looking up, he asked Perkins to have his mother and sisters join him. Of course, Perkins was nowhere to be seen, but the request had been heard and was being carried out. The two of them had an understanding. Unless something was of the utmost importance—that is, an out-of-the-ordinary importance in their world—Perkins would become one with the door and keep his eavesdropping skills finely honed.

Looking at his mother and sisters, Sar saw and sensed their guarded nature. There were far more pats of pockets and barely perceptible tugs on sleeves that alerted him to their anxiety. Of course, they were ensuring that their weapons were in place.

"Sar, we have to do something." Anne's wrinkled brow spoke volumes about the heavy weight of worry and concern.

"Mother, I know you believe I am not old enough to take care of you, but I will protect you with my life." Sar bent over from the edge of the desk and kissed his mother on the forehead. He couldn't let any one of them come to harm, even if they had all shaken hands with danger before.

"That's just it. I do not want your life in exchange for mine. Despite any and all odds, I want this family to live and flourish, especially my children."

"I know, Mother. How are you feeling?" To Sar, she still looked pale and weak. Their last day in the country had been filled with anxiety. Anne had come downstairs for breakfast and found herself leaning over a dustbin, emptying everything in her stomach. Weak and shaken, she had been carried by Sar back to bed. The images remained the same—still people and smoke.

When Sar wasn't with her, the ladies were. Checking on her frequently, Sar and Sebastian realized she could barely walk, and the steps she did take were slow and measured. "If you are going anywhere besides Paige's and Caroline's tomorrow, please let me know. Now that we are back, it is wise to be as careful as possible. You must let me know where you are going, please." Sar wanted to wrap his family in cotton wool, but he knew it wouldn't work.

That night, Berkley came to Anne in his usual manner—like a magician of the night. "Anne, I beg of you to listen to me carefully. You and the rest of your family are in danger, serious danger. Quinn and I have kept the prime minister up to date, and all we have are theories.

"As you had suspected, Jack is a traitor and a murderer. The why is still too deeply hidden. Has Sar notified Red Cloud to look for him at the docks? Regardless, Red Cloud will eventually pick up Jack's trail."

Anne knew how it worked. If they needed someone found, they sent Chief Red Cloud, who was currently in charge of the American side of the Avery Jacob Shipping Company. Thinking about Red Cloud, all she could do was sing his praises—he was savvy, bold, brilliant, and an excellent tracker.

Berkley almost smiled. "It appears I am a few steps behind everyone. Sar had Joycellyn make sketches of Jack, George, and Morgan and sent them to Red Cloud a few weeks back. Hopefully, he will be able to pick up Jack's trail. We don't know what Jack looks like now. He is in disguise, and I'll bet every pound note in my pocket, he'll find a way to stay like that until he knows he is safe."

"Red Cloud will get your man. What is it? Something else is bothering you."

"Yes, Jack is a turncoat, but the why of it is so elusive. Nothing connects, and all we have to show are pieces of a puzzle and an operative with a solid plan backed by some very high officials in government. Can't put my finger on it, but those on the inside are very aware of what we are doing. Then we have smuggling, espionage, and trafficking. All are treasonable offenses, and I always get my man or men. This could topple the government if not handled very delicately."

"I know you. Everyone will die before you let the culprits topple the government. Given that, what is your next step?"

"I don't know, Anne, I don't know."

Berkley sighed. He held out his hand. "I had a bath drawn. Come, let me bathe you." She extended her hand. He grabbed it as though it was his lifeline.

The thoughts of what she did with Berkley made her blush. A wanton at forty-eight. Without a doubt, she loved that man. It was not the same love she had with Avery, but a love just as intense. At this age, it was richer and fuller. Somehow, they would get to the bottom of the murders and the whys of it all.

The ton was nothing. Acceptance or not, the Roxburys were a part of the aristocracy forever.

"We fled America for safety just to run into international intrigue." Her soft laughter made him feel twenty-one again.

They opened the door to her private bath chamber. The steam rising from the old eight-foot round oak soaker gave everything a sensuous ethereal feel. Scents of sandalwood and vanilla heightened the tension of the anticipated moments of intimacy.

Berkley slowly undressed her and bit by bit caressed every inch of her body with his large hands. "I once told you every inch of you belonged to me from the top of your head to the soles of your feet and everything in between. Now, I will show you."

The steam from the water caused her hair to form tight ringlets around her face. As he gathered the soft hair in his hands, he moved closer to her. As he kissed her closed eyelids, her hands started roaming every part of his body. His heat was the only thing that mattered.

He rubbed the flannel over every conceivable part of her body, gently massaging her feet and toes. Anne sighed. When he reached her love center, the flannel became an extension of him. Over and over her mons he rubbed as sparks and tingles ignited her body and had her pleading for more.

Berkley worked back up her body. His kisses were soft as feathers on her neck as he started to work down her water-slick naked form again. Gently holding her left breast, he suckled the nipple and then laved until it was a peaked nib. Pulling the nipple, he feasted on the other breast.

Anne was beginning to moan as her moving body started making soft waves in the water. Her roving hands had found his extended member, and she was rubbing the appendage up and down until it was wide and hard as steel.

His hands had found her secret center and were brushing her mons. Her head began to thrash back and forth as she started losing control. Farther down her body he went until his head was below water and his tongue plunged into her.

Her Grace was barely holding on to any reasonable sanity when his head broke the surface. Picking her up, he carried her out of the tub and placed her on the padded chaise. "Look at me, Anne." Her eyes opened. "I want you looking into my eyes when I enter you—one of our forever joinings."

Berkley didn't take his time. He needed and wanted her now. He didn't wait for a yes. She reached for him as he entered her. Rocking back on his knees, he was captivated by the sight of their intimacy. Then he could see no more. All Berkley could do was feel—the heat of her sheath, the wetness of her canal, and the contractions that were beginning to hold him in a viselike grip.

He wanted to shout *mine*, but he couldn't get enough air in his lungs. All he could do was moan and whimper. Her release took them over the moon at about the same time as his. He wondered if he had enough energy to move. One powerful release after another curled her toes; she cried—for what was, is, and might never be.

Their lovemaking was that of two people who understood that life could be snatched away in a blink of an eye. The tenderness in each reach and touch had brought tears to Anne's eyes. The unspoken between them screamed, *We may never be together again.*

Life was like a deck of cards. You never knew what you'd get until the cards were dealt. The loss of Avery still caused her to choke. Telling her children they were Negroes had not been easy. But they needed to know. Regardless of how they were forced by the laws and precepts of America to pass as white, she wanted her children to be proud of their heritage. *Being white is not the key—the key is being who you are with a good heart.* Now all the madness in England.

Closely examining everything, Anne understood someone had given them gifts, and it was up to them to share their bounty with others. Would this create understanding and acceptance? She doubted it. Her Grace didn't need their acceptance, whoever *they* were. One thing was patently clear, she only had to fully accept and embrace herself.

• • •

In the former colonies, Jack sloshed about in mud alleys called streets. Everything oozed mud. He was making steady progress with contacts who wanted product and to be a part of their drug network. Today, he was meeting with men from the farthest region of the territory. Jack could feel the excitement of expansion when he spoke with them. Tonight, he would bring Morgan and George Mason up to speed. This and the destruction of the aristocracy were the only two things that kept him going on a day-to-day basis. With the Westmoures eliminated, he would be back in England within the year, a partner in a world empire.

• • •

The exquisitely appointed hunting lodge on the estate in the English countryside could accommodate fourteen, but today there were only two. Boss sat opposite the man who had made the offer. Her eyes followed him as he paced back and forth. Looking at him carefully, she didn't know whether to accept his offer or just kill him. *Killing him now might complicate things too much. After all, he is the higher-up with all the information. What use is he? What use is she? If our plan doesn't succeed, I will hang as will everyone else—we will pay the ulti-mate price.* Mentally going through their plan, she knew they would win.

. . .

Jay raced up the steps of the Duke of Westmoure's London residence. Behind him was a line of servants carrying food and presents. Today, he would introduce them to Holi, a Hindu religious festival known as the Festival of Colors. This group needed something to cheer them up. The pressure to stay alive and protect weighed heavily on them all. This was the celebration of victory of good over evil—something they could all use. The tempting Indian delicacies would bring the foreign soil a little closer to them and remind him of his home across the sea. Jay hoped the gods would understand and forgive them for being a few months late celebrating.

The early afternoon lunch achieved all his goals. Even though the women were continuously checking to ensure their weapons were in place, they laughed some, relaxed a little, and asked about the holiday.

"The Hindu religion helps make up the colorful landscape of India with the majority of Hindus living in India." As Jay explained, the tasty Indian food disappeared.

Anne pushed back her chair, ran to the nearest dustbin, and deposited what she had just eaten into it. Immediately, Sar was by her side supporting her. Berkley scooped her up and carried her upstairs. Towels, cold cloths, brandy, toast, and weak tea appeared.

The women stayed with Anne while the men retreated to the lower floor. "And that, Jay, is how it happens. Suddenly Her Grace is rushing for the dustbin, and unfortunately within a short time someone dies—or someone has died already, and we do not know about it yet." Daggs was pacing; Berkley was pulling his neckcloth apart.

"Do you think we could persuade Anne to stay in bed for the remainder of the day?" Berkley looked from one man to the other.

"No, Anne will proclaim that she is better and fit enough to stop by Paige's at closing. Caroline will claim they need the air and go along to make sure Anne is okay." Sebastian was pacing along with Daggs.

"Nothing we can do."

"Nothing you can do, Berkley. I suggest that you and Sar finish what you are doing at Whitehall. It appears we will have another murder to investigate." Sebastian poured himself more brandy.

• • •

Resting as much as possible before picking up Caroline, Anne dressed with meticulous care. There were enough people worried about her as it was. The two ladies reached Paige's just as the last customer was leaving and the doors were being locked.

"How did it go?" Things were scattered here and there—neatly, but it was obvious there had been a lot of people in and out. Anne took another look around.

"Oh my goodness. You won't believe it. Another dozen new orders for styles we sold out of." Joycellyn was like a child in a toy emporium. "I've sent material and patterns to the house so I can start working on everything tomorrow. Two of the seamstresses are willing to work with me."

"Let's put everything away. We are going to Caroline's for dinner." Her Grace needed to sit down. She felt worse than ever. "Caroline and I will close. The rest of you meet us at her house. We will be there shortly."

Making sure everything was in order, Anne and Caroline started turning off the gas lights. Outside, John the coachman felt the horses pull in their traces. He had no control over them whatsoever. There was a push and a swoosh; the horses took off as though they had nails digging into their flesh.

At the London residence of the Duke of Westmoure, a work wagon pulled up in front of the house. The worker jumped out, gave a friendly wave to the doormen, and went around the back to see what had to be repaired.

Then Anne heard Avery. *Grab Caroline's hand and the dogs. Pick up your skirts; run like hell out the back—now.* He gave her a push.

"Don't ask, Caroline, just hang on." The panic in Anne's voice was obvious. Clutching Caroline's hand, and ordering the dogs to lead the way, they ran like schoolgirls headed to recess. They had just cleared the back entrance when a *boom* rent the air. The force of the explosion propelled both women to the ground, dresses and hair aflame. Duchess and Felix started nudging their mistresses, so they were rolling on the grass and in the dirt. At the same time, the horses, with John the coachman hanging on for dear life, came barreling down the alley. He was jumping off the coach as he took in the scene. John took the horses' water and threw it on the ladies and reached for the blankets in the boot.

At approximately the same time, a blast at the residence of the Duke of Westmoure blew the roof off the house and destroyed everything within a ten-foot perimeter. Fire was shooting up from the hole that used to be the middle of the residence. There was no sign of either the wagon parked out front or the doormen. The worker had vanished in thin air.

The hair on the back of Berkley's neck was tingling. He hadn't had a sensation this strong since the war. "Sar, something is wrong. Send Perkins to the house. We are going to Paige's. Let's go." Both men rode as quickly as they could toward the new business. About five blocks from the store, they heard a blast. Tearing through the streets, they caught the acrid scent of bricks, wood, and plaster burning—the beginning and end of Paige's. Fueled by fear and anxiety, both men headed to what used to be the back of the store.

John was smothering flames and attempting to keep the hot embers at bay. The dogs kept nudging the ladies, forcing them to roll. The limp still figures on the ground were covered with ashes, soot, and dirt. Holes where fabric used to be revealed bloody hands and limbs. Their hair was singed.

"John, get Simmons. Tell him where we are and tell him he is to get here immediately. Anne and Caroline have been seriously injured. Then find Sebastian. He's probably at home. Perkins went to the duke's house. Tell Sebastian to meet us at the duke's. We'll tell the girls when we see them." The terse orders of the general were to be obeyed without question.

On full battle alert, Sar and Berkley went to work making sure the area around the women stayed clear of shooting flames and flying embers. The general felt his life falling apart right before him. Anne had known. He wondered if she might have sensed it would be her this time.

The mournful howl of the dogs sent a chill to his soul. A rage like no other welled up in him. Not a sound came from the lifeless forms. All he could do was hold his beloved. And then, the reality of the moment sank in.

To Berkley, it seemed like forever had passed before he heard the pounding of hooves. *Simmons*, he silently prayed. Sar was still sitting in the same position he had been in for the last twenty or so minutes. He was holding on to Caroline's hand as though willing life into her body.

Before the coach came to a complete stop, Simmons was barking out his own set of orders. "Blankets, good. Hand me the water and the spirits in the coach. Move it." Talking and working at the same time, Simmons examined the women.

"Need to get them to Berkley's house immediately. Don't ask, just do what I say as fast as you can." Her Grace was still bleeding from a cut to the back of her head. Not a good sign. Caroline's leg was clearly broken. Simmons didn't think they would awaken, but he had laudanum prepared just in case.

The urgency of the approaching rider could be heard through the cadence of the beating hooves. Perkins was wildly shouting something from a distance.

"Sar, the house has been blown up. The house . . . the house, it's been destroyed." Leaping off the horse, he looked at Sar and then Berkley. The scene playing out in front of him was worse than the loss of the house. Perkins almost fell to his knees when he saw the women.

"Calm, Perkins. Whatever it is, it can't be that bad."

Perkins looked from Sar to Berkley. Both acted and looked in shock, and not a word was uttered by either. Simmons was talking for them.

Perkins wanted to shake Sar or do anything to get him out of his stupor. "You didn't understand me, Sar. The house has been blown up." There was no sign of recognition in Sar's demeanor. He looked at Berkley. No help there either.

Simmons continued to examine the ladies while explaining some of the effects of trauma to Perkins. "They are not processing what you are saying. I am going to administer some laudanum to both shortly. Seeing the women is worse than the deadliest battle. They'll need something to offset the shock as reality begins to take hold. Let's get everyone to Berkley's house. Everything I need is there. It's the best place to work on the ladies. On the way, you can tell me what I can do to further assist."

With the help of the two coachmen, the women were gently placed in the carriages as Simmons watched over the process. "We will leave it to Daggs to sort this mess out. Perkins, have you sent for Daggs?"

There was no need for Perkins to respond. Daggs and his men were riding toward them.

"Simmons, Perkins, what happened?" The inspector acknowledged Berkley and Sar. One look at their catatonic stances and he realized another death warrant had been issued.

"Only the women know. I must get them to Berkley's now. You'll find us there. Tell Sebastian immediately."

"I will be along as soon as possible. My men are also at Westmoure's house. There will be a heavy price to pay for someone."

Silence was the underlying answer to the inevitable. Simmons nodded in agreement and climbed into the waiting coach.

As the two coaches made their way to the general's house, Simmons tried to stanch the flow of blood from Anne's wound. "You're going to make it, Anne; it's going to be tough for a while, but you will heal. If you don't make it, Berkley will kill everyone in his path. And that son of yours will be right behind him. Don't think I want to be killed twice. Oh, I forgot about those daughters of yours, and Sar's right-hand man Perkins. I won't stand a chance. Have pity on this surgeon." He chuckled at his own thoughts. There was no response, but he believed she heard him locked away in her deep shell of pain.

Halfway to Berkley's house, Simmons stopped the coaches. He checked on Caroline. The sooner he set the leg properly, the better he'd feel. It would take time for both ladies to heal. Thank goodness for that new device called the stethoscope. He listened to their hearts. Yes, they were beating strongly.

Berkley's London residence became a hospital and command center. The day had all but blurred. The women were thoroughly examined. Her Grace had the back of her head shaved and stitched. The bleeding had finally stopped, but she hadn't awakened.

"I created this technique on the battlefield. Broken bones

set straight, when supported, heal faster. Perkins, I will need you to hold everything perfectly taut like this. I'll put the leg in a wooden mold of sorts. Caroline will need a bath chair." Perkins silently did as he was told.

Berkley, Sebastian, and Sar were uncaged lions, waiting for the opportunity to pounce on anyone. Daggs hadn't reported in yet. The girls were sitting with their mothers. Julien and Royce were scurrying back and forth, updating everyone and making sure Simmons had everything he needed. Perkins was back in his usual position—ear pinned to the door.

"Have everyone join us in this study." Daggs kept walking as he talked. Opening the door, he started pacing faster than lava from an erupting volcano. "Waiting for the girls. It's best if everyone hears everything at the same time. My men are still probing through debris, searching for pieces to this ever-widening puzzle."

Berkley was the general once again. The look in his eye pronounced he was on the prowl, and he would get his man. A determined predator was on full alert.

Daggs was about to speak when Simmons popped in to give everyone an update. "Your Grace had a rather deep cut to the scalp. The bleeding has ceased; the gash was cleaned and stitched. There are other cuts and bruises, but not as severe as the head gash, and minor burns. I don't expect any scarring or other problems. Nothing seems to be broken on Anne.

"Caroline's leg is broken. It has been set and placed in a wooden support. From the looks of everything, she fell on Anne and tried to catch herself. They have not come around yet, but I expect that to change within the next twenty-four hours. But for a few minutes of exercise every day, I want both women to remain on bed rest. Caroline will need two strong, burly footmen to help her as she tries to walk a few paces on her good leg. They must always keep the bath chair behind her.

"Does anyone have any questions? I'll be around most of

the time. So do not worry. Please cancel all their engagements. I suggest we partake of Cook's meal as we get the report from Daggs." Everyone adjourned to the dining room.

CHAPTER 14

Picking Up the Pieces

Tonight, Daggs's eating was like his pacing—quick, precise bites—a rhythm all its own. "This is what we know. There were two explosions. Both deliberately set. From the bits and pieces, it appears that Paige's was blown up by someone loosening the wall lights—gas leaks. The escaping gas would eventually collide with the flames or embers in the fireplace. Instant explosion.

"As for the duke's residence, someone left a lot of black powder with the proper detonation as a gift. In the front of the house, there was evidence of a wagon. That was probably how the powder was left and could sit without suspicion. There was no sign of any staff. When the house exploded, everything in its path was blown to smithereens. My deepest condolences. My men are talking to your neighbors. The houses on either side of you were charred. Each had windows broken.

"Sar, my men are taking care of the remains of the footmen. We know how well you take care of your staff; I will go with you to inform their relatives in the morning. Thank goodness Your Grace had given the remainder of the staff the day off. Your household workers are staying with Simmons for the interim and awaiting orders from you."

"Is that all you got, Daggs?" Berkley was barking again.

"Yes, but I was hoping the girls might be able to fill us in. They left the shop right as it was closing." Daggs looked from one to the other, then at Frances. "Think back to who was in the shop, what they were doing, and any names you might remember, and distinguishing features."

The girls looked at each other. Beth chewed her lower lip. Frances shrugged.

"Let's just eat." Daggs tucked into his meal once again.

With assurances that Anne and Caroline would heal, and a lot of wine, everyone relaxed somewhat.

"Yes, that's it. I got it. I got it—measurements. The chest was wrong, too wide, and muscular for a woman, and perfect beautiful auburn hair. The shop girl who came back today and placed the order. Nancy . . . Nancy Smith." The words tumbled from Joycellyn's mouth.

"She was there twice before and very fascinated by everything in the store, especially the gas lighting." Joycellyn was twirling her fork in the air. "I have all the orders in the coach. I was going to take them home and begin work tomorrow."

"Perkins, send someone to the coach. Have the person bring Joycellyn's brown leather work satchel." The order from the general was executed without a word from Perkins. No need. Three minutes later, the work pouch was in Berkley's hands.

"Joycellyn, if you please." With a nod from Berkley, she opened the clasp and spread everything out. In a neat stack were all the orders placed earlier. She handed them to the general.

Keeping them in order, he shuffled through the work

orders and came to one for Nancy Smith. He knew as sure as he was the Duke of Hampton the address didn't exist, nor did the person. He'd send someone to check tomorrow anyway.

"Tell me about her hair. This may be our only real clue."

"It was perfect. What every woman dreamed of. Stunning, each strand glowed with . . ." Joycellyn gasped and stopped. "It was a wig."

"Yes, the woman at Newgate probably wore a wig also." The general nodded in agreement with Joycellyn's observation. They were back to the same Newgate clue, a soft feminine voice and possible wig. "We thought it might possibly be a man in disguise. You took her measurements. Did you notice anything else unusual, heavy hair on the arms, the color?"

Joycellyn thought for a moment. She had taken dozens of measurements as a seamstress. It was second nature to her. She could do them blindfolded. "Oh my goodness. Hand me the work orders." She almost snatched the orders out of his hand. "The person was in disguise. Look, the chest is far too large for such a petite woman, and the waist is off. The person had on a long-sleeved dress."

"Gentlemen, we are looking for a man, but we have no idea what he looks like. Another piece of vital information ripped from us." The general handed everything back to Joycellyn except Nancy Smith's order.

"Joycellyn, do you think you can make two drawings for us? We need a picture of Nancy Smith as she appeared in the shop, and a picture as she would probably look in men's clothing.

"Daggs, one more area for your men to keep under watch. There are places where men who dress as women frequent. Ask around. We might get lucky. Someone may have seen or know Nancy Smith."

After dinner, everyone went to check on the patients. All was the same. They were in a perpetual sleep. The men adjourned to Berkley's study. With their most recent clues, they started shifting the pieces.

"Somewhere in the midst of all this, a woman is involved. As Beth told us, only a woman could be that devious. I am putting Beth's theory to the test—a woman working with a high official in the government. We now know for a fact that only someone with connections at the highest level could be transporting women to Tangier.

"Perkins, summon Samuels in the morning. Have him here by seven. I am sending him to Nancy Smith's residence. Daggs, report here as soon as you get additional information from your men. I have a feeling there are more clues in the fragments of the buildings. We have men from the Home Office, the Foreign Office, and the Yard watching the house. I am ordering everyone to bed. We need some time to assimilate everything and look at every angle." What Berkley wanted to do was to watch over Anne. Trusting Simmons was right, he was willing her to awaken.

"Go to bed, you three. Your rooms are ready. I will watch over Anne and Caroline. All will be well. These aren't the typical ladies of the ton. I'll call you if they open their eyes. Before you start objecting, understand I got this."

Mer, Beth, and Alexius looked as though they would drop on their feet. They stumbled out of the makeshift hospital room.

Kissing Anne on the forehead, Berkley started whispering to his ladylove. "Don't you think this is a rather dramatic way of getting out of marrying someone?" He even laughed to himself. "We are going to have an incredible life, Duchess. However, I do think I shall retire you from government business. Ha, you will do what you want when this mess is over."

He didn't even look up when he felt the air change. The general had trained the man.

"I can't lose her, Berkley. She is my sun, my sparkling stars, the air I breathe, everything I am. Caroline makes me a better person." Sebastian picked up Caroline's hand.

"So, this is what love is really about." Berkley would have to get used to the feeling of someone else holding his essence in the palm of her hand. Could he live like that? What if he couldn't? If so, he wouldn't be a man but an empty shell without depth.

"This is what it is all about." Sebastian lowered his head as tears formed in his eyes.

Once again, Berkley didn't bother to look up. "Sar, I guess it was useless ordering everyone to bed. This is where we belong." The general took a very deep breath. *Love hurts.*

It was Simmons who eventually threw them all out. "I will sit with the women until morning. You aren't good to anyone without sleep. Out! Furthermore, for a lowly earl, I like ordering my betters about—dukes and a marquess. Now go. I am with them."

Berkley patted Duchess, giving her the order to stay *sur ses gardes* and left. Duchess climbed into bed with Anne. Felix snuggled up next to Caroline.

• • •

A sloop silently slipped into the Southampton dock. Waiting was Captain Coomes. The cargo was unloaded and placed on the wagon. Without a word, the wagon left the docks; the skiff returned to Cherbourg.

• • •

In the north of Italy, Sylvia Meacham, the Viscountess of Truvo, read the note again that the messenger had just delivered. *Headquarters for operation being moved to north of Italy. Boss, Jack, or Sam will join you. Former exchequer killed by the half-breed aristocrats. Send your husband back to England. Prepare to stay for a while. More information to follow. Acknowledge receipt.* Sylvia glanced at the husband she despised and decided it was his time to leave this world. She hugged her ever-expanding stomach and wondered what day she would deliver—today, tomorrow, or within the week. As she started to make plans, Sylvia threw the note into the fire and watched it burn.

• • •

Morning came as most mornings do. Before Berkley could start issuing orders, Beth, Sar, and Daggs climbed into an un-marked carriage and headed to the home of Arthur, one of the footmen killed in the explosion.

When Sar had awakened—or was it while he was still sleeping, he couldn't remember—his father had come to him. The words still echoed in his head. *I want you to put five pounds in an envelope and give it to the widow. Pretend that Arthur had been giving this to you for safekeeping from his wages. I am proud that you increased everyone's pay. We have more than enough, Sar. We don't have to be greedy.* Then Avery was gone.

"Daggs, I asked Beth to join us. From observing my mother in situations like this, a woman's comfort is needed." Sar sat on the coach next to Beth.

"Now, what are we going to do for the wife? Mrs. Spencer told me they have a four-month-old baby girl named Clarissa. Arthur's wife's name is Esther. It is going to be especially hard on her."

"I think Mother would approve if we sent them to Ivy Hall. Esther may not want to leave, but we will never know unless we offer. With training, she could become an excellent addi-tion to the staff. The baby would grow in a healthy environ-ment, and of course she would go to school."

"I agree, Sar. That makes sense." Beth was silently chewing on her lower lip while glancing at Daggs. Daggs was staring back.

"Daggs, will your men take care of all of the arrangements as per the widow's wishes?"

The inspector nodded.

Daggs must be at odds with himself. He can't pace. Sar almost laughed. They discussed Keith's family. By the time they reached Arthur's house, they had a plan to offer both widows.

Beth braced herself for Esther's initial response. The door opened, and a woman holding a baby stood in the doorway.

"What has happened?" The whispered words were out of the widow's mouth before Beth could open hers.

"May we come in? It is best if we sit." Without asking, Beth took the most beautiful baby girl she had ever seen from Esther's arms and followed her to the sitting area.

"There has been an explosion, and Arthur was killed."

Esther looked from Beth to Sar, and then to Daggs. Tears ran down her cheeks. Handing the baby to Sar, Beth embraced the mother and let her cry.

From somewhere, a hamper appeared; Sar handed Esther a small glass of brandy.

"What are we going to do? This is all we had. My daughter and I will be on the streets."

"Oh no, we can't let that happen. We have a plan." Explaining the plan took longer than expected. The shock of her husband's death was slowly sinking in. Patiently, Beth spelled out everything again.

Sar gave the baby back to Beth and sat next to the grieving woman. "Arthur was one of my favorites, because he always put his family first. He had been putting a little aside from each pay to save for you and the baby. Here, this is what he had saved."

Absentmindedly, Esther fumbled with the packet just

handed to her. "You would do what you said for me and my baby? You would do that for us? But I am a Negro."

"So are we. Yes, we will do that for you. It is the right thing to do. Arthur would approve." Sar could feel her pain. Life was always different and more difficult when your skin wasn't white.

"My men are taking care of the remains. We are at your service. Please tell us how to proceed." Daggs reached for the baby, pouring love into every rocking motion he made.

"Someone from our staff will be here within the hour to help in any way possible. We will talk about our plan next week. Just let the staff know what you need." Beth led the way out of the house but turned to hug Esther one more time.

Silently, the group made the short trip to Keith's house. The door was opened by a lad of about nine. "Ma, I believe the new duke is here. They all look important."

Petunia rushed to the door, but the minute she saw them, she froze. As if waving back time and wishing them away, she couldn't take another step.

A carrot-top girl grabbed her mother's hand as if sensing something was wrong. Sar led Petunia to the couch. Beth asked for a cold towel. Daggs handed Beth the hamper.

"He's dead, isn't he?" Petunia's face was flushed. Strands of red hair stuck to her cheeks.

Holding her hand, Beth simply said, "Yes."

After explaining everything to the widow and offering as much comfort as possible, they prepared to leave. The knock on the door stopped them. Beth answered, and she was never so happy to see a member of their staff. Susan was followed by someone carrying food.

"Petunia, this is Susan. She will help you in any way possible." Susan took one look at the widow and wrapped her in a warm embrace. As they left, Susan and Petunia were holding each other, crying.

By the time they returned, Berkley's cook had dishes on the sideboard ready and piping hot. A tray was sent to Simmons. One by one, they silently tumbled into the morning room. Quinn appeared.

"So much happened in one day." Beth was chewing on her lower lip, pushing food around her plate. Sar could hear Mer's foot tapping of its own accord.

"In life and war, that is how it usually plays out. There are always twists and turns beyond our immediate control." Berkley wondered what he had done with his life before the Roxburys. He had found Anne, and that was the most important thing. What if he hadn't? *But you did.*

"They are awake." Simmons rushed into the room. The room emptied before the next blink of an eye.

"Did they recognize you?" Berkley was worried. What if Anne's head wound had caused permanent damage?

"I said they were awake. I didn't say they were up walking around as though all things were normal. That will come slowly over time. For now, be thankful that two beautiful ladies have their eyes open. They aren't smiling; they are in pain. The next steps are to make sure they get the best care and are pampered. You understand that, Berkley?"

Simmons was going to get those two well using the old, trusted techniques of medicine along with some of the newer practices that seemed to work. "That's an order, General."

Berkley held up his hands in surrender. He had to see his duchess—had to see for himself. He had almost lost the gift he thought he'd never be given. Funny thing about love: It wasn't one perfect day after another. It was getting through all that mattered together with an unbreakable connection.

When he entered the sickroom, he was suddenly jealous of Duchess. This beautiful wolfhound was sitting next to her mistress and wouldn't let Berkley get any closer than the foot of the bed. "This is what you do to me, girl? I put you *sur ses gardes.* I didn't think that included me." Berkley took another step forward; a low growl erupted from the four-legged beast. Berkley knew he wasn't getting any closer.

"Anne." Berkley's reverent tone was almost like a prayer.

She struggled to answer. The words wouldn't come. "Don't bother. In a few days, your voice will be back." He looked over at Sebastian. It appeared he was having the same problem with Caroline, including a very overprotective dog.

"Anne, it looks like you are going to keep me waiting at the altar a bit longer. None of this is what we had planned. I thought I had lost you. Simmons said both you and Caroline will recover. One day soon, we'll have to talk about this.

"Beth's come-out at Almack's will need to be postponed. I am sending for the ladies and the Dowager Duchess Horton to put everything in order. They will know what to do and how to break the news to the patrons." With that last comment, he snorted. He could have sworn she smiled at that.

"Rest. Simmons has given me very strict orders. He will personally cause my demise if I overtax you." He reached out to squeeze her hand when the low snarl reached his ears. "You know Duchess, the four-legged human, won't let anyone get close to you. My feeling is that she would dismember anyone who tried to touch you or do harm to you. Do you mind calling her off?" Berkley grinned at that thought. *Not a chance that is going to happen.*

• • •

The next day, the men were in the general's study when Daggs burst in like a cyclone. "Daggs, more clues, I presume."

"This is going to take a while. I suggest you ask Cook to bring us an early lunch and we get to it." As soon as Daggs sat, he was up again and pacing.

"We'll start with the business. There wasn't much left

of Paige's. The scraps we found made one thing very clear, someone had tampered with the gas lighting. We were able to examine a few of the fixtures. First, there wasn't a clean break on any of them at the juncture where the gas flows into the fixture. Second, where they did break, everything was similar—too similar. It is one of those coincidences that can't be overlooked. Third, whoever did the job wanted to make sure there were no survivors. We were very lucky this time. If Anne and Caroline hadn't been able to get out of the building, they wouldn't be here today.

"One last very interesting bit. Julien owned the building and the candle shop next door. If he still does, this will make him a prime suspect as a spy." All eyes bored into Julien.

"When I thought I was losing Mer and told her we couldn't marry, for stupid reasons, that was the moment the sun went out of my life." Julien cleared his throat. The mere thought of not having her by his side for life brought pain to his heart and tears to his eyes. "I realized I could not go on without her. That was when it hit me, I loved her, truly and deeply loved her. To prove it, I bought the building, and my solicitor put the title in Mer's name."

Berkley blinked. He knew that feeling. It was what he felt for Anne. At that moment, he realized he was one with Julien and Sebastian. Their women held the power, and the men would move heaven, earth, and all England to please them. The general nodded his head in complete understanding. *Ah, this thing called love.* Of course, Sar, Royce, and Simmons had no idea what they were talking about. From the way Daggs looked at Beth, he might have an inkling.

"What about the duke's residence?" Berkley turned back to the inspector.

"Now, that is equally interesting. We interviewed the neighbors. Shortly before the explosion, a wagon pulled up in front of the house. A worker leapt off, waved at the footmen, and went around to the back of the house. Your neighbors never saw him again. The approximate area where the wagon was parked is deeply burned and charred. This indicates the origin of the explosives.

"I have squashed as much of the details and information as I could. The editor of the *London Daily* will put the item in the back. But watch out for the Society News."

As they took all their clues, tossed them around, and put them together again, their theories went from the obvious, practical, and logical, to the absurd. They realized that somewhere on the continuum was the answer.

The knock on the door was met with one clipped word: "Enter."

Samuels rushed in. "General, am I at liberty to speak?" Berkley waved his hand.

"I found Nancy Smith at the address, but there is something not quite right. Sir, she is blind and four years old."

"Thanks, Samuels. I didn't think you would even find that. Take this message to the prime minister and then report back here. This is your permanent post until otherwise instructed."

As Samuels left, Berkley heard the sounds of female voices. "The ladies have arrived. Perkins, ask them to join us." Without hearing so much as a *yes, my lord*, Berkley understood his order was being carried out precisely.

The Dowager Duchess Horton led the way, followed by Evelyn, Aurelia, Georgina, Diana, and Miriam. "Hot damn, ladies; this is serious. We've been invited into the inner sanctum. Where are Anne and Caroline?" Lady Hortense Horton suspiciously eyed the general.

Berkley started explaining what had happened. Somewhere along the line, Daggs took over, and then Sar. Six of the elite of the ton sat there with their mouths wide open, and not a sound was uttered.

"From now on, wherever you go, you will be followed by

men from one of our offices. We cannot allow any harm to come to you. Cancel all engagements, giving out only the barest of information. Good luck with the patrons of Almack's and Beth's come-out. We are keeping as much information as possible out of the newssheets. The Society News may have a blow-by-blow description. My wedding to Anne will take place as soon as she is strong enough. We will inform you." Berkley was at war again, issuing orders like retorts—short staccato sentences to be carried out without questions.

"I suggest you use this house as your planning center. My housekeeper has cleared my late mother's study. Ask for anything you need to make it more comfortable. My staff hasn't had this many people to care for in about three decades. Let them indulge you."

Perkins cleared his throat. "Luncheon is served."

• • •

The slow procession of carriages that rode past where the Westmoures' residence used to be was bigger today than yesterday. At any one time, the parade of strollers topped that of those trying to be seen at the Serpentine in Hyde Park. The address where the building once stood had been dubbed "Westmoure's Hole." Speculation was rampant and suspicious. Theories as to why the building had exploded ranged from the duke's involvement in drugs and smuggling, to the maintaining of the highest standards of society—that is, keeping the elite pure—to the king wanting the property for his next mistress. There were a half dozen or so additional ideas floated about. Westmoure's Hole became the place to be seen and heard.

CHAPTER 15

It's All About the Westmoures

The next afternoon, the patrons of Almack's arrived at the Duke of Hampton's residence. Their message from the Dowager Duchess Horton stated it was most urgent they speak. Led by Lady Sarah Jersey, they arrived at exactly one o'clock.

When they entered the receiving room, they were greeted by Evelyn, Aurelia, Georgina, Diana, and Miriam. Duchess Horton stood in the center of the room as overbearing and lofty as ever. The patrons were waiting for any information to add to the grist of the gossip mill. There wasn't a male in sight.

"Lady Jersey, thank you for coming. So much has taken place in the past couple of days, it just won't be possible to hold Beth's come-out as planned. It would be too much for the duchess and her family." The dowager duchess patted Sarah's hand. "I know you understand. Just think of having to replace everything you owned."

Miriam didn't let Lady Jersey get a word in edgewise. "Cook has prepared a special lunch for us, if you care to partake."

Evelyn, Aurelia, Georgina, and Diana, along with the staff, had worked their magic. Using only that china and silverware reserved for royal occasions, they ensured the formal dining room glittered and sparkled, further accented by the gold, gem-encrusted place settings and matching glasses. Showing Sarah Jersey to her seat, Aurelia reminded her that this was where the king sat when he came to dinner.

That was all it took. "Yes, this is his favorite seat. As you know there is always so much for the two of them to discuss. He was looking forward to surprising you at Beth's come-out."

Lady Sarah Jersey preened. "Yes, dear, we know how difficult this must be for all of you. We would have welcomed the king to our humble gathering."

Diana coughed to keep from laughing. "You and the patrons of Almack's have always been some of his favorites. You provide a wonderful service for the aristocracy."

"Yes, His Majesty mentioned that when we were at Ivy Hall. We always try to be of service to the Crown, doing our own bit in our own way." Lady Anne Stewart, Marchioness of Londonderry, nodded to the other patrons as she spoke. All the talk during lunch was about the king.

"Do send a message if you need anything. We are here to assist. Don't forget, if you need our assistance with anything at all, please let us know." Very pleased with herself, Lady Sarah and the remainder of the patrons marched out thoroughly pleased with themselves and returned to their lair to discuss what had just happened.

"I can't believe that. They didn't even ask about Anne and Caroline." Evelyn shook her head at the pettiness. "And to think they want to be involved with us. That would be like telling the world what we are doing."

"Oh, keeping them from asking about Anne and Caroline

was part of the strategy." The dowager duchess nodded in agreement. Georgina continued. "They came for information about Anne and Caroline. However, when the talk turned to the king, any information they were able to glean about him was much more important. All they know about Anne and Caroline is that they are alive. Sooner or later, they will begin to question why we are all at the Duke of Hampton's house."

"Remember the world we live in. It is always about showing off or having the upper hand. It's never about substance." Miriam recognized there would be a tiny entry in the society page of the newssheet about the king and his doings with enough information to pique the interest of those really in the know. She also understood that the patrons would hold what they had heard and learned today over the heads of everyone else.

• • •

On the other side of town, the men were in the private office of Daggs. "The captain of the ship detoured to Cherbourg, claiming a problem with the ship. He gave the men the night off and personally unloaded this pallet that wasn't on the original manifest. Two days later, the captain was en route to his original destination, Amsterdam. He thought it would be best to circumvent any question that he knew about the cargo. Here is his report." Captain Coomes handed the report to Berkley. Bella was already whining.

"She's telling us something." Jacob petted the animal's fur.

"Let's see what little gift we have now." Berkley ordered Julien and Royce to the back of the pallet. The rest started dismantling the front.

"As usual, they look like ordinary statues one would find in any working-class home. Shall we see what they hold? Bella, do you want first sniff?" Quinn held the statue out to her. Bella quickly tried to bat the pottery from his hand. "You're right, Jacob; she definitely does not like drugs."

"This is outrageous. There is at least four times the amount of opium in this shipment than the other shipments. I wonder just how much opium is really leaving the country through illegal means." Berkley was dusting the powder from his jacket. "Find anything, Julien, Royce?"

"Not a thing" was the answer.

"It's just as I thought. Opium is shipped out more frequently than documents. Coomes, have the captain of the ship report directly to me upon his return to Southampton. Daggs, have your men take over here. They are to let no one near this office. We will get everything moved before dawn tomorrow. Gentlemen, let's adjourn to my house." Berkley was halfway to his horse as he finished giving orders. He had to see Anne. His life would be nothing without her.

• • •

In the other fashionable house in Mayfair, the little red book showed two more deaths, but it wasn't the two people intended. *What is wrong with the plans? They should have worked.* Next time, more deadly and more accurate.

• • •

After checking on Anne, Berkley went to find the dowager duchess and ladies. They were with the other men. When they told them how they diverted the patrons of Almack's, Berkley threw back his head and laughed. "You mean to tell me they didn't ask one question about Anne and Caroline? They didn't even inquire about their health?"

"No, they were too busy being envious of Lady Sarah sitting

in the chair the king normally sits in when he dines with you. By the way, which chair does the king sit in?" Hortense was just as curious as the other ladies.

"Wherever he chooses to sit. That usually depends on where the prettiest woman in the room is sitting with the lowest-cut dress." *Yes,* Berkley thought to himself, *that is the way my cousin the king operates.*

• • •

That evening, Kiggins, the lifelong housekeeper of the dowager duchess, helped her employer to bed. The lady of the house was very tired. "Would you care for a glass of brandy to put you to sleep?"

"That would be perfect." She felt every one of her sixty-eight years. When Kiggins returned, Hortense was fast asleep with a smile on her face.

You did well, my love. It was delightful how you manipulated the patrons of Almack's. Ingenious tactic. Your time has not come yet; however, you will have to let Anne, Sar, Berkley, and the rest of the group know. Parliament and the king must be apprised of the situation. My solicitors have the original documents. You have a copy. There is the distribution of your substantial dowry and inheritance from your mother. You're being watched over by many. I love you, and I will come for you when the time is right. Sleep well, my love. Know that I am always by your side. Again, please accept my apology.

"Wake up, my lady. It's half past. The Duke of Hampton is sending his coach to collect you." The maid looked perplexed. The dowager duchess had the biggest smile on her face she had ever seen.

"Thank you; I'm awake. A bath please. The new blue dress will do nicely for the day." Even the steel-gray sky spitting rain could not dampen her spirits. She felt alive. Sterling had stayed with her all night. Of course, he was right. The world needed to know. *That will give the gossip mill something else to chew on.*

• • •

The Duke of Grayson appeared at Berkley's house before Cook had even laid out the morning meal. He had rushed back to town the moment he heard about the explosion.

"How is she?"

"Morning, Grayson. Caroline is better. Your daughter is going to be just fine. They opened their eyes three days ago. A little rest, pampering, and an overbearing Simmons were all they needed. Eat with me. I will try to answer your questions."

"I feel as though I am responsible for the explosion. I came up with the concept of ready-made dresses—an innovative way to help women who were working and were not supplied livery by their employers. Really, I thought it was a way to take one more chore away from a busy woman. Give her more time for herself or other things."

"The world is changing, Grayson, and ideas like yours are part of the change. You were not responsible for this blast. As we continue to try to get to the bottom of this craziness surrounding the Roxburys, your thoughts and theories are welcomed." The general realized a long time ago that fresh eyes may have insights overlooked by others.

By the time the ladies arrived, Perkins had the newssheet opened to the Society News. The article was longer than usual. It was all about the Westmoures.

"Our job is to deflect as much as we can. The Westmoures are the talk of the town. We'll have to be clever about this. Don't forget Anne's upcoming wedding. I shudder to think what will be put in print then." Hortense sipped on a perfect cup of tea. "Beth, will you please read the article?"

As Beth read, the ladies gasped. The column laid out in detail exactly what had happened down to the point that Anne and Caroline had been in Paige's at the time of the explosion.

The London Daily

Society News

Dear reader, it is safe to say that the uncivilized half-breed Americans were also involved in Paige's. According to what I have learned, the Duchess of Westmoure and Marchioness of Broadhurst were both in the building at the time of the explosion. They were the only two in the building. Are they still alive? No one has seen them since. If anyone knows of their whereabouts, please let us know.

"Well, at least the ton doesn't know where they are or whether or not they are alive. Just imagine if society knew. We would be bombarded day in and day out. Let's not think about the danger." Aurelia thought of all the precautions the men had taken since the explosions. She couldn't step out of her house without being followed by Berkley's men. On top of that, she was escorted by six outriders.

"We have our work cut out for us. Two deadly explosions and a killer or killers on the loose. Who wants more shooting lessons?" Every hand raised in answer to the question posed by the dowager duchess.

As Beth continued reading, it was clear to all there was a spy or spies within their midst. But who and why? Beth didn't get much further when the men joined them. Well, no one could say *joined* was the correct word. It was more like a charging calvary ready for action.

Berkley was barking out orders. "Joycellyn, you will work at Cummings from now on also."

"There are to be no walks in the park, drive-bys of the house, or trips to Gunther's. If you cannot live without an ice from Gunther's, we'll figure out a way to bring one here or one for each of you. Whatever is needed, make a list; one of our men will do the shopping." Before anyone could comment, the general continued. "Must keep all of you safe.

"In light of what has happened, we are asking all of you to move to this house for the time being. We know it is a major disruption, but this allows us to watch over you and everything else more closely. Are there any questions?"

Not waiting for a reply, Berkley continued, "Underbutlers, servants, and maids have been assigned to you to make this transition easier. They are all from one of our offices and highly trained and skilled. You will be moved by tomorrow. No, your senior and most important staff will not be merged with the staff here, except for Kiggins and Seymour." With that last edict, the general and his men turned and left.

The dowager duchess didn't blink an eye. "Ah, the usual Berkley. Exerting total control. Well, ladies, he doesn't take 'no' for an answer. Let's have Perkins send for messengers so we can tell our staff what to gather. Let everyone know you will be at a house party in the country. That will divert all attention as to our whereabouts. Might as well make the best of this. Besides, we have a wedding to plan."

She had just finished speaking when there was a discreet knock on the door. "Enter."

"Whenever you are ready, the messengers are waiting." Just as quickly as he entered, Perkins disappeared into thin air.

The ladies joined Anne and Caroline in the makeshift hospital for their daily update. "Berkley was in fine form this morning. He ordered us about as if we were some of his troops." The *huff* that followed from Aurelia spoke volumes. "It's almost as though we are prisoners."

Anne smiled and sighed. "But you are, and this is his jail. Now, let's get on with the planning of my wedding. If Caroline and I don't do something, we will go stark raving mad."

With their thoughts shifted for the moment, the ladies started planning Anne's wedding and wishing her the best of luck living with a man like Berkley. Anne laughed as though she had a secret.

For the rest of the week, Anne's wedding kept the ladies busy. The girls were working through the logistics of Cummings. Joycellyn's staff had finished the ready-made dresses. All dresses had been delivered and accounts settled except for Nancy Smith. The finishing touches were put on Anne's wedding dress. Her trousseau had been completed.

• • •

In the former colonies, Jack was reviewing his plan to return to England. It would take him about a year to get the plans in order. Then he would be on his way home. America was an uncivilized place. In reality, the streets were mudholes; makeshift buildings leaning from one side to the other were the scenic view. News was late, dinner was late, and it took forever to get a message to anyone. In disguise and without drawing attention to himself, he walked the streets of Boston. He was pleased with the plan so far. Thank goodness he had gotten rid of Brian O'Keefe. No one would ever know about the fake attack and amnesia. The plan had been seamless. With O'Keefe dead, there was no trace and no link.

• • •

Quinn was in Berkley's office. They were reviewing everything they had on the matter involving the Roxburys before the meeting with the prime minster. The knock on the door had them both wondering if someone had overheard their thoughts. "Enter!" Berkley all but growled.

"Sorry to disrupt you, Hampton, Quinn." His cousin Henry, the one who would inherit the dukedom, stood at the door. "In town again for more shopping. Women. Your cousin, my oldest daughter, is engaged. Do you have any idea where I can find the best seamstress in town?" Henry looked puzzled and perplexed.

"Sure, but I don't think she is available. There is Madame Burgoff, but from what I understand, she is not taking any new clients. She is excellent. I will ask the other seamstress if she is available. Where are you staying so I can get word to you?" Berkley didn't think Joycellyn was available, but he'd ask.

"We're staying with the future in-laws, the Earl and Countess of Lexington. With all this hoopla about the wedding, I was hoping I could find someone sane to stay with, but Lexington insisted we stay with them." All three men laughed.

• • •

"Anne, my household staff is as happy as it has been in years with all these people about. I didn't realize how much I had been missing by being a bachelor who was devoted to his work." Berkley was holding Anne's hand in the room she and Caroline had been sharing since the explosion. Duchess sat next to her mistress with her mouth open and tongue hanging out, watching the general. He knew the wolfhound had not let down her guard and wouldn't allow Berkley to get much closer. Anne was to be protected.

"I am feeling much better. I think the daily walks Caroline

and I take have helped tremendously. Can we marry three weeks from today?"

For the first time in over a week, the general had something to smile about. "I shall make all the arrangements with the archbishop. The ladies will take care of everything else." Today, Berkley didn't seem to mind the overbearing presence of the furry watchdog.

Once the general informed the ladies about the date of the wedding, the house seemed to spin with a magical energy. Even though the only ones present would be the group currently living in the house, say the word *wedding*, and all hearts were aflutter. Thinking of her own wedding, Hortense smiled and cried at the same time. *You have to tell them, my love. Life moves along rather quickly. One day you are a babe, and the next day you are facing your mortal demise. Within the week . . . that might be a perfect time. Have my solicitor come. He will help to make everything clear. I'm here, my love, waiting for you.*

"Is there something wrong?" Anne looked at the dowager duchess.

"No, I'm fine, but I am not fine. Oh, it is such a muddle. Do you think I could get a messenger?" Hortense knew if she was going to tell her secret, now was the right time.

"Don't worry. Perkins heard you. A messenger will be here shortly." Anne went back to her musings about her wedding, thinking nothing more about the dowager duchess.

That night, for the first time since the explosion, Anne and Caroline ate dinner with the others. To Anne, it was like the first time being allowed to eat dinner with the grown-ups. Halfway through the meal, Anne suddenly stood up and hurried as fast as she could to the nearest dustbin. The mood of their dinner went from merriment to the somber reawakening of impending death. Cold towels were applied to her clammy brow.

Once again, she found herself swept up in the arms of Berkley, who headed straight to the makeshift hospital room. He was followed by Sar and the rest of the group.

"You know I do enjoy being in your arms, but we have to stop doing it like this." Anne struggled to laugh and make light of the undeniable signal—death looming near.

Anne was tucked into her bed with the men fussing around her and the women standing back watching.

"Thank goodness we don't depend on men to soothe our aching brows. Look at what they are doing." Lady Horton added a "*tsk, tsk, tsk.*" One of Anne's legs was on the bed, the other was hanging over the side. Even though she was fully clothed with shoes on, the men were trying to tuck her in.

"Out, all of you except the ladies. You are going to make us sick just observing you." The dowager duchess spoke in her most authoritative voice. The men scattered like autumn leaves that had fallen to the ground, blown by a strong wind.

"Anne, what can I do? What do you need? Should I ring for your maid and sherry?" It was clear these spells of foretelling death were having an effect on her. She was pale, her hands were shaking as though she was having a fit, and her beautiful brown eyes were glazed and tearful.

"Nothing, Caroline, nothing. I am so glad you and Duchess will be with me all night." As if on cue, the four-legged beast jumped onto the bed and snuggled next to her mistress.

"Amazing animal. She was growling at Berkley until I told her it was all right. Even the general must keep a distance when she senses I am in trouble or that something is wrong." Anne looked over at Caroline's bed. Waiting patiently was Felix. "What did we ever do without them?" Both women smiled that look of understanding, when Simmons walked in and ordered them both to sleep.

After checking his patients, Simmons went to find Sar and Berkley. As usual, they were holed up in the study. "Need to talk to you both for a minute. I feel it is necessary to have Anne checked by a specialist. The blow to her head was not a light tap. It would make me feel better if he examined her."

"Just get her well. Whatever needs to be done, let's do it." Sar was in full agreement with Berkley. "We need her, Simmons, just as we need the air we breathe."

The general's statement caught Simmons off guard. Berkley was in love. Simmons was whistling when he left the study.

•　•　•

In Florence, Sylvia Meacham read the contract granting Severson Westmoure Shipping and the agreement written to her by Severson and approved by the attorneys. *Upon the demise of the current Westmoure Shipping, Severson is to be offered the shipping company at the price of two hundred million pounds. Due to the illegality of the Duke of Westmoure's involvement in smuggling and espionage, trafficking of women, and treasonous activities, the current duke will be hanged as so determined by the court.*

Then Sylvia's favorite part—*In the event something should happen to the Earl of Severson before the sale of Westmoure Shipping Company occurs, the shipping company is to be sold to Sylvia Meacham for the above amount stated. This is in consideration for her invaluable service in discovering the illegal activities of the current Duke of Westmoure.*

There was additional legal verbiage. The document was signed and pressed with Severson's seal and witnessed by the solicitor's clerk. His and her solicitors had made sure the transaction and agreement could and would withstand legal scrutiny, and the proper government officials had agreed to the sale.

Sylvia let out a sigh. She'd own the largest shipping company in the world. Feeling almost giddy, she dressed to take a stroll with her soon-to-be former husband. *Now to get rid of him and start the legal proceedings against Westmoure.*

• • •

The men were in the study trying to piece together the mystery of opium, espionage, and trafficking of women. They had put their men on every Westmoure ship and had men waiting at every port. If women or extra pallets that were not on the manifest appeared, the ship was to detour to a docking point in the opposite direction of the original port of call. Just as during the war, sloops would carry the extra cargo or women to England in the dead of the night.

Anne and Caroline were healing well. But for Anne's queasiness from her premonition, she appeared to be in good health. Work on Cummings continued. Caroline received frequent reports from Harson's.

"It's a good thing I started Harson's when I did. We have businesses asking for our students who have graduated." Caroline was filling in the dowager duchess about the school. "It is a different and new concept for women to be able to do accounting and business management and also to run an office. In the beginning, when I started this training school in honor of my mother, I didn't think we would ever be able to place our students. With the help of my father, we now have more positions than students.

"In order to graduate, the student must complete two years of classroom training and a one-year apprenticeship in an office that conducts business in the same field in which the student is interested. We make sure they are as prepared as possible. As you can imagine, many men won't recognize the competency of a woman. With the help of Grayson, we are able to get them the same salary as men who are doing equivalent work."

"Amazing. When I heard about the school, I was more than delighted. You're right about most men. They believe a woman's role is to make a man's every wish and dream come true. Good work, Caroline. After a tour of the school, I will help in any way I can. There are also several businesses I would like to see shaken to the core with the employment of women, especially those owned by my family." The dowager's mischievous glint was in her eyes.

Not far away, Westmoure's Hole was still the sight people clamored to see. The architects had a tough time surveying the land and coming up with a new design for the current duke. Every time they attempted to work, someone would wander by to ask questions about the explosion and the house to be built.

However, the big delay came when Roman artifacts were discovered in one of the holes blown open by the explosion. Then, the Royal Academy became involved. Everything came to a screeching halt as the artifacts were carefully unearthed. It seemed as though everyone wanted something from the Westmoures.

For the remainder of the week, Anne was too sick to move from her bed. The specialist, Dr. Langley, examined Anne. He concurred with Simmons. "Bed rest as you have been doing, good food, and a lot of laughter. Make sure she walks every day. Don't let her worry about anything. Let's see how things go, and next week, we need to sit down with her son or the duke. She must do everything we request."

"Agreed, Langley, agreed. This family keeps me on my toes." Simmons was thanking his lucky stars that the Roxburys had come along. Taking care of this family and Berkley's operatives was more exciting than being on the battlefield.

• • •

On the docks in warehouse number two, pallets and pallets

of opium-filled statues sat. Boss, dressed as a common laborer, inspected everything. She had thought about killing Sam today, but not yet. He was the big boss. The one with the power, the connections, and a thin blanket of integrity. But she would have to wait. She needed to kill that upstart Sylvia Meacham first.

That should be easy. The new headquarters for the operation were in Florence, Italy. Sylvia's current home. Once Sylvia was out of the way, she would eliminate Sam. Then she would own Westmoure's and run the operation with Jack. Boss turned, locked the door, and climbed into her work wagon to blend seamlessly into the crowds.

• • •

"Caroline, I feel like dancing. It is as though a burden has been lifted off my shoulders. I am famished." Anne was carefully attempting to climb out of bed to reach for her robe.

"You should be. You barely ate the last few days. A raid on the kitchen is the first order of business. Are you sure you are all right?" Caroline looked Anne over. But for the bandage on the back of her head, she looked great.

"Never felt better. I feel like a bride for the first time."

Both women laughed. They knocked on Berkley's and Sebastian's bedchamber doors. The two burly footmen walked beside Caroline, supporting either arm. Another was right behind her with a bath chair.

The kitchen was like a pirate's find. Food appeared from all directions. "You realize what this means, Anne—someone is not going to die."

"I didn't think of it, but you are probably right. More to celebrate. Plus, I will be a bride in two weeks." Anne hadn't felt this light and happy in months. She looked at Berkley—really looked at him. She knew he was the one, and her heart over-flowed with love, and every other emotion of ecstasy sang through her very essence.

In the makeshift hospital room, Anne and Caroline were trying to get into proper, clean nightclothes and into the bed before Simmons found them. Three burly footmen could barely stand on their feet; they were stuffed to the gills. All the two ladies could do was laugh. As soon as their heads hit their pillows, they sank into a deep sleep; Quinn's pounding on the front door did not wake them.

When Cook looked at her kitchen, she cried and then laughed. That morning, with his head resting next to a bowl of trifle, the Duke of Hampton snored peacefully. Sebastian was sleeping with his elbow on the table and his hand supporting his head. There wasn't a spot in the kitchen that wasn't covered with food or double-clotted cream.

Quinn found Berkley and Sebastian in the kitchen. "Strange bed."

"Would you care for something to eat?" Sebastian's expansive arm swept over the food. He didn't realize they had an audience. Cook was laughing; the other kitchen workers were all smiles. The general and Sebastian looked like they had slept in their clothes for the past week.

"Coffee, Cook, please. In my study. We are not to be disturbed. When breakfast is ready, bring that also." The Duke of Hampton was in complete charge again.

Quinn put his gloves in their usual place on the side table and sat to enjoy Cook's special blend of coffee. "By chance, one of our operatives came across a warehouse. It appears it is being used by those smuggling opium. A closer look turned up pallets and pallets of ordinary statues. If we could get one of the drug-sniffing dogs close, we might have our answer."

"Perkins, get Sar. We will need Bella and Jacob as well.

Have them come down at once. Tell them to be ready to leave." The general excused himself to change clothes. Sebastian was one beat ahead of him.

By the time they reached the warehouse, it was empty. But evidence lay everywhere. Bella wouldn't stop whining. The floor had spots of white powder here and there. Fresh footprints with wet mud indicated the smugglers had been there within the last hour or so.

"Find out who rents this warehouse. Get a dozen of our men here. They are to work in twos. Have them scour the area. We'll have the men from my office go over the warehouse thoroughly. Daggs, send your men to the docks. See if anyone is loading pallets. If so, get the names of the ship, the owner of the ship, and where they are sailing from the harbor master. Quinn, anything else?" The general was in fine form issuing orders.

"Look around carefully and surreptitiously. Commit to memory the description of anyone who looks suspicious or is a little too interested in the loading of pallets. Do not follow anyone just yet." Quinn was worried. He hoped this tactic worked.

• • •

The general read the note, and then he read the note again. The scrawl of Daggs's writing was unmistakable. The warehouse hadn't been leased in years.

CHAPTER 16

Surprise, Surprise, Surprise

Anne was getting stronger by the day. Caroline was lumbering along quite well, and the burly footmen were used to her habits. Every day the two ladies took a walk. Each day, they increased the distance by thirty paces. Life was moving along. The plans for the Westmoures' new house were just a mirage. The Royal Academy was enjoying every moment in the limelight they could wrench from the findings.

"So, they don't realize?" The general shook his head in astonishment.

Jacob, Sar, Julien, Royce, Jay, and Daggs had delivered five pallets of drug-filled statues to the private office. "No, it appears not," Jacob said. "They were aware something was amiss when the pallets sent on the Westmoure ships never arrived at their destinations. In their wisdom, they decided to use another shipping company. They chose the Avery Jacob Shipping Company. They aren't aware that this business is also owned by the Duke of Westmoure."

"Tell me once again how you came across these goods." Berkley wanted to make sure he wasn't overlooking anything.

"Last night, Bella and I were working late. We have a ship leaving at first tide, and I wanted to double-check everything. On occasion, Bella and I do this. I grabbed the manifest and checked the cargo. In the middle were five pallets not on the manifest. I sent a message to Sar and started unloading the pallets myself. Sar arrived with Perkins, Julien, Royce, Jay, and Daggs. Daggs suggested we bring everything here."

"Anything else?" Now Berkley was pacing along with Daggs.

"No. There they are." Jacob pointed to the five pallets sitting in the middle of the room. Bella wouldn't stop whining. "Shall we?"

They all knew what they would find, and they did. The gravity of the situation had reached new heights.

"Royce, send signals to the ship, putting it on high alert. Tell them to be prepared for an attack. That will get them battle ready. Hopefully this will circumvent any murder of the crew. Guard all cargo with extreme caution." The general was snapping out orders.

Berkley continued. "Jacob, are any of the men from Daggs's office on the ship?" They could hear the air crackling as Jacob checked the roster. He shook his head.

"They are not expecting us to know. Put our men on every ship you have leaving from now on. They know what to look for. Do we have any idea how long this has been going on?" Including Berkley, they all knew that would almost be impossible to determine.

"Let's look at it this way. The opium stopped appearing on the Westmoure ships after we confiscated that last set of pallets. They might have started using other ships then. Don't forget we still have a separate office for Avery Jacob Shipping." Sar looked at Jacob to see if he had any thoughts.

"I think Sar is right. Besides, that is the logical conclusion." Jacob took time out from petting Bella to add his thoughts.

"Jacob, gather the captains of all the ships that have sailed since then. Let's see what the captains knew or suspected. I'll send for Quinn; we will meet at my house for lunch." Berkley was in his battlefield mood. As he climbed onto his horse, he spoke to Sar. "Don't let me forget to pick up your mother's wedding present." The only thing Sar could do was grin.

Berkley was worried. He hadn't spent time wooing Anne. He hadn't thought she'd like flowers when the gardens surrounding the house could fill at least three dozen floral shops. With everyone at the house, he barely had time to steal a kiss. *Tonight, I think I had better change that.*

At dinner that night, the dowager duchess asked everyone to join her in the sitting room. There was something of utmost importance to discuss. Everyone at the table looked from one to the other to see if anyone had an inkling as to what this was all about. No one, including Perkins, had a clue.

After dinner, they gathered in the blue room, where three other gentlemen sat. No one knew them except the dowager duchess.

"There is no way to say this, so I had just better come out and say it. Right before the old duke died, we married." Hortense was gripping the hand of Kiggins. Waves of silence reverberated throughout the room until one of the solicitors cleared his throat.

"John Smythe, of Smythe and Sons, solicitors for the late Sterling Adam Roxbury," one of the gentlemen began. "We have the original wedding certificate and all the other necessary documents to prove the validity of the wedding. Before the duke and duchess married, Her Grace also became our client. There are matters of significance to discuss, and the king and Parliament must be notified, as is the requirement of the law. Due to the lateness of the hour, I suggest we meet here at ten in the morning."

During this entire time, no one else had uttered a word. "That will be fine, John. Perkins will see you out. I am sure my family has many questions to ask." The dowager duchess had to face them sooner or later, so now was the right time.

Go on, Hortense, talk to them. They are like this when someone shocks the living daylights out of them. Trust me, love. All will be well. These are the relatives I am proud to call my own. Sterling was gone with his whisper.

Inhaling deeply, Hortense looked around as though searching for the old duke. "After our former spouses died, we met at various social functions. There was a mad attraction between the two of us. One day, we just started talking. We talked for hours on end and every day thereafter. Realizing we had something very special alarmed us both. The question was what to do." The dowager duchess shifted in her seat.

"We were older, and we weren't two frivolous people looking for an affair, but for the love we had missed in our marriages. If you did not know, my marriage was a litany of one bad moment after another. I had to suffer through it for propriety's sake. My first husband and I married for all the usual reasons—an alliance, appropriate connections, and the merger of two wealthy empires. There was no mention of love, and there was none. After years of living on the periphery of life and happiness, Sterling and I decided to see if what we had was really love everlasting.

"That is why I know so much about the American Roxburys and some of the duke's business. I was privy to the letters Avery wrote to Sterling. The old duke and I talked about everything. Sar, your uncle Sterling told your father about the marriage. Sterling also said to me if I ever needed anything or was in any type of situation I could not handle, to contact Avery. Whatever it was, your father would take care of it.

"The few years we had flew by. Sterling realized he was sick. The physicians told him to make sure his affairs were in order. The only thing on his list that he had not taken care of was to make me his wife."

Hortense tried to stop the flow of tears. She needed Sterling now more than ever. Mer crossed the room and sat on the other side of the dowager duchess and put her hand over the beautiful ring that adorned the dowager's veined hand.

"He sent me a note, saying we would marry the next day at two at my house. All the arrangements had been made with the archbishop, and everyone was pledged to secrecy. His solicitor and clerk were the witnesses. He slipped the ring on my finger during the ceremony. This is the ring Mer asked me about as we prepared for her wedding." She held up her trembling hands. "The next day, he went home to die."

There wasn't a dry eye in the room. No one had anything to say. Tears were the unspoken words.

"There is much more, but I will leave that to the solicitors. If you would, I want you to accept me as part of your family. You had to know about this before anything else occurred. I am not getting any younger, and I need you. You bring light, joy, and love into my life. I have a substantial inheritance I am leaving to Anne, Mer, and Beth if that is acceptable."

As if on cue, the parlor door opened. With Perkins leading the charge, champagne, spirits, and food were brought in. "Congratulations, Your Grace." He bowed to the dowager duchess. His few short words seemed to snap everyone out of a daze.

Berkley was the first to stand. "Well done, Your Grace, well done." For the remainder of the evening, it was as though a wedding reception were taking place, and no one had a care in the world.

At precisely five minutes to ten the following morning, John Smythe and several other solicitors and clerks were sitting in the morning room of the Duke of Hampton's house. Also present was the enraged son of the dowager duchess, the current Duke of Horton.

To everyone's surprise, the Duke of Horton spoke first. "As usual, my mother is up to her insane antics. My solicitors will review all the documentation because this cannot be a legal union. Wrong, wrong, wrong."

While the Duke of Horton was pontificating, the door to the room quietly opened, and the archbishop stepped in. All eyes turned to him. "I can assure you that this union was legally solemnized before the Church in a manner befitting a duke. Sterling Roxbury was of sound mind, as was your mother. The solicitor was present at the ceremony and witnessed the entire proceeding. Here is the document with my signature affixed attesting to the validity of the wedding." He turned to Hortense. "I am sorry, Your Grace, if this has upset you in any manner." The dowager duchess just nodded her head.

For a timid-looking little man, John Smythe was very passionate about the law. He commanded the center of attention for the next hour. "As I stated, here are all the original documents for your inspection, to present to the king and Parliament. Having spoken to both Sterling Roxbury and his bride-to-be before the service, I determined that both were of sound mind. To the best of my recollection, the marriage was one of two people who had found their way to each other and were in love. Their commitment was sincere and honest."

"She cannot leave that amount of money to strangers. I am her son, her only son."

"According to the paperwork we have brought with us in case this question arose, the property and funds your mother is bequeathing to Anne, Meredith, and Elizabeth Roxbury are hers to do with as she pleases. This is her inheritance left to her and her alone." John Smythe was handed a stack of papers by his clerk.

"Also, I might not have mentioned this, but there is a gift for Kiggins, her lifelong companion, and a gift for Harson's, a school to educate women in areas of business."

Caroline gasped.

"If you want to review your mother's paperwork, please do so. We have it here. I do not expect the men handling your affairs to find anything amiss." John Smythe eyed the Duke of Horton without expression.

"You shall hear from my solicitors." The Duke of Horton rose and left.

"Our firm expected a challenge to this proceeding and the bequeathing of the funds of the dowager duchess. We have taken all precautions in handling this matter. From the reaction of her son, you can imagine that the amount is substantial. There are several million pounds at stake. To make things clearer as to the gifts to Kiggins and Harson's, they are also quite large. Are there any questions?" John Smythe looked around the room.

"Well done, John. Well done. This is what you warned me and Sterling of." The dowager duchess was smiling and crying. "Please forgive my son. He has ample to live on for at least three lifetimes. I wanted to make sure of that before I formalized my last requests."

The archbishop stood up and, in his most austere voice, asked when lunch was. As usual, in the manner of a household in which Perkins was a part of the door, he announced lunch.

Six days later, the archbishop stood in the middle of the same room and married Anne Roxbury, the Duchess of Westmoure, to the Duke of Hampton in the presence of the king. Hortense Roxbury just beamed. *Thank you, Sterling.* The quick reply was all the assurance she needed. *I love you, my dear, beyond eternity.*

The six days before the wedding had been a whirlwind of legalities. First, the king and Parliament were advised of the wedding between Hortense Horton and Sterling Roxbury. Due to the circumstances surrounding the succession of the late duke's title, the lateness of filing notification was conveniently overlooked. When informed of the impending nuptials of his cousin the Duke of Hampton to the American Anne Roxbury, the current Duchess of Westmoure, the king laughed and was heard to say, "Oh, this is royal."

Small entries as to both events were posted in the *London Daily*. The ton was hit by the cyclone effects of two marriages of the most elite of society; the gossip mill was buzzing once again about the Westmoures. The Society News set everything in motion.

The London Daily

Society News

Once again, dearest reader, the half-breeds from America are trying to disrupt the sacred lineage we all hold so dear, and there is much scintillating news. If you are not sitting down, it is best that you do.

The Dowager Duchess Horton married the late Duke of Westmoure (Sterling) shortly before his death. Our understanding of the matter is that it was a private ceremony at her home. According to our sources, the two of them had been meeting since the deaths of their former spouses. If you ever wondered about the ring on Lady Horton's, or I should say the Dowager Duchess Westmoure's, left hand, that was the ring given to her by the duke.

Furthermore, her son, the current Duke of

Horton, is very upset about this marriage. He was not apprised and called this "just another of his mother's antics." It has since been learned that he is going to challenge the legality of the marriage, because his mother is giving her enormous inheritance to the Westmoures. But hold on to your hats, there is more.

The Duke of Hampton, the current head of the Home Office and, may I remind you, a royal duke, married the uncivilized, mixed-breed American Anne Roxbury, the Duchess of Westmoure. What is happening to the men of the ton? Don't they realize the consequences of their actions and what this has done and is doing to our sacred world? She is now a part of the royal family and twice a duchess. At least they are too old to have children. We won't have to worry about any mixed-breed heirs. The title will pass to the duke's cousin. A line that respects the ton and what we represent.

We were told that when the king was informed of the impending nuptials of his cousin the Duke of Hampton to the American Anne Roxbury, the then Duchess of Westmoure, the king laughed and said, "Oh, this is royal."

The king was present at the small, intimate wedding. It is said that Lady Hortense took her place among the family as well. Yes, the proper notifications were given to the king and Parliament. To say the least, the Westmoure family has gone a little too far for the comfort of many of the established families.

The Duchess of Hampton was gowned in a periwinkle-colored dress, which skimmed the top of matching slippers. A silver lining made the gown shimmer. Crystals adorned the gown and the lining. The dress drew every eye to the bride. Yes, the dress was one of Joycellyn's creations. The child is talented.

It appears that Her Grace and the rest of the Westmoures had been sequestered in the London residence of the Duke of Hampton. We no longer need to wonder anymore where Her Grace has been since the explosion. Lady Caroline and her family are also there.

Well, we need not worry about ready-made dresses. Paige's was destroyed, and we hope that puts an end to that frivolous concept. However, it is still a mystery as to who did the explosive deeds. Two explosions in one day at approximately the same time. You never know where danger will strike, so heed my warning and stay away from the Roxburys. Mixing blood is not good. Maybe we will have something else to talk about in the future besides the Roxburys.

For the next week, there was only one place to be seen—the Duke of Hampton's residence. The stampede started the day after the article appeared in the Society News. Hordes came to see and speculate. They were getting a double dose of gossip in one place—the now Dowager Duchess of Westmoure, Lady Hortense, and the Duchess of Hampton.

Cook loved showing off her skills as an expert pastry chef. Her finger sandwiches disappeared the minute they appeared. Tray after tray was consumed along with liters of tea and sherry. The ton was at its finest, most glorious self-absorbed self.

"Don't you think it is a little soon to marry? Your husband only died what, five or six months ago. Was there a financial arrangement between your son and the Duke of Hampton? Don't worry, you can tell us; we would never repeat a word. It is a practice used among the elite. After all, we must secure our stations in life." The same questions were asked with each arriving group. Anne smiled as the buzzing in her head crescendoed. Lady Hortense held her hand.

As the cats sharpened their claws, no one was left unscathed as they set the dowager duchess in their sights. "Did you marry the old duke for his money? How many hours were you married before he died? What were you hiding from your son? I am surprised you didn't let him know. Was curious as to why you were sitting with the family when Lady Meredith married."

Categorically, Hortense listed each cutting remark in her mind for the time when karma visited each one of these lovelies of the ton.

As customary, Perkins held his usual post—one with the door—and did what all good right-hand men do. "Berkley, I think it is best if you go into the den of vipers and put an end to today's calls." He then repeated what he had heard.

"Unreal, Perkins. Unbelievable." Berkley was talking as he ran out of his study. He didn't need to hear more.

There was a hush over the room the minute the Duke of Hampton entered. No one bothered to congratulate the groom. He looked at the women. In his most sonorous voice, he simply stated, "I must borrow the two beautiful brides. King's business." He went over to Anne, then held out one hand for her and the other for Hortense. To dispel any thought of lack of love, he firmly kissed Anne on the lips and Hortense on her cheek. Not a sound was heard, but the sighs of some very jealous women filled the room.

As he led the women out of the receiving room, he leaned over to Perkins. "There will be no more receiving today or any time this week. Society be damned."

"Yes, my lord."

The house emptied quicker than a cattle stampede. Word was all over London within the hour.

Simmons and Dr. Langley met with Berkley and explained Anne's condition. They mapped out a plan for the best way to proceed. "When you speak to Anne, be gentle. I will be with you whenever you need. The important thing is bed rest. She should continue her daily exercise." Dr. Langley's kind demeanor was almost Berkley's undoing.

"Would it be all right if I took everyone to the country for the rest of the summer? The air is clean; it is cooler. Both women can continue to recuperate in peace and quiet. Anne and the children are who and what I live for. They are mine now, and I must do what I think is best. Simmons, will you come with us?"

"Berkley, of course. I can coordinate everything with Langley. I am sure he will join us from time to time. Let me suggest that we stay until mid-September or later if we can. Summer is almost half over as it is."

"Good idea, Simmons." Berkley turned to Langley. "Does this plan meet your approval?"

"Nothing strenuous, Hampton, Simmons." They both nodded. "Then I see no reason why you should not go. And no receiving or afternoon tea. Heard about how the entire ton tried to descend upon you in one day. This is serious; I feel a personal responsibility for the lives of my patients. Serious, gentlemen."

"The women of the country are gentle souls. I know them all personally and will have a word with the vicar's wife. She will let no harm come to either lady. Although she may become a little overbearing mother hen, I can vouch for them all." Berkley felt some weight slip off his shoulders.

"All right, then. Simmons, I am holding you responsible." Dr. Langley left the two of them to make the necessary arrangements.

"Perkins, whoever is knocking at the front door, tell them the ladies are not receiving. Please send for three of my messengers. I am writing as I speak." The general didn't expect a reply, and he didn't get one.

There was a soft knock on his study door. "Almost done, Perkins. Just a minute or two longer."

Perkins cleared his throat. "The Duke of Brockton."

"Brockton, what a wonderful surprise." Berkley clasped the old duke's hand. "Sit, sit. I will be with you in a minute." Berkley finished his notes and handed them to Perkins.

"Hampton, came to check on Sebastian and Caroline and have a chat with you."

Before Berkley could get out a word, the door opened, and in strolled Sebastian. "Brockton, thank you for coming. Berkley, I think we should gather all the men. Brockton's story is quite fascinating." Sebastian sat next to Brockton. "Maybe some refreshments would be in order."

"Trust me. The minute Perkins admits a guest, he lets Cook know. Should we time Cook's response?" All three men laughed.

Daggs was pacing as Brockton told his story. "I left my ancestral home because I was being poisoned by my nephew Basil. He is the one who will inherit the title. From personal observation, my nephew has become obsessed with spirits, dark prostitutes, and money. He drinks excessively. When with the ladies of the night, he frequently abuses them. I have received more than one medical bill for women he has badly beaten and battered.

"He is consumed by hatred of women who are not white. From what information I have been privy to, unless the women are Negroes or some other exotic being, he will not bed them.

What a contradiction. I am bringing this to your attention because your wife is a beautiful, exotic woman. I don't know who my nephew will lash out at.

"Basil has more than enough money. However, his father's bequest is that the unentailed property and money go to another. Basil is more than upset. My nephew seizes any opportunity to vent his rage. This anger and hate direct his life. Anyone who is close at hand can become the object of this wrath.

"Berkley, the men you placed in my household are of invaluable service, but the nuggets of information my butler Raymond ferrets out are priceless. Raymond reports to me frequently. I do not know what or why Basil is blaming people of color for all wrongs, but he has in his sight women of color. His goal is to destroy as many as possible.

"This is why I am in town. I need to speak to my brother's solicitors. I just don't have any answers yet."

"When will you know?" Berkley was barking again.

"That's just it. The solicitors are handling a major matter in Scotland. As soon as they return, I will have answers. No one seems to know when that will be."

"Are you sure, Brockton?"

"Berkley, my butler Raymond knows things your men would never be able to find out. Servants know everything. Raymond has been in my employ for over thirty years. He was of inestimable service to this country during the war. In the meantime, keep your wife close. Hate is the venom devouring my nephew."

"Thanks, Brockton."

Brockton rose to leave. "I will let you know the whys of everything as soon as I can speak with the solicitors."

As they tried to understand the meaning behind what they had just learned, Berkley was quickly changing their plans. They would leave for the country immediately. "Perkins, I need three messengers again." Berkley penned his notes while the other men discussed strategies.

"A man possessed and obsessed with anger and hate is a dangerous animal. Totally unpredictable." The general handed his notes to Perkins. "Daggs, put your men on double alert if anything is brought to your attention about abused exotic ladies of the night. We will start there. I shall also warn our men in Brockton's household. We depart for the country first thing in the morning."

The general was about to stand when the shattering of glass stopped him. "Sar, I believe little Elizabeth and Edward may need the country more than we do. They have a penchant for all things glass."

Peering through the newly minted hole, Sar saw two pint-size beings fleeing the garden. "I believe you are correct."

When he turned around, Berkley was grinning from ear to ear.

"Reminds me of when I was a child. I have ponies to help them wear off some of that excess energy. Such is youth." As though he didn't have a care in the world, Berkley got up, started whistling, and went to find his ladylove.

• • •

Unnoticed, the sloop docked at Southampton. Dressed as a dockhand, Captain Coomes helped to unload the schooner. The trip to London was of the utmost urgency, as usual. He would meet them at the private office. As he left the dock area, he knew he was being followed. *So much for being unnoticed.*

"Pull over." Perkins sounded almost like the general. In a matter of minutes, Perkins had lost the tail and was pushing the horses at maximum speed to the first safe house. There would be a quick change of clothes, wagon, and horses. The messenger was on his way to Berkley before the first pallet was put on the second wagon.

CHAPTER 17

Hampton Manor

Before they came to the manor, the men spent the night at Daggs's private office. A company they trusted had spotted the extra pallets in their cargo hold. At their first port, they had notified Coomes. With the greatest of secrecy and a little trickery with painting the boxes, they unloaded the pallets not on their manifest and sent them to Westmoure Shipping.

Again, they found the pallets stacked with boxes and boxes of statues filled with opium. "Let's see if the shipping label will lead us to an office or just another empty warehouse that hasn't been leased in years. Somewhere we are overlooking a clue." Berkley looked at the pallets. *Smuggling of opium is a larger operation than we thought.*

Sebastian examined the pallets. "We should look at this from another angle. Who would have the information about all the empty warehouses? Who would have access to them?"

Berkley stopped just short of the desk. "Those are the initial keys to this puzzle. We need to get that information immediately. Daggs, put a couple of your men undercover to get what we need. I can't go to Whitehall. Our enemy would know as soon as I made the request. The man with this information would disappear immediately.

"Also, look for someone who would do anything for a little extra money. Unfortunately, that is half the dockhands. Those pallets must get from the vessels to the warehouse.

"Once you find the warehouses, have teams of your men watching them twenty-four hours a day. No one is to work alone. I will inform Quinn, since the ships are crossing international waters. I'll be at Hampton Manor and can return at any time. I need daily reports." Having issued orders, Berkley headed home to wake his wife.

• • •

Beth had been in awe when she'd first seen Ivy Hall, the ancestral home of the Westmoures. But when the coach rounded the bend now, she gaped. Ivy Hall was a tiny country cottage compared to Hampton Manor, with its lavish decor and over three hundred and fifty rooms. Glittering glass caught the sunlight like prisms of rainbows suspended in time. Turrets stood guard over the arched brick entry. Behind the main house were acres and acres of land. Hampton Manor was like a country unto itself.

The inside of the house was unspeakably beautiful as well. One room flowed into another gracefully like the waterfall in the center fountain. Marble and hardwood floors were adorned with French-made Aubusson carpets. There were conservatories, music rooms, ballrooms, a grand dining room, and very large bedchambers. Beth wondered how long it would take before she got lost; they would search for at least three years to find her.

Complementing the house were exquisite grounds. Lush

fields of wild lavender grew adjacent to the most delicate roses, peonies, and hydrangeas. The greenhouses ensured there was an abundance of fresh blooms all year long. Almost every tree imaginable had its own special place on the land. The man-made ponds and the natural river, which meandered through the middle of the property, were full of fish.

"So, this is where you called home." Anne beamed up at her husband.

"I will try to make sure Edward and little Elizabeth enjoy it as much as I did, along with all the other little ones that fall under Sar's protection." Berkley hadn't felt this happy in years. It was due to Anne and her family. "Did I ever tell you how happy I am to be a husband?"

"You waited for me. Thanks, husband of mine." At that moment, Her Grace realized that this was all hers to watch over and care for. The coach had stopped, and she took a moment to take in the spectacle called Hampton Manor.

"Remember those promises I made to you on the dance floor? Well, I am about to fulfill all my promises and any requests you might have." The general looked down at his bride.

"I am holding you to it." Then Anne threw back her head and laughed. "I know you brought everyone along to make sure they are protected, but I would like some time with you by myself."

"There are a few beautiful cabins on the property I could show you. I am sure they would meet your expectations and also mine." As the footman opened the door, Berkley threw back his head and laughed with her. The footman almost lost his footing from shock.

The general had replicated his office at Whitehall in Hampton Manor down to the inkwell. Samuels carried messages back and forth every day. He was tailed by Dawson just in case there was ever a problem. Daggs went back and forth also. Sebastian, Jay, Julien, Royce, and Sar kept going through clues, adding the information that arrived in more than one diplomatic pouch. Jacob was usually at the shipping office. When not working, he was also at Hampton Manor.

At Hampton Manor, the ladies were as busy as the men. Anne and Caroline were making steady strides in their recovery. Cummings was thriving under the leadership of Alexius, Mer, and Beth. With the addition of shops in major cities in the former colonies, the business had a growth spurt no one could have predicted. The demand for graduates from Harson's School steadily increased. Miriam had more jobs than she had seamstresses. Joycellyn and Frances were in the country with everyone. Hortense, Aurelia, Evelyn, Georgina, Yvette, and Diana were helping wherever they could.

One afternoon, Frances pulled Anne aside and said she needed to talk to her and Sar. Sitting in the garden with them, Frances laid out her plans. "It is just time for a change. Fresh ideas, different fabrics for Joycellyn and Yvette, and I need a rest. I am coming to you for advice. With everything that's happening, do you think it is safe for me to go?"

"The enemy will strike at anyone associated with us. Here, you have protection. There, you do not. However, most people have only heard your name. They have not seen your face. Who would go with you?" Frances did not have to discuss this with them, but Sar was glad she did.

"I would take Martha and Frank. She has worked with me since I started Winters. Frank is the handyman."

"The big burly guy I have seen at the shop. Does he know how to protect himself and you?" Anne had seen this man on more than one occasion, and he was a brute with huge hands.

"Yes, at one time he was a pugilist. I have spoken with Joycellyn. She thinks it is a great idea and will help at the shop if needed. She believes if I go away, I will find true and eternal love. I imagine she and Beth have been reading one too many gothic novels." Frances almost smiled.

"This is wonderful. Go walk the ancient streets. Where will your adventure take you?" Anne couldn't wait to travel with Berkley.

"Paris and maybe Italy. I want to take my time—discover things and eat exotic foods." Frances imagined herself five kilos heavier, having to buy an entire new wardrobe. "I would like to leave next week if the arrangements can be made and return maybe by winter. I just want to be able to meander around and return when I am ready."

"I'll make the arrangements. Give Her Grace the given names of the two traveling with you. Will Wednesday work for you? You'll have to leave here on Tuesday." Sar smiled to himself—*an easy request for a change.*

"Is there anything else we can do for you?" Her Grace laughed. "Good for you, good for you, Frances."

"Thank you, everything is fine." Frances wanted to dance and sing.

· · ·

Quinn became a frequent visitor. "There is something we are overlooking, and I can't put my finger on it."

The general and Quinn were in their favorite after-dinner spot with brandy in hand. "I know Quinn, I know. Summer is more than half over, and I feel like we are sinking in a mud-hole rather than progressing. We have opium, espionage, trafficking of women, a dead former exchequer, and slain operatives. Women have been killed, and people are targeting the American duke and his family. Where do we go from here?"

"We keep digging, Berkley; we keep digging."

· · ·

A week later, in London, they were having their weekly

meeting. His short stubby legs were stretched out before the other man's desk. Fleshy fingers beat a steady staccato on the worn mahogany arm of the chair. He kept furtively looking around as though waiting for a shadow to attack from the outer recesses of the room. "Sam?"

"He won't be a problem."

"And the people Sylvia introduced you to after the wedding?"

"Lightweights with their own agendas but working for a common good, which we might turn to our advantage in the future."

"I understand that the Marquess of Dearne's half-brother is back. Is he going to cause a problem?"

"From what our reliable sources have told us, he is more of a ceremonial piece than anyone of importance. Everything for him is mostly show."

"What about this gossip I hear that he was trained by Berkley for over two years?"

"Speculation, pure speculation. He went to India when he graduated from university."

"What about the title he holds?"

"Again, for show. A brown Royal Highness. That's preposterous."

"Our job also includes eliminating anyone who is not white who claims to be a part of the aristocracy or of royal blood if the person crosses our path. Why can't they learn their place?"

"All of them will be eliminated at the correct time."

"Keep me posted on a weekly basis unless something important comes up. We can't afford mistakes." The top government official went back to his official work.

He looked up and added, "Make sure everyone is watched. You never know when opportunity will present itself." The other man stood, tugged on his waistcoat, and confidently left the office with the strut of one who owns the world.

• • •

At his London residence, Quinn gave the box to his valet. He checked the house again. Yes, that was the last item. The house was too large for him. Lately he could feel creaks and groans in his bones, going from one room to the next and climbing the stairs. He was always traveling for the Crown, and tomorrow he would leave again on government business. There was no wife and no children. So, he didn't need the mansion. It was the right thing to do—allow the next heir to take over the residence. He would be well settled in before Quinn left this mortal world.

As he had recognized some time ago, there was nothing left for him in London. It was time to leave and seek his pleasure elsewhere. Everything was in order in his office; he had submitted his letter of resignation four weeks ago.

The following day, Quinn boarded a ship to the Continent.

• • •

Back at Hampton Manor, Anne was eyeing the pastry cart—petit fours or cream cakes. Tea was being served along with delicate sandwiches shaped like Hampton Manor. They would all gain kilos if they weren't careful. The tea was forgotten when Evelyn announced, "We need something stronger." Champagne appeared as if by magic. Following the floating laughter, the men joined them.

More diplomatic pouches were delivered, and the men retreated to the study. "Let's see what we have here. More of the same—daily updates. Not much has changed. The attack is coming from all fronts, and to the best of our knowledge, not a shot is being fired. Now this is interesting. My office in Whitehall was ransacked. No one knows anything."

"That is a big clue."

Berkley quizzically looked at Sar.

Sar continued. "If someone is searching your office and no one can tell you anything, it means someone from a high office in the government is a part of the crimes. Hear me out. With you in the country, no one has access to your office except those higher up in government.

"Of course, a lock can be picked. But I studied the lock on your door. It would take a considerable amount of time to gain entrance without a key. But what are they looking for? Sensitive documents? Information about the drugs we have kept from entering the black market? Whatever it is, they know we are on to them. This makes the mission even more dangerous."

"Let's look at it from that point of view. That would mean one of the few people above me in the government is a part of the scheme. That would beg the question of almost infinite connections with endless possibilities. We could all be in deep trouble, because they are more than likely planning our demise as we speak." *What are we missing?* That question went round and round in Berkley's head as he spoke.

"Anyone have anything else?" The general was combating a well-organized and connected smuggling ring. His instincts were telling him that at least some of the smugglers were involved in espionage. "Then I think we should do this: Contact all the shipping companies we know are legitimate. We'll put a couple of men from Daggs's office on each ship. Give them the usual warning. Whoever these conspirators are have not put any goods on any of Westmoure's ships since we intercepted that very large shipment. We'll have to let the captains know."

A leisurely country summer at the manor continued. As the women were becoming more proficient, the target practice objects had been changed with added challenges. They were now shooting from moving bath chairs at shifting targets and swimming one mile a day and running two. Swords and knives had been added to their cache of defense. Their aim was deadly, and their language was becoming more sailor-like.

With the help of Perkins, hand-to-hand combat had been made a priority. The children watched, learned, and participated. Perkins was training two lines of defense.

• • •

The shadows danced along the corners of the tavern in the East End. The same two laborers were in their usual spot—heads hunched, solving their worldly problems. Jerkily, they stood. Staggering, they gave the impression of two drunken sailors on leave. They dropped the act as soon as they were safely enclosed in the warehouse.

Pallets of statues filled with opium stood in the middle of an otherwise empty area. "Berkley and Daggs have no idea. Just goes to prove we are smarter and cleverer." Kevin laughed. Their cursory inspection showed that all the pallets had arrived. "This load will be removed before sunup." The men locked the warehouse, turned, and walked into the arms of Daggs and his men.

• • •

The messenger leapt off his horse and took the steps to Hampton Manor two at a time. After a sharp rapping, the door was answered immediately. "Urgent message for Lord Berkley from Inspector Daggs to be delivered personally. I am to wait for the reply." He followed Perkins.

"Urgent from Inspector Daggs."

"Perkins, take the messenger to the kitchen. Please make sure he gets food. Cook will be happy to have someone else to feed." Berkley was looking at the missive, turning it over in his hand as he spoke.

"Gentlemen, let's see what surprise Daggs has for us." Opening the note, the general read it once and then again. Then he read it out loud. "'Caught two men, Kevin Michael and Elliot Jones, leaving a warehouse that had been previously empty. It was filled with pallets and pallets of statues bursting with opium. We emptied the warehouse. Kevin and Elliot are in separate cells at the Yard. Two men always guarding them. No visitors allowed. My cook brings three meals a day. Jay's men are keeping my cook company twenty-four hours a day. Jay's men are deadly. Kevin and Elliot still refuse to talk. Another couple of weeks and we will probably get something from one of them. Anything else? Daggs.'"

Berkley wrote the reply—*Add another guard. Someone is going to get anxious. Returning in another week. Will let you know when we leave. Berkley.*

"Perkins, is it September already? What a summer we have had. Why does summer always disappear so quickly? The children must get back to school, and we must return to the capital. Is there anything else we must learn before we leave?" Anne had just enjoyed her afternoon swim. She still wasn't able to beat Hortense yet.

"No. That should be about it for now. I asked Berkley to inquire of the king if we could use the park behind the palace three days a week for training. The king consented. Your training will barely stop." What passed as a smile was pasted on his face. Anne caught herself rolling her eyes.

"Does that mean six o'clock in the morning?"

"Most definitely, Your Grace, most definitely." Perkins's faint whistle trailed him as he went to find Sar.

"Men!" Anne stomped her foot and went to tell the other women of their fate.

"We are doing all we can up to this point. Don't worry, they will find other challenges. I am proud of us. We have done exceedingly well, and we even conquered Jay's strenuous swordplay." Her Grace smiled at everyone. Caroline was in fine form and walking without a limp. Anne looked robust and healthy. "However, we will be training three days a week in the park behind the palace. The king agreed. Six in the morning. Two hours each day."

"Might as well be as prepared as we can. Look at us, we have already turned into Amazon women." Lady Hortense smiled, giving herself a round of applause. She had done the impossible at her age, and all the other women tried to emulate her skills.

"Jay has been a tremendous help. Do you know someone was pathetic enough to start a rumor that he was no more than a ceremonial figurehead because his skin tone is brown? It was said brown people were not capable of feats and wisdom like the white man. Just don't get close to his sword in a fight. I can guarantee you won't survive." Caroline just shook her head. She had not been aware of so much hate until the Roxburys came into her life. *Why didn't I realize this before?*

• • •

"It's time to return and face the demons that have been plaguing the Crown's efforts and the why of it." The general pushed back the lock of black hair threaded with silver as if it were a pesky fly. "I want to return in the middle of the night. By the time most people rise, we will be conducting business as usual."

"It's time I kick the Royal Academy of Arts out of the hole that was my house and get on with rebuilding." Sar imagined the look on the face of Richard Earl, the head of the academy, as he evicted it from the premises. "Lives are starting anew.

My sisters are grown. Mer is married. Beth is a brilliant young lady helping to run a successful worldwide business. It's time we put every aspect of our lives in order."

"Couldn't have said it better, Sar. The directive ordering the inspector's men on any ship known to us that is leaving Southampton is already in place. Now, we wait. In the meantime, Daggs and some of his men are going undercover to find out who had the pleasure of rummaging through my files. Royce, you carry, send, and receive messages over the channel with the network. Julien, you are Royce's right hand in this. Sebastian and Jay, oversee everything, and by the process of elimination, let us get to the bottom of whatever we can. We will need to pay a visit to Scotland Yard to see what our prisoners can tell us. Usual orders. Watch your backs. Everyone is being followed."

Berkley stood and left the room to find Anne.

• • •

On a starry night at the end of September, the Duke of Hampton, his household, and several other prominent households, reestablished residence in the capital. At the bustling port of Rotterdam, Captain Coomes personally unloaded the mystery pallets, put them on a wagon, and drove them to the mouth of the river. Hans waited patiently as the transfer of cargo was silently made, a message sent to a contact, and the command to go like the wind given.

The signaled message was waiting for Royce. Royce and Julien were in work clothes before the others had climbed the stairs to their chambers. Julien hugged his Mer and then became one with the night. The note left for the general was self-explanatory. The wagon they pulled was empty. Samuels and Dawson covered their backs while Perkins covered them all.

CHAPTER 18

The Big Break

Everything was back to some degree of normalcy upon their return to the city. All the families returned to their London townhouses except for Lady Hortense. She stayed with the Westmoures at Berkley's.

On the morning of their return, the men went to Scotland Yard to pay a little visit to Kevin Michael and Elliot Jones. They were no more inclined to talk now than when they entered the cells several weeks ago.

"Daggs, offer one of them a one-way trip to America or both will probably hang. Have them think about that. Send a message when you get something. We'll be at my house." Berkley and the other men turned and left.

• • •

In Florence, Italy, Sylvia looked at the note again. Boss and M. N. were both moving to Italy. Arrival was within the next three weeks. Who was M. N.? She had seen the initials before when searching through the former exchequer's things. That could only mean he was probably the one in charge. This didn't sound good. If they were both moving to Italy, things in London must have changed. Thank goodness her husband had taken the baby back to England for an extended stay.

. . .

At Berkley's house, Mer was talking to Evelyn, Julien's mother. "Marriage? It's not what you expect, yet it is everything you anticipate. You're married, and he is wonderful. But it's different. You are responsible for each other twenty-four hours a day. That is a big responsibility. I want to wrap him in cotton wool to protect him."

Evelyn's light laughter filled the air. "Love has its responsibilities. However, the rewards of being with someone who truly loves you make everything worthwhile. Even when you are smiling and he has just made you angry." Evelyn hugged her newest daughter.

"You raised a wonderful man. He looks at people as individuals and is good and kind. I know you were not the happiest when he went to work for Berkley, but look at the strong, honest man he has become. What he does isn't easy. We were with them in France. At any time, an assignment could go wrong." Mer shuddered.

"Yes, we were there." Evelyn felt tears forming in her eyes. "I never fully appreciated what he did until we apprehended the former exchequer. It's not a pretty job, is it?"

Mer shook her head as they both sat there in silence, appreciating the calmness of home.

In the study, the men were figuring out what they did or didn't have. "Kevin and Elliot will talk eventually. My feeling is that Kevin is an underling and Elliot was just a dockhand hired to help move pallets when needed. Kevin can lead us to bigger fish. A trip to the former colonies is better than hanging." Daggs had circled the study several times.

"Let them sit another night or so. Sar, can you arrange for transportation?" The general kept talking, not really expecting an answer to his question. "Get as much as you can from them. If their stories have matching facts, they have both earned a one-way ticket. If not, we charge them with the crimes. That is about all we can do right now."

• • •

Anne sat in the conservatory with the orange trees. Wrapped in the cashmere shawl Jay had given her, she felt safe, warm, and protected. Duchess had her head in Her Grace's lap. On top of Duchess was the stray cat she had found—Starlight. When you saw one, you saw the other.

"Duchess, have you become a mother to Starlight or a best friend?" The cat heard her name, looked around, and promptly went back to taking her afternoon nap atop a snoring Duchess. Now Duchess was all black with a silver hump on her head. "I love you two." She petted both.

Anne was smiling from ear to ear. Life was not easier, but with Berkley it was definitely more interesting. *I told you he was good for you.* "Avery." But he was gone already. The men may spend their days together, but she had the general at night. If she thought the nights were exciting before they married, they were out of this world now. He had lived up to his promises made on the dance floor. She sighed with contentment, lay back, and closed her eyes.

"Gentlemen, I enjoy our time together, but I need to see my wife. I haven't had the pleasure of being in her company since this morning." The general stood and walked out.

"Berkley has a good idea. I'm going to see Mer. Coming, Sebastian? I'm sure Caroline is somewhere around."

Sebastian followed Julien.

"Might as well join them." Richard went in search of Evelyn.

"Married men. What is it about those four?" Royce watched as Richard made a beeline to find Evelyn.

"When you find the love of your life, you'll understand. Brandy, gentlemen?" Grayson went to the sideboard to pour.

• • •

Quinn returned to England about two weeks later. He had one last thing to check on. Being on the docks reminded him of his early lean years. When the man he had called father found out he was not his get, he threw him out. Four years later, he begged him to come back, because he was dying without an heir. There had been no one else. Now, he had the title and the power. No one knew who his real father was.

He met the dockhands, and together they unloaded pallet after pallet of statues filled with opium. This was their largest shipment yet. It was important to get everything to the right contacts. When they finished, he looked at the prized packages that filled the warehouse, lined up in correct order for the buyers. Quinn spoke to the men behind the warehouse and paid them, and he and the line captain went to close the warehouse. In a few days, someone else would deal with the buyers. This area was safe from the prying eyes of Berkley and his operatives.

Captain Johnson of Scotland Yard was taking his usual evening walk in the dock area. Dangerous though it was, he loved this part of town. Johnson could smell the sweat of hard-working men and vividly picture barrels being rolled, pallets being loaded, and dock children breaking into the various warehouses. It was his nature to notice the constant changes of the docks.

His meanderings had him uncovering things he had never seen before. As he was about to turn around, he noticed something. A warehouse that had been recently boarded shut for months was open. *Children of the docks fooling around again.* They knew everything, including how to get in and out of buildings. He'd look, notify the watch of the situation, and be on his way.

As Johnson got closer, everything felt wrong. There were no children about, and light was shining from within. The closer he got, the quieter it became. He reached for his whistle and felt the knife slide in between his ribs. Johnson was quickly losing consciousness as the knife was removed. Down he fell; he attempted to grab anything for purchase.

"Drag him in there and dump him in a corner. Someone will find him eventually. His decomposing body will attract attention." Johnson was dragged into the warehouse. The two locked up and left everything to someone else.

The next morning, Quinn boarded a ship to the Continent. Smiling to himself, he was very proud of the job he had done. He had made himself a few million pounds and could supervise the private endeavors from afar.

• • •

"Men, Anne almost upcasted her meal for a second time. I say *almost*. She saw a figure on the ground lying in white dust. This left her shaking and in tears. Caroline was with her and verified everything. Does anyone have any ideas?" Berkley saw his wife crying and hated the fact he couldn't do anything about it.

"Does that mean someone almost died or is dying? Can

we do something to prevent the death?" Sebastian looked at Daggs.

Daggs was pacing as usual. "My feeling is that Sebastian is right. How do we find this person?"

"Daggs, is there anyone missing who might be connected to the smuggling that you are aware of?"

As he thought, he shook his head. "Wait. Captain Johnson hasn't reported to work for two days. That is not like him at all."

"That's a start. Anyone else?" Sar was on his feet, but before he could say anything else, the door opened.

"Messengers ready whenever you are, Sar."

"Thank you, Perkins."

"Daggs, you leave for the Yard immediately. Talk to everyone who knows Johnson. Find out what his habits are, especially after work. Get as many men as possible. We'll organize as soon as we find out what we are dealing with. Where were his lodgings? I'll send two people there. Everyone is to meet at the Yard as soon as you gather the information assigned to you. Also, we'll need to know the name and address of his intended if he has one."

Working in twos, the men gathered the information. "Lucy, his intended, hasn't heard from him in two days. She is getting concerned. It is not like Stephen at all." Sar glanced at his notes again. He and Jay had left a teary-eyed woman at the door of her house.

"They could tell us nothing at his favorite pub, but he hadn't been in. Nice chap though." Julien spoke, and Royce concurred. They knew they had run into a stone wall.

"The agent at his quarters couldn't tell us anything. He paid his rent—on time." Sebastian and Richard didn't have much more to report either.

"Got it. I think this is our clue. He liked to walk in the dock area after work—meandering around, looking about."

"That's it, Daggs. He is either working with them, dead, or near death. Divide your men into four groups. Search every meter of the docks and surrounding area. Perkins, send for Simmons immediately. I'll be at dock one. Be thorough and hurry. His life may be hanging in the balance." Berkley headed to dock one, and everyone else split into various teams.

Daggs kept abreast of the groups. When one team finished, it went to help another.

Sar and Jay broke the lock and knew this was what they had been looking for. Pallets and pallets of boxes were neatly stacked. If Johnson was injured or dead, he was more than likely inside. "Wait a minute before you enter. We need help." Sar let go a shrill whistle three times.

"That's Sar; he needs help. Follow that sound." Perkins gave a silent thanks the signaling process for the Underground Railroad worked everywhere. Gathering the other men, they followed the sound. Simmons led the way.

"Okay, Jay. They are on the way. Look in the corners and all dark places first." As they started checking the corners, Simmons arrived.

"Nothing yet. Wait, I spoke too soon. A small stream of blood is flowing from the corner. Get over here, Simmons, and tell us what to do." Slumped in the corner was Captain Johnson.

"Let's get him out of here. Easy, Sar, easy. He is barely alive." Simmons helped to carry Johnson to the carriage. "We're taking him to Berkley's."

As Berkley was arriving, Simmons was leaving. "Your house, General." Then he was gone.

The remaining teams gathered around Berkley. "Some of you form a perimeter around the building. The others of you form a second perimeter. Samuels, get some men to secure the area. Perkins, wagons to get this stuff out of here. I don't need to guess what it is."

"Daggs, once we get the pallets moved, set up around-the-clock guards for the next forty-eight hours. They should remain behind the building. Your men are to arrest anyone who attempts to come near the warehouse. We'll see who is anxious to get inside. As soon as you can, meet us at my house."

For the next few hours, Sar, Jay, Julien, Royce, Richard, and Sebastian moved pallet after pallet of boxes. Bella stood guard, whining intermittently and batting at the boxes. Wagon after wagon was filled. As soon as they were full, they departed. Perkins drove one, Her Grace and Caroline another, and then the men another. Dawson watched their backs.

• • •

On a rooftop not far from the warehouse, a man peered through a telescope. Standing in front of the building were Berkley and Daggs. *Not good, not good.* He closed the telescope, ran down the stairs, and jumped into the coach.

• • •

At the general's, Simmons, with the help of Beth, cleaned and stitched Johnson's wound. "Berkley, Daggs, I don't expect him to awaken for several more hours or longer. I assume he was on the ground bleeding for two days. According to Daggs, that is how long he missed work. Please ask Cook to make a broth. I will watch over him."

"As you say, Simmons. We'll be in my study. Perkins will bring you brandy."

"A little food also. I haven't had dinner yet."

"Perkins heard. Dinner and brandy coming up." The general returned to his study.

"This is what we know. The shield Joycellyn and Yvette designed, which Daggs passed out to all of his men, saved

Johnson's life. The rest is a mystery until he can talk to us. We took more opium out of the warehouse than I dare to guess. Someone is going to come looking for it. We will all have targets on our backs and that includes the women. Go out in groups. If you have to do something alone, have Perkins or Dawson be your shadow.

"Cook has made us a late-night repast. I suggest we eat, and everyone get a good night's sleep. We'll talk to Johnson as soon as we can. Since the ladies are here, everyone stay the night." Berkley was looking at his men. Moving all that opium had taken herculean strength, and they appeared to be dragging.

Berkley found his bed before midnight. Anne was half-asleep. "Come here, my duch . . ." Before he could finish saying *duchess*, he was snoring.

The morning light filtered through the windows. "I've missed you, Anne. Do you want a quick update?"

"No, Berkley. I'd rather have my way with you." The general rolled on his side and laughed.

"Can you wait until this evening? We found Johnson. He's in the makeshift hospital. All the men are here. Cook will have breakfast waiting." Berkley gave her a toe-curling kiss and went to submerge himself in the tub.

• • •

The next forty-eight hours went by faster than a blur. Johnson woke. His breathing was still labored, and his voice sounded like a rusty gate. The men listened silently. "I like walking in the dock area, and I frequently do it. It's as though I can smell the sweat of the men, hear their comments, and see the children playing. I was passing a warehouse that had been closed for a long time. That late afternoon, the door was partly open and there was light."

The ragged coughing kept him from continuing. Simmons

handed him some water. "So, I was thinking dock children. They know how to open everything. As I got closer to the building, something struck me as odd—no noise. That's when I picked up my whistle and was ready to blow when something stuck me deep in my side.

"I was falling and reached for anything to gain purchase. Nothing would support me. What I grabbed was soft. When I hit the ground, one of the men ordered the other man to drag me inside and dump me in a corner. He was an aristocrat with a very cultured voice and said, 'Someone will find him eventually. His decomposing body will attract attention.'

"I don't remember anything else. Very tired." He closed his eyes and was asleep in seconds.

The men headed to the study. "Daggs, it appears your man is not a part of the criminal activity. He just happened to be in the wrong place at the right time. Perkins, send a coach to pick up his intended. That will cheer them both up."

Daggs sat and then stood up again to pace. "Daggs, get as much information out of Kevin and Elliot as you can. If their facts don't match, they hang. Otherwise, it is a one-way trip to America. Is transportation arranged?" Berkley was barking out orders.

Sar nodded his head.

"Berkley, do we know what Johnson grabbed as he was falling? Johnson's recollection was something soft and small." Sebastian had been curious about this since he heard this bit of information.

"No, if he is awake, ask him. Now, let's start with the information we have so far on the government officials. Where's Royce?"

"One of his contacts needed to speak to him about someone in government. Dawson is trailing him." As he spoke, Julien handed over the written reports to the general.

Sebastian strolled back in carrying a soft well-worn glove

and plopped it on Berkley's desk. "Johnson probably pulled it out of a pocket as he was falling."

"Okay, let's get started." The general had switched to command mode. Royce walked in with another stack of papers and put them on the desk.

"Why do you have Quinn's glove? Is he here?"

"What did you say, Royce?"

"Quinn's glove. Is he here?"

"No, he is not, but I believe his true presence is about to be known. How do you know it's Quinn's glove?"

"Because he'd put his gray gloves with the half monogram on the back on that side table whenever he came. Check the back of the glove."

"Who is investigating Quinn? What do you have?"

Royce started. "I have just left his new lodgings. His valet said he was out of the country and had no idea when he would be back. He wanted to tell me Quinn had a lot of mysterious meetings with the former exchequer late at night and his safe was full of cash. About six hundred thousand pounds, give or take. The valet counted it."

Julien continued. "Quinn moved out of his London residence. The heir apparent has moved in. According to him, his uncle told him the house was too large for one person, and he was getting too old to climb so many stairs. The nephew hadn't heard from his uncle in years."

"There are a couple of curious things, but this is the one we found most interesting. The former exchequer has a house in the country. It is a pleasure palace."

"From what we understand, it is still operating. The reason we couldn't interview his staff is because he had sent most of them to work there. I think we should all make a visit. This place will probably answer some of our other questions." Royce gave the final page of the report to the general.

• • •

On the other side of Mayfair, the man rushed up the stairs. "Reid, tell Lamont that Eric is here."

"What is the problem, Eric?"

"I was checking the warehouse as usual. When I looked through the telescope, I saw Daggs and Berkley standing outside. The warehouse was empty. They have everything."

"Wait, Eric, we have to come up with a plan." Lamont stroked his beard. "These are some of the things we need to do tonight. Tell everyone to stay away from the building. Take this note to our signalers. We must get this information to M. N. I'll notify our other boss. We will have to be more careful."

• • •

In the general's study, Sebastian had just finished detailing his report about another person who needed to be watched.

"We only have one other person who is somewhat suspicious. Keep an eye on him and continue to gather evidence." Berkley's heart had dropped to his stomach when he heard the name.

"We'll be leaving for Caen two days hence. Must meet with Rue. Royce, Julien, Sar, Jay, you come with me. Richard, Grayson, Sebastian, Daggs, be waiting on the shore when we return. The rest of you men keep the ladies busy. I suggest a wonderful dinner with lots of champagne. We're going and coming back in one day. Perkins, do you hear that? You can keep them home for twenty-four hours, can't you?"

"Royce, the message for Rue. 'Meet at Caen two days hence. Usual place. Midnight. B.'"

In the morning, the reply was waiting for the general. *Received. Understood. Rue.*

CHAPTER 19

Return to Caen

All the women were well aware where the men were going. True to their word, they promised not to follow them to a foreign country. Anne wondered if crossed fingers behind her back would work with a master spy.

"Ladies, where do you think they will run into trouble, if any?" Anne looked around the table.

"If I overheard Sebastian correctly, he said on the way back it will be night, and there is a stretch of land that is forest on either side with a side road here or there. Bands of highwaymen can come and go easily after a theft."

"Good work, Caroline. Your eavesdropping skills are coming in handy." Anne smiled at the thought of Perkins and his students.

"He was talking to his valet. They were deciding on which weapons to take." Caroline laughed. "My husband did not even detect I was eavesdropping."

"Did Sebastian say how many men were in a band of rob-bers?" Anne asked.

"Usually three to five."

"They will be fine. Don't forget Jay's men won't be too far behind. They will slice anyone in two if they think His Royal Highness might be harmed. No, I wouldn't want to be there." Aurelia laughed at the picture going round and round in her head. The men charging forth with scimitars twirling. *I would run for the hills and hope not to get caught*, she thought.

"Don't forget Samuels and his band of merry men." Anne was beginning to feel sorry for the band of robbers. They didn't stand a chance.

• • •

Sylvia sat on her balcony overlooking the stately trees of Florence, seeing nothing. She had heard from neither Boss nor M. N. *Are they working together, or are they just taking their time getting here, or both? My actions must be quick and final. Now for a plan.*

• • •

Quinn, traveling under the name Madison North, should have been in Florence by now, but there was one delay after another. The missive waiting for him in Paris had to be answered. Sitting in the café, he wondered about the many solutions Lamont had proposed. Their base for shipping operations had to be changed. Quinn agreed it had to be Southampton. Even though he had no desire to return to England, he would have to go set up the shipping through his line of contacts. Everything had to be worked out on his end. He would go in the spring.

Frances, known as Boss to a small group of people, was

in Milan buying things for Joycellyn and Yvette. The fabrics were superior. She was having bolts and bolts of cloth sent to them. Sometimes she felt sad that she would not be returning to England, but a better life waited for her in Italy. Now all she had to do was figure out a way to get rid of Sylvia Meacham immediately.

• • •

On a sandy beach in Caen, two nights later at exactly midnight, two men clasped hands. Not a sound was uttered. Soft crunching filled the night, then nothing. The men crossed the strip of ground and entered the deserted house. Shutters were closed, and someone lit the lamps. The look on Berkley's face announced the seriousness of the matter.

"*Mon ami, dis-moi.*" Monsieur Rue leaned in close to Berkley.

"*Nous avons découvert qui est l'un des hommes clés de l'opération.*"

"One of the key men in the operation. *Ce n'est pas bon, hein?*" Rue knew one thing for sure, Berkley always got his man.

"*Non, pas bon.* No, not good. It's Quinn."

"*Mon Dieu, mon Dieu. Chef de votre Foreign Office Quinn?*"

"*Oui, oui.* He is working with another."

"*Savez-vous de qui il s'agit?*"

"No, I don't know who it is yet, but I suspect someone." Berkley moved closer to Rue and whispered, in a tone only the two could hear, the name of Quinn's accomplice.

"*Mon Dieu, mon Dieu. C'est ce que vous diriez qui ferait s'effondrer votre gouvernement.*"

"Yes, yes. It would topple our government."

"*Quel est votre plan?*"

Berkley sat a little straighter. He looked as though he was carrying the whole world on his shoulders. "First, we need to find Quinn. He is either in France or Italy. Then I want him tailed twenty-four hours a day, seven days a week. This will probably go on for months," he said to Rue in French.

"Fait. De quoi devrions-nous êtreconscients?" Rue sat back, thinking about which of his men would be best for the job.

The general thought a minute about the things they should be aware of. "The women, especially Sylvia. She is deadly; she will kill first and ask no questions. Her favorite way of killing is through the ribs to the heart with a stiletto. Anyone in her way will be removed permanently." Berkley spoke in English first and then French.

Rue was nodding his head. *"Compris, compris."* He pulled out his stiletto to demonstrate.

Berkley continued in French, "We have sketches of Quinn and Sylvia. We don't know what name Quinn is using, but we have seen the initials M. N. As for Boss, all we know is that she is a female. We have never seen her, or we have and didn't know who she was."

Berkley handed the renderings to Rue. "One other thing. Joycellyn and Yvette created these shields to help protect the men from these attacks. We have brought you some for your men. These save lives." As Berkley spoke, Julien and Royce showed Rue and Jacques how to use them. "They don't offer total protection, but they prevent the blade from getting to the heart."

"C'est génial. Protection contre les attaques. Ils empêcheront la lame de percer le cœur." Jacques was explaining everything to his father.

"We must be very careful with messages. There are too many prying eyes and attempted interceptions. Everything must be sent in code that can't be broken. If it is very important, we visit each other. Code names—Quinn, turkey; Boss, buzzard; and Sylvia, vulture. Let me know when you find them. Royce, Jacques, see to the codes."

"It's time to leave." Berkley turned to Rue. "Thanks, old friend." They silently walked back to the channel and clasped hands, then the men disappeared into the mist.

• • •

While the men went to visit Rue and take care of matters at Whitehall, the women had traveled to Hampton Manor under heavy guard. The sun hadn't started to rise when the men entered Hampton Manor. By the time he reached the ducal chambers, Berkley realized how tired he was. Anne was asleep in the middle of the bed. Thank goodness the women hadn't followed them. He fell asleep in the duchess's chambers.

Later that morning, the women weren't hard to find. They were in the morning room looking and talking madly about the pile of jewels and money in the center of the table.

The other men were looking at the spoils. "May I ask where you got these from?" Berkley looked down at his wife.

"Oh, these?"

"Yes, Anne, 'oh, these.'"

"These are the spoils from the highwaymen the other night when you went to visit Rue." Her Grace smiled her prettiest of smiles.

"I thought you said you didn't follow us." The general tried to calm down.

"Well, we did kind of, sort of. We had Jay's men clear out either side of the highway. You didn't meet highwaymen, did you? We asked them not to kill anyone. They are very persuasive with their twirling scimitars. Jay's men took all the spoils the robbers had taken.

"Now, if you men would please get the jewelry back to the rightful owners, we would appreciate it. We are taking the money to help change the children's home we are sponsoring.

There is so much to do." Her Grace pushed the pile of jewels and watches toward the men.

Berkley started laughing. His wife.

CHAPTER 20

This Can't Be

Everything seemed to be back in order, or as much order as can be in the household of a master spy and head of the Home Office. The extended stay with the duke was a wonderful adventure for everyone. They had it all—work, pampering by a most attentive staff, and the opportunity to look at the mysteries surrounding the Westmoures from different perspectives. The staff loved the new duchess and her friends.

Trees quickly became bare as the kaleidoscope of colors gave way to Mother Nature's call for change. The crisp smell of fall gave way to winter. The Society News kept up its usual tirade against the Westmoures, lambasting any and all who were not pure and preaching the disgrace of mixed blood, especially in the aristocracy.

Berkley, Sar, Sebastian, Royce, Jay, and Julien headed to Whitehall. Daggs was meeting them there. They bundled up. It was the first real cold snap. The air had the feel of snow. The last shipment of illegal opium intercepted had also produced documents stolen from the general and the Foreign Office. Their vigilance had stopped some of the smuggling, but far too little. No one had sighted Quinn yet.

Four officials in government had been identified as possible suspects involved in smuggling, espionage, and trafficking. The why of it hadn't been figured out, and that is where the trail ended. Today, the men were at Whitehall searching every inch of Berkley's office, looking for anything that might be a clue for the plundering. Except for the four government officials who had to be handled very carefully and circumspectly, and until they found Quinn and his female counterparts, they were up against a brick wall.

• • •

The person watching the Duke of Hampton's house crawled out of his hole, casually walked down the street, and mounted his horse. As soon as he could, he raced pell-mell for the Duke of Brockton's house.

"All the men are gone. It is just the ladies."

"Perfect. I will send Otis with the note. Go clean up as we wait for our guest." Basil's laugh made the hairs stand up on one's arms.

• • •

At Whitehall, the men were beginning to take apart every piece of furniture in Berkley's office. "There must be an answer or clue somewhere in the office. Why would someone turn it upside down?" The general was not used to elusive things. This one was bothering him to no end. The lives of his family were at stake.

• • •

At the Duke of Hampton's house, Anne received an invitation to have tea with the Duke of Brockton. He had to unfortunately request that Duchess remain at home. He sneezed profusely in the presence of dogs and would have to be put to bed for several days after a sneezing bout.

"Caroline, I can't take all the ladies with me. Why don't you come? We'll only be gone a couple of hours. The old duke acts more like my grandfather than just another member of the ton."

The two looked quite fetching as Perkins escorted them to the waiting coach.

About thirty minutes later, the knock on the door startled Perkins. When he opened the door, there stood the Duke of Brockton. One look at the frazzled duke, and every alarm bell in Perkins went off.

"Your Grace, the duchess and Caroline are on their way to your house. Our messenger delivered the acceptance to your invitation for tea." Perkins's face was blank as he spoke.

"No, I haven't been to my house. Perkins, I am afraid that Anne and Caroline are in great danger. Where are Berkley, Sar, and Sebastian?" There was no doubt of the fear expressed by the old duke.

"At Whitehall. I will summon them at once." Perkins had his great coat on and was halfway out the door before Brockton responded.

"I shall wait for them in front of my house. You must hurry, Perkins. I fear we have very little time."

A winded Perkins reached Whitehall, jumped off his horse, and took the steps two at a time. He sprinted down the hallway. Without knocking, he opened the door. "The Duke of Brockton's house now. Anne and Caroline may have been abducted. The old duke will be waiting for you outside."

"Anything else, Perkins? I won't ask why you let them go."

The men already had their great coats on. Sar's left eyebrow was raised in a questioning manner.

"No, you won't. She was in one of her *I am going out, and don't try to stop me* moods. We must hurry."

Before Perkins could say anything else, Sar asked, "Where are the girls?"

"I left them at the house."

"But are they there now? Let's go, everyone, we must beat the girls to the duke's house. I know Mer; she eavesdropped and overheard everything. Mer, Beth, and Alexius will think they must protect their mothers. If anything happens to any of them, I will kill and ask questions later."

"Sounds fair to me." Berkley was already racing down the hallway. It appeared all the other men were of the same mind.

The men were coming from one direction, and the women from the other. Upon seeing everyone, the old Duke of Brockton eased out of his coach as quickly as possible.

"I believe my nephew will harm the ladies. I can explain more once we get everything under control. The object of Basil's obsessive behavior is your wife, Berkley. The solicitors were quite informative." The old duke checked to make sure both pistols were loaded. Brockton wanted to apologize for his nephew's repulsive behavior, but an apology wouldn't help with murderous intentions at hand.

"What? Anne? But why? You can't be serious." One look at Brockton and Berkley knew this was an additional life-threatening danger coming from another direction. If Brockton's looks were any indication of his feelings, he could probably demolish his own residence with his bare hands.

• • •

At the Duke of Brockton's house, Basil was enjoying center

stage. "I am going to kill both of you. Must get Her Grace out of the way. No one will care that one more Negro is dead. No one will miss either of you. Before I kill you, Your Grace, I am going to show you what it is like to be made love to by a real man."

The stiletto was just as dangerous as the gun he held in his other hand. Before Anne could react, there were three successive pings. The buttons on the front of her dress had been cut, and they landed in a neat pile beside her. It was done so quickly. She only saw a flick of a wrist.

This is a deranged man. Be careful what you do, Avery whispered. *Keep your wits. You know help is on the way. Keep him talking.*

"Why do you want to kill us?" As Anne spoke, she continued to loosen the rope binding her hands. Once they had arrived in the receiving room, his kindness had stopped. They had been roughly grabbed and shoved into chairs by two of his henchmen. There had been little use in struggling. Caroline was next to her now, taking deep breaths.

"Why do I want to kill you?" Basil repeated. "Interesting question." The sound erupting from Basil's mouth was deadly. "Because, Duchess, you are taking what is mine. No one takes from the future Duke of Brockton, especially a Negro." He pointed the stiletto and ran it across her neck and down the buttonless bodice of her dress.

"This just happens to be my lucky day—two for one." He sliced the sleeve of Caroline's dress. In two swift strokes, it was on the floor. "The only question now is who to kill first. Should I have the duchess watch her friend die, or should you watch the duchess die?" He ran the cold steel barrel of the gun up and down Caroline's neck.

"Why would your father leave me money?"

Keep him talking, Anne; the knot is almost loose enough. Avery's words resonated in her mind.

"Who is your father? I don't know him."

"Regardless, he left you what is mine. The hell if I know why, and I do not care. I repeat, no one takes from the future Duke of Brockton. With you and my uncle out of the way, it is all mine."

The last knot was just about to be undone, and then she would be free. As sure as the pistol in her garter, she knew that Berkley and Sar would arrive soon.

Just keep this idiot talking, Anne. Help is near at hand. Don't panic. Avery was gone as quickly as he'd come.

Caroline, watch Anne. Just focus on Anne. Caroline didn't know where that thought came from. She found herself silently mumbling, *Will do.*

Outside, Berkley took the key from Brockton and quietly opened the front door. The house was eerily still. Basil's shouting could be heard from the front room through the closed doors. With Berkley on one side and Sar on the other, they pushed open the doors.

The look on Basil's face was pure hate of demonic proportions. He looked up. "Go away, Uncle. This is something I must settle. My father gave my money away to the lowest of the low, a Negro; it is a disgrace to the aristocracy. The world will appreciate the elimination of one of them." He waved his gun at Anne and Caroline.

The ball hit the ceiling with a thunderous clatter. Shards of plaster rained down. The current Duke of Brockton threw the pistol he had just discharged to the floor and pulled another loaded weapon out of his pocket.

"Basil, put that pistol down. Even at my age, I am a deadly shot from this range." The Duke of Brockton cocked the pistol. "Don't even think about it. You'd be dead before you could pull the trigger. I shall not allow you to kill your half-sister." The air in the room shimmered in silence.

"What?" was the only word spoken by Her Grace, frozen in

shock. Berkley rushed to her, easing her hand out of the loosened knot. Sebastian was cutting the rope holding Caroline bound. Berkley wrapped Anne in his protective arms. Sebastian picked up Caroline. Sar none too gently removed the gun from Basil's hand.

Before Sar could say a word, Beth raised her arm. A knife went sailing through the air and lodged in the middle of Basil's hand. Blood spurted everywhere. His stiletto dropped to the floor as if jerked forcibly from him.

Beth raised her other arm. "Stop, Beth, you already made your point." Beth's other knife slipped into throwing position. She looked at Sar and nodded in agreement.

"No one hurts our family. Is that clear, Basil? You attack one Westmoure, you receive the wrath of us all." Beth lowered her hand but kept herself in a ready position just in case.

Daggs and his men were busy rounding up the other scoundrels in the house. They found Raymond beaten and unconscious.

"Samuels, get Simmons at once." Berkley was barking out orders.

"No, I shall not have a Negro as a relative. What outrageous trick is this?" Basil's body shook in rage and disbelief.

"Berkley, help your wife to the couch. She will feel better with you sitting beside her. Sar, Royce, stand on either side of Basil. Do not leave his side. Jay, stand guard. Sit, my nephew. Julien, if he makes a move, shoot him. There is a lot to tell."

Shaking his head, the Duke of Brockton found a chair and continued. "Some time ago, I came across an unopened trunk of my brother's. Basil, why your mother never opened it upon my brother's demise is a mystery to me. When I opened it, I found items he had brought from America, and his will drawn up by an attorney in the former colonies. Immediately, I sent this information to my solicitors. They contacted the lawyers in America and my brother's solicitors here." Brockton settled further into his chair. Someone had passed glasses of brandy to everyone.

"Perkins, do you want to come in?"

"No, Your Grace. I can hear everything perfectly well with my ear to the door."

"All right then, as you wish. Unknown to everyone except Sebastian, his family, and a few other people, I have been in town and staying at his home.

"At my ancestral home, Basil was poisoning me. I was very aware that I had to escape his clutches. With the help of my butler, cook, and physician, we were able to flee in the nick of time." He raised his hand to stop Basil from the denial or excuse that was about to be uttered.

"My solicitors confirmed the will is valid, and I have the duty of fulfilling my brother's wishes. Basil, your father found true love in America, but through a twist of fate created by man's hate, it was never meant to be.

"Anne, your father did not die years ago as you were told. My brother, Robert, your father and Basil's father, wanted to return to England. Although your parents held themselves out as married, we all know that marriages between Negroes and whites are not allowed in America. According to what we have been able to piece together, your father begged your mother to join him in England. She refused."

Taking a sip of brandy, the Duke of Brockton continued. "So, they made up the story that he went fishing and never returned. He landed in England and was welcomed back into the family fold. Knowing we needed an heir, my brother set about looking for a *suitable* wife. When I say *suitable*, I mean ton suitable. It took some time, but he eventually found Basil's mother, who was much younger than him. Several years later, they had Basil. My nephew, and you, Your Grace, are approximately thirteen years apart in age.

"Anne, let me fill you in on parts of your family history you are not aware of. The solicitors will speak to you at any time you wish. We will discuss everything in depth later.

"Your mother's parents were slaves to a Jewish family. There were very few Jewish slave owners in America. Unlike the slaves from Ireland, whose families had been practicing organized religion for generations, most of the African slaves did not have established religions. Some adopted the religion of their slave masters. Your mother's family adopted Judaism."

Before he continued, the duke looked up to make sure he had everyone's attention. "Under the laws of the Torah and other laws of Judaism, one person cannot completely own anything or another. At some point, your grandfather's owner freed all his slaves, citing the Torah and Talmud for justifying his actions."

Silently yet reverently, the duke pulled a fragile, browning paper from the file.

"Anne, this is the paper announcing to one and all your grandparents' freedom. In this document, the slave owner also mentions the biblical and religious laws. This belongs to you, my dear."

Brockton was ready to hand Anne the document, but at the last moment, he returned it to the file. Anne's quiet sobs told him now was not the time.

"Anne, you may not remember this, but according to my brother's note, your mother wore this Star of David until she gave it to my brother." The Duke of Brockton held it up for all to see, then passed it to Berkley. "The family menorah is in the trunk. You are Jewish by birth.

"My brother made one firm request—since he could not claim you legitimately due to the laws of America, he asked that all his unentailed property be given to you. This includes unentailed money.

"Basil, your father may not have been perfect, but he was

ashamed of your behavior and what he had heard through others of your proclivities. However, I do not believe your father would even consider that you would stoop to the lows you have."

"A Negro as a relative. Are you crazy? What happened to breeding and purity? Negroes are nothing. Even the former colonies recognized that. Nothing, Uncle, nothing. On top of that, she is a bastard."

"Enough, Basil, enough! You disgrace yourself in front of your sister and your nephew and nieces."

The duke turned to Her Grace and other members of her family. "Please excuse him. I do not know how he got these crazy ideas of hate and purity in his head. Hate has never been taught by the family. As for purity of lineage, every person with any common sense or who has studied history knows that is impossible. Somehow, he missed those important history lessons. Roxburys, welcome to the family. In time, I do wish you would call me Uncle."

Looking at his nephew, the duke raised one finger and pointed. "Let me make this very clear to you, my nephew. If anything should happen to Her Grace or her family under suspicious circumstances while I am alive or after you become duke, I have left orders that you are to be shot on sight. No questions asked. Have I made myself clear?" The duke's bushy white eyebrows scrunched up as if making their own emphatic point. "Probably, my men wouldn't have to do a thing. Berkley will protect his wife and family in the manner befitting a master spy."

Basil stood dumbfounded as he listened to his uncle's edict.

"Julien, Royce, my nephew is to be on the next Westmoure ship bound for America. I'll pay for the passage. He is not to return until after I have been buried." With stooped shoulders and a hesitant shuffle, the Duke of Brockton crossed the room to his desk. Fumbling, he pulled out his book to write a banknote.

Tears formed in his eyes. "You shall not draw another penny from the coffers until you return from America." Brockton threw the fifty-pound banknote at Basil. "While you are there, hopefully you will think about your actions and the hate you harbor. Julien, Royce, get him out of here. I never want to see him again." The Duke of Brockton turned his back as Basil was escorted from the room.

The silence spoke volumes as Her Grace watched her brother leaving the room. She was tired. Too tired.

"Perkins, send for Dr. Langley now! Have him meet me at my house immediately." No one saw Perkins, but Berkley knew the order had been executed in most haste. The general bundled up a wilting Anne into his arms and held the pale, sobbing form to him. *God, don't let me lose her.*

Langley was waiting for Berkley and Sebastian when they arrived. One look at Caroline and Anne and he knew his two patients had suffered a severe shock. "Into bed, in the hospital room, both of them. I'll examine them there."

Langley's assessment was thorough. "Berkley, you must keep Anne calm. First, it was a severe deep cut to the head, and now kidnapping and the threat of her death. They are both in shock. I do not consider that calm. Caroline is not used to this either. Get Simmons, Sebastian, and Sar in here."

Simmons was working on Raymond in the adjacent room. He popped his head into the makeshift hospital and knew by the look on Langley's face that he was about to issue a list of commands.

"All right, gentlemen, this is what must be done. I emphasize the word *must*. There can be no deviation." Langley cleared his throat. "The ladies are to remain on bed rest until I say otherwise. They are to take daily walks in the garden. Both are to be assisted by footmen; both are to have separate bath chairs. Have Cook make their favorite foods to entice their appetites. And bring those dogs in here. They calm them. Both women have endured massive trauma.

"Let them cry when they need to. Talk to them, but don't pretend this never happened. It did, and they survived. That is the important point. We let the healing occur naturally.

"Physical and mental injuries can have long-lasting effects. In time, they will gain some perspective, but it won't be today or tomorrow. They have experienced what most women and many men of the ton never will—the dark side of life.

"The shock to the body may have been too great. Both women have endured massive distress and may suffer serious consequences. All we can do is watch and wait. They must have someone in attendance through the night.

"Gentlemen, am I making myself clear? Are there any questions?" Langley looked at each one of them. "Then I expect my orders to be carried out. I am holding you responsible, Simmons.

"Until tomorrow." Langley washed his hands again, packed up his instruments, and left.

The women gathered around Anne and Caroline, soothing them, wiping tears that were streaming down their faces, and holding their hands. They were unable to talk. Someone sent for hot broth and spirits—strong spirits.

Progress was slow for both women. Sometimes it appeared as though they were automatons. Other days it was forced gaiety laced with deep worry and concern. Days passed and then a week and then another. By the end of November, Caroline was declared well enough to be moved to another bedchamber and join the others with some restrictions. Anne remained where she was.

During this time, the hunt for Quinn, Boss, and Sylvia continued. Operatives had scoured France. Since he was a master of disguise, it would be more difficult to pick up Quinn's trail. Sightings had been reported, but all leads turned into dead ends. They knew what Sylvia looked like, but Boss was a mystery. Sylvia hadn't surfaced at all.

They were now fanning out to other major cities—Florence, Venice, and Milan—looking for English citizens trying to be Italians. The end result was like looking for the proverbial needle in a haystack.

One day in late November, word reached Berkley that a woman matching Sylvia's description had been spotted in Florence. Berkley's reply was simple: *Keep under watch at all times. Two others may be with her. Keep track of all.*

Shortly thereafter, a suspicious-looking nun was questioned in the same area. Unfortunately for the operatives, she was just as she appeared, a nun. When the nun reached her lodgings in Florence, she ripped off the disguise, bathed, and became Quinn. Laughing out loud, he was more than happy. Money had changed hands, more opium was to be shipped, and men in Morocco, Algeria, and Tunisia wanted the prized beauties of England.

• • •

The Christmas season was upon them, and all eyes and concern were on Anne. Espionage and smuggling kept the men busy in England. The trafficking of women was on and off. The watch had learned to spot women more easily. More pallets of opium were confiscated. Daggs had men on every legitimate ship that left English soil. Red Cloud and his tracking brigade were busy pursuing Jack, Morgan, and Mason in America. With their business acumen, the girls were making Cummings the most talked about company in the business world. Dowager Duchess Hortense Westmoure took over Harson's for Caroline. In her usual general-like fashion, she kept everything in top order.

Anne took daily walks, sat in a chair, and went back to bed. Christmas week came and Her Grace became sicker by the day. Although the house was decorated, the only sounds heard were the muffled painful cries of Anne.

A dark pall descended over the house. Besides the doctors, Cook wouldn't let anyone but Arthur's wife and herself attend to Her Grace. Soothing towels were placed on a sweaty brow. Hot scented therapeutic oils were massaged into Anne's skin. There was no relief for the body wracked in pain.

By early Christmas morning, earsplitting screams resonated throughout the house.

Berkley looked at Sar and saw him flinch; beads of sweat formed on his forehead. "Damnation, I'm losing her!" Berkley shouted to no one in particular. His hand shook as he hurled his tumbler into the tongues of fire dancing in the fireplace. The flames greedily absorbed the brandy, shooting spirals of blue up the chimney. Just like the brandy, his life was being consumed by a force beyond him.

Again, sharp, mournful screams rent the air. They didn't stop. At some point in time, they seemed to collide with each other. The reserve that had helped Berkley remain completely intact throughout all his covert missions or had given him the grit when he was a hairsbreadth away from death or had allowed him to do his job, which included killing to survive or watching his men die around him, had been stolen from him by the mere thought of losing the woman he would love beyond death.

His job and missions paled in comparison to what was happening right then and there in his house. His constricted chest was like a death toll; the beating of his heart was the tone that was rapidly fading. This was his fault, and he would live with these agonizing moments until he left this earth.

Sar sat stunned, frozen in his chair. This was his mother. They had taken a risk, and his mother's life was slipping away with each shock wave of pain. So much had happened to bring them to this point. As his mind cataloged everything that had occurred in the past eleven months, he wondered how she had been able to withstand the onslaught.

Then there was utter silence. Berkley looked at Sar; Sar looked at Berkley. For a half second, two faces drained of all color stared hauntingly back at each other. They both reached the stairs at the same time, and shoulder to shoulder, elbowing and shoving each other, they raced up the staircase to the ducal bedchamber. Silence filled the rooms of the house like a shroud.

EPILOGUE

———

Just as Berkley opened the door to the ducal bedchamber, they heard the strong, lusty wail of newborns. Her Grace, with hair plastered to her face and a smile wider than the room, gazed at the children. For once, Berkley had nothing to say.

As Langley and Cook finished wrapping the babes, the general took in the scene as though he were observing from another planet. Looking between Anne and the babies, he couldn't decide which was more beautiful. Cook placed the babies in Her Grace's arms.

"My lord, your son, the next Duke of Hampton, and his sister." Anne lovingly grinned at her husband. "Let's say we won't be doing that again regardless of how much I love you, Berkley."

The current Duke of Hampton hadn't found his voice yet. He moved humbly toward Anne.

"I have a brother and a new sister." Sar, like his mother, was grinning from ear to ear. "I'll inform Mer and Beth if Perkins hasn't told them already." Whether anyone heard Sar was dubious. The new parents were wrapped up in each other and the newborn babes.

"I never thought . . . Thank you, Anne. It felt as though I was losing you."

"No, my love. Just the natural process of childbirth. Women are tougher than you think. We have a lifetime together." Anne tried to talk as the new father smothered her in kisses.

"We agreed on a name before the child was born if it was a boy, but we hadn't planned on a girl and a boy. Do you still want to go forward with what we planned?"

Anne nodded.

"Maximillian Avery David Hampton it is for our son. Now, for the most beautiful name for our daughter." The duke swooped in and kissed his wife.

"That's what got us into this trouble in the first place." Anne's laugh could be heard throughout the house.

"Berkley, out. I need Her Grace to rest for a while. It's Christmas, and everybody will stop by to see your son and daughter. They are healthy and both have a head full of hair like you." Langley did not have to say another word. Kissing his wife again, Berkley backed out of the room.

Langley was right. Food and champagne had appeared, and the ladies and their husbands drifted in one by one. Cook was over the moon, and the most delicious smells drifted from the dining room.

"To my wife and son and daughter, the greatest gifts of all." Everyone raised a glass.

*   *   *

"What? That can't be possible. They're too old. A son and daughter! Are you sure?"

Their operation had run smoothly until the Roxburys came along. Everything was perfect without an heir. Now, there was one.

"They must all die, even Berkley. The sooner the better."
"He won't even see it coming."
"Take care of it."
"No problem, at the correct time."

• • •

The London Daily

Society News

Dear readers,
I have news that will rock our revered lineage and the ton to the core. There is a new future duke and lady among us, and they are mixed breed. If you wondered why the Duchess of Hampton has not been seen, according to my most accurate sources, she was in confinement. On Christmas Day, the future Duke of Hampton was born, along with his sister. He is said to be a healthy boy who looks like his father.

The daughter looks like both.

Well, the aristocracy will never be the same. Don't forget the Duke of Westmoure's sister married Lord Julien last spring. There will be more mixed-breed children. Will someone tell this writer how this happened?

But there is more we are just learning about. I trust all of you are seated when you read this. Yes, it does involve the Westmoures. Basil, the Duke of Brockton's nephew, has been exiled to America. Why? No one really seems to know the answer. The speculation is the Duke of Brockton was so enraged with him that he banished Basil.

However, and this may be the true reason, Basil has a half-sister. She is none other than the Duchess of Hampton. Remember when Basil's father, Lord Robert, was in the former colonies for years? We understand he fell in love with a freed slave. They had one child—Anne Roxbury, the wife of the Duke of Hampton.

Oh, dear reader, there is much, much more. The duke's brother, Robert, returned to England and married Basil's mother, Catherine. Robert never spoke about his life in America, nor of the child he had fathered out of wedlock.

Most African slaves did not have a religious affiliation. In many instances, the slaves adopted the religion of the slave owners. Anne's grandparents adopted their owner's religion. Anne Roxbury is Jewish by birth—a Negro Jew.

Well, that is the tip of the iceberg. As we learn more, we will inform you as soon as we get the details . . .

Dear reader,
Welcome back to the exciting world of the Roxburys. It's all about love, everyone. Whatever happens, the Roxburys support and care for each other.

As passion overflows for Anne and Berkley, they understand that loving someone involves an unbreakable connection through the good moments and the challenges. Love is never straightforward, especially so for the Roxburys, but they endure together as one.

The ton is up to its usual tricks; the gloss of a perfect life that it wants to reflect to others is filled with hate, greed, ignorance, dishonesty, and arrogance. Even though this book is set in the Regency era, there are striking similarities with events in today's world. It makes one wonder if we have changed and advanced.

Life is short, and we never know what the next chapter will bring. Laugh and smile as much as you can even when things are not going your way. As we journey through life, the Roxburys wish for us to find ways to make life easier and happier, and of course, they wish for us to find love.

It has been my pleasure to bring the Roxburys back to life

in this adventure of the American Duke series. Love comes when we least anticipate it and from those we least expect. Be open to receive. Regardless of what is going on in your life, take time to smile, laugh, and love more.

The Roxburys thank you for welcoming them back. Anne and the general send special hugs.

—August Jade Sterling

P.S. The historical facts woven throughout the book are true.

---

1. There has never been a law in England prohibiting interracial marriages. In America, there was.

2. A judicial ruling in 1772 by Lord Mansfield, chief justice of England, was the initial impetus that resulted in freedom for slaves. It wasn't until 1833 that slavery was abolished in Great Britain.

3. The time-honored principle of international law, which made the union of Avery and Anne legal, has been in effect for centuries. Captains of ships can perform legally binding marriages. Under the principles of international law, a wedding on the high seas in international waters is legal and binding if the country in which the ship is registered and sails its flag under recognizes the marriage as lawful. The mare liberum rule decreed waters beyond national boundaries were considered international waters, free to all nations but belonging to none of them.

4. Irish women were bought and sold as slaves. After the Irish Rebellion of 1798, official records show more Irish women were sold to America than African women. Irish women were less expensive to buy. Like the African slaves, they were bound, branded, and sold, and became the property of the

slave owner. Do not confuse these slaves with indentured servants.

5.　Indentured servants usually came to America as the result of a financial arrangement entered into with the family of a woman. Many times, the family desperately needed money. For a monetary sum, the young woman would work for several years for the person making the purchase. Upon completion of the agreed-upon time or indentured period, the woman was allowed to leave. Most never returned to Ireland.

6.　On March 25, 1807, An Act for the Abolition of Slave Trade was passed in Parliament and became effective May 1. This act abolished slave trading, rendering the transporting of slaves illegal. Thomas Clarkson, William Wilberforce, and Olaudah Equiano were the real forces behind the twenty-year campaign to end the slave trade. Duke Sterling Avery Roxbury is the fictional character added for the purposes of this book. You might be familiar with the name William Wilberforce. The film *Amazing Grace* is the story about the fight to abolish slave trading and his active participation, along with others, to end this inhumanity against man. Wilberforce University in Wilberforce, Ohio, was named in honor of this abolitionist.

7.　*Shenanigans* was first used in 1854. I am taking literary discretion and using it in the 1820s.

8.　The British Empire was the world's leading drug trafficker in the nineteenth century. Although the Chinese used opium as a medicine, there was no widespread addiction before the British arrived. In the late 1700s, imperial decrees prohibited the smoking and then importation of opium. Opium addicts and corrupt officials collected bribes to allow smuggling; they effectively became allies with the British in subverting the efforts made by the Chinese government to stop opium smuggling. In 1821, the

British responded to the Chinese government's attempt to stop opium importation by moving the base of its opium-smuggling operations out of Canton to the small island of Li Tin inside Canton Bay, where the Chinese navy could not threaten it. By 1831, the opium trade to China was two and a half times greater than the tea trade. It was probably the largest traded single commodity in the world.

9. Hoby boots were made by probably the best-known London bootmaker, George Hoby (1759–1832). He was the bootmaker to at least four royal dukes; Hoby also made the iconic Wellington boots.

10. Nostalgia, Da Costa's syndrome, combat exhaustion, neurasthenia, shell shock, PTSD: In the late 1600s, Swiss physician Dr. Johannes Hofer coined the term *nostalgia*. This word was used to describe Swiss soldiers who suffered from despair and homesickness and classic PTSD symptoms like sleeplessness and anxiety. In 1761, Austrian physician Josef Leopold Auenbrugger wrote about nostalgia in trauma-stricken soldiers in his book *Inventum Novum*. As a result of his observations, he noted soldiers became listless and solitary, among other things. Efforts made did little to help them out of their lethargy. Nostalgia was a phenomenon noted throughout Europe and the US Civil War (1861–1865).

After the Civil War, US doctor Jacob Mendes studied Da Costa veterans. He found that many of them suffered from specific physical issues unrelated to wounds, such as palpitations, constricted breathing, and other cardiovascular symptoms. These symptoms were thought to arise from an overstimulation of the heart's nervous system, and the condition became known as "soldier's heart," "irritable heart," or "Da Costa's syndrome." Posttraumatic stress disorder was a major military problem during World War I, though at the time, it was called "shell shock."

However, medical and military authorities documented shell shock symptoms in soldiers who had been nowhere near exploding shells. These soldiers' conditions were considered neurasthenia—a type of nervous breakdown from war. This condition was also classified as "shell shock" (or war neurosis). In World War II, British and Americans described traumatic responses to combat as "battle fatigue," "combat fatigue," and "combat stress reaction." Today it is termed PTSD, posttraumatic stress disorder, a diagnosis related to psychological issues stemming from traumatic events and sometimes associated with other mood states (depression), as well as angry or reckless behavior; it's now in a category called "trauma- and stressor-related disorders."

According to the Anxiety and Depression Association of America, about 12 million American adults have PTSD. The National Center for PTSD reports 6 percent of people will have PTSD at some point in their lives. PTSD is more common in women than men. The American Psychiatric Association's Diagnostic and Statistical Manual of Mental Disorders, Fourth Edition (DSM-IV), states the one-year prevalence of posttraumatic stress disorder has been found to range from 1 to 6 percent in the general adult population samples across the world.

11. Queen Charlotte of Mecklenburg-Strelitz (1744–1818), wife of George III, was descended by six separate lines from Margarita de Castro, the daughter of Alfonso III of Portugal and his mistress, Mourana Gil, an African of Moor descent. Queen Charlotte and King George III had fifteen children, of which thirteen lived to adulthood. Among those children was Prince Edward, the father of Queen Victoria. Queen Victoria's great-great-grandchildren include the late Queen Elizabeth and her husband, the late Duke of Edinburgh. Queen Charlotte,

a botanist, expanded Kew Gardens and introduced the Christmas tree to England. Charlotte, North Carolina, is named after her; the city's nickname is Queen City, and it is in the county of Mecklenburg. There is a sculpture of her in the city's international airport.

12. Philippa of Hainault (1314–1369), wife of Edward III, was rumored to have African ancestry. She was from the Low Countries; that region is now Belgium. African Moors had ruled the area. No one knows what she looks like because all her pictures were anglicized with Caucasian features. That was standard practice then.

13. Buck breaking was the disgracing, demeaning, degrading, dehumanizing practice of stripping a male slave, usually a very strong slave, tying him to a stump, and flogging him. The white slave owner or slave master ordered the other slaves to watch. Then the white slave owner would sodomize the beaten slave. Frequently, the slave owner invited other slave owners to observe and sodomize the slave. This form of degradation was practiced more regularly in the Caribbean than in the former colonies. However, this act was committed in America and documented. The slave owner used sex to control the other slaves. Some of these sodomized slaves were so humiliated that they committed suicide.

14. Almack's assembly rooms were the place where the elite went to see and be seen. It was the marriage mart for those of its class, and it existed to exclude the nouveau riche. Breeding, along with wealth, behavior, and address, were crucial factors for being granted a voucher by the lady patronesses of Almack's. The cost of the voucher was ten guineas (a guinea is a little more than a pound). During the height of Almack's supremacy, it was ruled by six or seven patronesses. The number of patronesses changed depending on who was involved with Almack's at the

time. The lady patronesses were the Countess of Jersey, the Marchioness of Londonderry, Lady Emily Cowper, Lady Sefton, Countess de Lieven, Baroness Willoughby de Eresby, and Countess Esterhazy. Their reign lasted until approximately 1824, when the exclusivity and strictness of the rules were no longer in effect. Today, a high-rise building stands where the elite once danced and were matched. A plaque on the building commemorates the existence of Almack's.

15. Dueling eventually came to an end in England in 1852. Dueling was alive and deadly for nearly three centuries.

16. Richmond Park was created in 1625 as a hunting park by Charles I. To this day, it is one of the beautiful attractions of the London area. Charles I planted trees that are still standing.

17. Pen Ponds in Richmond Park provided a food source of fish. The ponds were formed in the early seventeenth century when a trench was dug. Today the ponds take in water from streams from higher ground and release the water into Beverley Brook.

18. St. George's in Hanover Square in London, England, was built by John James between 1721 and 1725. The organ in the west gallery is housed in a five-towered case. George Frederic Handel was a parishioner from 1724–1759. It is a favorite venue for society weddings.

19. Oilskin is a type of waterproof fabric.

20. The stethoscope was invented in 1816 by the French physician Rene Theophile Hyacinthe Laennec. It looked more like a telescope than the modern instrument we see dangling around the necks of medical professionals.

21. According to records, Jewish slave owners in America numbered about five thousand, representing approximately 1.25 percent of all slave owners in the South, and most of them were relatively small-scale slave owners.

22. According to the Torah, you never have complete ownership over anything. Many African slaves adopted the religion of their slave masters. Slaves of Jewish owners rested
on the Sabbath and Jewish holidays.

23. Holi: the significant Hindu celebration of colors, love,
spring, and the triumph of good over evil.

August Jade Sterling is allowed to live with her cat, Sir Prince Charming, in Minnesota. Like all good cats, he runs the house. While she is busy working away, he takes his daily naps in between thoughts of food. August Jade holds a graduate degree from the Maxwell School of Citizenship and Public Affairs at Syracuse University. When not writing or singing jazz, she creates programs for television.